PRAISE FOR JAMIES(

"Jamieson Wolf is a gifted writer!"

Kelley Armstrong, New York Times Best Selling Author

"As I read, Jamieson Wolf taught me to dance to the beats of his heart. Tender, heartbreaking and beautiful."

Caroline Smailes, Author of In Search of Adam, Black Boxes, Like Bees to Honey and The Drowning of Arthur Braxton

"Jamieson Wolf writes like Augusten Burroughs without the cynicism."

Nasim Marie Jafry, Author of The State of Me

"Jamieson Wolf has written a compelling story about navigating multiple sclerosis and cerebral palsy. His story will touch your heart, make you cry, then laugh, and inspire you. A touching memoir with a hint of magic...and tarot!"

Theresa Reed, Author of Twist Your Fate: Manifest Success with Astrology and Tarot

I have had the pleasure of reading this collection a few times and will many more I am sure. Jamieson's words provokes the entire spectrum of emotions in his words, allowing feelings to surface in the reader easily. There is an almost haunting permanence in the stories he weaves, one that has taken me to my own experiences that I thought were long lost.

Dava Gamble, Author of Silver Journey's and Silver Cusp

"With his unique style and powerful imagery, Jamieson Wolf lures us into this beautiful volume of poetry. Colors splash across the page, emotions are captured in a single word or phrase. We ride the city bus and see a woman's tears, feel the touch of a caring hand, experience the joy in a child's smile. Each poem is a stolen moment in time, raw, vivid, and intimate.

Dianne Harstock, Author of Alex, Without Aiden and Philips Watcher

The Queen of Swords

Jamieson Wolf

Queen of Swords

    ISBN: 978-1-928101-32-1

    Text: Jamieson Wolf

    Cover: Dominic Bercier

    Editor: Christine Moore

Wolf Flow Press

www.wolfflowpress.com

Dedication

For Michael,
Who knows the dark reaches of my mind
and still loves me.
For the real Jackie.
Thank you for following along
on your doppelganger's journey.

The Queen of Swords

Jamieson Wolf

0

"Would you like a warm towel?"

Jackie looked up at the stewardess and smiled. She had never travelled first class before, so this was a whole new experience. The plane hadn't even taken off yet, and she was already half drunk on red wine. She hoped they would bring some food soon, she needed something to absorb the booze.

"Yes please." Jackie replied. She gave the stewardess a smile as she took the towel. She looked at it for a moment. "What do I do with it?"

The stewardess gave her a kind smile and said "Here, let me." She took the towel from Jackie and unwrapped the plastic covering. She then handed it back to Jackie. "You wipe your hands and face with it. It's supposed to refresh you and get you ready for travel."

"Oh!" Jackie said. She wiped down her face and hands as instructed. "Thank you so much."

"Not a problem, that's what I'm here for. Is it your first time on a plane?"

Jackie could feel herself blushing. "No, but it's my first time in business class. I've always only flown on coach before."

The stewardess smiled. "Well you are in for a treat. You just settle yourself in and I'll bring you another glass of wine."

"Actually," Jackie said sheepishly. "I've had a lot of wine already. I would love something to eat first. Is it long until dinner?"

"We don't usually serve the meal until we're in the air, but I can find you some snacks in the meantime. Would that be all right?"

"Yes please. Thank you..."

"You're welcome. I'll take care of you on your flight, Ma'am."

"Jackie."

"Well, pleased to meet you. My name is Vanessa. I'll be right back with something for you to eat."

Jackie gave Vanessa another soft smile, leaned back in her seat and closed her eyes. A woman could get used to travelling like this. The ticket had been a splurge. She had always flown coach or on a bargain airline and tried never to pay full price, but she had been well paid for her last job, so she had just

1

gone with her impulse and paid the fare. Looks like it would be money well spent.

Her cell phone rang. Looking at the number, she felt her smile falter a little. Jackie sighed. Why did she even bother resisting taking the call? He knew that she would answer, and so did she. She sighed again and answered. "Yes?"

"Hey." He said.

Even the one word greeting sent her heart into overdrive. It was her mind that stopped things from getting messy. "Hey yourself." She responded. "What do you want? I can't talk long."

"You going out?"

"No, *away*. You have one minute."

"Listen, Baby..."

"No, *you* listen." Jackie said. She kept her voice light, but there was an edge to it, and she knew that he would hear that edge. He had always told her that she was one of the only people he knew that could threaten to rip your gut open, in an upbeat voice with a smile. "You don't get to call me Baby anymore or any other name. You lost that right."

"She didn't mean anything, honest." He said. "It was a one-time thing."

"Sure it was."

"Baby, I love you!"

The captain began to speak over the PA system. "I loved you too." Jackie said.

She hung up and put the phone on airplane mode, not caring whether or not he would call back. She didn't care...she really didn't care.

Then why was she running away? True, spending thousands of dollars on a flight to wherever she was going just because a guy cheated on her? She gave her head a little shake. Jackie didn't think of it as running away. Maybe she was finding herself.

She hadn't packed much, just a few changes of clothes. Her carry-on held her makeup and her Kindle. Jackie also brought her tarot cards. She didn't go anywhere without them. She put her phone away, and placed the bag on the floor of the cabin in front of her feet like the stewardess was demonstrating. Laying back, she hoped that there was good food in first class. She really needed to eat something soon.

QUEEN OF SWORDS

As if on cue, Vanessa slid up to her seat and handed Jackie a few packages of cashews and a small bag of chips. "I hope these are okay. We will start serving food about twenty minutes into the flight."

"These will be fine, thank you."

"Don't mention it. Just make sure to keep your seat in the upright position. We'll be in the air before you know it."

Jackie nodded and gave her a smile. She watched Vanessa walk to the front of the cabin and disappear behind a blue curtain. She couldn't help but think of the Wizard of Oz. "Do not pay attention the man behind the curtain..." She said to herself.

Putting the cashews and chips in her purse, Jackie decided to save them for later and grab a little shuteye instead. She laid her head back and closed her eyes, letting the thrum of the plane and the wine she'd had lull her to sleep. She heard the plane take off, the chatter of people, and then nothing.

When she woke, the world around her was in darkness.

"Hello?" She called out. Jackie knew that was stupid. Didn't the monster in horror movies kill the kid who called out each and every time? Fuck it. She undid her seat belt and looked around her. The airplane appeared to be empty and in complete darkness.

She tried again. "Hello?" She hated the sound of her voice and how afraid it sounded. Jackie hated how her insides were vibrating and how her heart had started to speed up. She was not good with scary movies. She always preferred a romantic comedy or the odd biopic. Her reading tastes ran the same way, the occasional Stephen King with a lot of what was called chick lit.

Jackie didn't do very well with fear. Often, she turned to her cards when she was feeling afraid and she itched to do so now. To lay out a tarot spread that would make things easier to see and provide her with clarity in her current situation. She longed to pull out he cards and hear the soothing whisper of them when she shuffled, but it was pitch black except for the light coming in through the windows.

With how little light was coming in, she knew that it must be nighttime. Leaning over, Jackie opened her window shade. Expecting that she would be looking out at the tarmac with the night sky shining down upon her, she

3

was surprised to find herself looking out at what appeared to be an airplane hanger.

"What the fuck is going on?" She said.

She called out again, hoping that her voice could be heard from the outside of the plane. However, after nearly ten minutes of banging on the window and screaming, it didn't look like anyone was going to hear her, let alone come to her rescue.

Her palms stinging, she got up and got her carry-on bag from the floor of the plane. The first thing Jackie looked for were her tarot cards. The purple velvet bag had long ago lost its sheen, but she had never wanted to replace it. This bag had been a gift from the last person she had truly loved. Holding onto this bag was like holding on to the one person from her past for whom she had felt anything.

Jackie itched to take the cards out and find out what they had to tell her, but now was not the time. She had to find a way to think her way through this, to rely on her smarts without the aid of her cards. She had to stand on her own two feet, at least for now. She wondered what to do, where she was, and how long she had been here for.

Pulling her cell phone out of her bag, she turned it back on. Waiting for it to load was torture. Even though it was only a thirty second wait, it felt like thirty years. She waited for the little bars to light up and tell her that she had cell service. Instead of the anticipated little bars, there was a big X, meaning that she had no cell service. *The hanger must be blocking the signal,* she thought.

Jackie wondered what to do. She couldn't stay on this plane forever. There had to be someone around who would come and help her. With nothing left to do, Jackie wandered the aisles of the plane. There were things left behind on the seats: sweaters, purses and bags, the occasional stuffed toy; she even stepped on a child's soother. "What the fuck happened here?" She asked out loud. Her voice seemed muffled by the confines of the plane.

She looked under seats and in the overhead compartments. There was a surprising amount of carry-on luggage left in the overhead compartments. There were women's purses and small pieces of carry-on luggage. As she was alone on a plane and there didn't appear to be anyone in the airplane hanger, Jackie was pretty sure that no one would be too pissed off if she went through the bags. She would leave that for later, though. When it came time to leave the plane.

Knowing she would eventually have to leave the plane filled her with more terror than waking up on the plane and finding herself alone. Shoving her fear down, she kept searching. She went to the back of the plane where the stewards prepared food for the passengers. Looking through the fridges, she saw tray upon tray of food. It looked as if none of it had been touched as the fridge was full.

"What the fuck happened here?" She asked again. There was fear deep in the pit of her stomach now, though she could not explain why she was so terrified. Her stomach growled, seeming to know that she was near food. It occurred to her that she hadn't had anything to eat for a long time, and she had no idea how long she had been asleep. All she'd had were those glasses of wine. She had fallen asleep before the meal was served. Looking at the fridge and the full assortment of meals, it looked as though the meal hadn't been served at all.

Taking one from the fridge, a covered tray that promised meatloaf with vegetables. She looked at it. Who would serve meatloaf in first class? Looking at the other meals, she saw that her choices were macaroni and cheese or rice pilaf with beans. "What kind of shitty airplane food is this?"

Her stomach decided for her, and she tore open the package. She looked in the small airplane kitchen, found some cutlery and dug in, too hungry to see if there was a microwave. She would heat up the next meal. After a few bites, she had to admit that the food actually tasted pretty good. Her stomach didn't really care at the moment, it was just happy to have food.

Going into the washroom to clean her hands, Jackie looked at herself in the mirror. She was shocked by how normal she looked; she didn't feel normal, not really. Her blond hair had body and lustre. She had it done before she left, figuring that if she was going to ride first class, she might as well feel classy. Her light blue eyes actually looked alert, contrary to the growing fear that was making its home in her stomach. She was always good at lying with her eyes, at least that skill had come in handy.

Her skin looked a bit pale, and that was all right, given the current circumstances. Her face was a long oval shape, with a bump out for her chin.

She loved her face; it was the stuff that the face hid that she had difficulties with.

Striding to the other end of the plane, Jackie wondered at how quiet a plane was with no one else on board. She could hear every footstep she took, and she wondered if she should be louder; if anyone would hear her. She saw that the cockpit door was slightly ajar. She opened the door and tried to take in what she saw.

There was a lot of blood. She didn't know where any of it came from, as there was no body. It was splattered across the front windows of the plane. It looked as if someone had bled out. The red of the blood had turned a dark black colour. *Shit, how long had she been out?* She thought. What had happened here?

She was about to back away from the cockpit when she noticed the radio. With a grimace, she stepped gingerly into the cockpit making sure not to step on any blood. She had worked a radio several years ago when she had been a long-distance truck driver for a short period of time. She hadn't liked the long drives, but she had loved forming relationships with people she had never met, how just hearing their voices could brighten a long shift. Looking at the radio, she said a short prayer: *Please fucking work.*

Picking it up, she pressed the talk button and heard static. Jackie tried anyway, "Is there anyone out there?"

There was only the sound of static in response.

She tried again. "Please. If there is anyone out there, please answer. I'm stuck on the plane."

There was the sound of static, but she heard a voice speak softly over the static: "Then you'll have to find a way out, won't you?"

The whisper of the voice coupled with the snow sound of the static sent shivers along her skin. She thought of what she knew about planes, and it wasn't much. Jackie knew she was really high up in the air and without a flight of stairs, there was no way out. She pressed the talk button once more and listened to the sound of snow for a moment. Then she pressed the button again and somehow found her voice. "Please, can you help me? How do I get out? I must be ten feet above the ground."

Listening to the snow, Jackie wondered if the voice would respond. She waited a few moments, and was slowly stepping out of the cabin when the voice spoke once more. "You'll have to take a leap."

Then the sound of static snapped off, as if it had never been there in the first place. The sound of silence after the snow of static was deafening. The whole plane's absence of noise was too loud. *What the fuck happened here?* She thought again. *And do I want to find out?*

She looked around her, the meal she had scarfed down lay heavy in her stomach. She ran to the plane door and tried to see if there was any way out, any way down, any way she could jump from the door without breaking her fucking legs.

Jackie saw the emergency exit and knew that was how she would have to leave, but how to do it? She turned and looked to her right and saw a notice on the wall. The notice talked about emergency procedures for evacuation, what to do to make sure the air masks fell properly from above the seats, and how to help passengers in the event of an evacuation over land or water.

She got to the part about the slide and her heart skipped a beat. That was it. That was how she would get out of the plane without hurting herself. But would it fucking work inside of a garage? It didn't matter, it was a way out. It was a way down.

Looking at the sign again, she read the instructions and wondered what she would do. There didn't seem to be anyone coming for her, or for the plane. Jackie thought there was really only one decision, and she read the sign over one more time to make sure she did everything in the correct order.

She turned the emergency lever one-hundred-and-eighty degrees and opened the emergency door. The sign said that the emergency system would take over. Jackie heard a loud hissing noise and she watched as the slide began to inflate in front of her. It stretched itself out like a long, silver snake. She knew that this snake would be her salvation. The whole inflation process took only about six seconds. The slide was twice the size of the exit door, and she wondered if she would bounce off and hit the concrete. The hissing stopped and the slide was inflated. Freedom was mere moments away. She checked her purse to make sure she had her tarot cards, her phone, and her Kindle, and then said a small prayer; she didn't know to who, as she hadn't prayed in years. Still, she prayed to whoever was listening. Jackie heard that whisper filled with snow once more: *"You'll have to take a leap."*

So, she did. Letting herself slip onto the slide, she let gravity claim her. The ride to the ground was remarkably fast and she got there in no time at all. Standing, she turned to look up at the slide and the open door of the plane. It waited there for her, looking as if it would swallow her whole.

Shivering, she dusted herself off and looked for an exit sign. She saw one in front of her a short walk away, the light in the sign burnt out, the red still visible due to the light filtering in through the door. Taking a deep breath and letting it out, she walked towards the door and tried to push it open. The door was stuck and, though it moved, it would not open.

Letting out a sound of frustration, she pushed with all of her might, using every muscle she had. The door moved a little more. After ten minutes, the door opened a little further. After another ten minutes, the door was almost open, and the air beyond the door was rank and a little foul. She didn't pay that any mind, but kept pushing. Jackie threw all of her weight against the door and it finally opened with a snap. Jackie let out a loud yell, one of release. She didn't know why the door wouldn't open, but got it open she did.

Looking out at the world beyond the door, Jackie wished she had kept the plane door shut.

I

The first thing she saw was blackness.

The large expanse of land in front of her looked as if it had been covered in tar and charred rock. Interspersed amongst the black space were things she recognized: car tires and hubcaps, a shopping cart, something that looked like diamonds but was probably shards of broken glass. There were overturned cars, and ones that were burnt as black as the pavement they sat upon. One of them was still smoking, a tongue of red flame peeking out and waving at her in the distance.

Looking closely, she even saw a child's soother, and close by, a Raggedy Ann doll. Its white face and smiling red slash of a smile seemed to be mocking her, and the situation she found herself in.

"I always hated that fucking doll."

Her voice sounded loud in the half-light of this wasteland; everything was too fucking quiet. There should be noises of traffic and people and music and sound. The world was always too loud with it. Now, all that greeted her was the wind, the flickering and cracking of the fire in the distant car, and the sound of her own breath.

Now that she was out of the plane, she didn't know what to do. Jackie looked around her and saw only destruction. It was as if something had chopped up the streets and turned them into a mockery of what they once were. And that fucking doll. That was a child's doll. Where was the fucking child?

Taking a step forward, and then another, Jackie kept looking at the world around her. Every step revealed something new. A building in the distance with broken windows surrounded by more broken glass. There was a truck used for luggage, with suitcases strewn across the ground, their contents littering the pavement, some of them still smoking. She kept walking, waiting for when she would wake up, when this dream would end, when the light would turn on and all of this would be over.

Jackie pinched herself. Stupid thing to do, but her overworked brain couldn't think of anything else. She pinched herself so hard she was about to draw blood, when she stopped herself. She had almost broken the first layer of skin. The pain running along her arm helped her focus and clear the almost euphoric-like terror filling her mind.

The pain brought the reality of her situation home.

Jackie desperately wanted to take out her tarot cards and find out what they had to tell her, wanted to be comforted by the knowledge and wisdom that they would share, but now was not the time. She put her hand into her purse and just held the bag that hugged them. She drew comfort just from their touch. They were like her talisman, and brought her comfort in what was an unreal situation.

Walking further, she passed more burned-out cars and trucks. There were smashed windows of buildings, and more mangled vehicles. She walked on, past the point of caring, past the point of thinking that this would somehow resolve itself.

Looking up, she watched the sky darkening, watched it turn purple and a dark blue. There were far-off shades of pink and an almost orange colour that made her ache. She wondered how something so beautiful could exist in a world that had changed so much.

With the night coming, Jackie knew that she had to find somewhere to rest. Looking around, she saw that she was on the tarmac of an airport. She looked around, and saw the airport in the distance. It was far away, but not too far.

She didn't really have a choice. Jackie couldn't see anywhere else for her to take shelter for the night. Something told her that she didn't want to be outside in this world, even though it was her own. The wind blew, she heard beads of glass tinkle along the ground, and the fires snapping and crackling in the distance.

Jackie shivered, even though the air was warm. She kept walking as she didn't want to stop; she didn't want to admit her fear. It hummed inside her as if her very lifeblood had been replaced. She ignored it and started to jog towards the airport. She could see it in the distance, most of its glass still intact. It shone like a beacon, beckoning her. She focused on that as she jogged, and then tried to outrun the coming darkness. As she ran, Jackie saw things on the pavement out of the corner of her eye that would have caused her to stop had she not had a goal in mind: more children's toys, a cassette tape with its tape ribbons running out onto the ground as if the wind had tried to steal it away. She saw purses and wallets that had been left, identification spilling out amongst lipsticks, compact mirrors, cell phones and packs of cigarettes. There were pieces of jewelry amongst shards of glass and bits of metal, left there after something had exploded. In some places, the pavement was covered in a tar-like blackness, which was still emanating smoke. There were bits of hair, and then there was the sheer volume of blood.

As she ran, she watched the colour of blood change from a red that reminded her of strawberries, to the red of a lollipop, then to the red of a tomato that had begun to rot from the inside out. Then she saw a trail of blood that looked like it had turned to tar, and something even blacker than tar. It was as if the blood had become a part of the night itself.

She ran now, not caring about the stitch in her right side or the pain in her legs. She was also thankful she had worn her sneakers. Running as fast as she could, Jackie watched as the trail of blood she was following led right to where she was headed. She could see the end of her path now, and it ended in a broken window whose sharp edges were covered in the black tar blood. She didn't bother looking for another entrance or another way in. She gazed upwards and saw that the colours had left the sky; now the dark blue of the sky was sliding gracefully towards black. Jackie did not want to be outside when the sky was completely black, though she had no idea how she knew this. She just had a feeling that she would be vulnerable, if she remained out here, to whatever had caused all this blood to be shed.

'Yes, but what if the thing that caused all this blood is inside *the airport? Ever think of that? Huh?'*

She let out a groan and kept running. Stupid fucking inner voice. "No one asked you." She said out loud.

The voice remained quiet; this time.

She fell to her knees and touched the glass just as the night fell completely. As if they had been waiting in the wings, the stars began to appear as though someone had pulled a blanket off of them. The sky was filled with a symphony of stars. At any other time, she would have stopped to admire them and take in their beauty. Right now, though, she was keen to be inside. She would not sleep, she just wanted to hide until she figured out what she would do next.

Jackie pulled herself though the broken window, being carful to avoid the shards of glass, thankful that she had worn her leather coat. At the very least, she could use it as a blanket or pillow, but right now it was keeping her skin from being punctured.

When she got herself through the window, it was as if she had entered a different world entirely from the one outside. There was light here, though dim. It looked like the emergency lights had come on. Everything was illuminated in a pale, shadowy glow.

The world outside had gone dark. Looking out through the broken window, Jackie jumped when she heard the sounds of animals, followed by what sounded like human screaming. The sound set Jackie's teeth on edge, and she moved slowly away from the open window.

The airport was empty and seemed larger without people there. One of the luggage carousels was still turning, but the light on top had stopped blinking long ago. She watched it and wondered about the people that used to work here, those who had been travelling and waiting for their luggage so that they could take off on their next adventure or go home and wait for the next journey to start.

Sitting down on one of the plastic chairs, she pulled her tarot cards from inside her purse. She had been itching to take them out since she had found herself alone on the plane. Jackie's hands itched as she pulled the cards out of their deck bag. Looking at the colourful drawings was like seeing old friends again. These cards had seen her on many a journey before the one she found herself on now.

Though she had an extensive collection of tarot decks, totalling some seventy-eight, she always travelled with her copy of the Rider Waite Smith. Indeed, it was the deck with which she had learned to read tarot cards. Even though she read with all of her decks, for clients or herself, she always came back to the one she now held in her hands. It was comforting that she held this touchstone that was so familiar to her when the world around her had become something that was so foreign.

Closing her eyes, she shuffled her cards and, though she regularly thought of a question to ask, it made more sense to let the cards read her current energy, and tell her what they had to say without the anchor of a question. Shuffling a little more, she stopped and cut the deck twice, then pulled the first card from the top of the deck.

She looked down at the comforting sight of The Queen of Swords.

Knowing the tarot as well as she did, she knew that the Queen of Swords was an intelligent and self-aware woman. She was a teacher, a writer. Jackie knew that she was also overly critical of herself and that her tongue could often be sharp when offering advice. She occasionally lacked compassion toward others, and especially herself. She was also pursued what she wanted with clarity of thought and thrived best in solitude.

Looking back down at her deck, Jackie let out a sigh. She hated when the cards were unclear. She resisted the urge to pull another card for clarity. "Thanks for trying, cards." She said, putting them back in the deck bag and then safely back into her purse. Standing, she realized how hungry she was. She dug into her purse and pulled out the package of cashews the stewardess had given her. Ripping open the bag, she devoured them in a few minutes. She was still hungry.

Jackie started to walk, knowing that there had to be a restaurant around here somewhere. She left the waiting area and walked deeper into the airport. Her sneakers were soft-soled, but they still made noise on the floors. Her footsteps sounded louder than they actually were, the sound not softened or muted by the noise of other people and their own footsteps.

Resisting the urge to run or walk faster, Jackie kept wandering and looking for a restaurant. Along the hallway, she saw the familiar sign of the golden arches and sped up her pace. It hardly counted as food, but she would settle for anything at this point. When she came upon the restaurant, she looked inside. There was no one, and the television showing the menu was flashing, as if it had forgotten how to maintain its light. At least there was no blood, Jackie thought.

She felt odd going behind the counter and pulling open one of the warming trays, but when she reached her hand in, she immediately pulled it back out again. There were burgers there, but they were covered in mold. How long had she been asleep? She mused. Letting out a sigh, Jackie went deeper into the kitchen and found a working freezer filled with uncooked meat. It was still cold, so that meant that there was some power somewhere which was still functioning. She pulled out a pack of hamburger patties and a package of buns. She would have to guess at how to cook this, but she was reasonably sure she could warm something up that would be edible. She had never been great in the kitchen, but she was really good at warming things up in a microwave.

Turning on a burner, Jackie heard the tell-tale sound of gas coming to life. She located a frying pan, dumped the patty in, and placed the bun nearby to warm up. Hopefully the nearby heat of the burner would defrost the bun so it would be edible.

Soon, the kitchen was filled with the scent of frying meat...and the sounds of animals outside the airport crying out into the wind, their wild cries sending a shiver down her spine. There was also the sound of footsteps. Grabbing the finished burger from the frying pan, she placed it quickly into the thawed bun, and held the frying pan aloft in defense of whatever was coming her way. Her heart was beating a loud tattoo under her skin, and she wondered at what was coming.

A man ran into the restaurant, red-faced and out of breath. "What the fuck do you think you're doing?" Looking at him, Jackie saw he had dark hair and tattoos that covered his face, so that his blue eyes looked all the more startling in contrast. The tattoos were black scrollwork that traced his forehead and cheekbones.

Jackie was taken aback. "Making something to eat. What the fuck does it look like?"

"Turn off the burner, grab your burger and come with me. You're going to attract scavengers, and did you not hear that animal cry a few moments ago?" He shook his head. "You have no idea what's out there."

"No, I don't." Jackie said.

He gave her a startled look, perhaps expecting her to argue with him. His eyes narrowed, as if he saw something within her. "Come on if you're coming, then. I don't have all day. Drop the frying pan, I have much better weapons than those."

Jackie turned off the burner with her free hand and dropped the frying pan. She didn't know why she should trust this man, but Jackie always trusted her gut. Right now, her gut was telling her that this guy was her best chance at surviving whatever was out there. Stuffing most of the burger in her mouth, she followed the tattooed man out of the restaurant kitchen.

He was waiting for her in the hallway and when he saw her, he nodded. "Excellent, now follow me and be quiet."

"Where are you taking me?"

"Nowhere. I'm merely letting you follow me. Now, please whisper if you have to pepper my ears with inane questions."

Jackie decided not to talk, thinking it would be better not to, at least until they got to what the tattooed man considered safety. As they strode quickly, the screams from the animals outside filled the air, still muffled from the walls that stood between them and the outside. Their footsteps made a staccato of noises as if they were lending a beat to accompany the animal screams from outside the airport, like some kind of eerie techno music.

The tattooed man scurried on, and took several turns; down one hallway and then another, through the hallway and down a flight of stairs. Gradually, the animal cries sounded farther and farther away until they ceased all together. There was a stich in Jackie's side and her lungs were filled with fire. She had been somewhat physically active in the world that she knew before today, but that didn't mean she could keep up this speed for much longer.

"How much further?" She asked quietly.

The tattooed man shot her a look; his blue eyes warm despite the coldness of the glare they gave her. "We're almost there. You'll have to toughen up. We're not even running. Imagine if we had to run the entire distance we just covered."

"Would that be necessary?"

Now the blue eyes gave her a look of wariness. "Surely you know what waits for us out there in the dark? And you walking around with nary a weapon to defend yourself!" He let out a small scoff and quickened his stride.

Walking faster, Jackie kept pace with the tattooed man. He looked behind him and nodded his head at her again, as if coming to another judgement about her. They came to a door marked with the word "Maintenance" and he opened it. There was light coming from within. He gestured for her to go in. She hesitated.

The tattooed man sighed. "I promise no one is there to capture you and you won't be hurt, at least on my watch. Inside lies safety and the promise of food. What would you like to do?" He sounded both impatient and kind, if such a thing were possible. "And not to rush things along, but while we are safe here, we are safer inside."

The tattooed man gestured once more, and Jackie stepped through the doorway. She blinked a little to clear away the darkness that filled her vision. Eventually, Jackie could discern shapes in amongst the shadows. As her eyes started to get used to the dark, she was able to see more and she realized that there was indeed light here, but it was very soft. She looked back at the tattooed man. He nodded at her again. "It's okay." He said. "Go forward, not backwards."

"That's awfully deep." Jackie said.

She watched him shrug, his shadow moving in the dark. "I'm a deep person." He said.

"Clearly." Despite her slight unease, she moved farther into the room.

Her eyes became more adjusted to the darkness. She could see the light settling on dust that floated through the air. It made Jackie think of fairy dust, though there was nothing magical here, she was not in some dream. She was in some basement room with a man who appeared to be covered in tattoos and surprisingly, she was not afraid.

Going through a doorway, she found herself in what looked like a small bachelor apartment, except for the fact that it was in an airport basement. There was a bed at the far side of the room, what looked like a hot plate, and a small fridge. She saw clothes packed neatly into a cupboard that had been turned into a closet. There were even a small table and chairs. There was a television on the table, and what appeared to be a walkie talkie.

He motioned at one of the chairs. "Sit." He directed. "I'll make us something to eat."

"I already ate, thank you." Jackie said.

"That was hardly a meal. Let me make you something to eat." He said. "Please."

It was the please that softened her. "All right."

She sat and looked around while he cooked something on the hot plate. There was a small collection of photographs in a multi-frame. It looked like it could be folded up and placed in a pocked at a moment's notice. In fact, all of the belongings looked as if they could be given away or left behind. The place had a temporary feel to it, as if the tattooed man were himself just temporary.

Watching him as he cooked, Jackie took in his purposeful movements; not a step was wasted in the small space, and she thought that he would be like this in every aspect of his life, whatever life he had now. He didn't speak as he cooked, but focused on the task at hand with intensity. She wondered if she had ever been so absorbed in anything. Jackie didn't think so.

He turned, holding two plates. Sitting them down in front of her, Jackie was treated to a scent that sent her mouth watering. "Pasta?"

He gave her a look. "Beef stroganoff."

"Really?"

"It's pasta, canned mushroom soup, and hamburger. I got patties from the restaurant freezer earlier today."

She picked up a fork and eyed the concoction warily. "Is it safe to eat?"

"You just saw me cook it." He said, a note of warning in his voice. "Here." He took a bite of his own dish and chewed.

After he didn't immediately get sick, Jackie dug in. She had eaten beef stroganoff at a fancy restaurant a few years ago; it had been made with fancy creams, home-grown mushrooms, and free-range beef. It had been good. Though her current dinner looked like roadkill on a plate, when Jackie took a mouthful, she had never tasted anything so good. She didn't realize how hungry she'd been.

Her fork hit an empty plate and Jackie looked down at it, wondering where all the food had gone. The tattooed man let out a small laugh, refilled both of their plates, and got glasses of water for each of them. She thanked him and continued to eat.

"How long have you been here?" He asked her.

"Not long." Jackie wrinkled her nose. "Does it show?"

Shrugging, the tattooed man said, "Only a little." He looked at her with those deep blue eyes that sparkled like sapphires. "How did you come to be here?"

"You wouldn't believe me if I told you." Jackie said.

He motioned around at his room of with a sardonic look. "The world around us has gone to shit, and I have an inkling that you have no idea what you've found yourself in." He said. "Why don't you try me?"

She looked into his eyes and saw only kindness and that same rugged determination. For some reason, Jackie knew she could trust him. "What's your name?"

He looked taken aback for only a second. "My name was Xander."

"Was?"

"I don't think this world has names anymore. It's just live or die trying."

He didn't elaborate further, nor did he ask for her name. Jackie sighed. "I was flying to Hawaii. I had a lot that I had to get away from." She took one more mouthful of food before continuing. "I fell asleep on the plane. When I woke, I was here. I don't know where I am. This isn't Hawaii. Do you know where we are?"

He took a moment before answering. "Things like where we are don't matter anymore. You must understand that, and you can't tell anyone else what you just told me." He said. "People would eat you alive here, Jackie."

Jackie sat up straighter. "How do you know my name?" She asked.

"I know many things; some I can tell you and some I can't. Some others I will show you."

"Well, that won't help me much." She said.

"What do you mean?" He asked her, giving Jackie a look of patience. "I will tell you what I can to prepare you for the world outside these walls."

"What world is that?" Jackie asked. "I boarded a plane and woke up on one, I assume in the same world." She huffed out a breath. "There's no way this is a different world." However, even as she said it, she wondered if he was right. The world felt different than it had a day ago.

Giving her a look that somehow deepened the blueness of his eyes. "You have no idea what the world is like now." He said. "Come on, I have something to show you."

Standing, Jackie followed him to the left wall of the suite and stopped in front of a door. He took a key from around his neck and took hold of a padlock that was holding the door closed. Looking up at her, the tattooed man looked grim. "What I'm about to show you will keep you safe. There are a lot of dangerous things in this room. Please be careful."

Jackie nodded at the serious tone of his voice and a shiver ran down her spine. She stepped through the doorway into an even darker room. The walls were covered in metal caging and metal shelving. There were all kinds of weapons here: guns, tasers, batons. There was also a shelf of what looked like newer weapons. Indeed, they shone brightly in the soft light coming in from the other room. The guns looked cold, even in semi-darkness.

The tattooed man flicked on a light, and Jackie saw the entirety of the room. It was filled completely with weapons, though not the usual kind, not like the guns and modern weapons she has seen thus far. The majority of the room was filled with knives and what looked like...

"Swords?" Jackie tried to keep the note of skepticism out of her voice, but wasn't entirely successful.

"Weapons like guns and tasers are useless here."

"Since when? People have been using guns for as long as history can remember."

"Yes, this is true, but guns break down. They require maintenance. It is harder to kill with a gun than with a sword. You have only to depend on yourself, not the use of a man-made machine."

"I can't use a fucking sword!" Jackie said almost laughing. "Who do you think I am?"

"A woman who wants to stay alive, I'd wager." The tattooed man said.

"Of course I want to live."

"Then you will have to learn how to fight. There are many weapons here that don't depend on technology. You will need to learn to use one of them if you want to survive."

"I was only on the plane for a day. The world can't have changed that much, could it?"

He blinked and looked at her, seemingly deepening his gaze. He was silent for so long that she didn't know if he would speak again. Minutes passed by in silence. When he finally did, his voice was softer, as if he were worried. "You've seen the area outside the airport. There are other places in this world that are worse than what you've seen already. You will need to prepare yourself. There are things in this room, other than guns, that can help you."

Jackie shrugged and walked around the room. She saw more swords, even small round discs for shields. "Where are we, in the fucking Middle Ages?"

"We might as well be. There are pockets of power throughout the land, but they are hard to find. You will also need to learn to defend yourself."

"How the fuck am I going to do that?" Jackie asked, her voice climbing in volume and reaching a level of hysteria unfamiliar to her. "What the fuck happened out there? There was so much blood and shit all over the tarmac and in the grass. Why was there no one working in the garage? Where are all the other planes?" Once the questions started, there seemed to be no way to stop them. "Who the fuck are you and why are you telling me that I will have to defend myself? Defend myself against what? What the *fuck* happened?" She ran across the room to the tattooed man and clutched his shoulders. "There were fucking children's toys out there, just sitting in the road. Where *is* everyone?" She looked into his too-blue eyes, and saw that her fear was reflected there. "Where am I?" She whispered.

The tattooed man closed his eyes and when he reopened them, the coldness seemed to fade a bit. Jackie watched warmth spread into that sea of blue. He took both of her hands in his, and spoke to her in a soft, calming voice. "You have only to go on. You have just begun your journey. I can't see its outcome, but there is much work left for you to do, and much left for you to learn."

"Go?" The very idea frightened her. She had no idea what kind of a world she had stumbled into, but she wanted out. "Where the fuck am I going to go?"

"There is a woman who will help you answer what you ask. She is just a short walk away from here, but it's a walk that is best done during the day. You can sleep here tonight. We will head out tomorrow."

"We?" Relief ran through Jackie like water. "You'll come with me?"

"I don't see any reason why not." He looked around the weapons room and through the doorway that led back into his bedsit. "I've hidden here for too long. I'd like to feel the sun on my face again."

He bent closer to her and Jackie breathed in a scent of woodsmoke and citrus. When he kissed her on the forehead, a calm serenity ran through her that took away all the fear that had been building in her. "I will train you to use the swords on the way. It wouldn't hurt to learn how to use a knife, either."

She looked at Xander's tattoos which ran along his forehead and face. They framed his face and made his cheekbones stand out, making him look like some kind of scarecrow man. Taking in all the different tattoos, Jackie saw that there was an infinity symbol on his forehead in the very centre. While all the other tattoos were done in black ink, the infinity symbol was tattooed in yellow ink, standing out against the black ink of the other tattoos.

"Who are you?" She whispered.

Xander gave her a small grin. "There will be time for that." He answered. "For now, it's been a trying evening for you. I suggest we sleep."

Jackie grew instantly uncomfortable. "I don't think I can sleep," She said. "I mean, I'm too wound up, and there's only one bed..."

He nodded as if he understood what she was really saying. "I will make us both a tea that will bring sleep. I will also rest on the floor with a blanket and a pillow. You can have the bed. You have nothing to fear from me, and I will keep you safe should there be anything to worry about."

"Do you think that's likely?" Jackie asked, hating the worry in her voice.

"I wouldn't rule it out. For now, tea and then sleep, and we will see what the morning brings. Okay?"

Jackie nodded her head. "Okay."

As Xander went to make the tea, Jackie followed him out of the weapons room. She watched him ready the tea by placing two tea bags of camomile in two mugs, and putting a pot of water on the hot plate to boil.

Watching Xander as he poured the tea, the smell of camomile filling the small bedsit, it occurred to her that Xander had never answered any of her questions. She wondered if the answers she sought were too hard for her to hear at the moment, or if Xander knew more than he was letting on. She sipped the tea, and halfway through the cup sleep began to claim her. She put the cup beside the other dirty dishes and lay down on the bed.

As she slipped into slumber, she pondered what Xander had said, and what he had not answered. She thought of the infinity symbol tattooed on his forehead and was not surprised when the sight of it followed her into her dreams.

Jackie woke to the sound of water running.

She sat up and blinked her eyes. Xander was washing himself in front of the sink, shirtless and wet, with his back to her. Though she experienced no sexual attraction towards him, she couldn't help but appreciate the thickness of the muscles that ran underneath the skin of his back.

The tattoos on his forehead marked his back as well. Much like his face, the swirling scrollwork covered his back. Peering closer, she saw that something was contained within the scrollwork. She tried to make out the shape, but he kept moving, and the light was muted in the small room.

Her voice came out before Jackie could stop it. "What do the markings on your skin mean?"

When Xander turned, his blue eyes were filled with all the light in the room. They seemed to glow brighter than the light itself. His eyes were wide, perhaps at finding her awake. He grabbed a towel from the counter and came towards her. She saw that the tattoos covered his front as well, that same delicate scrollwork that looked as if it had been painted on with a quill, rather than a tattoo gun.

He pointed to the tattoo on his chest. A pair of hands was clasped in prayer. From the hands, the scrollwork flowed down his chest and ended in the area between his belly button and groin. Though she could not see all of the tattoo there, it looked as if it were a wand of some sort.

"They mean that we are all connected." He said, his voice gruff in the dust-filled air. "That we are all creators of our own destinies, even in a world that we no longer understand." He put his own hands together like the hands that graced his chest. "That we are all connected and that we have the power, should we wish to claim it."

Blinking at him, Jackie let out a breath. "That's pretty deep for so early in the morning."

"It's the middle of the day, actually."

Jackie blinked at him again. "How could that be?"

"There's a clock over there," he said, pointing at a clock that sat behind her on a small crate that served as a bedside table. "You looked like you could use the sleep. I'm sure that the world as it is now must be quite an adjustment."

"I'll say." Something occurred to her then, and she wondered if she should voice the question.

"I let you rest, but now it's time we get ready."

Jackie nodded. "You want to go already? Set out to see this woman that you spoke of?"

"Yes. There is much you need to learn about the world that you're in. We leave soon. I made a small pot of coffee, there should be enough for a cupful for you."

Jackie was touched at the thought. "That would be wonderful. I normally have to kill for a cup of coffee."

"Well, now I've saved you the trouble of committing murder." He grabbed a shirt from inside a cardboard box that looked to hold all of his clothing, and put it on. She tried to look at the tattoos that marked his body before the t-shirt covered them, but he was too quick.

He was silent as he went about packing some of his belongings into a rucksack. Studying him for another moment, Jackie roused herself when she smelled the scent of coffee filling up the room. Getting out of bed, she went to the counter and poured herself a cup. The first taste was like heaven, and it almost made her feel normal for a moment, even though nothing about her current situation was anywhere near normal. To think that the last time she had coffee was yesterday morning, when she had been preparing to leave, gathering together things for a small bag she no longer had, lost to the bowels of the plane. To think that her life had changed so much in such a short time. She had no idea how to make her way through the world she was in now, but she would damn well try.

"After you've had your coffee, I would like you to look over a bag that I've packed for you, and you should choose weapons."

"Weapons?" Jackie thought of the weapons room that Xander had shown her last night. "I've never had to use one."

"Well, you will have to learn. The world has changed, Jackie, and we all must learn to adapt. Everyone must learn to defend themselves in order to survive."

"I don't know how to do that. I've never had to defend myself."

"Then I will teach you. If you know nothing of the world as it is now, you must prepare yourself or find yourself vulnerable. Everyone is alone in this world unless they can find people they trust."

"I trust you."

"As well you should. Em lives not too far away, but even in daylight there might be things we have to watch out for. If you're going to go out in the world, you must prepare yourself and learn everything you can."

"Who says I need to go anywhere?" Jackie asked, a bite to her words. "You're the one telling me that I need to go out there in the world, that I can't stay here. What if I do just that? What would happen then?"

Xander gave her a look that contained patience and wisdom. Jackie wondered how deep that patience ran in him, and if she would be wise to test it. "You would prefer to stay in an abandoned airport where the resources are running out and you're vulnerable?"

"You're here. Have been for quite some time, by the looks of it." Jackie said.

He blinked once. "I've been waiting for you. You took a long time to get here."

"What do you mean you've been waiting for me?"

"Just that. Sometimes good things are worth waiting for."

Jackie wondered if this was more nonsense that Xander would not explain. She tried to control her anger at the situation that she found herself in; she knew from past experience that it would not do to get pissed off. As good as it felt, it very rarely solved anything.

"I want to stay here. There's food and we're safe here." She said.

Xander eyed her with what she could only call tolerance. "You can do this, by all means, but your path has only just begun. Can't you feel it?"

She did. Jackie could feel her life changing around her, from the moment she had glided down that slide out of the airplane. Looking at Xander, she saw understanding of the acceptance she felt. "I do. I don't know what I'm doing or where I'm going to go, but I trust you. You've already saved me once."

"Then let me save you again." He said. "Here."

He placed a rucksack on the bed. Jackie looked inside and saw a few things that would be useful. There was a change of clothes, some toiletries, a small gun, as well as non-perishable foodstuffs and some portable cutlery. "It's not much, but you don't want to carry much with you. There's room for what's in your purse and some smaller weapons, but you want to pack light."

Tossing her a cookie out of a bag, Xander said "Let's go choose your weapons."

She caught the cookie and ate it quickly. She took her coffee with her, and followed him to the room that held the weaponry. He turned the light on, and for some reason, the weapons frightened her more now, seeing them in the full light. The metal of the swords looked lethal. Jackie supposed that was the point.

Xander approached the swords and touched their blades lightly. "Swords are wonderful but dangerous things. They can protect us; cut down wood to build shelter, defend ourselves. However, they can also make us bleed. You must approach every sword with respect and reverence, and know that if used incorrectly, the sword could kill you."

Jackie looked at the swords and imagined them shining with malice. "Look, I don't think these are for me. I'm better with throwing shit at people. I have good aim."

"That skill will help you with the swords." Xander said. "Aim will be important if you have to throw them. Now," He pointed to the row of swords. "Choose a pair."

Jackie looked at him, astonished. "Two of them? You want me to carry *two*? I don't even want to carry *one*."

"You will have to learn quickly. Life on the road is dangerous."

"Which again makes me wonder why you're so keen to get on the road."

He took both of her hands in his. "Jackie, we need to choose our paths, not lie down and take the ones given to us. Would you rather spend your time here alone and frightful? You don't strike me as that kind of person."

The compliment caught Jackie off guard. She wasn't someone who would just lie down and take it, never had been. She had stood up to that asshole back home, stupid fuckwad. She had always fended for herself. She had packed her carry-on and had gotten the fuck out, so she could figure herself out. She had made that choice on her own. Jackie had always stood up for herself and done things her own way. Why was she so afraid?

"You're right." She told Xander. "I'm not that kind of person."

"Then choose your swords. I recommend one for short-handed combat and one for long-handed combat. You don't have to know how to use them yet, I will teach you on the road. Plus, Em will be able to give you some insight as well."

"Who's Em?" Jackie asked. "You keep mentioning her."

"The person we're going to see, and the woman who will help you learn about yourself."

25

"Sounds mysterious."

"She is. Now choose your swords."

Looking down at the swords, Jackie had no idea what she was looking for except one with a short blade and one with a long one. She had no idea what she should do, but in the end figured that it was easier to just go with her gut. That approach had never led her wrong in the past.

Running her eyes over the blades, she saw two that gleamed more than the others: one had a long thick blade that looked as if it could impale someone. She wondered how she would lift it, the sword being half her body length, but was surprised when she wrapped her hand around the handle and pulled it free from the stand. It was light in her hands, betraying its size. Looking down at it, the sword seemed to gleam even brighter than before. When she looked down at the second sword, it looked as if it were pulsing with light. Reaching down, she took it from the stand and looked at it. It had a short, curved blade that was thick at the curve and thinned out to a point. It looked almost like play swords that actors used to play Aladdin or knights from Egypt. Though it looked like a plaything, the heft of it told Jackie otherwise.

"These two." She said. "I want these two."

"Good choices." Xander said, offering no further explanation. "You'll carry them in this." He handed her a shoulder harness. "You will be able to pull them out when needed. Don't worry. I will show you how."

Jackie nodded, not trusting herself to speak. Where had she ended up that the world was now so completely different? Where she had to arm herself with swords and weapons against whatever foes lay outside? "What will I have to use these against?" She asked. "What kind of animals are out there?"

Xander raised an eyebrow when he looked at her. "What makes you so sure that you'll be using your swords against animals?"

"Well, the way you're talking, it sounds like it's a savage world out there."

He raised another eyebrow. "You went outside. You saw the blood marking the ground?"

"I did, that's why I'm asking. What kind of animals would do that?"

He waited a moment before responding. "What makes you so sure those animals weren't human?" He let her process that for a moment, the silence between them stretching for a few seconds before he spoke again. "We should get going. I've put the contents of your purse and carry-on in the duffel bag."

"How will I carry the swords and the bag at the same time?" Jackie was confused.

"Have you never gone hiking before?" He asked. "You will wear your coat, strap the duffel to your side, then the swords, which you will carry on your back."

She was going to make another comment, but then something clicked inside her. Jackie had carried a lot of weight in her life, this would be no different except for the fact that the weight now had a physical presence.

"Okay." Jackie said. "Let's load up."

Xander looked at her face and perhaps he saw what he needed there, for he gave her one of his nods and then began to compile his own clothing and supplies. She watched him strap a sheath of knives to his leg, a pair or swords to his back, a gun tucked into his boot and one at his waist. Then he began to load clothing into his bag, most of it black and some of it covered in writing. She wondered what those were for, if the clothing held a special significance. Xander moved with precision and she was lost in the observation of him. It looked as though he were dancing, and not a single movement was wasted. She wondered if it was the same when he fought a foe.

When he picked up one of the discs and strapped it to his arm, she spoke up. "Why do we need one of those?"

"Why not? We need some way to protect ourselves. You will have one too, you'll carry a small one in your duffel bag. While you are still learning the swords, you will need some kind of shield to protect yourself."

"So now I have to learn how to use a shield as well as a sword?"

Xander snorted. "When you are good enough, the sword will be your shield. Until then, you will need to defend yourself."

"I thought you were coming with me."

"I am, but I'm not going the whole way. Here, let me help you with the swords. I will teach you to pull them and place them when we have time." He placed the harness along her back and shoulders and, when it was secure, placed the swords within the holders. The harness held them so that they sat diagonally. "You can pull them out easier this way." He said. Jackie went to try, and he guided her hands so that she could grasp the handles of each sword. "This will become more comfortable and natural over time."

"What do you mean you're not coming the whole way?"

He took some time in answering once again. "We all have our own journeys to make." Was all he said. "Are you ready?"

Looking around her, Jackie wondered what would happen if she did stay here. She assumed that she would likely die or perish when the food in the restaurant went bad when the power finally went, because she imagined the power at the airport had couldn't last for too much longer. That would leave her vulnerable to the animals, or whatever the fuck was outside this place. Xander was the only person she had seen so far, so she had to assume that she would be alone in here, but her mother had taught her that to assume made her an ass, or something like that, so she knew that to do so was foolish; it would be tantamount to a death sentence.

Jackie also knew that she couldn't go out there into the world alone. She had no idea what she would face or how to deal with what could be waiting for her. Looking him in the eyes, she nodded. "Yes," she said. "I'm ready."

Jackie was already loaded and ready to go. She reached into her duffel bag and touched her deck of tarot cards. They were like a talisman for her and they would light the way into the future or whatever lay ahead. They just had to. She knew that her cards could be vague, contrary, blunt or antagonizing in their advice. They could also be helpful, comforting, supportive and encouraging. It just depended on the advice the cards held for her. Either way, they'd been with her for so long that they were an extension of her hands. They were a comfort and a barrier against the dark. Xander noticed but didn't say anything.

"Let's get going." He said.

Trying to walk with the weight of the duffel bag on her side and the swords at her back was going to take a bit of getting used to. With every step she took, she felt the soft *thump* on her side from the duffel and an answering *thwap* form the swords as they clapped against her legs. Instead of being annoyed by the movements of the bag and the swords, she thought of the sounds as music that would intermingle with the steps that she took or the beating of her heart. Jackie felt larger than herself.

Xander led her through the labyrinth of the airport they had moved through last night. She tried to keep a mental list of the twists and turns they made, but stopped when she realized that it didn't matter. She doubted she would ever be back here again.

When they were up on the main level, the first thing Jackie noticed was the sunshine pouring in through the windows. She could see that the sun was shining through a haze that looked like smoke, or was it gas? She didn't stop to wonder, knowing they were going outside anyway.

Xander made his way to the cracked window and beckoned her through. She managed to get out without cutting herself. Instead of going towards the plane which is where she thought he was headed, Xander led them in the other direction.

There was blood here too, she saw. It looked as if it had rained down from above, and she followed the droplets as they arched along the grass. She wanted to reach out and touch the droplets, but she had no idea what could bleed blood that was so dark.

When Xander started walking towards a dirt road that led away from the tarmac and away from the airport, Jackie followed.

She had no idea where she was going; she was at Xander's mercy. She knew this, but she wasn't afraid. She didn't know why she trusted him so completely, but she knew deep down in her gut that she could. Her gut was her intuition, and it was spot on. Exhibit one was the cheating asshole she had left behind. If she had listened to her gut in the first place, she wouldn't have had to fly away, and she would not have ended up here in a world that was so like her own, but couldn't possibly be.

They walked on with only the sounds of their swords and their footsteps as their music. When the sound of the occasional breeze was added, along with the sound of a faraway animal, she couldn't help but be swayed by the music. When the sounds of animal calls were cut short in what sounded like a guttural fight that ended painfully, she was less enchanted.

"What was that?" She asked Xander.

"Nothing to concern ourselves with at this time. Though if the animals come closer, then we need to worry."

She took a few more footsteps, bringing up dust clouds. "I thought everything bad came out at nighttime."

Xander stopped walking and turned to look her. "Not everything dangerous thrives under a cloak of darkness. Look at us. We're a prime example."

Jackie snorted. "We're not dangerous." She said. "I'm far from dangerous."

"And yet, you are walking with swords strapped to your back and a loaded gun that could best any animal here." He said. "You need to rethink who you are. Don't forget you have power of your own that you have yet to tap into."

She snorted. "Yeah, whatever you say. I'm a fucking warrior." She said sarcastically.

Xander chose not to reply. Instead, he walked on, and Jackie had no choice but to follow him. She sped up her stride and walked beside him, throwing him a dark look. "You could wait for me you know."

"Why? I know you will catch up eventually."

Jackie chose to keep her words to herself. What she wanted to say was something along the lines of 'Go fuck yourself', but a little more eloquently. She had been told what to do by the fuckwad she had left to come here, wherever here was. He was always sharing advice, but Xander wasn't like that. Though she wanted to tell him to take one of his swords and fuck himself with it, she didn't, mostly because he was telling the truth.

Where else was there for her to go? He was the only person that she knew in this place, and he hadn't done anything but help her thus far. She knew in her gut that she was right to trust him. Keeping her words to herself, she kept up her pace and walked beside Xander, instead of behind him.

They walked on for quite some time. She lost track of how far they had travelled, even of the direction they were headed. All she knew was that they walked forward. All she heard was the beating of her heart and the slap of the swords on her legs. All she felt was the ground under her feet. There was less blood along this path. She wondered if the gore was only at hubs of the city. The city seemed to go on forever. Though there were fires and carnage here, the damage didn't seem as violent.

As soon as she had this thought however, they turned down a street to find it covered in droplets of blood, and great slashes of it across the pavement. There were clothes, car parts, children's toys, and a television in the street. They had to pick their way around them. There were a few burning cars sending black smoke into the air, and she was reminded of what she had seen at the airport. Her heart filled her chest, as if it were too big to be contained. Xander felt her fear. He reached out and took her hand.

"They've already moved through here. We're safe for now. We're close to our goal. It's just down this street. You're doing well, Jackie."

"Thanks, I think."

They walked a little further and Jackie had to step over a pothole filled with blood. There was a gold watch with a shattered face on the ground nearby, it and though she was tempted to pick it up, she left it where it was. She had a feeling that time didn't matter here. She now lived in a world beyond time

Xander stopped in front of a house. When Jackie stopped to look at it, her mouth dropped open. The house couldn't be called a house. Mansion was the only word for it. By the looks of it, the house took up half a city block. The exterior was done in pink stucco that made Jackie think of sunsets on the beach. There were wide picture windows and sweeping green lawns. The effect of the house was marred by the slash of gore on the front driveway and the blood that was trickling in the fountain in the centre of the driveway.

"Em lives here?"

"Yes."

"A bit grandiose for my taste." Jackie said. "But it certainly makes a statement."

"I don't know." Xander said. "I always preferred a country home."

Jackie looked at him and a smile was curving her lips. "Did you just make a joke?"

"I believe I did." He said.

They walked up the driveway and the front staircase. It was a massive affair that reminded Jackie of Gone with the Wind. Then they stood in front of the door, the duffel and swords making their *thwap* and *thump* sounds. Those sounds hid the pounding of her heart which beat a loud tattoo in her ears. She was not afraid of what was behind that door, she told herself.

She looked at Xander and he nodded at her, and she knew from that nod that she must be the one to knock. This was her journey after all, and Xander was merely along for the ride. Not knowing what could be waiting for her on the other side of the door, Jackie knocked.

Nothing happened. Jackie looked at Xander. He shrugged.

"Well, you've been here before, right?"

He shook his head. "She was staying in a smaller house down the street. She only moved here last month. I would try ringing the bell."

"Oh. Right."

Jackie pressed a finger to the white button on the right of the doorframe. They heard a soft peal of chimes ring throughout the house that made Jackie think of butterflies in flight. It played on for almost a minute, and Jackie was standing there thinking about what a lovely sound it was, when the door opened, and she was looking down the barrel of a gun.

"Who the fuck are you?" A salient voice said.

II

Jackie blinked and tried to look beyond the revolver. The woman had sleek red hair that had been done in an updo. It fell around her face in a riot of curls. The eyes that looked at her were jade green, so bright you would swear there were real jewels in those eyes. They looked at Jackie now with fierce intensity and an unblinking stare.

The woman flicked the gun. "I asked you a question."

"Um, I'm Jackie."

"She speaks! Well then, um I'm Jackie. Why are you here?"

Jackie turned to look at Xander and the woman followed her gaze. She took Xander in and snorted. "Well fuck. You better come in then." She turned and walked back into the house.

Jackie and Xander followed after her, closing and locking the door. The woman who she presumed was Em didn't look back but walked towards a bar that held glasses on the sideboard. She took hold of a bottle of whiskey and poured a few inches of the warm brown liquid into a glass. Taking a sip, she regarded Jackie over the rim of the glass. Jackie didn't know what she was seeing, but her eyes widened and when she took the glass away from her lips and smiled.

"Well, aren't you a young bird fallen from the nest." She said.

Jackie looked at Xander for an explanation, but Em said "I'm over here, honey. Look at me when I'm talking to you. Don't you have a mouth of your own?"

"Yes." Jackie wasn't entirely successful keeping the heat out of her voice.

"Good! And such spirit! You are a feisty bitch when poked, aren't you?" She looked over at Xander. "Where did you find this one?"

"She was trying to make food in one of the restaurants. I'd been waiting for her for a while."

"Everything comes in its own time. You knew this already." Em turned back to Jackie. "Well, either you're very brave or very stupid. You probably had no idea the danger you were in, did you?"

"I was fucking hungry." Jackie said. Once again, she tried to soften the edge to her words and was far from successful.

Em let out a laugh and looked at her, eyes twinkling. "Oh, and you have bite to you as well as spirit. This is going to be so much fun!"

"I'm sorry, but what is going to be fun?"

Em looked at her and blinked. "Why surely the magician told you why he brought you to me?" Em asked.

"For training. He was going to train me to use my swords, and he said you would train me too." Jackie said, feeling as though she was missing a piece of the puzzle. Em didn't look like someone who could handle a sword, much less use one.

"Honey, do I look like I've ever picked up a sword?"

Jackie looked at this woman, the mysterious Em. She was wearing a light blue robe, with hints of white throughout. On top of her head was a small blue cloche hat that somehow worked well for her. She was adventurous in fashion at any rate. Jackie tried to picture her hands working with swords and couldn't see it.

"No." Jackie told her. "No, I don't see you ever picking up a sword."

"That's right. That's more his territory, playing around with his swords and his shields." Em took a swig of her drink. "Has he showed you his wand yet?" Em gave Jackie a wink and barked out a laugh at the shocked look on Jackie's face. "Oh honey, aren't you going to be fun." Pouring another part-way full glass of the shining brown liquid, she sent the glass sliding across to Jackie.

Quickly reaching out her hand to stop it from falling to the floor, Jackie looked at the drink and then at Em. "Thanks."

Em nodded just like Xander had nodded at her, as if she had decided something. "You'll do. You've made me laugh already and that's pretty fucking hard to do in this day and age."

Jackie felt confusion rolling around in her. It wasn't just the fact that she was in a world that she had known but was now completely unfamiliar to her, it was that the people around her lived as if they had been dealing with this reality for a very long time. She thought back to the conversation she had with Xander and the things he had decidedly not told her. Looking this woman in the eyes, Jackie saw depths there that were undammable. She knew that Em had seen things that defied description. Em's eyes looked as though they contained the heart of the cosmos within.

"Thank you."

Em pursed her lips. "That's all that you have to say? I can see your mind whirring like a demon behind your eyes. You're thinking at an incredible pace, my girl. You'll burn yourself out. Don't look out here for answers, look within yourself."

"I have no idea what you're talking about."

"No, you don't. But you will." Em turned to Xander. "I suppose you want to stay, too?"

"If you have the space." Xander said.

Em barked out another laugh. "Honey, you know I have the space. It's a matter of whether or not I will let you stay."

They waited in silence for a moment while Em regarded Xander. Jackie watched both of them, wondering at the animosity that ran between them. There was clearly a past there, more things left unsaid. She didn't get the feeling that Em hated Xander, only that there was something that that lay between them. Jackie could almost see a chasm between them, though there was no actual body of water.

"Um," Jackie said, feeling that she had to say something to break the tension. The words stuck in her throat when they both turned to look at her with their eyes filled with so much left unsaid. Still, she pressed on. "He has to stay. He said he'd train me on how to use my new weapons." She indicated her swords, as if the weapons were not obvious to Em and to Xander. "I'm sure this place is plenty big. Aren't there any free rooms?"

Em's mouth curled up at the edges and the smile widened before she opened her mouth. "Why yes honey, there are. And you're right, there is plenty of space here. You up for a sleep over, magician? Do you want to make yourself at home?"

A grimace crossed over Xander's face. "If you'll have me."

"Of course I'll have you. Thing is whether or not you want to stay. What do you say, Xander?"

Xander nodded. "I'd be delighted." He said, sounding anything but delighted. "Thank you for having me."

Jackie just about threw up her hands. "Oh, for fuck sake, will you both just get over yourselves? I know there is a past between you two but the world looks pretty fucked up right now and I could really use some help."

Both Xander and Em's faces showed shock. "So, I need you both to get over yourselves." She looked at Em directly. "We're staying here, both of us."

Em blinked and let out another loud laugh and her eyes twinkled like pieces of jade. "Honey, you will do fine! Where you'd find this one?"

"I told you, I was waiting for her at the airport." Xander said cordially.

"Well, isn't it lucky for her that you were there." She gave him a bright smile, but Jackie noticed that the smile didn't reach her eyes. "Xander, you can go and get comfortable. I have to talk to Jackie, so you just make yourself at home. I know that this house is larger than the hovels you're used to, but I'm sure you'll manage."

Jackie watched Xander swallow thickly and pictured the words he wanted to say sliding back down his throat. "Of course."

"All right then." She turned her gaze to Jackie and her gaze became considerably warmer. "Pour yourself another tumbler of hooch and take a walk with me."

Jackie did as she was told, then joined Em at the doorway of another room. Em led the way as they walked through what looked like a ballroom, with splatters of blood marring the bleached wood of the dance floor.

"Mind the blood, honey. You don't want to walk in that. I keep meaning to have it cleaned, but good help is hard to find these days."

The ballroom had big picture windows covered in thick gold-coloured draperies. She saw chandeliers that glittered, even in the half-light of the room, as if they were made of diamonds and for all she knew, they might be. She looked up as she walked, taking in the sculpted ceilings, the decorations that made it look as if there were angels flying above them.

"Aren't the angels beautiful?" Em said. "Though I do wonder if the owners confused this place with the Sistine Chapel, but still, pretty, right?"

They walked through another door and Jackie wondered if she had died without being aware of it and had found herself in heaven. Looking around, there were books as far as she could see, covering every wall. Shelves made of dark wood almost gleamed, but that was nothing compared to the allure of the books. It was a fairly large room, and the books were the focal point. The books were the room, and they ran from floor to ceiling. There must be thousands of books here, more than Jackie could read in her entire lifetime, though not for lack of trying. Jackie walked away from Em and made her way to the shelves.

The books didn't seem to have been organized in any manner, and this was how Jackie preferred them. Books shouldn't be organized by colour, subject or alphabet; they should fill a room haphazardly, given space to breathe and let the stories ruminate. She ran her fingers along the spines, seeing old friends there: The Art of Racing in the Rain, Harry Potter and the Prisoner of Azkaban, Zen and the Art of Motorcycle Maintenance, Salem's Lot by Stephen King. They were mixed in with classics like The Three Musketeers by Alexandre Dumas, Little Women by Louisa May Alcott, Anne of Green Gables by Lucy Maud Montgomery, and A Midsummer Night's Dream by William Shakespeare. As her fingers brushed the spine of each book, it was like she was reconnecting with old friends. She tried to remember the last book she had read and realized that she couldn't. That saddened her.

"You like books?" Em asked.

"I do, very much. The people that owned this house had an eclectic reading taste." Jackie said.

"I know, marvellous, isn't it?" Em walked along the walls of books, trailing her finger along the spines much as Jackie had done. "Books hold a certain kind of magic, wouldn't you agree?"

"Of course, they do. They're the only magic that we can carry with us."

Em's eyes widened slightly, as if Jackie had said something that had impressed her. Her smile also stretched and, unlike the smile that she had given Xander, this one was genuine. "My dear, you are a surprise to me. Do you have any idea why the magician brought you here to me?"

"Why do you keep calling him that?" Jackie asked. She wanted to give some room between Em and herself, so she crossed the floor and sat down on a comfortable-looking plush peach fabric settee and put her drink down on a small wooden table beside her.

Em shrugged. "People have lots of names for different things. For instance, what's your full name? I assume that Jackie was not the name you were given at birth."

It wasn't a question. "No, my full name is Jacqueline."

"And yet you have claimed the name of Jackie. Does that give you a certain kind of power?"

"I don't understand."

"What I mean is does the name feel like it is more *you*?"

"It does. Jacqueline is too stuffy. It's a name for pretty girls."

"But you are pretty my dear." Em came closer and reached out a hand to softly touch Jackie's hair. "You mustn't sell yourself short, that dilutes your power." She stood straight. "No, you chose your name, much as you chose to go down the airplane slide. You took a leap."

Jackie let out a gasp. She remembered those words. She had heard them on the plane, whispering at her through the plane's radio: *"You'll have to take a leap."*

"That was your voice I heard." Jackie said. "In the airplane."

Em nodded. "And here you are. We all make choices. What I'm about to teach you is also a choice, about taking control. Tell me, do you dream?"

Jackie barked out a laugh, not unlike Em's own laughter. "Isn't this a dream?" She said. "I keep wondering when I'm going to wake up."

The other woman regarded Jackie with eyes that saw right into her. The silence stretched between them for so long that Jackie wondered if the other woman was going to speak. "Would you want to wake up if it turned out that you were dreaming?"

That was an odd question, Jackie thought. "Why wouldn't I want to wake up?" Jackie said. "Wouldn't you? I mean, have you been outside lately? What the fuck happened here?"

Instead of answering her, Em came over and sat beside her on the settee. "What do you see when you dream, Jackie? When you are completely silent, what goes through your head?"

"Why can't you answer any of my questions?" Jackie spat. "You're a lot like Xander in that way you know."

"How do you mean?" Em asked.

"He doesn't answer any of my questions either." Jackie said, frustration building inside of her. "He told me that I had to come here for training. What kind of fucking training could you possibly give me?"

Em took Jackie's hand and turned it over. "Well, the magician will teach you how to own your power and choose your path. You've already done a bit of that when you chose to accompany him when he brought you to me. I can teach you something different. While he will teach you to defend with your body, I will teach you to trust your intuition, to delve into the knowledge that you already have within you."

Jackie snatched her drink from the small table. "I already know how to do that."

"In what way?"

"You're talking about listening to my gut. I know how to do that. I've been doing it for a long time." Jackie said defensively.

Em barked out another laugh and clinked her glass against Jackie's. "That's a girl. That will help you here. You have to listen to what you already know."

Jackie took a sip of her drink before she answered. "What the fuck does that mean? Are you fucking high?"

"Honey, I've always got my feet on the ground but my head in the clouds. It's the only way that I can truly see."

Jackie took another sip of her drink. She looked at Em's face and it appeared honest, though her eyes were shrouded in shadows. Looking into them, Jackie saw depths of flowing water that flowed from Em and into her. Jackie could see the stars contained within her and the rolling waters below. Had she wanted to, Jackie could have dived into that ocean and swam forever. She blinked and the vision was gone. "Woah."

Patting her on the hand, Em gave Jackie a bright smile. "Yes, honey, I suppose that 'woah' does cover pretty much everything." She took Jackie's glass and stood, moving to the bar on the other side of the room with such grace, she hardly looked as if she were walking. Instead, Em seemed to be floating. She didn't walk so much as glide. Em poured both glasses full of whiskey and came back to the couch. Jackie watched her and wondered how the woman had ever become so sure of herself. Jackie had confidence in spades, but she could never look around at the world as if seeing it for the first time. Jackie had seen too much of it.

Em handed Jackie her glass. "Drink up now."

"Are you trying to get me drunk?" Jackie asked.

"What if I am? There is precious little alcohol left in the world and it's nice to have someone to share it with. I hate drinking alone." She gave Jackie another smile. "Indulge me a little while I look for a particular book that I want you to read."

Going to the bookshelf, Em looked for a bit, running her hands along the spines. Stopping at the end of one of the shelves in front of a large leather-bound tome, Em put her drink down on a side table and pulled the leather tome off the shelf. She came back to the settee where Jackie was sitting, and held the book out to her.

Looking at it, Jackie thought she had never seen such a large book. "It's the size of a small child." She said.

"That's a good way to think of it. Here, take it."

She handed the book to Jackie and Jackie had no choice but to take it. It was surprisingly light and not at all heavy. Jackie had expected to have to use all of her arm muscles to handle the book, but she was able to lie it across her lap where it rested. The leather was old, but still gleamed with a bit of its old shine.

There were the remnants of a title in gold leaf on the cover. She traced her fingers over the it, trying to read the words, but could only see a few letters. "What does the title say?" Jackie asked. "I can't read it."

"That will become clear as you read the book. Go on, open it." Em said.

Jackie did so and found herself looking at blank pages. She flicked through, running the pages through her fingers so that they whispered. When the book closed, Jackie swore that the book was vibrating softly. "What kind of book is this?" Jackie whispered.

Em looked at Jackie with deep eyes once more. Jackie wondered how she was able to switch moods like that, how she was able to go so deep into herself and let all of that be seen. Jackie was so used to keeping everything closed off; she would feel vulnerable showing her true self to people, let alone to herself.

Em nodded as if she had heard what Jackie's thought. "It's your story Jackie. You'll have to look inside of yourself to find the story and fill the pages."

Jackie stared at her and tried to keep exasperation from showing on her face, once again unsuccessfully. "You want me to write my own story."

Letting out a laugh, Em sat down beside Jackie and patted the book. "Sorry, I didn't explain. I know I don't make too much sense."

"You make more sense than Xander does. It's like he speaks in riddles. I just want someone to give me a straight answer."

Em shrugged her shoulders. "I'm sure you'll find that in life, there really is no such thing as a straight answer. Every question has a million answers."

"No it doesn't. It's yes or no."

Em raised an eyebrow. "And here I thought you were smart, honey. There are a million answers to every question, never just yes or no. How about maybe, not right now, later, never in my life, just to name a few?"

Jackie had never thought of it that way. For her, it had always been yes or no with no grey areas in between. That had always been her way. It looked as if things would have to change to adapt to what the world had become. "What do I do with the book?" She asked.

"Honey, you have to fill it with your story. Do you ever meditate? I want you to sit with the book in your lap or in your hands, and concentrate at letting the words flow. Only that it's less like writing and more like telling the book what you want to say."

"That doesn't make any fucking sense."

"The world doesn't make much sense, if you stop to think about it. Which I suggest you don't as it will just drive you fucking nuts." Em took a sip of her drink. "You don't have to do it all in one sitting, either. We have time. You still have to work on your training with the magician and practice your sword work. So, we have time."

Jackie looked down at the big book that lay on her lap. She ran her hands along its cover. "I don't know how to tell a book a story." She said. "It's normally a book telling me a story."

"Well, all books have personalities," Em said. "What personality would yours have?" She patted Jackie on the hand. "Don't make it too complicated. How does every story start?"

"Well, that's easy. Once upon a time..."

The book in her lap started to hum. There was no other way to describe it, the book *hummed* and grew warm in her lap. She flipped the book open and looked at the first page. Words were being written there by an unseen hand, the very words that she had just said out loud. She watched them being written and then looked at Em. "What the hell was that?"

Giving her a brighter smile, Em said "You've just started telling your story. Good for you. Now you and the book are linked. I'm so proud of you."

Jackie shook her head. "What the hell do you have to be proud of me for?"

"Honey, not everyone is brave enough to tell their story and let someone else read it."

Jackie looked at her open mouthed. "Who is going to read it?"

"Well, anyone out there in the cosmos. Stories have a way of getting told. You will have to look deep within yourself to tell your whole story, but think of how freeing that will be! How much weight you can cast off."

Jackie shook her head. "I still don't understand what this is all about."

Em looked at Jackie, and there was such a depth to her gaze that Jackie once again wondered if it was possible to swim within her eyes. When Em finally responded, she said "Let's get you another drink and I'll start on something for dinner."

Jackie was trying to be patient, she really was.

However, she also really wanted to hit something, break something, anything to get the anger out, anything to work through her frustrations. She went back into the living room of the large house and went to her swords. She grabbed the shorter curved one and headed straight for the front door. Pulling it open, she stepped outside and went to the backyard. If she didn't find anything that she could stab into submission, she was going to lose it.

She looked up and in front of her was a pile of wood. It looked like it had been part of the fence that surrounded the house, but it had been broken up to make firewood. It was perfect for her purpose, so Jackie headed towards the woodpile, intent on venting her rage.

She didn't get very far. Xander was standing there, his own swords in hand, shirtless. His chest was shining with sweat, and he looked like he'd been working out for quite a while. "Fuck." Jackie said. She didn't know if this was due to the fact that he was shirtless and covered in sweat or because he was in front of the wood pile.

"Get out of my fucking way." She said.

"By all means, but would you mind telling me what you intend to do with that sword?" Xander's voice was all smoothness and warm honey.

He was trying to calm her down, manipulative fucker. "I'm going to attack that woodpile and work out some of my rage." She said. "I'm so fucking angry and if I don't vent my fury soon, it won't be pretty. So, get the fuck out of my way."

Xander's eyes widened and, to her surprise, he stepped out of the way. "By all means, Jackie. But if you don't mind me suggesting another sword? The rounded one is suitable for impaling a person, so the blade is really sharp. It will be wasted hacking away at the wood. Might I suggest your broadsword?"

She blinked. "Oh." She blinked again. "Okay, let me go get it."

"No need, you can use mine. It's similar to the one you will be wielding. I am surprised by you actually."

"How so?"

"I would have lost my temper a long time ago. You've been handling the situation rather well with no one telling you anything of great importance."

"Including you."

"Yes, including me."

"Does this mean that you're going to tell me some of the shit I need to know?"

He looked at her and she saw a great expanse within the blue of his eyes; it spanned to the mountains and through them she saw the sun, the sky and the heavens. Then she blinked and she was back to looking at him and the drops of sweat that still covered his face.

"No," He said. "Now is not the time."

Looking back at him, she held out her hand. "Give me the fucking sword."

Xander grinned at her and he was lucky that she didn't ram that sword through that smug little grin. The sword was heavy in her hands, but not as heavy as she thought it would be. She held it in two hands as if it were a bat and looked at the wood pile.

"Am I holding this thing correctly?"

"You don't have to worry about grip and stance right now. You want to beat the crap out of this wood pile? Have at it, let your rage out. If you keep it inside, it will not do you any good. Part of finding your way through the journey you're on is finding out what your capable of."

"That sounds like more of the shit that Em was spewing!" She almost screamed this at him.

Xander leapt out of the way as she charged at the wood pile, letting out a scream of rage at the wood instead of Xander. Jackie threw herself into it and began to swing the sword down, gripping it with both hands. The first *thwak!* into the wood shook her slightly, the force of her hit travelling up her arms. This made her angrier and, with another guttural scream, she pulled the swords free and swung down again. She did this again and again and again, until she had lost count of how many times the had tried to attack the woodpile. In a way, she thought that with each *thwack!,* a bit of her anger was appeased.

She was angry at what they weren't telling her, at her shit job back home, at that fucking asshole of a guy who had screwed someone else and had sent her running away from herself. She was angry at herself for the direction that her life had gone, and the fact that she had no idea how to change it, no idea what to do.

Finally, she couldn't attack anymore. The sword fell from her hands and her whole body was vibrating. Her breath was coming out in hard, rough gasps and she stood there, pain running up and down her body, and wondered when she had ever felt so alive.

She let the sword fall from her hands and looked over at Xander. He was smiling at her, the smug bastard.

"Feel better?" He asked.

"Much."

"Good, now we can begin your training." He said. "For now, rest. You've earned it."

III

She was given a bedroom. She wasn't sure how long they would be here, but she could get used to this, Jackie thought. The bedroom was as big as her whole apartment back home. In fact, it was twice as bit as her apartment had been. Large windows overlooked the grounds of the house. Jackie could see large trees surrounding the perimeter of the property.

Looking around the room, Jackie took in a large queen-sized bed within hangings that made it look as if a fairy princess slept there, with a desk and a bookshelf nearby. There was a bedside table with a book which was still open and placed facedown. Jackie wondered who had slept here, who's room this had been.

She approached the bed and trailed her fingers through the gauze. It felt almost normal being here, other than the fact that there was nothing normal about this situation, this house or the two people downstairs. Jackie wondered if she had been slipped some pot on the plane, but that seemed unlikely. "This is the new normal." She said. Jackie didn't know how she felt about that.

The tarot cards in her purse were calling to her. She had been desperate to draw a card to see what they would have to say. She walked over to the desk, sat in the leather chair and pulled out her deck.

Though she had collected tarot decks, she always took the Ryder Waite Smith deck with her. Jackie was once asked how many decks she had, and at the time, she thought she had somewhere around eighty. That had been years ago. Who knew how many decks she actually had back home? She loved the art, the different styles, and the way the message coming through the cards would be different, depending on the creator's voice. Tarot was fluid.

Pulling her deck out of its bag, Jackie always experienced a moment of anticipation. What would the cards have to say to her? What message would spirit bring her? What voice would come through? Would the message from the cards be soothing, or stern and direct? Jackie never knew what she would draw. There were some tarot readers that said they could, but she had never been one of those readers. Instead, she used her gut, or what Em called her intuition to read the cards.

Taking a minute to clear her mind, Jackie thought of her question. "What the fuck do I need to know?" She was sure that spirit would forgive her if she swore, it being the end of the world and everything.

She shuffled until it felt right to stop, broke the deck into three piles, and chose the one that called to her the strongest. She pulled the topmost card and looked at it. It was The Queen of Swords. When Jackie had first seen this card, she thought that the Queen looked like one tough bitch. Having read the cards for years now, she had grown to appreciate the deeper meaning of the card. The Queen of Swords was always truthful, she communicated clearly with others and didn't mince words. She was also fiercely independent. She was a teacher and a writer.

Looking at the card, with the Queen of Swords sitting in her throne, one hand clutching a long silver sword and the other hand outstretched to someone or something beyond the edge of the card, Jackie always thought that the Queen was saying 'Bring it on'. She knew that when a person read the cards, it was what they understood intuitively that mattered more than the card's meaning according to a book. Looking at the Queen of Swords, Jackie thought that the Queen was telling her that she had this, that whatever this new world presented, Jackie would be able to take it all in stride.

Drawing another card for clarity, Jackie was shocked to pull another Queen of Swords. This one was slightly different than the first, which had red hair and a large golden crown. The new one had blond hair and a small silver crown. Jackie shook her head. "That's not right," She said out loud. There aren't *two* Queen of Swords."

Putting the cards back in the deck, she shuffled the cards the same as before, cut the deck and drew a card. She wasn't surprised to see that she had drawn the Queen of Swords again, but this time, the Queen had black hair and the crown was a bright brilliant bronze colour.

"What the actual fuck?" Jackie whispered. She put the card back in the deck and then shuffled again. She quickly pulled a card from the top and this time the Queen of Swords had brown hair and wore a crown that looked as though it were made of glass. At this point, Jackie let the cards fall out of her hand, and watched as they fell to the table, some of them sliding to the floor. Those that landed face-up were blank, as if something had wiped them entirely clean. One of the cards wasn't blank though. Jackie reached down to pick it up, and saw that it was the Empress.

Letting out a breath that blew her hair away from her face, Jackie muttered "Fuck", picked up the cards and put them back home in their bag. "Maybe spirit is having a bad day, I know I am."

She caressed the bag and then patted it as if it were a living thing, which in a way it was. The cards lived through her. Tucking them back into her bag, Jackie wondered how long it would be until sleep claimed her. Would she ever be able to sleep again? She didn't think so. There was a small part of her that hoped she was dreaming, that she was still asleep in first class on the plane, on her way to a week in the warmth and sun. Pinching her arm, Jackie sucked in a breath at the pain and assumed that meant that she was awake.

"Fuck." Jackie said again.

She had no idea what to do. The cards had always been there for her, giving her sage advice when she needed it, even though she may not have wanted to listen to it at the time. It had always given her a direction at the very least, even if the meaning of the cards wasn't very clear.

Sighing, she turned to the bed and spotted the large leather-bound book upon it. Em must have brought it up to her room while she had been outside with Xander. Looking at it from across the room, Jackie remembered what Em had told her: *"You've just started telling your story. Good for you. Now you and the book are linked. I'm so proud of you."*

Jackie wondered if the book had recorded everything she'd been doing since she had first linked with it. *That would be cool*, Jackie thought. *Like a metaphysical Kindle downloading from the cloud of me.* She walked over to the book and looked at its old leather surface. Jackie could actually feel the pulse of the book from where she stood. Reaching down to pick it up, she fully expected to feel an electric shock of some sort, but when she did pick it up the book let out one final pulse as if it had finally found its home.

Shaking her head, Jackie said "I'm going fucking nuts."

She opened the book and saw only the words that had been there before. "Once upon a time..."

"What the fuck do you want from me?" She asked it. "We're linked now, right?" She sat on the bed, cradling the book in her lap. "Can't you just download what I'm thinking?"

The book ruffled its pages and fell still. "I take that's a no."

Jackie let out a long sigh. "I've never been good at telling stories, do I have to speak to you out loud? I'll sound like an idiot doing that."

The book ruffled its page again.

"Fucked if I know what to do, then. I have no idea." She sat looking at the book and stroked its pages softly. "I have no idea where I am anymore and have no idea what I'm doing."

She set the book down when she heard Em's voice calling her for dinner. "I'll see you later." She went to the door and opened it. Stepping out into the hallway, she closed it behind her. In the silence of the room, there was the hiss and whisper of a pen writing across paper.

*

When Jackie came down the stairs, neither Xander or Em were visible. "Hello?" She called out, feeling too much like a potential victim in a horror movie.

"We're back here!" Em called. "In the kitchen!"

Now that she was listening, she heard the sound of voices, Em's and Xander's being easy to pick out. However, there was a third voice she had never heard before. From a distance, it sounded deep, as if it were coming from the basement of someone. The closer she got to the kitchen, the more she heard the voice in her bones, so deep was the voice. Though she didn't know who this person was, the voice immediately made her feel calm, as if wrapped in a warm blanket.

Stepping into the kitchen, Jackie's first thought was that the voice matched the man perfectly. He stood well over six feet and was broad shouldered. He had a thickly muscled chest and his arms held more muscle. Her eyes were drawn to the rope-like veins that ran up and down his arms. He wore a vest that looked as if it had once been made out of denim, but had things added to it. It now looked as if it were armour, and the weather had turned it hard and supple. Leather had been sewn overtop of the denim. There was a black tattoo that covered his arm. She was into astronomy and the planets, so she recognized the symbol as the planet Venus. It was surrounded by a heart which had been made to look like barbed wire.

Whereas Xander's eyes were a brilliant blue and Em' eyes a rolling green and blue, this new man had eyes that were a warm golden colour. That was Jackie's first thought, but as he continued to look at her, Jackie saw that there were flashes of silver there too. It was as if his eyes were filled with the stars and the lightning that graced his arm. His lips were formed in a thin line as he took her in, and like Em and Xander before him, he seemed to come to some internal decision as he smiled.

"Jackie, how nice to meet you." His voice was even deeper than it had been on the other side of the doorway. "Xander and Em were just telling me about you."

For some reason, this pissed Jackie off. "Yeah, well I don't like people talking about me behind my back." She looked this hulk of a man in the eyes and saw them widen with either shock or amusement, she couldn't tell. She also didn't care.

His smile broadened and he let out a little laugh that shook his whole body. To Jackie, it felt like the earth itself was moving around her. "Oh, you're right Emogene, she is a fighter!" He held out his hand to Jackie and said "My name is Gabriel. It is a pleasure to meet you."

Jackie's hand was enveloped by Gabriel's, his hands being twice the size of hers. "I suppose it is nice to meet you, too. Now are you going to do what these two are doing and tell me fucking nothing? Or are you going to talk to me plainly?" She sighed and tried to calm her anger, as she felt it rising within her. Nothing would get accomplished if she was pissed all the time. "Between Xander and Em and the fucking book, I've had it up to here with knowing just enough to keep me hooked but not enough to really know anything."

Gabriel let out another deep, rolling laugh. "You're a spitfire, aren't you?" He smiled at her again. "That will serve you well here. You need the will to fight," He inclined his head toward Xander. "In order to choose your path, you must have all the weapons you need. As well, you need to know yourself completely." He inclined his head at Em. "Only then will you know where you are going."

Her anger was boiling over now. "And what will you teach me? How to be a fucking warrior? How to look into a glass and find my spirit self waiting to sit down and be best buddies? What the fuck is going on here? That's all I want to know."

"That's the one thing that we can't tell you." Gabriel said. "Yet," He added, taking note of the fire in Jackie's eyes. "Everything will become clear in time, but for now Emogene has made us a beautiful meal and there is a freshly opened bottle of wine on the table. I suggest you take food with us; you must be starving."

At the suggestion of food, Jackie's stomach grumbled loudly. *Fucking traitor*, she thought. "I could eat." She said.

Em gave her a kind smile, a soft curving of the lips, and ushered her into the dining room. It looked as though it had been set up for visiting royalty, not a ragamuffin collection of people. She wondered if everyone else smelled or if it was just her. Jackie wondered how long it had been since she last showered. Hope they don't breathe in too deeply, she thought.

She turned around to ask Xander something about her training, when she realized that Em and Xander had not entered the room. Jackie could hear them making dinner in the kitchen. She sighed and turned to look at the mysterious Gabriel. She tried to look at him with her most pissed off expression.

He gave a little chuckle. "I do love a woman with spirit. They make the best warriors and will do anything to defend home, honour, and their lives. They also know how to love fiercely and with fire." Gabriel said kindly, gesturing to a seat close to him.

Jackie let out a *harrumph* as sat across from him, and crossed her arms in front of her chest. "I do have to admit that describes me."

Gabriel let out a loud guffaw. "I'm glad you take that as a compliment. It's how it was intended. Life can be too short sometimes." A look of sadness entered his gaze that pushed the smile off his face. Jackie wondered what despair he had known in his life. It seemed odd to her that these people had existed before she had gotten off of the plane, and had lived a whole life before she came into the picture.

He looked at Jackie once again and a bit of the light came back to him. "You must be finding this all too much to deal with."

Gabriel's voice was even deeper when she was so close to him. She could feel it in her chest as he spoke. A little bit of the fight lessened in Jackie as she looked into his kind gold eyes. She decided that she needed to speak honestly to him. He would understand her. "I don't know where I am." She said. "The world was one way when I fell asleep on the plane and it was this way when I woke up. I don't know anyone, and I don't think I trust myself here. I'm too unsure. Xander thinks he will train me with a sword when I've never held a weapon in my life. I'm not that brave."

"I beg to differ. You have more courage in you than you give yourself credit for. How many others would have been brave enough to take that leap onto the plane slide?"

"Well, I couldn't very well stay up on the plane, could I?" Jackie said. "I mean, I would have run out of food eventually. It's not like I could have stayed there for very long."

"Yes, but there was food there and you could have made something of a home for yourself in the seats." His voice glowed with something like pride. "Yet, even with all of that, you chose to find your own way down, to inflate the slide and glide down into the unknown. I think that's plenty brave, don't you?"

"I don't know what's brave about wanting to survive."

"Plenty, even the will to survive is brave. I have great respect for you, and you're so hard on yourself."

Jackie felt her cheeks reddening. Even so, she kept her gaze on him and her arms crossed. "Thank you. Are you going to tell me what the fuck is going on?" She asked. "Tweedle Dum and Tweedle Dee out there won't tell me anything."

Gabriel gave her a look and she knew that his answer would not be the answer to her question. "You're forgetting what you need to do, Jackie. You forgot it a long time ago."

"What did I forget?"

"How to love yourself of course. Do you have respect for yourself anymore?"

Jackie looked into Gabriel's face again and actually let out a snort. "Really? This is what you want to talk to me about? The all-mighty power of love?" She blew a raspberry at Gabriel. "It hasn't done me very well, just so you know. It's how I ended up here."

"Well, sometimes love hurts. Sometimes, those we love hurt us. It doesn't mean that we have to love ourselves any less."

51

Jackie let out another snort. "All this talk of love. You're nothing but a big softie."

Gabriel shrugged. "I suppose I am. Love can heal all wounds, you know?" He eyed her with narrowed eyes from across the table. "Actually, you don't know, do you? You're walking around with a lot of wounds that are still bleeding."

"Well, what the fuck do you want me to do about it?" Jackie said in frustration. "I don't suppose you have a metaphysical band-aid, do you?" Gabriel gave her a look. If she wasn't trying to be such a bitch, she would probably have cried.

Reaching out with one large hand, he took one of Jackie's and squeezed it. "Oh honey. Who hurt you?"

Xander and Em came into the dining room at that moment. They both had platters of food, more food than Jackie had seen in days. "You two having a good talk?"

Gabriel gave Jackie a soft look. "We're having a great gabfest. Talking about love and self-love."

"One of my favourite topics." Em said. "You make any headway with the book, Jackie?"

Jackie shrugged. "I don't know. I don't think it hears me very well."

"It hears you fine. Books can be stubborn about listening. You'll learn how to talk to it, and to make the book listen."

Xander and Em piled the table high with corn on the cob, slices of roast beef, green beans, potatoes, green salad, and a roasted chicken. Jackie's stomach growled despite her wish to keep it quiet. Gabriel looked at her with a knowing smile and patted his stomach.

They all sat around the table and Jackie watched as Em poured three tall glasses full of red wine. She passed out the glasses and said, "To new friends."

Jackie clinked her glass against the others and took a moment to enjoy the ringing that filled the air. Then she spoke: "How about to finally telling me what the hell is going on here?" She smiled amiably at all three of them and took a sip of her wine which she had to admit was very good, and looked at them all as sweetly as she could. *Fuckers*, she thought.

Gabriel looked at Xander and Em, and shrugged his shoulders. "I'm just along for the ride here, folks. It's all up to you, Jackie. Keep that in mind, okay? It's all up to you."

Em looked uncomfortable and Xander still looked surly. "You have to understand-" Em began.

"No, you have to understand. I've arrived in a world that should be like home, but I don't recognize it anymore. *You*," She pointed to Xander, "tell me I have to learn to fight and get me prepped with swords. And *you*," She pointed at Em, "tell me that I have to connect with some fucking book, that it will complete me somehow." She turned to look at Gabriel. "Now *you* tell me to love myself more and that my love will help me with what is coming."

Putting down her glass, Jackie folded her hands politely on the table in front of her. She let Xander, Emogene, and Gabriel squirm in the silence for a bit before speaking again. "You want me to fight, give me the weapons I need." She gave them all a stare that was as cold as steel. Jackie was gratified to see them all looking slightly uncomfortable. "Won't anyone tell me what the fuck is going on?" She let out a rough breath that blew her hair out of her eyes. "Please?"

It was the please that made them look uncomfortable. Em said nothing, but started to serve the food. Jackie was happy that they all looked so skittish, but that happiness began to fade when she realized that these were the only people that she had here. She couldn't be starting off this way. Her grandmother had always taught her that you catch more flies with honey than with vinegar.

"It's just that I have no idea what is going on. No idea what you're preparing me for. You want me to fight and be ready, but fight against what? Be ready for what? You're not giving me a lot to go on here and you're leaving me in the dark." Jackie made sure to look at all three of them in the eyes and made sure that she held their gazes upon her. "I'm lost here. I don't like being in the dark, and you're keeping me there for a reason. I don't like being in the dark." She said again. "It's been like that for most of my life. In this new life I'm now living, is it going to be the same thing?"

Em had finished dishing out the food. Jackie waited for Em to respond, but to her surprise, it was Gabriel who spoke first. "Let's eat and enjoy this wonderful meal and then you and I will go have a walk outside, okay?"

"It's getting dark outside." Jackie well remembered the noises she had heard as she ran from the airport. "I don't want to be outside in the dark."

"Sometimes you'll have to be. But Xander will come with us to make sure we have light. Em will stay here and guard the house. Okay?"

Jackie didn't have to think about it. "Okay." Although after she said that, she wondered what Em would be guarding the house against.

"All right then. Dig in, I can hear your stomach from here."

*

Jackie pushed back her plate away, her stomach satisfied.

The meal had been filled with idle chatter and the music of knives against cutlery. Jackie watched each of them as she ate, content to listen rather than talk. Thankfully, no one commented on her silence, perhaps wanting to avoid another confrontation.

She tried to pay attention to the way that these people, her supposed protectors, interacted. Jackie wanted to see if they had any tells or facial expressions that she should pay attention to that might aid her in the future. She trusted Xander without question, but there was something about Emogene that gave Jackie pause. Emogene was kind, yes, but there was a darkness between her and Xander that needed further explanation. Jackie also wondered if Em had any tattoos or markings like Xander and Gabriel sported.

Gabriel was someone else who gave her pause. All his claptrap about love and self-love and healing herself had sounded truthful, but he couldn't possibly believe that loving herself could heal her. He couldn't be that simple. What was she missing? She didn't like to be so distrustful of the people who had taken her in, but her gut, or her intuition to us Em's word, was in overdrive. Something else was going on here and she was at a loss as to what it was. She had to find out more.

When Jackie had pushed her plate away, Em turned to look at her. "Was everything okay, dear?" She asked.

"It was wonderful. First real meal I've had since I've been here." Jackie said. "Thank you."

"You're welcome. Now go ahead with Xander and Gabriel." Em looked at her, and Jackie knew that her deep green eyes saw more than Jackie could know. She was being peered into completely; Em was looking through her, and her eyes grew brighter for a moment. Then she nodded her head. "Trust your intuition, dear. It won't lead you wrong."

It was as if Em had seen the words she had just been thinking and brought them to the surface. "What do you mean?" Jackie said, almost in a whisper.

"Just that. Now go on, the boys are waiting. Leave your plate, I'll clean up."

Jackie felt helpless, if only for a moment, and that pissed her off. Squaring her shoulders, she turned to find Gabriel and Xander waiting for her by the back doors. Xander was holding out her swords to her.

"You'll need these." Xander said. He helped Jackie pull them into place, making sure the straps were comfortably snug, but not too tight. "Soon you'll be able to do this by yourself. It takes practice though."

"I still don't understand why I need them." She said.

"You'll see." Xander said. "Let's go."

Gabriel opened the door and they stepped out into the inky blackness of night. Their only light were the stars and the moon which shone down upon them. Jackie marvelled at how brightly the moon shone, how brilliant the stars were. She hadn't had time to stop the other night to look at the stars, too intent on getting inside the airport to safety.

The moonlight highlighted the fact that, even here, there was grit and grime. Jackie could see dark slashes that marked the grass that she knew was blood. She wasn't paying attention to where she was going and tripped over a loose stone. Gabriel caught her before she fell.

"Oops, careful honey. Don't want you to hurt yourself. Xander, a little help here? Care to shed some light on the path ahead?"

"Sure thing." Xander said.

Jackie turned when she heard the *chik fizz!* and watched as a ball of blue fire, like the blue colour of his eyes, bloomed in the palm of his hand.

Jumping back, Jackie almost fell again, and would have if Gabriel hadn't steadied her. "What the fuck is that?" She almost yelled.

"This?" Xander tilted the blue flame this way and that. "This is how we will see in the dark."

"You know what I mean. How did you do that?" Jackie asked.

Xander gave her a wry grin that looked almost demonic in the half light from his blue flame. "What?" He brought the flame closer to her face, and though the light was bright, she could feel no heat from it.

She glared at him but it didn't do her much good in the dark, even with the light he was casting. He seemed to get the hint and let out a little chuckle, giving her a smile. His teeth looked bright in the shadowy darkness highlighted by the blue flames.

"Sorry." He said. "I knew what you meant." He snapped his fingers and the flame changed into a tongue of blue flame that sat in the centre of his palm for a moment before growing into a ball of blue fire once more. "We all have talents, Jackie. You are learning what yours are. Mine is magic."

"Like pulling the rabbit from the hat magic?"

He shook his head. "No, more like the real kind of magic. There's a reason that Em calls me the Magician." He said.

"Come on folks," Gabriel said softly. "We should get going. We've got some distance to go."

"How far are we going?" Jackie asked. She was nervous about being outside, even with Gabriel and Xander by her side. She had no idea what was hiding in the dark, not anymore.

Pointing to a copse of trees near by, Gabriel said "See those trees? We're going over there."

"Why?" Jackie said. "Is there someone else for me to meet out there?"

Gabriel's eyes widened and he let out a soft laugh. "You're smart. No, there's no one out there for us to meet. I just figure that a walk has to have a destination in mind. That copse of trees is our destination."

"Okay." Jackie said, not feeling at all as brave as she sounded.

They began to walk toward the trees. Their steps whispered over the grass, and Jackie tried to avoid the darks spots that shone even in the darkness. She had no intention of finding out what it was, but she was pretty sure that it was blood.

The lawn here was littered with other forgotten things: a bicycle tire, a few pieces of furniture that had been broken into shards, what looked like a woman's purse, and a leather jacket that had been shredded to pieces. Jackie was beginning to feel ill.

"I'm not sure that I want to be out here." Jackie said.

"You have to be brave honey. Be a warrior." Gabriel said.

"Fuck that. You're the one built like a brick shit house. You be the fucking warrior."

Xander let out a snort. "She's got you there, handsome."

"Shut your mouth. You just concentrate on being our glow worm, okay?" Gabriel said acidly.

Their steps continued to whisper and hiss over the grass and the copse of trees seemed no closer. "What are we going to find in the trees anyways?" Jackie asked. "A troll that hides in amongst the leaves?" When Xander snorted, she turned to him. "What? I suppose a fucking rabbit made all that blood?" She gestured at the grass. "The world is so fucked up right now that it seemed the most likely guess."

"Not a bad guess, honey." Gabriel said. "Nope we won't find that." Gabriel said. "I want to find someone else who's going to help you."

"Who's that?" Jackie asked.

"Yourself." Gabriel said and stopped walking.

Jackie stopped walking also, but the whispering continued. Jackie had good enough vision to notice there was something moving in the trees. What could move along the grass like that and make that kind of noise? Did she want to find out? Jackie didn't think so.

"Do you hear that?" She whispered.

"Yes." Xander said. "And now they've heard you. Get ready."

"Ready for what?"

"Don't ask stupid questions and grab a sword." Xander said.

There was the metallic whisper of metal being pulled free, and Jackie turned to look at Xander holding a sword in one hand and his blue flame in the other.

Reaching up, her breath coming fast and quick, Jackie pulled out the long sword just as Xander had. The whispering had begun to increase, and it now sounded as if a whole chorus of shadows were chattering in the darkness.

"I can't do this." Jackie said, hating how her voice shook.

"Yes you can, honey." Gabriel said softly. He stood beside her, holding a small shield that looked like the shape that had been tattooed in his arm, with a symbol shining brightly in the shield's centre. "You can do this. You have been training for this your whole life."

"No, I haven't. I worked as a fucking office manager in the tech industry back home. Far from wielding a sword."

"The sword is but the mind." Gabriel said. "Just like in your tarot deck. Only this time, you hold on to the sword, you direct its power and force, rather than be at the mercy of your mind. You hold the sword. You control what you do and how this goes."

"Why are you doing this?" She asked with a bite to her words. "Why did we come out here at night?"

"So you could see what you're up against, and learn a bit about the fight that we have ahead of us." Xander said. "Get ready now."

The whispering had reached a fever pitch and Jackie wanted nothing more than to cover her ears, but she didn't. She stood her ground with her back straight even though her insides were shaking. She was made of jelly and her legs would give out at any moment, they would give away and she would fall and the thing that was coming would take her. *No!* she said to herself. *No, I won't let that happen!* She tightened her grip on the sword, grasped it with both hands. She didn't know what was coming, but she would be ready.

The wet whispering stopped, and the silence of the air around them was deafening. Jackie was a mess of emotions and she felt like she was going to piss herself she was so afraid, but she kept looking forward; her gaze locked on the grass in front of them which had started to sway as if moved by a soft breeze, but there was none.

Jackie took in a breath as the night sky filled with darkness. She thought that her nightmares had come to life and were flying towards her. She didn't know if they were birds or beings, feather or fur, but all she knew was that the darkness was coming towards her she didn't ever think she would breathe again.

Gabriel maneuvered so that his back was to hers, and Xander moved so that his back was to both of theirs. Swords, shield, and light out in front of them, they waited. They didn't have to wait long. Jackie screamed as a piece of darkness came towards her. Something bit her arm, and she screamed again,

58

QUEEN OF SWORDS

trying to use the long sword to cut off its head, but there was no way she could angle her sword that way. She threw her arm out and the beast flew out into the darkness, charging towards her again. Jackie reached up to grab her short sword, an pulled it free, and faced the oncoming hoard. She was ready.

"Fucking thing fucking bit me." She said, spitting out the words. She hacked with focus, making sure to try to keep them farther way from her with her long sword, and decapitating what got too close with the short sword. Bats, birds, and animals with fur. She didn't know how many she had killed. She had no idea what Xander and Gabriel were up to, if they were able to hold their own, but she was reassured every time she saw a flash of blue light and gold sparkles from Gabriel's shield.

A sound drew her attention on the right, and she saw what looked like a pig running towards her, but she had never known any pig that looked like that. It was twice as large as any pig she had ever seen, and the blackness just oozed from it. She saw no eyes, just a black void of darkness. "Just fucking shadow." Jackie said gritting her teeth. "Just spit and fucking shadow."

Slashing out with her long sword, Jackie let out a gasp as the sword didn't even cut the beast but slipped right through its shadowy form. Then the thing was closer, and she took a swing with her short sword, knowing as she did so that it was to no avail. Then the thing was on her, and she let out a guttural scream as the pig opened its maw to take a bite out of her neck. She reached up and pushed it down with her left hand, trying to keep the pig from her jugular.

Letting out another scream, but somehow cheered on by the blue and gold lights she could see, Jackie pushed the pig off of her with every bit of strength she could muster. Digging deep, she found more strength and more courage and thrust downward with her short sword, knowing that she wanted to be close enough to witness the thing's demise.

As she thrust down, Jackie felt a heat begin in the middle of her stomach. It was as if her whole body was on fire, and she let it flow into her. She pulled on the fire, knowing without knowing how she knew that it would not hurt her. With every bit of strength she had left, she thrust downward with her blade, the red fire from within her erupting in a dark red light, tinged with orange and yellow. The fire took over the beast, consuming it in flame and turning it to dust in a heartbeat.

Then there was silence again, a silence so loud it was deafening. She looked around and saw no beasts left. It was as if they had just faded away to nothing. Jackie looked at Xander and Gabriel and found they were looking at her. Tears were streaming down her cheeks and her legs were now really shaking.

"Well, what the fuck was that?" She said. Letting the swords fall to the ground, Jackie tumbled into blackness, and she let it claim her willingly.

IV

When Jackie woke, the first thing she heard was the sound of wind and leaves.

It was making the leaves whisper. She tried to listen to them to see if they had anything to say to her but could make no sense of them. Blinking her eyes, she looked at the sky above her and could see the sun shining through the foliage. The light was tinted green and red, gold and orange.

Sitting up, Jackie looked around her and tried to ignore her growing sense of panic. She was surrounded by trees. They were old, and aged, and stretched to the sunlight filtering through their leaves. While the leaves were full of colour, the trunks of the trees were so dark they were almost black. She wondered how long they had grown here to have stretched so high. Jackie didn't need to count the rings inside the trees to know that the trees of this forest were very old.

Nearby, Jackie heard the crinkle of leaves. A shiver ran along her skin that had nothing to do with the colder air that was blowing through the trees. The idea that someone, or some*thing*, might be in the woods with her did not instill within her a feeling of comfort. Her mind showed her what she had seen last night, a flurry of beasts and birds that were made from shadows, but were so much more terrifying. Blinking, Jackie tried to think of something else, anything else, but then she heard the crinkle of leaves again. She looked around for Gabriel and Xadner but didn't see them. Perhaps they were the ones making the noises? She certainly hoped so. She saw her swords laying nearby.

Standing, she went to them and slid them with some difficulty into the scabbards. Then she made her way as quietly as possible towards the noises. It was difficult to walk on a dirt floor that was covered in leaves without making any noise, but she tried to walk as quietly as possible.

The trees around her provided cover, but they also provided cover from potential harm. Either way, she didn't meet any more of the shadow beasts. The rustling of leaves she was headed towards grew louder, almost in anticipation of her arrival. Jackie kept going anyway, knowing that her curiosity left her with no real choice. She had always been this way, too curious for her own good. Jumping off of the plane and down the slide had been the least cautious thing she had done in a long time.

She approached carefully, the rustling growing louder. Jackie tried to look around the trees, but could see only more trees. Walking a little further, she was rewarded for her curiosity by a light that had begun to grow and grew brighter as she neared. The rustling almost filled the air around her; it was louder than her breathing, louder than her heartbeat.

Looking down, she saw a leaf shaking on the forest floor. The closer she got, the more it shook, and she realized that it was this leaf that had been making all the noise. She bent down to pick it up. From her days as a Girl Guide, she knew that this was a leaf from a rowan tree. Twirling it in her fingers, Jackie admired its jagged and symmetrical edges. Letting the leaf fall so that it lay flat on her palm, Jackie let out a small gasp. The leaf had begun to glow a soft golden colour. The glow brightened until it was almost blindingly bright. Jackie couldn't look away though; she had never seen anything so beautiful. There were tears sliding down her cheeks, which had little to do with how bright the light had been.

When the light cleared, the rowan leaf was no more, however there was now a rowan leaf tattooed on the palm of her hand. She ran the fingers of her right hand along her left palm, trying to see if the leaf would rub off. It didn't. Tattoos were nothing new to Jackie, having gotten quite a few of them over the years. This was the first time that something had tattooed her without pain. She wasn't sure she would have chosen a rowan leaf, but there were some strange tattoos out there in the world, and this one was no exception.

The golden glow that came from between the trees grew brighter still, as if it had absorbed some of the glow from the leaf that now graced her palm. No longer afraid, Jackie walked towards it. As she did, she noticed that more flowers had begun to grow in this part of the forest, but they were all yellow or red in colour.

Looking closer, she saw that the flowers were actually leaves, all kinds of them. As she walked by them, they followed her movements, seeming to bend and twist towards her. Walking towards the light coming from a little grouping of trees, Jackie wondered how her life was about to change again.

"This whole world is always changing." Jackie said out loud, merely to hear the sound of her own voice. She wasn't afraid, but she was apprehensive.

She hated not knowing what was going to come next. It drove her mad. Christmas had been torture for her as a child, and things hadn't much improved. She sighed. If she could jump off of a plane and onto a slide that led her into the unknown, then she could walk through a fucking forest; but that didn't mean she had to like it.

As she walked further into the forest, Jackie began to hear the sound of soft music, as if there were someone drumming a beat. It filled the forest with a tattoo of rhythm that didn't make her want to dance. It was more a beat to mark time, or her steps. The light kept brightening and she could almost taste it on her tongue. It smelled of autumn, like dirt and leaves that had been crunched under her feet. The leaves around her had lost their green colour; now they were the reds and golds of those leaves she had seen before. She stood and watched the colours of the leaves change right before her eyes.

A breeze willowed through the crowd of trees in front of her, and it almost felt as if it were pulling her along, into the small gathering of trees. Stepping through the outer edge of the circle of trees, she was momentarily blinded by the bright light that had been trying to find its way to her through the forest all this time.

When it cleared, there was a throb of warmth on the palm of her left hand. Looking down, she saw that the rowan leaf tattoo was glowing. She marveled at it and looked around her. Inside the copse of trees was different than it had been on the outside. Inside, the air was warm and the breeze within smelled of spices. It was also a lot bigger than the small circle of trees had led her to believe. Within the centre, she could see a large throne.

It was made from aged stone. Though old, the stone held warmth and glowed softly from within. Of course, the glow could have come from the woman who was sitting upon the throne. The woman was looking at Jackie with a stern expression on her face. Not foreboding, but more that it would not be wise for Jackie to step out of line in her presence. Her eyes saw too much.

Jackie approached the woman slowly, and the woman continued to look at her, as if she were taking all of what made Jackie complete under consideration in one glance. The woman was dressed in red robes and a cloak. Jackie could see silver armour covering her legs. There was a gold crown sitting on her head, on top of a riot of curls that framed her face and fell past her shoulders. The woman had a face unmarked by time. She could be twenty or sixty-two, Jackie had no way of knowing. She held a golden staff in her right hand.

Slowing her pace, Jackie walked towards her, even though her feet wanted to stay still, nestled in the leaves. Still, she tried to calm herself as she approached the woman by listening to the music she made as she walked, the crinkly music of crushed leaves. She took solace from the scent of earth and the warm breeze that flowed around and through the ring of trees.

Looking into the woman's eyes, Jackie saw that the eyes, though they saw too deeply, were kind. They widened slightly as they looked at Jackie, and then nodded, much as Xander or Emogene had done. Jackie resisted the urge to curtsy, but instead nodded back.

The woman let out a peal of laughter, and the air around her filled with several blue butterflies that flew away into the canopy of the trees. "I see you have a spine." The woman said.

"I should hope so." Jackie replied, speaking without thinking. "Otherwise, my head would flop all over the place."

"What I mean, as I'm sure you know, is that you are strong and you can take care of yourself."

"I am and I always have." Jackie said. "Look, not to be rude, but who the fuck are you?"

"True, I have not introduced myself." She looked at Jackie a moment longer. "You may call me Theodora, but I prefer the name Dora."

"Then Dora it is." Jackie looked at the woman. She exuded power, and Jackie could feel it from where she stood. She felt like she was standing in front of Oz the Great and Terrible for some reason. "Are you going to tell me why you're here with me in this forest?"

Looking at her with narrowed eyes, Dora responded "They weren't following the rules."

"I'm sorry?" Jackie said, even though she was not. "What the fuck do you mean?"

Dora stepped down from her throne and came towards Jackie, leaving the gold sceptre by the throne. "They were not following the rules. They know how this is all supposed to go. They know the rules. They can *help* you but they can't *lead* you." She said. "This is your journey to make, not theirs."

"I'm sorry," Jackie said, though she was far from sorry. "But who are you talking about?" She thought she had an idea of who Dora was talking about, though.

"The fools in that big house." She said, almost with venom. "They walk around, treating you like a doll when you are so much more than that. You are a *warrior*."

"Well, now you are speaking some sense. By the people in that house, do you mean Xander, Em and Gabriel?"

"Is that what they are calling themselves now? Interesting."

"I'm sorry, but are you going to spout off more stuff I don't understand?"

The woman gave her a wide-eyed look. "More of what stuff?"

Jackie let out a snort. "Please, if you know them, you know how they fucking talk." She tried to mimic their voices. "You have to choose your path Jackie, you have to bond with the book Jackie, you have to learn how to love yourself, Jackie." She let out a harsh laugh. "At least that's what I think they were saying. It was all a bunch of gobbledegook to me."

The woman let out a laugh and beckoned her closer. "I would hope as much. They can be tiresome, but they mean well. We each have our part to play after all, and some of us are better at playing our part than others."

Jackie let out a groan. "Here we go. You're going to speak to me in riddles too."

"I shall do no such thing. There are things that I can't tell you because you're supposed to find them out on your own. It would be a disservice to tell you everything. There would be no sense of adventure."

"Then what did you mean by them not following the rules? About the parts that they have to play?"

"All in good time, Jackie."

The woman came closer to Jackie. She could tell that the woman was not someone to be fucked with. The air around her seemed to crackle with electricity. It was as if she held all the fire of the world within her, but held it in complete control. Jackie watched the woman as she approached. She moved like army sergeant or military personnel, with not a step wasted.

"Walk with me."

"Now why would I do that?"

"Isn't that what friends do?" She asked. "They take constitutionals together? Talk amongst themselves? What do you normally do with your friends?"

"Yeah, well friends usually know each others' names. I don't know yours and you want me to walk with you?"

The woman's eyes widened again, and Jackie was about to shout something at her, when she spoke. "My name is Marie-Claude."

The name didn't really mesh with the woman in front of her. "Really?"

"Yes." Her tone made it clear that she knew what Jackie was thinking. "It means the one who raises. I prefer to think of that meaning the act of raising or rising up to take control. Do you see what I mean?"

"Yes and no."

Marie-Claude held out her hand again. "You will. Walk with me."

Jackie put her hand in Marie-Claude's and felt the warmth coming from her touch, chasing away the cooler air of the forest. Looking at her, Jackie thought that a lot of people had probably been fooled into believing that Marie-Claude was simply a beautiful woman, when Jackie knew that the woman was an inferno.

They walked along a path made by fallen leaves. Their steps sounded like rough music and whispers. The whispering sounds were amplified by the trees that replayed the echoes of their footsteps, and Jackie found herself being lulled by it. She wasn't sure how long they had been walking, but Marie-Claude had still not said anything.

"So are you going to tell me what is going on, Marie-Claude?"

The older woman cringed. "My full name is so formal, don't you fine? . You can call me Marie."

"Fine then, Marie. Are you going to tell me what is going on?"

"But you already know what is going on." She said.

"What? That the whole world has gone to shit and the only people that survived are fucking crazy?"

"Essentially."

"What, really?"

"Well, that's the simple version of events."

"Yeah, but what caused it?" Jackie asked. "What's with all the fucking blood everywhere, all the burning cars? All the missing people?"

"I can't tell you that right now. That's for you to discover on your own. You have quite the journey ahead of you, Jackie."

Inside her head, Jackie screamed at her. "You're not the first person to tell me that. You won't tell me anything? You're just like the magic trio that landed me here."

"You're right about that. They were helping you, and they should not have helped in that way. They did not follow the rules. As to what I can tell you, I am limited in what I can share."

"What the fuck can you tell me?" Jackie said, trying desperately to keep her temper under control.

Still holding Jackie's hand, Marie walked on, gently tugging Jackie after her. As they walked, the forest seemed to part before them, filling the air with the raspy music of leaves. Jackie could see the whole world laid out in front of her, and she wondered at her place within it and what she could do. She thought briefly of the leap she took down the slide and where it had brought her. How far could she go in the world as it was now?

Marie let go of Jackie's hand and pointed at the hills. "You must make your way to those hills. There you will find a mystic who will be able to help you further on your path."

"I have to do that all on my own?"

"I said no such thing. You will have help along the way from those you have already met, and more besides them." Marie made a face. "Despite the fact that those people may have hindered your growth, they will be a great help to you. There is one more thing that you will need as you go forward."

"What's that?"

Taking Jackie's hands in her own, Marie held them both together. Jackie felt Marie's magic, warm and soothing, run through her. Light began to shine from between her closed palms. Though she could see it out of the corners of her eyes, she did not look down. Instead, she looked at Marie.

Her brown eyes were filled with more of that light, and her face was beautiful and serene. Jackie had never seen a more beautiful woman. She could also feel the strength that ran through Marie, strength that she hoped to embrace and emulate.

The light faded, and when it was gone, Marie took Jackie's hands and spread them apart. Now there was a rowan leaf tattooed on her other palm.

Looking at it, Jackie wondered at the magic that had made this happen. Had magic always existed in the world, or was it new to the world as it was now? *Whatever*, she thought. *The world has gone to shit.*

"Why did you do this?" Jackie said. "I already had this tattoo on my right palm."

"Because there must be balance in all things. Sometimes, finding that balance within yourself will be difficult. These leaves will help you find that balance." Marie rubbed her thumb gently along the tattoo on each palm. "The rowan leaf symbolizes courage and strength, just like the courage and the strength that you carry inside you."

Jackie didn't say anything for a while, but merely took in more of the warmth that Marie emanated. Finally, after the silence between the two of them had stretched on, Jackie spoke. "I don't know what to do. I don't know anything about climbing a mountain."

Marie-Claude smiled at her, but there was a steel within that smile. "You will have to show this world who you are. You will have to show it what you're capable of and exercise your authority over it."

"But I don't understand this world."

"This is your world, Jackie. You may not understand it as it is now, but you know how it was. You can see that, underneath all the blood and carnage. You can see the good beneath the dark. Just because you don't understand it doesn't mean you can't have authority over your involvement with it."

Jackie sighed. "More fucking riddles."

"No, not riddles. That's sound advice and something you need to remember. You have always been strong Jackie, but you have never truly ruled yourself. Now is the time to do so."

"What about the fucking mountain?" Jackie said, a tinge of panic reaching her voice, despite her best efforts to remain calm. "I don't know anything about climbing a mountain!"

Marie patted her hands and the rowan leaf tattoos responded by sending a thrill up Jackie's arms. "A mountain is only as big as you want to make it. You must find balance within yourself and authority over yourself if you want to move forward."

Jackie blew out a raspberry. "I think I might have preferred the riddles over the directness."

"I see no point in telling riddles. You need to know how things are. I can't tell you everything that you want to know, but I have armed you with the tools you will need to go further. You can do this, Jackie."

Jackie resisted giving her the finger. Marie seemed the type of woman to cut it off just to spite her. "What comes after the mountain? You're asking a fuckload of me, to just go on this journey, willy nilly. Why should I? What will it do? It won't accomplish anything."

Marie gazed at her and the building warmth she had been seeing in the woman's dark brown eyes turned to fire, and the look she gave Jackie was terrifying. "What *good* will it do?" She said, every word a hiss. "It won't accomplish *anything*?" Marie's eyes narrowed, and the leaves began to flutter and fly around them.

The leaves all rose into a circle, formed a cyclone around them, and Jackie knew that Marie was causing this, that her energy was responsible. "Look, I'm sorry okay?" Only she wasn't sorry and didn't sound like it. She just wanted the leaves to stop whipping around.

The cyclone around them moved faster and Jackie could feel the wind and the air getting fiercer and more violent. The breeze was no longer making music with the leaves as it had before. Now, it was screaming around her. It was pulling at her body and she had difficulty staying in one place, the wind wanted to pull her off of her feet.

"This will make all the difference for you!" Marie yelled, her voice somehow louder than that wind. "You have no idea, none at all! You have no idea of the steps you have already taken and what you will be able to do!"

Jackie tried to press against the cyclone swirling around them. It was growing smaller and smaller and Jackie was being whipped by the wind now, the leaves that had looked so beautiful cutting her face. "Look, I'm sorry okay?" She said again. "I'm sorry!" She reached out and took one of Marie's hands. "I mouth off when I'm nervous. I'm sorry. Please stop this!" Jackie cried. "I have been afraid before but now I'm fucking terrified!"

Perhaps it was the act of touching Marie's hand, but the golden flame within Marie's eyes started to dim and the wind around her started to lessen. Looking at her, Jackie wondered if the woman was some sort of Goddess or if she was just full of magic, if all the people she had met were. If they were filled with magic, what did that make her?

The wind mellowed to a soft breeze, no longer howling in her ears. Jackie looked at Marie and watched the woman become human again, the anger fading from her. "I'm sorry." Jackie said again. "I know that you're just trying to help."

Nodding her head, Marie said "That's all right. I'm sorry for frightening you."

"It's all good. It's not the most fucked up thing I've seen since I've been here."

Marie looked calmer now. She gave the hand that she still held a soft squeeze. "Shall we walk on?"

Jackie knew that though Marie had phrased it as a question, it would be foolish to refuse her. "Yes. Okay."

They walked a few steps and the forest was beginning to thin. Jackie noticed that there were a smaller number of trees that surrounded her. She knew that her time in the forest was coming to an end, and she wasn't sure that she had actually learned anything about what she was supposed to do.

Marie squeezed Jackie's hand. "You have learned so much." Marie said, as if she had read Jackie's mind. "I know that this is hard for you, that you wish your life to have the structure and the balance that you so crave." Marie gestured forward again at the landscape before them. "There is a balance to be found out there, even though all you see is chaos right now. You will have to find your own balance, your own stability."

Marie stopped walking and Jackie looked around her. The trees had thinned to bush, and there was nothing around them now but the rough ground that was the landscape leading to the mountain. "I know you want to find your way out of this world, but it is *your* world too, Jackie. You're not just passing through. You will need to find out what happened inside yourself before you can find out what happened here."

Jackie nearly choked on the fear that filled her. "How am I supposed to find out what happened here?" She whispered urgently. "I don't even know why I woke up here. I have no idea what I'm doing or what I'm going to do." She tried to keep the panic from her voice, but wasn't entirely successful. She hated sounding fearful and weak, always had. She thought it made her less in some way.

Marie leaned in and kissed her, first on one cheek and then the other. "Sometimes, it's when we have no idea what we're doing that we find out who we are supposed to be. Sometimes, the greatest struggle can bring the greatest clarity."

Reaching into the air, Marie pulled Jackie's bag and swords from nowhere. Jackie had seen plenty of magic thus far, but this simple act took her breath away. "You will have to lead, Jackie. It will be difficult work, but you can do it. I believe you can. I just hope that you believe in yourself."

"It can't be that easy, can it?" Jackie said in a hoarse whisper.

"Sometimes it is." Marie turned slightly, then turned back. "Help will be given to you if you ask for it. You will find salvation at the top of the mountain, though not the salvation you think it will be." Marie smiled when she saw the frustration on Jackie's face. "Have faith, Jackie. The highest mountain is climbed one step at a time."

Marie turned and began walking towards the forest. Jackie watched her for as long as she could, but eventually the trees and the mist swallowed her and Marie was no more. Jackie stood on the terrain of rough stone and dry earth and looked at the mountain in the distance, sitting in front of her like an insurmountable wall.

Jackie took in a deep breath. "Fuck." She said.

V

"Fuck." Jackie said again.

The breeze that had seemed so comforting in the forest as it whirled through the trees now let out a lonely and haunting whistle out here in what looked like a stone tundra. She watched as the shadow the mountain cast along the ground shifted and stirred as clouds moved across the sun. She walked a little closer, looking up at its mighty height, wondering how she would get up there, how she would find a way to scale the rockface that stood in front of her.

"Fuck and shit." Jackie said. *Hey,* she thought, *you had to change it up a bit, right?*

Walking closer to the mountain, she took a deep breath in and let it out slowly to calm herself. It was something that she did often to still herself when she was upset or anxious. She had to change her way of looking at this obstacle. It was just a mountain, right? She had conquered many tougher things in her life, like being married to her ex-husband. She deserved a fucking medal for that.

Jackie had hoped that by doing some deep breathing that the mountain would somehow magically change shape, that it would somehow morph into a pathway that led to a magical meadow, beautiful and alluring. However, the mountain stayed a mountain and didn't morph or change or become something else. "Everything else is magic here, why can't the mountain be magic?"

She sighed, thinking that it probably already *was* magic. *It wouldn't be here otherwise, would it?* Jackie thought. Letting out a long breath, Jackie squared her shoulders, put her head up and walked onward. There was nothing else she could do.

As she walked towards the mountain, getting closer to it with each step, she listened to the music created by the wind and the sound of her duffel back and swords. *Thwap! Thump! Thwif!* She took a step to each noise, trying to keep the beat of the sounds around her. *Thawp! Thump! Thuf!* She walked onward, even when her body wanted to give up and fall to the very ground upon which she walked. *Thawp! Thum! Thwoo!* Jackie didn't know how long she had been walking, had no idea how far she had come, but the mountain still seemed so very far way.

"What gives?" Jackie asked out loud. She listened to the wind, wanting to hear a response, but heard nothing besides the endless whispering. Looking back in the direction from which she had come, Jackie received a shock: the forest was so far away that it was but a black pinprick in the distance. She stood there, looking at that pinprick, wondering how it was possible that she had come so far, but not far enough.

She looked in her bag to make sure that her cards were there, something that she should have done a long time ago. They were there, thank goodness, as well as a few other things she didn't remember packing: a small rolled up sleeping pallet and blanket, a couple changes of clothes and, thank goodness, a small package of food and a bottle of water.

Sitting on the hard earth, Jackie unscrewed the bottle cap and took a few cautious sips. She didn't want to guzzle it all down right away, and she didn't know how long she would be out here amongst the rocky terrain. She tightened the cap, put it back in her bag, and pulled out the small packet of food. She wondered who had put it there. It didn't seem like a thing that Marie would have done, but Jackie had just met her for the first time. What did she know about these people that she had met anyways? They could be anyone, her mind said. However, her heart said that they were being genuine. Jackie trusted them, no matter how frustrating they were or how little information they gave her. She had gone on journeys blindly before, and wasn't this just another journey? All she could do was take one step in front of the other and go forward. All she could do was walk onward, no matter where this journey led her.

The small packet of food had been wrapped in muslin and cheesecloth, then placed in a plastic bag. Unwrapping it, Jackie revealed some pieces of chicken, and a mixture of fruit raisins, and what looked like dried cranberries. There were also some pieces of cheese. She ate a little bit of everything, then wrapped it all back up in the muslin, cheesecloth, and plastic. The cheese had tasted of dill, and the chicken of mustard. The food had reminded her of Em, and the meal that she had made in her massive house. That seemed ages ago now, having fought and survived by the blades of her swords since then.

Tucking the food back in the duffel bag, she rooted around for her cards and found them, but there was also something else. Pulling it out of the bag, she put her cards aside and looked at what she held in her hands. It was a journal made of the thickest leather. The paper within appeared handmade, and there was a long leather thong that tied it closed. When she undid the leather cord, she saw a cover much like the one from the book that had been in her bedroom at Em's. She thought longingly of the bed now, sitting on the hot and hard earth.

Letting the cover of the book fall open, a white piece of paper fell into her lap, but it was what was on the aged paper that drew her eyes. There was small, neat writing that lined several pages of what she now understood was a journal. Looking more closely at the words on the page, she knew that it was her journal, her book, the one that Em had told her to fill with her story. Jackie had no idea how it had been done, but she knew that this was *her* book, the one that had been in her bedroom. How Em had shrunk it down so that it was the size of her palm was something that Jackie couldn't explain, but she just *knew* that it was her book. She was actually happy to see it.

Looking closely at the words on the first page, Jackie saw that they began with 'Once upon a time...' like all good stories did. She wanted to keep reading to find out what the book had written about her, what she had written about herself, but she tucked it back into her duffel bag along with her cards. She picked up the piece of paper that had fallen into her lap. On it there were a few words written in a curling black script: *If you should lose your way, the words contained within this book will lead you back to yourself.*

Jackie was warmed by this, but somewhat annoyed. "I don't suppose you have any information on how to climb a fucking mountain, do you?" She fished the book out again, and flipping forward to the last entry, she looked at what was written there: *Jackie looked at the words written on the page and hoped to find clarity there. She found none.'*

Closing the book, Jackie blew a raspberry at it. "Well fuck you very much." She pulled her cards out, thinking that at least they would provide her with some kind of clarity, if not a direct answer to what was going on. She thought on her question, trying to make sure that it was clearly worded. She wanted to have a conversation with the cards, encourage a dialogue within herself. She asked the cards "What do I need to know about getting to the top of the mountain?"

Shuffling, she laid down three piles on the hard earth, chose her favourite one and drew the card. She got the Queen of Swords. Jackie let out a snarl followed by several choice swear words. "I'm beginning to hate that bitch." She sighed and drew another card and laid it face up beside the Queen of Swords. It was the Hierophant. "Great, so I'll receive some mystical advice that will somehow enrich my spirit, but be really pissed about it?" Jackie didn't understand it. Her cards had always led her down the right path, or at least reflected what was going on in her life. What was she not seeing? She drew another card; it was the Lovers. This card related to love and self love, or the love of another.

Jackie snorted. "Yeah, like that will happen!" She put all the cards back into her satchel and stood, strapping the swords and the duffel back on. Looking at the mountain, she tried to see if there was a path over it.

Looking up at the mountain, she reached into her duffel bag, took out the water bottle and had another swig. It still seemed so far away. What was it that Marie had said? *'The highest mountain is climbed one step at a time'.* That was fine, but what about reaching the godforsaken thing? She let out a growl of frustration. Why did she have all these people around her "helping" her, but they didn't actually help when it got right down to it? She was supposed to train with Xander on the swords. Did that happen? No. Gabriel had wanted to show her how to love herself more. Did that occur? No, it didn't. And Em, wanting her to let her internal self fill up a book? What fucking good would that do her?

She looked down at the bag where the small book rested. "No offense." Jackie said.

Jackie looked up at the mountain again, and then looked at how high it went into the sky. There was no way she was going to be able to climb that, not without any mountain climbing equipment, ropes, or proper boots. All that shit that mountain climbers wore. She could feel the frustration building in her, the panic that left a taste in her mouth that made her think of rust and metal. She had struggled to keep the panic contained as a kid and as an adult, but it was growing stronger here. Jackie had only been here three days, but it felt like she had been here for years. She had no idea what she was doing, and now she was heading towards a mountain that she swore was just moving itself farther away from her out of spite.

The panic ran up her spine and was beginning to turn her stomach into a mass of knots. She looked to the sky again and threw her arms out at her sides and let out a loud and resounding "FUUUUCK!" She could hear it echoing off of the rockface of the mountain: *ukkk...ukk...uk.*

Feeling only a little better for having let off steam, Jackie wondered what she was going to do. "I need help." Jackie said out loud. "There's no way that I can do this alone."

The air around her seemed to fill, and then there was the sound of a voice behind her. "Well, finally!" The voice said. "I was beginning to get worried honey!"

Turning around, she saw the hulking form of Gabriel, looking somehow bigger when surrounded by so much open space. "What the fuck are you doing here?" Jackie gasped, clutching her chest in fright. "You scared the heck out of me."

"Sorry honey, I tend to have that effect on people." He gave her a big smile and pulled her into a soft hug. "How've you been, honey? You look like shit."

"Why are you here?" She asked. "Marie-Claude was pissed because you and Em and Xander weren't playing by the rules."

He blew out a raspberry. "She always was a big stick in the mud, that one. Never wanted to have fun. Now, give her a throne, and she thinks she's all that." He shook his head. "Don't you worry honey, I got her number."

"Fat lot of good what with phones not working."

He gave her a mock look of shock. "Honey, did you just make a joke?" She grinned. "Maybe."

"Well, get over your bad self."

Jackie wrapped her arms around him again. "It really is good to see you."

"You too, princess. Now what have you been doing out here? Going for a leisurely stroll?"

"More or less." Jackie said. "I've been trying to find out how to climb that mountain."

Gabriel looked shocked. "You've got to be joking."

"I'm not. Marie said that my salvation would be found at the top of the mountain, that I would have to climb it."

"Did she really say you'd have to climb it?" Gabriel asked. "Seems like a silly thing to do."

She thought back to that conversation: 'You will find salvation at the top of the mountain, though not the salvation you are thinking it will be'. On hearing the words in her head, she questioned it. "I don't think she said I had to climb it." Jackie said. "If not climbing it, then what am I doing here?"

"Sometimes obstacles are just that: *obstacles*."

"Even so, how do I get to it? I've been walking for hours!" Jackie gestured at the mountain, and let out a growl of exasperation. "I've been walking all this time and it hasn't gotten any closer, but the forest is farther away." She looked behind her and tried to spot the forest in the distance, but could only see a dot of shrubbery that might be the forest. "How is that possible, Gabriel?"

"How is anything possible? Especially today?" He shrugged. "You gotta live and let live honey."

"Yeah, well it's fucking hard right now to have such a blasé attitude. Where have you been? Last thing I remember is the black mass of animals in front of the forest, and then I was in the forest and you weren't anywhere."

"Well, I won't be able to answer all of that right now. I don't have a lot of time."

"What do you mean? You just got here!"

"I did, but Marie is keeping a careful eye on things. We're supposed to help you find your own path, not lead you there."

"You weren't leading me there." Jackie said. "You were all confusing the fuck out of me. That's what you were doing."

A look crossed over Gabriel's face, one filled with remorse and regret. "There is so much I wanted to tell you, but we didn't have the time. We still don't. Do you have the book that Em gave you?"

Jackie reached into her bag. "Right here."

"Good, she told me to tell you to pay attention to it. Also, you have to change your perspective."

"What? What are you talking about?"

"Just that. You have to change your perspective."

"You keep saying your helping me. What fucking help is that?"

Gabriel sighed, and took both of her hands in his. "Listen, stop thinking about going over the mountain. That's not going to work. You'd be walking for a few more days if you just keep moving towards it. You're just supposed to get by the mountain, not conquer it. Sometimes the surest way to get past the mountain is to avoid it. Why not change your direction."

"I don't know any other way over a mountain." Jackie said. "The only other thing I can think of doing is to go around it."

Gabriel said nothing but bowed his head to her with a bright smile. "There you go." He took his hand away from hers. "I'll be seeing you."

"Wait, don't go. I don't think I can do this alone."

"You have to. This is your story, your tale. Besides, you'll be fine. I know you can do this. It may feel like nothing makes sense, but it will...eventually."

He kissed her on each cheek and began to walk away. Jackie kept her eyes on him, hoping to watch him until he was but a dot in the distance, but after a few steps, Gabriel disappeared, as if he'd never been.

Watching Gabriel vanish, something else occurred to her. *'You will find salvation at the top of the mountain, though not the salvation you are thinking it will be.'* She looked at the spot where Gabriel had been and said "Well, shit."

Standing there, Jackie let out a long breath, and made the decision. She thought of what Gabriel had said and decided to go around the mountain on the left side. Even though Marie had said that she would find salvation on the top of the mountain, she couldn't worry about that now. She just had to get past the mountain, or find a way to get closer to it.

As soon as she had made the decision to go around the mountain, it appeared to be growing with each step she took toward it. Soon, she was running toward it, and the mountain was growing bigger. It was as if by changing the way she thought of her obstacle, it changed the way it presented to her.

Jackie was full out running now, her swords slamming into her leg, the sound of wind growing stronger the closer she got to the mountain. The leaves that had been floating in the air in the forest flew around her as she neared her destination. As the mountain grew larger as she approached, she began to see something that made her want to stop in her tracks. There was a man waiting for her at what looked like an altar made out of the rockface of the mountain.

The altar seemed to have been eaten from the rock, as it was in a large circular cave-like space. Jackie wondered what kind of monster had come by and eaten the rock, or if it was a natural formation of the mountain. Stalactites hung like fingers from the ceiling of the rock formation, and to Jackie, it looked as if they were reaching down towards the man to gather him up into their embrace. More frightening than that, the entire area, from the altar to the carved-out piece of rock, was bathed in a red hue. Jackie blinked several times, wondering if the red would fade away, but it remained as red and as vibrant. She had the sneaking suspicion that it was blood.

Turing her gaze to the path that led towards this man and the altar, Jackie saw the ground leading to them was covered in what was unmistakably droplets of blood. In fact, it looked as if the blood had been slashed across the rocky terrain, or as if the ground itself was bleeding as it neared to the man and this altar. It looked like the maw of the worm god was waiting to swallow her whole.

The man himself was somewhat emaciated. He stood, repeatedly touching the items on the altar, which she couldn't make out from far away. He looked to be wearing a long robe made of red silk, but as she watched, she noticed that the ground behind him was being stained red as he walked; she wondered whether or not the robe had been dipped in blood or whether he had been bathed in it.

Jackie realized that she had a decision to make. She could turn around right now, or she could go forward. Frozen in place, she thought of turning back for one millisecond, but knew that this was the way forward. That if she turned back now, she would never be able to find a way through the mountain, and her journey would stop here. She had been faced with these decisions before in life and had always chosen the easy way around, the way backward so that she could make a different choice. When Jackie pulled a tarot card and she got one with a negative theme, she would often put the card back in the deck and reshuffle after asking a different question. Jackie knew better, but she did it anyway. She had always chosen the way that caused the least amount of fear and rejection. Jackie had thought it was moments of bravery, but she was beginning to wonder whether she had just chosen the easier path. Was that why she had ended up here, in this world that she knew but that was also so foreign to her? She wondered if this was some sort of karma for choices left untaken?

Even though she was terrified, she stepped forward and found herself actually following a trail of blood that had either been made by the altar man, or by things that had been on their way to be sacrificed. Shaking her head, Jackie focused only on the altar. She didn't want to think of stuff like that, even though it was more than likely true.

As she neared the red crevice carved into the mountain, her footsteps sounded like they were whispering as they moved through the dust, grass, and hard rock of the earth. The whispering stopped as she would step over a patch of the ground that had been marked by what she was sure was blood. It wouldn't whisper, it would merely make a squelching sound.

With each step, her heart beat faster. As if he had heard her heartbeat, the emaciated man tuned to look at her. Jackie paused when he did this, but she kept going despite how afraid she was. The man had large eyes, in two different colours; black and blue. He had sharp cheekbones and dark hair that flowed to his shoulders, which was also covered in blood.

He gave her a wide smile and then bowed to her, his arms out and fully extended. Then he rose again, his arms still outstretched.

"You have come! Oh, I thought you might. I said to myself, self, she may not find her way, she may not find the true path as it is hidden in the other path." His smile widened and he held his hands together. "But she did find it self, I told myself, she did find it. You are wise beyond your years Jackie, oh brave lady. Self says that you are most marvelous, and I agree with self."

Unsure of how to respond, Jackie just said "Thank you?"

"Oh no, it is I and self who should thank you, for you have faced your fear. You have shown that you have a belief that is stronger than the belief in yourself, for why would you have walked onward towards this if not in fear but also in courage? You are a wise student; I have been listening. I know that you have studied under Xander who is skilled at wielding magic, Em who uses knowledge, Gabriel who holds love above all. You have even survived the hard hand of Marie-Claude, she who rises or brings up, who lifts and separates the wheat from the chaff, the sparkle from the star."

Jackie was stunned to discover that the man's words were making sense to her, even though the spoke in a mishmash of first and third person. "And who are you? Are you one of my teachers?" Jackie asked.

"I am the one and the self and the not self, who taught all those who came before me. We all are on our own paths, but as long as we believe, as long as we look into the unknown and judge it worthy of exploration, we have won, you have won, Jackie. Did you know that your name is derived from the name of Jacob which means that God protects you, even if you don't believe in God. You believe in God, don't you?"

Jackie started to shake her head, but then nodded it instead. "I suppose I do."

"Well of course you do!" He came forward and hugged her in joy, and she was horrified to discover that his robes were in fact wet with blood, and now hers were marked with it too. He saw her face. "Oh, do not fret, she who is protected by God, it is the blood of animals which blessed me, they always bless me and now they in turn have blessed you." He reached up with a thumb and drew a circle on her forehead. "Come, come, there is much to see, much to do! Much to see and say to self and your self and each other."

He beckoned her forward and held out his hand. Jackie took it, discovering that she trusted him, as bizarre as he was. There was so much joy in him that she couldn't help but smile. They walked closer to the altar and Jackie was able to see what its contents. She had thought it would be objects filled with great reverence; what else would deserve the sea of blood that it was bathed in? However, they were merely trinkets: coins and pieces of wire, glass and bit of string, marbles, small cups made of glass, even a doll with only one arm.

"What the hell is all this junk?" She asked. "Why is this here?"

"Junk?" The blood-covered man said. "Junk? This isn't junk! These are offerings and givings, stuff that was left in order to gain light and direction. Self, I say, self, she does not know what form a wish can take in its physical embodiment. She does not know that wishes have power too, that wishes are another way of believing. Self says that they are another way to pray, to find the direction that has been lacking. Self says this is true."

He clasped both of her hands in his, and now her hands were covered in blood, but she couldn't pull away. She was mesmerised by him, enraptured by his speech and the fervor with which he spoke.

"You may call me many names." He said as if she had spoken. "I go by many words and many phrases, just as many sounds make up your name. I can be called Solomon or Alfred or Hudson." He smiled at her. "I go by many names as does self, self says he goes by many more names than I do, but the spirit is infinite, so that has always been the way."

"Were you always this way?" Jackie asked softly. She did not know what made her say such a thing, why she would ask something so bold. However, he did not show shock for her having asked it.

He shook his head, and she watched as tears began to flow softly from his eyes. They ran down his face and left clear marks on his skin where they fell through the blood that specked his face.

"What name are you going by today?" Jackie asked, not wanting to know what brought him to this state, and unsure whether or not she would receive an actual answer.

He looked up to the sky as if in thought, but Jackie could almost hear the question that he asked of himself internally. He nodded as if he was agreeing with the answer that she could only hear in whispers. "Self says that my name is Aldrich. I am Aldrich today." He smiled. "Self says that it is a very good name and means wisdom. I can see through the stars."

Aldrich motioned Jackie to come forward, and they walked deeper into the cave. This area was covered in blood, too. "What caused all of this, Aldrich?"

"All of what, Jackie of God and who is gracious? The universe or the spark that started it? Both would take a very long time to explain, and the explanation is usually best started with once upon a time. Self says that I tell really wonderful stories."

Jackie stopped walking and took his other hand in both of hers, much as he had done to her. "All of this. All this blood and the carnage that the world has become."

"The carnage here? Self says it has always been this way, for this is a blood mountain that was made to test people such as yourself. I say it's because it is the way it is. The carnage of the world that you speak of? Self says that there are many secrets that you have yet to discover, but Aldrich can tell you one of them. It has to do with that book inside your bag."

Jackie clutched her bag, dug into it, and pulled out the small leather-bound book. "This one?" Jackie asked, watching Aldrich's eyes as they widened at the sight of the book in her hands.

"That is your book, the book to higher knowledge, yes? I know that you are on a journey to tell your story, and tell it you must or you may never find your way out of the world as it is now. The altar is covered in blood because the mountain offers its tears, the animals offer their blood, all for the sake of cleansing, for the sake of giving and going free. Do you see what I mean? Self says that you look confused."

She was so fucking lost and had no idea what he was saying. "I'm a little lost." Was all that Jackie could muster.

"We are all lost. Here, we must fill your book with stars. Then it will work better for you. How can you tell your story if you don't know the words? You need to find a way for the words to show themselves to you. Can't you hear the pens writing and scratching in the paper? Can't you hear the voices that are telling your stories? You need to find the words in the stars."

Holding back the scoff that threatened to escape her mouth, Jackie just said "And how do you want me to do that?"

Aldrich took his hands from hers and made that come-hither motion again. "Come we will show you; Aldrich will show you, We will all show you. We will all show you what you need. You need to talk to the stars."

Taking Jackie's hand, Aldrich led her further into the mountain, further into the shadows, until they were standing in front of a door. He put a finger to his lips and made a soft *sssshhhh* sound, his lips curved in a smile. Jackie nodded, feeling a deep sense of quiet around this door anyhow. There was almost a reverence coming from Aldrich and the door. She wondered what was behind it? She didn't have to wonder for very long. Aldrich pushed the door open softly and stepped in, closing the door only when Jackie stepped through.

At fist, she could barely see. The very air around her seemed to sparkle. The light in the room made her blink several times until she could see, but she still had to put a hand up to shield her eyes. Looking over at Aldrich, Jackie whispered "What is this room? What is making the light?"

Aldrich looked at her with eyes that were even brighter than before, and whispered one word: "Stars." He said simply.

Jackie looked around her. What she had taken for crystal formations in the rockface were in fact formations of stars. Looking up, she saw that the stars covered every surface of the room, every crevice of the rockface, every rock and speck of dust. She saw that a small stream flowed through the centre of the room. There were stars upon the surface of the water, too. Looking around again, she wondered how long the room went on for. It seemed to go on forever.

"Self says that you are awed and impressed." Aldrich said in a whisper. "As you should be. I often withdraw from others when my light is low and I can't see my way forward. Sometimes, you need to step into the darkness to see which way your light is going to go, or to find the light within you that is buried so deeply that sometimes you can't find it, but the little speck of light will shine, leading you to it."

Aldrich took her small leather book gently from her hands. Jackie watched as he shuffled over to the small stream and kneeled before it. He motioned for her to kneel beside him and she did. Gently, he dipped the book into the water three times and took it out again. When he handed the book back, Jackie expected it to be wet, but it wasn't. Instead, the small leather-bound book sparkled.

When she opened it, the pages were filled with writing in an unknown tongue. It wasn't any language that she knew, but even so Jackie could read it. She could understand it. Looking up at Aldrich, she asked, "Who wrote this?"

"Why, you did!" He said in a gleeful whisper. "While your body and mind sleep, your spirit is active! Very active indeed! They are like the stars!" He motioned at the stars which filled the cavern around them. "Though they seem to be in one place, they are in constant movement. We are looking at their selves from hundreds and thousands of years ago, from time that no longer exists. Spirit is like the stars, that is why it takes so long to know it."

It felt eerie to Jackie, sitting in this cavern of stars and whispering to Aldrich about spirits and stars, but it also felt like something within her clicked into place, like she had found a part of herself that she had lost long ago. Aldrich stared at her, and his eyes widened as she nodded in understanding.

"So, you see and your spirit sees, my self says and your self agrees! Spirit is a lifelong journey and you can't do it in a day. You have to get to know it, and to nurture it, and to hold it closely to yourself; embrace it. It takes time. You can't learn who you are in a day."

"Xander did mention I'm on a journey."

"We all are, all of our spirits and selves and the people and masks we hold within." Aldrich said. "We are merely stardust given shape. Delving into spirit is like taking an intimate look at each of those pieces of stardust, and then stepping back to see how they make up the whole. It's a long journey, self says."

Something Marie said occurred to Jackie once more: *"Help will be given to you if you ask for it. You will find salvation at the top of the mountain, though not the salvation you are thinking it will be."*

"Aldrich," Jackie said. "How do I find my way to the top of the mountain? It's why I came here."

"Your body came here, but your spirit will show you the way." He said.

He went towards the rock wall, and stopped in front of a constellation that shone brighter than all the other stars around it. Jackie looked at the shape of the star formation, and Aldrich nodded. She reached out with one finger and traced the line. It started as a slanted line and then went upwards, sloping to the left. It dipped and curved slightly towards the right, and then went straight up. When Jackie's finger touched the topmost star, the whole formation glowed even brighter.

"The Hydrus represents the snake." Aldrich said. "Explorers saw them on their journey as they made their way over the land, and saw them in the skies. The believed that the snake could show them the way forward, and not the way backward."

A line began to show itself, four lines that formed what looked like a door. She watched it open, sliding slowly into the rockface and revealing bright light thorough which Jackie could see a flight of stairs leading upwards. The light was almost blinding, but cold like the stars that were found within the skies above.

"Just as you have to look at things a different way to find your destination, sometimes the destination is within." Aldrich said.

"Thank you." Jackie told him.

"No thanks needed. Just thank yourself and learn to know yourself more, Jackie of the swords and the blades of light."

Leaning forward, he lay a kiss upon her brow, and she could feel it shining upon her face, beside the kiss that she had received from Marie. Jackie regarded him for a moment, words failing her. He seemed to understand her, for he nodded and motioned her forward into the light made from stars.

Stepping onto the first step, Jackie looked back at Aldrich one last time as the door made of stars slid slowly closed. He made a sign of benediction, and the kiss that he had placed upon her head led her as she made her way upwards to whatever waited for her.

VI

Jackie climbed the stairs for some time.

She had no idea what would be waiting for her on top of the mountain, but kept climbing, comforted by the light that led her path. She wondered if it was the light of the stars, shining through the rock. Either way, it seemed to be urging her upwards along the stairs. With each step she took, her appreciation for the position she found herself in grew; here was a chance for her to *do* something, to make a difference, and find out what the fuck was going on and what had happened. There had to be a way to put the world right. She was feeling very hopeful...until she came to the door.

It looked so big and imposing, made of more rock from the mountain. On the front door was a silhouette of a woman. Her hair looked to be moving of its own accord. Jackie learned closer, and realized the silhouette was made of stars. Marvelling at it, Jackie thought that the shape looked like her. She could even see the outline of a sword. Her hand was on the doorknob when a thought struck her. If she opened this door, was she going further into herself?

Squaring her shoulders, Jackie turned the knob and pulled the door open. The first thing she saw was the peaks of the mountain which surrounded her. They were covered in snow and droplets of blood, yet there was no mass carnage up here like there was below. Jackie wondered if the wind that rallied around the mountain had carried some droplets up here so that they would land on the snow, or maybe the droplets came from above?

Stepping through the door frame, she watched the outline of the door shimmer for a moment and then it faded in a shower of mist. Holding out her hands, Jackie felt sparkling dust land upon her skin. Looking behind her, she saw that the door was gone.

"Guess it was a one-way ticket." Jackie said out loud.

Looking around, she saw the rough outline of a path cut into the snow. She wondered if someone had been here before, or whether Aldrich had made the path for her. Walking a little further, she came to a clearing in the snow with a small bench. Nearby there was a little table. This seemed like as good a place as any to lay out some cards for some guidance, and maybe even check out her little leather-bound book to see if she could make sense of it.

Sitting on the bench, Jackie pulled out her cards. Feeling the current that ran through them, she shuffled her deck thoroughly and then cut it into three piles and stacked it. She drew a card. It was the Queen of Swords. "Mother fucker!" She swore. "I'm getting so sick of seeing you." She knew that if you saw a repeat card that meant you hadn't learned what you were supposed to, or fully received the guidance that spirit was trying to give you. Even knowing that, Jackie was pissed off to see the fucking Queen of Swords again. She was so tired and wanted a clear direction as to what was going to happen or what she was going to find.

She sighed and pulled another card. It was the Chariot.

That was more promising, but why did the Queen of Swords keep popping up? She knew that the tarot deck had three different sections to it: the Fools journey, the pip or numbered cards, and the court cards. She knew that the court cards represented someone in your life or yourself, but she was so sick of seeing that judgemental bitch. The Queen of Swords was one tough bitch, but she was a total mind fuck. Sighing again, she put her cards away and wondered where she was supposed to go next. She wondered if she was the Queen of Swords. "All right already," Jackie said. "I get it, okay? Leave me alone."

There really was nowhere else for her to go but onward, along the path. Normally pretty sure of what she wanted to do and where she wanted to go, Jackie found herself filled with confusion. She had no idea what she was doing or what she was supposed to fucking do.

Pulling out her small leather-bound book, she flipped through it. She saw scratches of ink, and there were even drawings along the margins. It looked like her writing, and flipping through the book, she saw that a quarter of the pages were already filled. She saw that the book was only keeping notes on where she had been and who she had seen. She flipped forward to see if there was anything at the end of the book, but the pages were blank.

"Well, what the fuck good are you?"

The words she had just spoken were written onto the page, and she watched the words appear in her own handwriting, even though she didn't write them. The writing looked hurried and frantic. It reminded her of the journal that she kept in her bedside table back home. She would write her dreams in it when they woke her from a deep slumber. Jackie would try to read the writing afterwards, but could only ever make out a few words. It was the same thing here. The book was supposed to hold answers, it was supposed to hold her story, but it could only take her so far.

She thought of something that Aldrich had said: "*Just as you have to look at things a different way to find your destination, sometimes the destination is within.*" She had thought that by going through the door at the top of the mountain, she was going further within herself, but introspection was done in moments of quiet, like this one. It finally occurred to her what Aldrich meant: *she carried the answer to where she was going and what she had to do inside of her.*

"That makes no fucking sense." She said out loud. Her voice was gruff and she knew that it sounded as she felt, defeated.

Either way, there was nowhere to go but forward. It was the only direction she had left. Tucking her cards and book back into her bag, Jackie stood and continued down the path. As she kept walking, the landscape changed once more.

The sky was beginning to darken. The droplets of blood which covered the grass and rocks started to lessen with each step she took. The rocky gravel underfoot changed to gravel, then grass, and she could hear the sounds of each footstep. She tried to slow her walk so she wasn't making so much noise, but after a while there didn't seem to be much point. She hadn't seen anyone for a long time.

The path led to a small grove of trees. They looked so green, and in the distance, the apples growing in amongst the leaves looked like blood. She hoped that was a trick of the light. It had been a long time since she had eaten something, and she was so tired. With each step, she became more exhausted. It was no wonder, she had been travelling for what felt like forever.

As she neared the orchard, she wondered how long ago she had slept last. She thought of the bed in Em's house that she never slept in. She thought of the airplane where she had woken from slumber into this terrible world. She thought of the night she had spent with Xander.

Out of everyone, it was him who she missed the most. Jackie thought that this was why she thought she saw him amongst the trees. A form seemed to waver in front of her eyes, and she put this down to fatigue. Honestly, she didn't know how much longer she could keep going.

The shape was tall, and he was standing near a tree. He seemed to meld in and out of focus, and she wondered if he was part of the tree, or if he *was* the tree. She tried to focus on the shape. Not knowing what else to do, or if the shape was even real, she kept walking. She kept moving towards the trees along the path because she didn't want to stop going. She had to keep going further. Marie-Claude had said *"Help will be given to you if you ask for it. You will find salvation at the top of the mountain, though not the salvation you are thinking it will be."*

What kind of salvation comes at the top of a mountain? What could salvation be to her right now? Jackie felt as if she would pass out. Looking at the sky, she saw that the sun was fading quickly, and there was nowhere to go, nowhere to hide. Only the forest ahead of her, and she hadn't enjoyed her time in the last forest, regardless of Marie and the power that the woman had held within her.

The shape moved towards her and she could see a flash of blue at his fingertips, if it was indeed a man. She tried to run off the path, but her feet were heavy and she found the effort of moving tortuous. "Fuck," she said. "Fuckety fuck. Now my legs decide not to work, that's *so* convenient." She stopped and did the only thing she could do and pulled her long sword free from her scabbard. Sprinkles of magic sparked from the sword and she stood firm, holding it in front of her. She was ready.

"Come with me, Jackie." The shape said. It was a man; she had been right.

"Fucking asshole, you think I'm just going to go with you?" She held on tighter to her sword and fixed her stance.

"You will if you want to survive." He said. The blue light flashed again, brighter this time, and she saw that it was Xander.

Letting out a cry, Jackie nearly dropped the sword. "Why are you here?" Jackie asked. "What are you doing here?"

He shook his head. "We don't have time for that. We have to find shelter."

"Well, if you haven't noticed, we're kind of out in the open here. Besides, there's no blood here, not really. Are you sure we're in trouble?"

Xander grinned and put a hand to his ear. Jackie humoured him and listened. All she could hear was her heartbeat for a moment, but then, she heard the sound of birds. They sounded large and angry. *Just what they needed*, she thought. *A bunch of angry fucking birds.*

"Does it ever *stop* here?" She asked.

"What do you mean?"

"There is always some kind of danger. It just keeps going. Does it ever stop?"

Xander shook his head. "Not that I've ever known it to. Though there are some moments of joy."

Jackie let out a snort. "Yeah, I'm having a fucking ball."

"Come on, I will take you to shelter."

"Like I said hotshot, there isn't anything here except the trees and I've had enough of forest, thank you very much."

Xander shrugged. He took out a wand from the pack hanging from his waist. He traced what looked like the shape of a door in the air in front of them; a rectangle. The outline began to glow as he put the wand back in his pack. He took her free hand, and Jackie tried to ignore the feeling that ran up her arm. "Hold on to me." Xander said.

Jackie was trying to ignore the rush she felt from his touch. *Man, I need to get laid.* She thought. "All right." Jackie agreed, unsure whether it was safe to say anything else.

The outline of the door glowed brighter still, and then the dark blue of the sky faded to an almost inky black. She could see a bits of shadow but a whole lot of nothing else.

"Where does the door take us?"

"You'll have to trust me and find out. Come on."

"Okay." Jackie was searching for alternatives, and she didn't see any other option. With the sound of approaching birds behind and above her, she followed Xander and stepped through the doorway that had been drawn in the air.

And found herself back in the bedsit she knew well.

It was Xander's room within the airport. "Now, you wait just a damn minute." Jackie started.

"I can explain, but you really don't have to be upset about anything."

"I have plenty of right to be upset. Let's count the ways, shall we?"

"Aren't we in a place of safety? Aren't you safe?" Xander asked.

"Safety is a relative term in this world."

"Well, you've been given the tools to help you find your way."

"Is that what I've been doing?" Jackie said. She could feel the anger rising in her, could feel the heat running along her skin. It was always like this when she got royally angry. "Let's see what I've been given, shall we? Two swords I barely know how to use, a fucking book that writes itself, just repeating what I've said or done when the moment strikes. And let's not forget the lovely, picturesque stroll I've been on, shall we? I've met some kind of mad woman in a forest, was abandoned by you and Em and Gabriel, met a mad fucker named Aldrich who was covered in so much blood, yet he was trying to give *me* advice!" She took a breath.

It was in this breath that Xander spoke. "He's still there? He is still at the mountain?"

Jackie widened her eyes, and watched him shrink away a little. Serves you right, you jackass. "You *know* about him? You've been there before?"

"We all have in one way or another," Xander said. "His name was Balthasar when I met him."

She threw her hands up in the air. "All these fucking riddles!" She was screaming now. "Why can't any of you speak normally? You and Em and Gabriel kept talking about what I would have to do without telling me anything! You just expect me to keep going?!" She went to him and rammed a finger into his chest. "And now you've taken me back to the beginning?" She was screaming in his face now, so thick was her anger.

Sparks were flying from her eyes and her fingertips, but only Xander could see them. He marvelled at the fact that she looked more beautiful the angrier she became. He didn't think such a thing was possible, yet the woman in front of him was proof that the impossible existed.

"What the fuck am I supposed to do now?" She yelled. "Do you want to teach me how to use my swords again, something you failed to do the first time? Or we could go see Em and Gabriel at her fancy fucking house, or maybe you want to go meet Marie-Claude in the forbidden forest? That's one fucked up place too!"

"Jackie, listen to me." Xander said softly.

"No, I don't have to listen to you. I don't have to listen to anyone. All I've been listening to is a bunch of people telling me to keep going, that this will all make sense, that I will understand in time. But it doesn't even feel like I'm halfway there! How long is this fucking journey? How long do I have to keep going?"

Jackie let her hands fall to her sides, sinking down onto the bed and putting her head in her hands. When she looked back up at him, Xander's face had softened. "Don't pity me." She said. "Just tell me what the fuck I have to do."

He took a while before responding. When he did speak, his voice had lost the gruffness it normally held. "Maybe it's not about what you have to do, more how you approach the journey."

"Gods, more fucking riddles?"

"Hear me out. Why did you leave?"

"What do you mean?"

"I mean why did you leave? Why did you leave your life and board a plane with a first-class ticket for the first time in your life? Why did you do that?"

"If you know about the plane then you know why."

"I do and I don't. I want you to tell me."

"I don't think I can do that."

"Well, you're going to have to, okay?"

Letting out a groan, Jackie stood and started to pace in the small bedsit. She wrung her hands as she spoke. She hadn't thought of Daniel in a while. Ever since she'd hung up on him when she was on the plane, in fact.

"I was leaving a guy." She said. "I found him fucking my best friend."

"So rather than have it out with him, you chose to run?"

"No, I had it out with him. I told him what a fuckwad he was. I screamed at him for hours. Kept telling me he was sorry, sorry, sorry. It would never happen again, it was just a few times, that she meant nothing to him, and I was the one he truly loved - you know, all the usual bullshit."

"So why did you run?"

"I didn't run!" Jackie screamed.

"Seems like a weird thing to do, to run away from your life to leave everything behind, all because some guy couldn't value you for what you're worth. Why would you run?"

Jackie shook her head. "I don't know." She said. "I *didn't* run."

"If you didn't run, what were you doing? Why would you make that decision to run away?"

Jackie shook her head. "I wasn't running away...more like I was running toward something? That's what it felt like, like I was trying to find myself and had to get to the right starting point, you know?"

Xander nodded. "I do know. I do." He went to her and took one of her hands in his. "We've all been there. You made choices that put you on this path. It's time for you to see it through. But you have to think of *why* you chose to find your starting point. What was the one thing that pushed you to leave? The one thing running through your head that made you want to run towards something else?"

Jackie thought about it, really contemplated what had moved her. Looking Xander in the eyes, she thought she could get lost in there, so she looked away. Why had she left? Why had she run away from her life?

The answer came to her in a spark of bright light that filled her head. "I wanted to love myself instead of letting someone else love me. I wanted to be worthy of my own love and not settle for someone who only wanted to love me in his way. Does that sound stupid?"

Xander shook his head. "You acted with love. Love is always the right choice."

Jackie let out a snort. "Doesn't seem like it. It landed me here."

"Yes but look how far you've come."

Jackie thought for a moment before asking her next question. "How much farther do I have to go?"

"I can't answer that."

"Yes, but you've been on this journey!"

"Wrong. I've been on *my* journey. This is yours. Each journey is different. Yours has already gone down different paths than my own."

"Don't I get an idea of what's to come?"

He shook his head. "No, that would ruin the surprise. You like surprises, don't you?"

She shook her head. "No, I don't. I hate surprises."

"Well, then, you'll have to get used to disappointment." He reached down to his waist and held his hand there. A shining blue light began to glow brightly, and a wand materialized in his hand where none had been before.

"You and that fucking wand." Jackie said. "Going to make another door?"

Instead of answering, he opened the door to the weapons room. "This space is a hub that connects many roads. I'm not supposed to pull you off of your road, but you looked like you could use some help."

"So, help me."

"I am." He held the wand in front of her; she could hear it hum. "This is the embodiment of my magic. It's physical form," he said, when he saw her look of confusion. "The swords are yours."

"Yeah, but you gave those to me. And my swords don't glow blue like your wand does."

"You have to find your magic." Xander said. "It's deep within you. When you go through the door within yourself, you'll find your magic waiting there."

"In case you haven't noticed, there aren't a lot of places for me to sit and have a good talk with myself."

"You carry your book with you, do you not?"

"I do." She pulled the leather-bound book out of her bag.

"And you still have your tarot cards?"

"I always have those." Jackie replied, almost defensively.

"Then use them. Aren't the cards supposed to tell you the direction you need to venture in, or the kind of work that you need to do on yourself?"

"Yeah, but I've been dealing the same cards. It's always the Queen of Swords."

"Can you not think of why?"

"No, I can't, and it's getting fucking annoying. They're usually a lot clearer than they've been lately. I think this world has them all screwed up."

"Can you really not think of a reason the Queen of Swords keeps coming up?" Xander pressed.

"I already told you, no."

Xander raised an eyebrow and pointed at the swords Jackie carried on her back.

"Oh." Jackie said softly, as everything clicked into place.

"Have you taken the time to read through your little book?"

"Yeah, it's just what I've been doing, right? It just repeats every action I make."

He shook his head. "I think it's time that you read your book more closely. You sit and read. I will make some tea and food for you."

Jackie nodded and sat down on the bed, taking out her cards and the book. She looked down at them. "So, you both be good to me, okay? I could use a break."

The book began to make scratching sounds even as she picked it up. She had a funny feeling that she would not be getting the break she had requested. Opening the book, Jackie looked down at the first page.

"Well, fuck."

VII

Jackie read her book with a scowl on her face.

Xander came and brought her tea and a sandwich, which she thanked him for, and then quickly got back to reading. It was the first line that had gotten her. It read: "Jackie doesn't know that she's made of magic."

She had flipped through the book to the pages she had read before, and they had all said something slightly different than what she remembered. When she had read the words before, it was just a word for word tally of what she had done and where she had been. Now there were different words written on those pages in a different hand, as if she had been having a conversation with someone...or her book was. "Why are the words on the page different?" She asked Xander.

"You see them more clearly now."

"What the fuck does that mean?"

"You have spent the past while journeying onward to find yourself and find your spirit, have you not? Maybe the words upon this page are just one of the rewards that you've been able to gather."

"Rewards, huh?" Jackie said. "What's my other reward? You'll finally teach me to use my swords?"

Xander touched his nose with the tip of one finger. "I suppose that could be one of them. What does your book have to say on the subject?"

She flipped back to the section where she had first gotten the swords from Xander. The main story was written in black ink but the instructions on stance and balance were written in red ink. She had never seen Xander's handwriting but wondered if it was his.

"It's got a whole wealth of information here."

"Well, let's put it to the test, shall we?" He made for the door that led upwards towards the ground floor.

"What, are we going to go outside?"

"We're relatively safe during the daylight hours. There may be a few things that we can practice on, however." He opened the door. "Coming?"

"Fuck yeah!" She got up and followed Xander out of his bedsit quietly. She walked with confidence toward where the broken window was. She remembered it well from when she had first found her way into the airport. She wondered if the airplane still held all of that food or was it useless now? As if in answer, her stomach growled.

"After we practice, I will feed you." Xander said softly.

"All right. Lead the way." It astounded her that she was so willing to learn how to battle with her swords when she had never handled such an object before in her life. "Is it odd that I'm excited?"

"Odd that you want to learn to defend yourself?" Xander asked. "I don't think so."

They found the broken window and Xander went outside before Jackie to determine if there was any pressing worry. When he saw that there wasn't, he motioned for her to come out. Jackie did so carefully.

She scrambled up to him, looking around them at the gore which seemed to have intensified. Could blood grow thicker over time? She had a thought of Aldrich and the altar carved out of the mountain, the blood covered clothes he wore. Why did it always come back to blood?

Looking away from the blood, Jackie looked at Xander instead. Her pulse raced just seeing him. She took a few deep breaths to try and centre herself. He nodded at her.

"That's right, take some deep breaths. You need to focus on what you're going to do with a calm mind. Are you ready?"

"Yes." She was ready for a lot of different things at that moment.

"You have the stance correct. I want you to hold the sword like a bat."

"How would I know how to do that?"

"Haven't you ever played baseball?"

Jackie snorted. "Do I look like I've ever played baseball? I mean, seriously?"

Xander sighed. He held a hand to his side. Blue light began to glow from underneath his black clothes. He put his hand down around it the blue light which ran from just under his right armpit and ran down to the middle of his thigh. As he held his hand there, the glow intensified and then faded.

Blinking a few times, Jackie saw that Xander was now holding a sword.

"How did you do that?"

He lifted up his black shirt to reveal a red splotch along his skin that looked like it would match the sword outline along his skin. Xander said nothing but let her stare. She reached out a hand to run it along the markings on his skin.

She thought of the shapes that she had glimpsed when she had slept nearby in this very bedsit in what seemed years ago. "Your tattoos?" She asked, whispering the words.

"My tattoos," he said nodding.

Jackie resisted the urge to ask if she could see the rest of them. She had an inkling that he would do just that and if he did, she didn't think she could concentrate on the job at hand.

"Show me how to hold the damn sword." She said.

He grinned as if he knew why she was so agitated and held his own sword like it was a bat. Jackie mirrored him.

"Good. Now this two-handed grip on the sword has advantages and limitations. It gives you a stronger base from which to swing, but it also limits your range of movement. Only use this for close hand-to-hand battle." He swung his sword and she saw blue light tracers in the air.

"I don't know if I can do this."

"Of course, you can. You only *think* you can't. It's okay, Jackie. I think you can do this. I haven't been wrong yet. Go ahead and take a swing."

She did so and his sword of blue light rose up to meet her metal sword, filling the air with the sound of singing metal.

"Like I said, this stance has limitation. You can only use it for the killing blow or hand-to-hand combat."

"So that will do me okay if I'm close up, and or if I'm barbequing food and need something to clean up." She gave him a cheeky grin. "What will I do in other situations?"

"You'll use your longer sword. Pull that out now."

Jackie did so and though she wanted to grasp the sword with both hands, she did not. Xander looked at Jackie and must have seen something within her.

"I know what I need to do." She said.

She gripped the sword only with one hand, letting it swing from her as if she were using it like a magic wand. Jackie saw her light begin to glow throughout the sword, but where it had been blue before, it was now gold in colour. In fact, it looked as if her sword were made of magic. Letting her arm become part of the sword, Jackie took a swing.

"Do you see?" Xander asked.

"Yeah, I see my sword is sparkly. What the fuck is that about?"

Xander smirked a little. "You are finding your magic. You see how the light changed? That is the colour of your magic."

"Why couldn't it have been a sexy colour, like slut red or vivid vixen?" A picture entered her mind of Aldrich covered in red and she was suddenly glad that her magic was not red.

"Everyone's colour is different." Xander took a swing with his sword which Jackie blocked with ease. "This is all part of the journey of becoming."

"Well, what the fuck does that mean? Am I learning to become some sort of butterfly?"

"Very wisely put. Maybe there is hope for you yet."

Xander took another swing that brought them up close. She blocked the attack with her short sword using only one hand. Moving quickly with her long sword, she held the blade to his neck. He had been too slow to try and block her blades. They regarded each other, both of them breathing heavily.

Jackie's heart was beating quickly, and she doubted whether it was just the workout with the swords. Uncrossing her blades, she backed away from him. "Why is it important for me to learn to use the swords anyways?"

"Are you not the Queen of Swords?"

He was taking deep breaths, too, trying to steady himself. *At least it's not just me*, she thought.

"Yeah, I guess I am, but there has to be more to it than that." Jackie said, finally able to get her breathing under control.

"I keep telling you that you are on a journey."

"Yeah, I feel like fucking Dorothy in the land of Oz."

Xander smirked again. "Funny. Actually, you would look good in pigtails."

"I can still kick your ass with one of these swords."

"Yes, you could. Did you ever stop to wonder why you are on this journey?"

"Because I woke up in an airplane and the world as I knew it changed?"

"Smartass. It's because you are *becoming*. Using the swords teach you about willpower and control. You are choosing to control one part of your destiny on this journey. Amidst all the things which you have no control over, you are learning to control something."

"Why?" Jackie said. "So, I go on some journey to find myself, what's the point?" She was beginning to get frustrated. "You all fill my head with riddles and half-truths, with hidden lies and you expect me to be excited that I'm learning to control something?" Gold sparks shot along the length of her long sword and Xander looked down as the sparks shone momentarily and then went dark.

Xander lost his casual grin and when he glared at Jackie, blue flames snapped in the air around him. "Do you think I like having things this way?" He asked, trying to maintain control. "Do you think I enjoy seeing you being put in danger? No, I don't, but it has to be this way." He reeled in the blue flames and took another deep breath. "This is the way that it has to be. I don't make the rules. You are living your story. Just like your cards, your story is a series of moments. You have to decide what you do with what you are presented. You are on this journey for a reason and you have to learn to fight and learn to control yourself for what is coming."

"Why can't you tell me what's on my path? You've already lived this before."

Xander's face hardened. "I've already told you that the journey is different for everyone, and the steps to get there are changed each time. Don't you realize that this isn't a game?"

"What do you mean?" Jackie tried to control her own supposed magic but failed. The gold sparks shot down her sword again. "Of course, I know this isn't a fucking game!"

"You've just been traipsing though everything, hoping that someone would tell you the answers. You're afraid to do the work. You ran from a man and the life you knew because he was an asshole, you left everything behind, to go where? To do what? Are you just waiting for someone to save you instead of saving yourself? When will you take some fucking responsibility for yourself?"

A gold flame leapt along her sword and she let out a loud cry, flying at Xander with both swords raised. They slashed and fought, the sound of metal rang through the air. Soon, gold and blue flames danced so close together that the air was filled with an emerald green cloud that seemed to wane and build at will with each sword thrust and parry.

Jackie let out a guttural sound every time Xander blocked one of her thrusts or jabs. After some time, the clang of metal began to feel good. It began to fuel something within her, and she gave into the dance of it, let herself be pulled along by the song of the swords. She was their Queen after all.

She moved as if the swords were part of her arms and they powered her soul. Jackie didn't know how she understood them so well in such a short time, but she had come to believe in magic. What else but magic could explain them or the world that she was in? Having witnessed all kinds of magic so far, she knew that it had a light side and a dark side. The swords felt as if they were somewhere in between.

Their song was coming to an end, though. The dance was rounding its last few movements. She could feel the magic that had come so readily to her when she had begun the dance begin to fade and splutter. Jackie knew that it wasn't gone, no. It was within her to call upon whenever she needed to.

When they stopped, the blue and gold light began to fade around them, and Jackie put her swords away. She watched as Xander pressed his sword back into his side, the blue magic flickering, then going out.

"Why is it so easy, now?" She asked.

"What do you mean?"

"I mean, I've been carrying these swords for some time. Why are they just revealing their magic now?"

"Because you were under threat of attack." He said. "Your magic had to bond with you in order to work. You can continue to strengthen it by reading and knowing your book and using your cards. Magic is real here, as it is within you. Your book has things to tell you that you must know if you're to survive what comes next."

"I suppose you can't tell me what's coming up, can you?"

"No, I can't. You've begun to learn how to control yourself tonight. You will need more practice, but we don't have the time. I'm working on borrowed time anyways."

"You're not dying, are you?"

"No, but we've spent enough time together and it has taken you away from the journey you're supposed to be on. You have to get back."

"Back to where?" Jackie asked. "What's the next step for me?"

"You'll have to find out on your own. Take this." He took a long chain with a star-shaped pendant from one of his pockets. "If you need help, merely hold this in your hand and think of one of us and we will come to you."

"Can't you just come with me?" Jackie asked, knowing the answer already. She slipped the necklace over her head, somehow knowing that their time together was coming to an end. Jackie made sure her bag and swords were in place, her cards were tucked safely beside her leather-bound book.

"You remember what happened last time. We can come to aid you, like I am now, but we can't see you through until the end. It's *your* journey.

"I'm so afraid. I'm afraid all the time, even more so now." It hurt Jackie to admit this, to say this thought out loud, but it was the absolute truth.

"I know you are."

Xander reached to his leg and blue light came to life. He pulled the wand from his thigh as he had before. He drew the outline of a door in the air in front of him and gently pushed it open. She couldn't see what was on the other side. It was just a swirl of lights and sparkling magic.

"I'll miss you."

"I know. And I you. You will have to be strong, Jackie. Be the Queen of Swords that you are."

"I will."

They said no more, the words left unspoken hanging in the air between them.

She reached out and pulled him to her, pressed her lips to his - they were salty and soft and supple. Then, turning away, she walked through the door that led her back to the path that she was on.

VIII

"Fuck." Jackie said.

She looked out at a landscape different than the one she had left behind. Gone were the grass and rocks of the mountain. Now there seemed to be nothing but a wide expanse of hot, dry earth that reminded her of the land that surrounded the mountain, aside from the occasional tuft of grass growing through the cracks in the ground.

She scanned the land for signs of people or buildings, wondering if she had to look at things in a different way in order to get to where she was supposed to be, like the mountain;but she couldn't see anything. All she could see was a wide expanse of bare earth marked with the occasional splatter of blood.

Not wanting to exhaust herself as she had before, Jackie sat right down on the hard earth and rummaged in her bag. She pulled out her cards and journal, but she also found a sandwich filled with ham and a spicy mustard and a bottle of what looked like beer. On the paper which wrapped the sandwich was a large black X with a heart underneath. She wondered when Xander had had time to pack a sandwich and beer in her bag but was so grateful she didn't ponder long. When she saw him again, she would give him the biggest kiss she could.

Unscrewing the bottle of beer, she took a big swig. It tasted heavenly and was oddly refreshing. She wondered if the food here had been made from magic. How else to explain a bottle of beer in a world where it shouldn't exist.

Next, she unwrapped the sandwich. It had been wrapped in wax paper and tied with string. The sandwich was indeed filled with ham and spicy mustard, those she had smelled through the paper, but it was also made with lettuce and a slice of tomato. She meant to eat it slowly, to take her time and maybe save some for later, but she happily sat there on the dirt ground stuffing her face with ham and guzzling from her beer. As she did so, she looked through her book.

Her previous observations had been right: the book told her what had already happened. However, peppered throughout, there were other wisdoms that she didn't remember having. In one way the book was hers, but it also belonged to her spirit which saw more than she could with just her eyes.

As she ate and drank, she read. She was surprised by how much the book had to tell her. She read a passage about the plane: *I had woken up on a plane, alone and in the hanger, but why wasn't I afraid? Why wasn't I worried?* That had been in her own writing. **I was terrified. I should really have taken more food with me. I wish I had thought to take more food from the plane.** That was the book. It still looked like her writing, but it was thicker, as if an invisible hand had pressed the pen into the page. These were the books words, not her own. As she was sliding down the emergency slide in what felt like forever ago, she *had* thought of that airplane dinner and wondered if it would be her last meal, if she should have taken some of the meals with her. She flipped through the book wondering what else it had to say.

The book was speckled with its own thoughts. She wondered how it had begun to write its own words, her words. Had the books words been there all along and all it needed was to have the light of her own magic to see those words by?

Didn't stop her from being creeped out, though. The book knew Jackie better than she knew herself. Em did call it the book of knowledge, but a better name for it would have been the book of *self*. She knew that as she continued on her journey, the book would have more to tell her. Jackie wondered what it was about this world that revolved around secrets, hidden meanings and symbolism hidden in the shadows. Why couldn't anyone just *tell* her what they wanted and what they meant? She supposed that some journeys were just like that.

Sighing audibly, she put the bottle and wrapper back in her bag. Jackie almost didn't want to pull a card from her deck, but she had to admit that this seemed like the most appropriate time. Pulling out her deck, she shuffled them and stopped when it felt right. She cut the deck and pulled a card.

It was the Queen of Swords. "For fucks sake." She said. "Not you again. Why must you keep showing up?"

Now that she knew that the cards were actually referring to herself, this card didn't bother her so much. In fact, looking at it more closely, it seemed it *could* even be her. Was the card changing? It looked slightly different. She knew that previously the card pictured a woman with horrible reddish hair.

It looked almost as if the woman had a mullet, a poor choice for a Queen. She wondered if she could change the cards with her power of thought and imagination so that the Queen of Swords would have a better hairstyle.

Pulling another card, she looked down at the Two of Cups. "Oh well now, you can really go fuck yourself." Jackie knew that the Two of Cups was about being open to love, about a bond between two people which was strengthening or growing into something new. It represented the emotional need to be open to love, and everything that came with it.

She couldn't help but think of Xander and the obvious attraction there. She wanted to again see him shirtless and study all of his tattoos. She looked down at the rowan leaf tattooed on her right palm and wondered at the meanings of all of Xander's tattoos.

Drawing one more card, Jackie looked down at the Hermit. "Great, so time alone? Yeah, well, I've got that here in spades."

Looking around her, she saw nothing for miles except…she was probably imagining it, but it looked like a patch of grass. Even from this distance, the grass looked lush and thick. With nowhere else to go, Jackie headed there.

She wondered how long it would take to reach it. While she walked, she listened to the *thwap* from the swords against her legs and the *thump* of her duffel bag against her side. She loved the music that she made, combining those sounds with the *rustle* of her steps. Jackie enjoyed the ability to make her own music. Soon, she was making up lyrics in her head. She wondered if she should write them down, or if her leather-bound book would write them down for her. The book was buried deep inside her bag next to her tarot cards, so she wouldn't be able to hear the whisper scratch of writing while she walked.

As she walked, the grassy knoll was drawing closer. Unlike the mountain that she had walked toward before which had seemed to avoid her for hours, the grass neared with her every step, looking even more lush as she approached. Unless mistaken, she could hear the sound of water nearby. Jackie could even see trees not too far away. She wondered how long it would take to get there and what she would find when she set upon the grass. Thus far, every location had had something to offer, some sort of lesson that she had to learn. Jackie wondered what this lesson would be.

She looked down when she could feel grass under her feet. Jackie wondered how she had come upon it so quickly; she had only been walking for what seemed like an hour and the grass she had spotted in the distance had seemed lifetimes away. She bent down to touch the grass, and looking around her, didn't see any blood. Could it be that this was the first place she had discovered that wasn't touched by gore?

Standing, Jackie drew in a deep breath. The air even smelled better here. She walked towards the sound of water and was looking forward to at least dipping her toes in when she heard a sound from behind her. Turning, Jackie took in a very large lion standing there, regarding her with fierce yellow eyes. "Fuck, it probably thinks I'm lunch." Jackie whispered. She wished for a wand like Xander's, but she didn't have anything except herself and her swords.

Seeing that Jackie was paying attention, it let out an ear-splitting roar, and then another. Jackie wondered what she had to do, what the point of this part of the path was. Thus far, she had had to learn something in each stop along the path that she found herself on. Aldrich taught her about reaching for the stars, Gabriel had taught her about being loving and kind, Em had been so focused on gathering knowledge and getting to know herself inside and out and Xander...she didn't want to think about Xander right now.

What was she supposed to learn here? On a knoll of grass with a lion in front of her? The lion let out another roar and it was so loud, the force of it ruffled the grass around her. "What the fuck am I supposed to do?" She asked out loud. Only the sound of the wind and the lion's steady grumbles found her ears. "Fuck." Her cards wouldn't help her in this situation. She wondered if the book would help her or have any information? She started to reach into her bag but the lion let out another roar, not as loud this time, but more of a warning.

She tried to move around the lion, but it moved with her. There was anger and madness in its eyes. Jackie had no idea what to do, but she did know that she had never been so afraid on this journey as she was now. Noises of animals in the night that she couldn't see were different than a threat that was standing right in front of her.

She gazed at the lion and tried to calm her heart; it was beating far too fast, and she wondered if the lion could hear it from where it stood. Bending down, she grabbed a rock she had seen in the grass and wondered if it would be a suitable weapon. *Can you kill a lion with a rock?* She wondered. The lion growled as if it had heard her thoughts.

Jackie was quaking inside herself. She had no idea what to do. She thought of the five-pointed star on the chain that Xander had given her. Jackie thought about using it for a moment, but chose not to. He had said that this was her journey and it was *her* path. She had to do this on her own. She would only call upon the people she'd already met when she was in complete dire straits. This frightened her beyond any and all reason, but she knew that she could do this; that she had to do this. She knew that she could only go forward, unless Xander pulled her through one of his fucking doors again.

Gathering all of her courage, she looked at the lion. It gazed back at her with eyes that seemed almost human, but there was a ferociousness in that gaze that frightened and excited her at the same time. *What would it be like to be so wild?* She mused. *What would it be like to be so* free?

Staring at the lion, Jackie gathered all of her courage and looked around. She saw the trees in the distance, the grass and the hills that lifted up the terrain beyond. She could hear the water nearby and it sounded cool and delicious. Looking back at the lion, she noticed how hot its gaze was. It stood rooted to the spot and growled again. It tensed as if it was ready to spring at her.

Jackie did the only thing she could think of to do: she pulled out her long sword and held it properly with one hand outstretched to keep the lion even further from her. "Don't make me fucking kill you." She warned. She hoped that the lion didn't know that the only thing she had killed was a fucking crow made of shadows. The less the fucking lion knew the better.

She reached out with her other hand and gripped the sword with both hands to keep her arms steady until it was time to swing, to stab and perry. The sword seemed to anger the beast and it tried to approach her, but Jackie kept it back. She moved with the lion and read its body language. In a way, Jackie felt as if she were dancing with the lion. She wondered who was leading and who was following.

The sword was getting heavy, but she didn't dare let it fall. Still though, the thought of killing the lion made her feel ill. A being made of shadow and darkness like that flock of fucking crows and ravens? No problem. But a fucking lion? The beast was out here just looking to survive, just like she was.

"What do you want from me?" Jackie asked.

The lion growled at her and made an advance, but Jackie thrust the sword at it. The lion took offense, letting out another roar, shaking the ground around her, as if the lions roar was a call to the wild and it was responding to the sound.

"What the fuck do you want from me?" Jackie asked again. "If you want treats, I'm all out of giving a fuck."

Holding the sword higher, Jackie struggled to keep it from wavering. The lion let out a louder roar and the earth shook even more beneath her feet. Jackie stood her ground. "I'm not afraid you." she stated, even though she was lying through her goddamned teeth. "I am not *afraid* of you."

Then the lion lunged, and Jackie let out a groan-like scream but she still stood her ground and was all set to attack, to conquer over the lion. She sprung at the beast, but missed, and tried again only to miss once more.

They were dancing again, and she didn't know who would come out on top. She was becoming more erratic with her movements. She was trying to read the lion's body language but it kept changing the pattern of its steps. Of course it did, the lion was a wild beast. It didn't believe in routines or precise movements like Xander had shown her. The lion was untamed, and it just moved. She had to think like the lion. Jackie had to let embrace the power of the beast within her.

For too long, she had been afraid of being confident. Jackie had always been afraid of letting herself shine. She didn't want to outshine anyone. The ex who she had run away from was proof of this. He always told her that she was too loud, too much, too everything and could she tone it down? She had. She had done what he had asked her to do, and had shoved everything within her down. Jackie had done whatever he had wanted to keep him happy. She realized now that she had given everything of herself away, and the asshole had still cheated on her.

"Well, fuck that!" She yelled out loud. "You can't have all of me! You can't have any of me, not one fucking piece!" Jackie was unclear to whom she was yelling; the ex, the lion, or herself. It didn't matter. What mattered was that she was taking herself back. She had been too fucking meek on this supposed journey. It was time to embrace the wild child within her and see what she could do.

The lion let out a roar at the noise she was making, so Jackie let out a roar of her own. It was a primal sound, filled with torment and all the suppressed anger that she had shoved down into the pit of who she was, the pit to which she had locked up and thrown away the key. The pit where every dark thought and angry retort had been rotting away for so long. She had put so much of herself away into that darkness that she didn't know where she began and where she ended anymore. Jackie didn't know these lost parts of herself, but that would end now. She would embrace the wildflower child of herself from the past, only that she didn't feel so much forgotten as shoved aside.

Now, Jackie held out her hands, or rather held her hands inward to the self that she had done away with, and she felt the wild child grab hold. Jackie pulled her to the surface and felt her body fill with a fire. The rowan tattoo on her left palm lit up and its light ran along the blade of the sword. For the first time on this adventure, she actually felt like the Queen of Swords. She took no shit from anyone, least of all herself. She was the lion and the whole world would hear her roar.

All of this was contained in the primal noise she was making.

When the noise stopped, when the scream ended, she found herself standing with the sword held high and it shone, much as she shone with a soft golden light. Looking up at the sun, it was a moment before she realized that she was crying. Great big tears were sliding down her face, and she made no effort to wipe them away. She looked down and saw that the lion was looking up at her with huge, frightened eyes.

"Oh!" Jackie said. She put the sword gently down on the ground beside her and held her hand, still glowing with a faint golden light, out to the lion. "I'm sorry to frighten you. Come here. I won't hurt you."

Holding her breath, she let it out when the lion came slowly towards her. The lion sniffed her hand and rubbed at it with its muzzle. Jackie let it, and then reached to run her hands through the lion's mane. It was softer than it looked. "See, I won't hurt you. You're safe with me."

The lion lowered its head into a submissive position, Jackie knew enough about cats to recognize this behaviour. Then it rolled over and showed its belly. Jackie pet the belly briefly, thinking of regular domesticated cats. They would show you their belly but that didn't necessarily mean they wanted to be petted there.

"Come on," Jackie said. "Let's go find that watering hole, okay? Feel like taking a swim? Is it okay if I walk on with you?"

The lion let out a loud purr that made the ground under her vibrate. It was a good feeling and seemed to energize her. She had read that a cat's purr had healing powers. She wondered if that was amplified because this was a lion.

The rowan leaf was still lit up on her left palm and as she stroked the lion's fur, it purred louder. The glow from her hand made it seem like the lion was growing. She looked into the lions' golden fur and wondered what had brought him here, to the world as it was now.

The energy that Jackie had released flowed through her body still. She still felt the tingle of the suppressed energy along her skin. There were all the other thoughts there, too. The men who had tried to keep her down, she had given away her power to them. She couldn't continue to be that way.

Whatever was coming, she would face it head on and with her head held high. She would try not to be afraid. If she had to find out why this world had become so foreign to her, so be it. What's more, Jackie *wanted* to find out what had happened. She wanted to find out what had turned the world from the one she had known into one that she barely recognized underneath a layer of so much blood.

Jackie also wanted to know what the cause of the blood was. Though her body chilled at the thought of finding out what could wreak so much violence on the world, she knew that it was up to her. This was her journey. She had to be the one to find out.

Standing, the lion stood too, and she walked on towards the pool of water she could hear in the distance. It had been so long since she had gotten truly clean, and she planned to enjoy the feeling of the water on her skin as she washed away the rest of who she had been so that who she was now could shine through completely.

As she had hoped, the water was cool and welcoming. As she disrobed and let the water slide over her body, she let her head go under the water so that all the thoughts of how she had held herself back, how she had let men change her, how she had changed herself for other people, washed away. When she rose out of the water, she was completely herself once more, all the thoughts of who she had been were left in the water.

When she emerged, she was who she had always been, but had been too afraid to be. She shook out her hair and the electricity crackled. The tattoo on her hand glowed, the rowan leaf looking as if it were a light that would show her the way.

Slipping out of the pool, she let the sun dry her and fill her skin with heat. Gradually, the magic that she had called to the surface, past the wall that she had broken, began to fade back into her. Jackie could feel it thrumming underneath her skin, waiting to be called upon when she needed it. She dressed and put on her swords, then started walking once more, the lion following close behind her.

IX

Jackie and the lion walked on.

The land around her became filled with hills and what looked like small mountains. Jackie didn't know where they were going and did the only thing, she could think of doing - she followed the path.

There was less gore here, only the wildness of the grass and the rolling hills. The lion kept good pace beside her as they walked together. Jackie had to admit that it felt good having someone else walk with her, even if they weren't capable of human speech. A tamed lion was good company indeed. Jackie knew that she had the talisman Xander had given her, and that she could call on him or Gabriel if she was in trouble, but she didn't want to use it for casual conversation and a want to have someone nearby. She had to do this on her own.

Jackie wondered where this fear had come from. In the past, she had never had a problem being on her own. Somehow, she had gotten to a point in her life where she needed the constant company of other people. She had even found herself in a relationship with a man who was a complete and total fuckwad. She was still angry at herself for having sold herself short, for even giving that man a moment of her time.

As they walked along the rough path, she watched the land around her become rockier and soon, there was no grass. She was left with the dirt that she walked upon and stone as it overtook the ground around her. However, she kept walking; she had to find somewhere to sleep before it got dark. Though she saw no blood along the ground here, she had no idea if the land around her was safe. She thought not. Jackie hadn't felt safe for a long time, except when she slept in Xander's bedsit. It had helped that she had been in a protected basement room and there had been a crapload of weapons around them.

Jackie also hated that she was afraid. She had never been one to give in to fear. She had always gone on, always chosen the most difficult road on purpose. Jackie learned about herself in those moments, but she wondered if that explained why she had stayed with a guy who she didn't love. She wondered when she had stopped loving herself and selling herself short?

The lion let out a snort. Looking down at it, Jackie let out a snort of her own. "Sorry, I'm not good company right now."

In response, the lion rubbed its head on her legs and she stopped to run her fingers through its gorgeous, thick mane. It looked up at her with golden-green eyes and she saw the intelligence there, she could *see* the love. She gave its fur another quick tussle and they kept walking. Soon, the pathway stopped being dirt and now they were walking on gravel. She knew that the land around them was changing.

She could also hear the *swoosh!* of water nearby.

What was more, Jackie could feel the wind change. The air that had been filled with the scents of smoke, fire and grime and the dry heat of the mountains. Now it was filled with the scent of water and something deeper, something more primal. She could hear the call of the ocean and wanted to run towards it. She didn't, though. Jackie kept her pace the same. She would get to where she was going when she was meant to.

Walking up a small hill, she finally saw what was waiting for her. There, on the rocks surrounded by water that crashed against the rocks with a loud smash, was a small hut. There was light coming from inside and Jackie wondered if this would be their salvation. Already, the sky around her was becoming darker. She was able to pick out some stars in the sky, others waiting to make their appearance.

Looking down at the lion, Jackie knew that it shared her thoughts. They both quickened their pace towards the hut. There was a brief walk down the hill they had climbed, and there was still a short way toward the small hut when the sky around them went dark. It was as if the darkness, instead of inching toward night, had been switched off abruptly so that she could see the stars.

Around them in the dark, there were noises. The lion began to growl as they walked and looked to the left and right, even as they moved forward. Jackie began to grow afraid when the noises coming from the shadows began to grow louder than the surf that surrounded them. The lion looked at her and raised an eyebrow.

"Don't fucking look at me." Jackie said. "I don't know what that sound is, and I don't really want to find out."

They hastened their pace towards the little hut on top of the rocks. It became even darker still and the noises grew even louder around them. It was as if whatever beasts were hiding in the shadows had been waiting for darkness to fall. Jackie well remembered the sound of the creatures that had roamed outside the airport and the fear that had run through her. While she had resolved herself not to be afraid anymore, she knew that fear could be a smart thing. She quickened her pace and so did the lion.

The noises turned to growls and the occasional hiss. They strode faster towards the little wooden hut, but it seemed to be even father away than before. Jackie wondered if this was like when she approached the mountain. Should they try to reach it from another angle? She looked around her quickly and didn't see any other way. They hastened their pace.

The growls changed to screeches that made the hair on her arms stand on end. She was flat out running at this point and the lion was ahead of her and she followed its lead, praying that she didn't fall on her face. There was a wet sound behind her as something hit the ground and she could hear whatever it was moving along the gravel behind her. Sweat was falling off of her face and her feet felt as if they were running on hot coals, but she kept running, hoping that she would reach the hut.

A light went on inside the hut and it shone brightly in the darkness. The screeching howl grew louder and the thump and drag of the thing behind her grew quicker. It sounded like it would be on her at any moment, so she ran even faster still.

A door opened, and the figure of a rolled out onto the ledge of rock the hut stood upon. Jackie saw the gleam of a wheelchair. His hand raised a lantern, and she could see his face. It was aged by wrinkles and a white beard that grew so long it curled in his lap.

When he spoke, his voice rang clearly through the air. "For God's sake! Ride the lion, girl! He can run faster than you can!"

The lion understood the words and it slowed for Jackie to get on, slowed, but did not stop. In the space of a moment, Jackie had climbed onto the lion's back and had entwined her fingers in its mane. The lion let out a roar but kept going. It kept running towards the man that was lit up like salvation and Jackie kept her hold on the lion for all it was worth.

The thumping wet sound was coming close to her. Indeed, Jackie felt as if she had almost missed getting swiped at, the beast was that close to her. The hut was nearer and nearer now, so Jackie held on tighter and prayed to a god that she hadn't believed in for many years that they would make it safely.

The night around her was screaming, her own cries joined theirs. Still, she didn't take her eyes off of the mage in the doorway and the salvation that he promised them.

With a burst of speed, the lion leapt the remining distance and landed softly in the mans hut. The door closed and she tumbled off the lion even as the sound of something slamming into the door reverberated throughout the hut. The man with the lamp stood looking at turned his chair .

Jackie lay there looking up at him and wondered what a man not living in a town or village represented to her. He regarded her silently, and while he looked at her, she looked at him and took in everything about his appearance.

He looked genuinely worried. His head was framed by white hair his long white beard shone.. He rolled towards her, holding the lantern whose light showed the deep blue colour of his robes. Though he was not smiling, Jackie saw kindness in his eyes.

"Bringing the lion with you was ingenious. You normally get taken somewhere along the rocks by the things chasing you, though why you never think to turn around and strike at them with your sword is beyond me."

He held out his hand to Jackie. Taking it, Jackie sat up. "What do you mean, I normally get taken somewhere along the rocks?" Jackie said.

He looked at her and Jackie could have sworn she saw the seas within him, full of waves and white foam. Then she blinked and what she had seen was gone. "I meant nothing by it." He shook her hand. "I suppose you are hungry."

The lion huffed. "My friend is, too." Jackie said. "But you probably don't have food suitable for a lion."

"The lion will be the one to decide that. Come with me, Jackie."

"How do you know my name?"

"I know many things. Would you like something to drink? A relaxing tea after your journey to get here perhaps?"

He turned and rolled away from her, down a small hallway that Jackie hadn't noticed before. She let the lion follow the mysterious man and she looked around. The small hut was wooden on the outside, but it appeared that the wooden layer was a shell overtop of the stone within. She turned around in a small circle and saw how the man had used the stone walls to great effect. He had made storage areas out of holes in the rockface and had even used part of it to create a cooking area that even now had a fire burning merrily and a large black pot over the fire that had something bubbling within that smelled heavenly.

As she followed the route he had taken with the lion, Jackie saw that the crevices had been filled with candles that increased the glow of the place. Running her finger through one, Jackie realized that the flames were somehow magical. Though they gave off light, there was no heat to them. Pausing in the hallway, she could hear the beasts trying to find entry but knew without a doubt that they were safe inside the hut.

When Jackie came into the kitchen, she saw the lion. He was lying down in front of the hearth, soaking the warmth from the fire that has been created there. The man had made a pot of tea and was pouring out two cups.

"Look, I don't mean to be rude," Jackie said

"Yet, sometimes we are rude or we have to be. It can't be helped."

"Yes, well I still don't know your name. You somehow know mine but I don't know yours."

"My apologies." He came towards her with a cup of tea and held it out. "My name is Ethan."

"Ethan?" Jackie said. "Really?"

"What? Were you expecting something different?"

"Well, a mysterious man living in a hut on the rocks surrounded by the sea? I thought it would be something like Apollo or something, but not Ethan."

"Sometimes, there is more to a name. Here," Ethan handed her the cup of tea. "Come, let's eat.." He motioned to a table that had been laid out with bread, cheese, meat and small round cookies. "I made those hermit cookies myself, this morning." Ethan said.

"If I sit down with you, will you tell me more of what you were saying before?" Jackie asked. "More about me being stuck on repeat?"

"I said nothing of the kind."

"You said that I normally get taken along the rocks. What did you mean by that?"

"I meant nothing." He said, not unkindly.

Jackie sighed. She knew that he would be another person along this path she found herself on who would not tell her everything that she needed to know. Jackie respected that everyone wanted her to find her own way, but at the same she wished they would give her a fucking clue about what she was supposed to do or where she was supposed to go. Jackie let out a breath and took a sip of her tea. She tasted an ocean of flowers and sunshine, she could even feel the sun upon her skin.

Putting down the teacup, she looked at Ethan. "This is wonderful tea."

"Thank you. I've had plenty of time to perfect it."

"You make this yourself?"

"Yes, I can show you my gardens later."

"I would love that." Jackie said sincerely. Taking another sip, she tasted mint and the stars, and could hear the planets moving around her. She looked quietly around and wondered how it was that she was not swimming in amongst the stars. Blinking, she came back to herself. Looking about, she saw books covering all tables and stacked within shelves made of stone. Reaching out with her free hand, she ran her fingers over a few book spines. She could hear whispering from her book and knew that she would find more writing in her leather-bound book later that had not been there before. She looked forward to reading it. She decided to try another tactic with Ethan.

"How long have you lived here?" Jackie asked.

"Quite some time."

"Define quite some time."

"I've lived here for many years..." He looked somewhat uncomfortable. "Truthfully, I've forgotten how long it has been."

"You don't remember? Why would you stay here for so long?"

He shrugged. "I meant to only get away for a little bit. Sometimes you just need to get away, to leave and take yourself away from society so that you only have your own voices in your head." He took another sip. "I think you know about this kind of mindset."

"I do." Jackie said. Wasn't it the need to get away that had put her on a plane bound for somewhere across the ocean? She had just wanted to get away, to just be on her own and know that she held only herself accountable. "I do indeed."

"Well, one week became a month, a month became a year and so on. You know how quickly time can move, don't you? Soon, it was just me and my voices, and I would carry out conversations with them so that I wasn't so alone."

"Why didn't you try to leave?" Jackie asked.

"Truthfully, I didn't know my way back." He looked sad at this, and the ocean within his eyes returned. Though he was looking at her, she didn't think he actually saw her. He could only see the ocean and the wind. As the ocean in his eyes stormed, she could hear the waters outside the hut growing stronger. She wondered at what kind of magic this mage held. All the other people she had met so far had some kind of magic. There was no reason for Ethan to be any different.

When he blinked, the storm in his eyes faded and the waters outside calmed at the same time. He wheeled over to the counter and got the teapot and poured more hot tea into her mug. Jackie nodded her thanks.

"You might think I'm lonely, but in reality, I was able to find myself. The world around me just became too *much*. There was always too much going on, too much happening and all of it was happening now *now* **now**. It was an age of instant gratification. No one worked for anything anymore but yet they wanted anything and everything. It was so loud, so incredibly loud. All of the lights were so bright and I found myself turning away as I walked down the road. I started hiding in my apartment more and more. I would embrace the darkness and the shadows. Even surrounded by so many other people, I was so lonely. I didn't know where I was going or what I wanted out of life."

"Does anyone?" Jackie replied.

"I should hope so. Everyone has a spark inside them but I'd lost my spark somewhere in the shadows. Do you know what I mean by this?"

Jackie nodded, feeling a warmth of understanding blooming through out her. "Yes, I do. My whole journey here has been like that."

"But there is so much light if you want to look for it. If you welcome it in." He took hold of her left hand and turned her palm upward. "The rowan is a tree of healing. You are healing. You are on a journey to find yourself, just as I went on mine."

"What happened to you? Did you lose yourself?" Jackie asked. "I find myself pulled into the shadows too often. I deal with depression a lot."

Ethan patted her hand. "Yes, exactly. I fell into the shadows as if I were Alice falling into a rabbit hole. I knew nothing but the shadows, and when they started to speak to me, I knew that I had to get away."

"How did you find this hut?"

"A friend of mine had told me about it and had offered me refuge here. When I found it, I knew that it was home, and that find my soul again and let my spirit soar. I knew that it would take some time though. Sometimes, you really only find yourself in the silence that is within you."

Jackie heard the sound of purring and felt a presence at her feet. The lion had curled himself up and was lying on the floor, gently purring. She reached down to pet him, and the purring increased. The sound filled the hut and echoed gently off of the stone walls.

"How long have you been here?" She asked Ethan.

"I don't know, exactly. I meant to stay here only a few days, but the days became months and then I stopped marking time." He motioned to a stone wall in the small kitchen that had marks etched into the wall. The notches covered the entirety of the stone wall and had begun to spread onto the floor and the ceiling. Jackie couldn't help but be reminded of the marks on the walls that prisoners make.

"But surely you want to go home?"

"Why would I when this has become home?"

"What of your family?" Jackie asked. "Surely you miss them?"

"I don't know, I have not seen them for so long. I think they all might be gone from me; I do not recall them except in fondness." He poured more tea into both their mugs. "What of your family, Jackie?" Ethan asked. "I'd wager that they miss you, do they not?"

Jackie hadn't thought of her family in a long time. She was an only child, and both of her parents had passed on. Jackie supposed that her family was the friends she had around herself, but she wondered if they even existed any longer in the world as it was now. Was there anyone to miss her now that her world was gone?

"I don't know." She said truthfully. "I haven't really had a family in a long time."

"Perhaps your family are closer than you think they are. Not all family is family by blood."

The lion purred even louder and Jackie ran her finger though its fur again. She wondered who her family really was. "When did you last leave your hut?" She asked.

"Why would I leave when I have everything I need here?"

Jackie was shocked by his words. "Do you mean to tell me that you haven't left in all this time?" She motioned at the wall that had been marked by days or months with notches. "You've remained alone?"

"I see nothing wrong with that. I have my lantern if it gets dark. It's the only thing that calms the beasts and the waves when they get too loud. They are afraid of the light."

"Aren't you afraid as well?" Jackie asked.

"There are all kinds of fear. I just choose to live with mine."

"Huh, yeah.. right. What I was going to say is that don't you think your being cowardly? I mean, getting some alone time is one thing and this is a pretty nifty hut."

"I have everything I need here," he said again There are birds that live within nests that they have built and they sing to me when I get lonely. There are gardens that I have built in the earth below this hut, and I have watched the plants grow with the joy I give them. There are other creatures here that burrow under the ground and in the walls, and they come out from time to time. I am never truly alone."

Jackie looked at Ethan, really looked at him. Far from the serene person who she had met when he saved her from the dark beasts, Jackie thought that the turbulent waters she could see in his eyes were filled with sadness rather than strength. He was strong, yes, but taking a deeper look at him, Jackie could see a layer of despair within him that she hadn't noticed before. She didn't feel sorry for him, he wouldn't want that. However, it did make it clear to her that she didn't want this life for herself.

"Here, we should enjoy a repast. I've been a neglectful host; you must be hungry." He stood and busied himself by the fire pit and opened the post that hung there. A gorgeous scent filled the hut, and he took out two earthenware bowls and filled them with what looked like a stew. He took down a plate and piled it with thick crusty bread and took out a dish that was filled with rich creamy butter.

"Did you make all of this yourself?" Jackie asked.

"I did. You learn how to fend for yourself if you have to. As you have done." He bowed his head to her and then filled their cups with the final drops of tea.

"I haven't had to fend for myself." Jackie said.

"What do you call the journey that you are on if not fighting for yourself and your survival? You are in a world that is full of things that would kill you, many you have already met, and yet you continue to thrive. You continue to *fight*." He looked down for a moment and muttered "Something that I could never do."

He set the bowls down in front of them and the plate of bread. Jackie chose not to comment on his last remark, not sure of what she would even say to him. She knew now that he wrestled with the choices that he had made.

Saying her thanks, Jackie took a piece of bread in hand and dug into the stew. It tasted of winter and spices. The stew tasted of yuletide and it filled her whole body with so much warmth that she hadn't realized how cold she had been. The lion looked up at her and made a small mewing noise, but Ethan was there right away with a bowl of chopped up pieces of meat and vegetables for the feline. They all ate in companionable silence for a while and the small kitchen was filled with the music of cutlery and a good meal.

Finally, Jackie spoke. "Did you make all of this here? The stew is fabulous."

"Yes, I grow the vegetables in the gardens out back and I keep chickens here that I've hatched from eggs. I live completely off this land. That's enough for me." The last phrase was as if he were answering a question that she hadn't asked.

While Jackie finished eating, and her thoughts moved to Xander, but she pushed those away. Instead, she wondered at Ethan's wisdom and thought about what she had learned from him. She knew now that, although she was afraid, she did not want to turn away from the complications that life required of her. The very idea of going on this trip was her way of deciding not to deal with the issues and problems she had faced. She knew that although some time by herself was a good and even necessary thing, that she didn't want to shut herself off from life either. Jackie wanted to live. She had spent her life hiding what she wanted and hiding from what she deserved. That couldn't happen any longer.

"Thank you for the food and the moment of comfort." Jackie said.

"No thanks needed." He said. "You've always found your way here, what choice do I have but to help you?"

There was a mountain of unsaid words and information unuttered. Jackie knew this. Rather than fight against it, as she had with Xander, Em, or Gabriel, she accepted it. This was her journey, and it would take her where she needed to go. She had to accept that as well. Sometimes faith was like that, Jackie knew.

"Well, thanks anyways." Jackie said. "I think it's time that me and my friend go on our way. I have no idea how much longer this path will last, but I know all I can do is go forward."

"Spoken like a true warrior. You will need light to see your way forward and to give you clarity."

Jackie motioned to the lamp that was on the table. "Should I take this?"

The mage snorted. "And how will you fight with your swords if an enemy tries to best you? Hold out your right hand."

Jackie did so. He took the lamp that was on the table and pressed it to her right palm. "I thought you said I won't be taking the lantern."

"You won't, not in this form. Now hush while I finish this."

Jackie nodded and watched as Ethan pressed the lamp onto her palm gently, as if he were working it in. Slowly, so slowly that she wasn't sure it was really happening, she watched the lamp start to come away, as if it were made of snow and not metal. Flakes of it began to float around her hand as if it were a cloud made of magic and wishes given form. Jackie stared as the lantern came completely apart. The pieces of the lantern, shining like magic like bits of snow, began to flow into her right palm where Ethan had been pressing. When the cloud of metallic snow cleared, there was a tattoo of an eye on her palm.

"There. Just as the rowan leaf is a symbol of grown and bravery, the eye will see into the darkness and into the beyond, whichever direction you want it to see. Now keep in mind, the eye and the lantern are powered by your own light, so make sure that it is always kept at the ready for when you need to see. Do you understand?"

"I think so." Jackie said. She closed her hand into a fist and then opened it up but nothing happened.

"Think of the light within you like the light of the lamp. You have to will it alight. Think of blinking within yourself, if you know my meaning."

Nodding, Jackie closed her eyes turned inward and tried to visualize the barrier that kept the light hidden. She could see the light glowing within her. When she opened her eyes, the light shone out from her palm, and she could direct it into the dark corners of the hut. When she blinked again, she imagined a temporary door sliding down around the light again and it went dark.

"Thank you so much for this." Jackie whispered.

"Not much good trying to see into your future without light to lead the way." Ethan said. "Come, I will show you the exit. You'll have to go out the back way. The darkness is quiet during the day, so you will have time to quickly move on."

He stood and led Jackie and the lion to a door that was hidden behind a shelf filled with cans and dishes and more books and there was the click of stone. When Ethan moved the shelf aside, she saw the door there, cut into the stone wall. When she pushed it aside, she saw that the path she walked alone continued from here, the rush of the sea giving way to birdsong. Turning to Ethan, Jackie threw her arms around him in a hug.

"Please come with me." She said. "Come and see the world."

He shook his head. "I have had my fill of the world. Besides, this journey is for you and you alone."

"I'm walking with a fucking lion." She said. "That's hardly alone."

"Still, it is your journey. It's not mine to take with you. You must go forward, and I must remain here. That is the way it has always been."

A tear slid from her left eye. "Won't it be dark without your lantern?" She asked.

"I have more." He said. "Aside from that, your light will fill up the skies so that I will know you are okay." He kissed her on the forehead, and she could see his eyes, usually filled with the roiling seas, were calm. She found comfort in that.

"Thank you." Jackie found the words lacking.

"Thank *you*." Ethan said. "Now go and use your talents. Don't turn away from challenges, but stand and face them head on, okay?"

"Okay. I promise."

"Good, now go. Please and with my blessing."

She nodded and the lion came to her and walked beside her. As she strode away from the small hut on the rocks, Jackie felt hollowed out, as if a weight she had been carrying had slid from her and landed at her feet. She took a step, leaving the weight behind.

Jackie heard the door close behind her and knew that Ethan had retreated inside once more. Looking down at the lion she said "So it's just you and me." The lion purred at her and licked her hand.

Jackie walked on. She didn't know what was coming, but she knew that she was face everything head on, no matter what it was.

Coming from the the direction she was walking, she heard an unearthly noise that sounded like the very earth was coming apart. The sound sent shivers down her spine and her skin broke out in goosebumps.

She stopped walking. "What do you think?" She asked the lion. "Do we keep going?"

The lion looked at her and pawed the ground and kept walking forwards. Jackie breathed a deep sigh. "Well, fuck."

X

"Well, fuck me indeed." Jackie said.

The screaming sound was increasing with every step. She didn't know if it was people or animals making the sound, or if it was something else. Whatever it was, the sound was scaring her shitless. The lion wasn't faring any better. She looked down. "What do you think? Should we go back?"

The lion shook its head and started forward. Jackie let out a sigh and followed, walking quickly so that they were walking side by side again. "You're really going to make me do this, huh?" Jackie said. "I don't suppose now would be a good time to draw a card, huh? The lion let out a snort loud enough to be heard over the ear-splitting noise.

As they walked on, Jackie kept looking around. She could see birds flying through the air and other wild animals in the distance, but none were running or walking away from the noise Jackie couldn't understand it.

"Are we the only ones who can hear that noise?"

She could have sworn that the lion shrugged. There was blood here, too and it looked like it had been thrown a far distance. It splattered the ground in front of them.

Jackie looked at the arc of blood splatter and thought it was very telling of what she could look forward to. The splatter had come from the direction they were heading, towards the noise she could hear ringing through the air. It was like a siren song, and it pulled Jackie towards it. The landscape around them looked as if it belonged to an old town with cobblestone streets, with trees and gardens planted all around her. The houses they passed by were older wooden homes with inviting hedges and front gates, thick glass windows and roofs that looked as if they had been cut from gingerbread. It looked like a merry and happy place, except for the blood that covered everything from the flowers to the windows to the front doors of the houses. It shone wetly in the bright sunlight. Jackie wondered if it was one of the animals she had heard back at the airport that was making the noise.

She was walking faster towards it as the lion followed beside her. They passed fountains and a gazebo, what looked like a small park with swings. The swings were swaying slightly as if a child had just recently left. There

126

was no breeze to move it, leaving Jackie to wonder what had caused the movement.

Looking at the lion she said, "I don't know about you, but this place is creeping me out." The lion nodded and let out a snort of agreement.

They walked onward towards the loud noise which was a fever pitch. Jackie wondered if her ears were bleeding, and she checked just to be sure. She wouldn't be surprised by anything at this point.

Rounding a corner, Jackie's mouth fell open. There was a small fair or carnival set up inside the town square. None of the rides or games seemed to be working except the Ferris wheel, which was brightly lit and spinning at a lazy pace. Her mouth hung open and she knew without a doubt that this was where she was meant to go. This was the next stop on her path. She thought of Xander and each step that she had taken on her journey so far. Jackie wondered what she had to learn here.

The screaming sound increased to the point where she was sure that her ears were going to split open and start bleeding. Motioning to the lion, they ran the last few feet to the fairground, keeping her eyes glued on the Ferris wheel, their steps hard on the cobblestone streets. Finally, they reached the fairground. The moment that Jackie's foot made contact with the grass, the screaming noise stopped completely. In the silence, they could hear the nearby flapping of fabric and the creak of wood moving in the breeze.

Jackie stood there, the lion looking up at her with wide, concerned eyes. He looked as shocked as she was. "What the fuck was that?" She whispered. The lion let out a soft growl. They moved forward on the grass and saw that there was more blood splatter here, too. In fact, it looked as if it had begun here as the blood droplets seemed to fan out from the Ferris wheel. She traced their arc along the grass and the stone.

The lion let out a small snort. "I guess we should look around," Jackie said. "Just do it quietly. It's fucking weird that there's no one here."

They passed a few stalls where games sat waiting to be played, darts waiting to be thrown and bottles patiently waiting to be knocked over. Everything looked to have a light patina of dust. "What happened here?" She whispered.

As they neared the Ferris wheel, Jackie heard a soft tune filling the air. It reminded Jackie of the old carnival music that she had heard at the fair when she'd gone with her parents. The sound of that music used to fill her with such a thrill, it was a preamble to the fun that would come afterwards and the thrill that would last for days. She loved the feeling of the wind in her hair as she rode the rides and sampled the food and candy on offer.

Her favourite ride had been the Ferris wheel, mostly because it had been her mother's favourite ride. It had been the only ride her mother had been able to stand, having found all the roller coasters and other rides too much for her to handle; but she could do the Ferries wheel and Jackie remembered riding on it, clutching her mother's hand while her father watched from below.

She hadn't thought of that in a long time, but it had been an even longer time since she had been to a fair. This one didn't look like it would cause children to laugh and cry out in joy. It may have caused them to cry, given the state of the place. She saw bumper cars nearby, a ride that looked like a Tilt-A-Whirl , something called the zipper drop, a kiddie slide, a couple of roller coasters, and the Ferris wheel itself. The fair had many places to eat, but even these were all closed up. Whereas the blood had appeared fresh before, here even the droplets of blood were covered in dust.

Jackie headed for the Ferris Wheel and the lion walked beside her, a worried look in its eyes. "Hey, you're not allowed to be afraid. You're supposed to be brave. You're the king of beasts, right?"

The lion let out a snort.

"I suppose now isn't a good time for me to draw a card or write something down, is it?"

The lion rolled his eyes at her.

"I didn't think so. Thought I'd ask anyway."

They walked further into the fair. There were a few games that had been hidden from view and her heart skipped a beat when she noticed a fortune teller tent. She walked over to the tent slowly, not too sure if she wanted to go in. Her curiosity got the better of her, however, and she moved closer to the tent. It had been draped in purple that had gone dusty with time. Her heart somewhere in her throat, she pulled the curtain aside.

Jackie was surprised to find a man waiting for her. The inside of the tent was well-lit with candles that sparkled in the half-light. She let out a small cry and the lion growled softly beside her. The man gestured to her. The man was short, no taller than five feet, and had a tiny white goatee. He was wearing what had once been a purple fez hat and purple robes, but the colour had faded to maroon over time. He wore pince nez glasses perched on his nose.

"Come in, come in. Don't stand out there; it's not too pretty out there, it's so much nicer in here, don't you think?" The man stood and went to the chair across from him and actually patted the seat. "It's comfortable, I assure you! I just had the chairs redone. Mine has a little bit more padding as its not very comfortable sitting here all day waiting for you." He stood and gave her a smile. "Would you like a cup of tea?"

He said this all very quickly, but with a genuine smile on his face. Not waiting for an answer, he busied himself with a small kettle that sat on a hot plate and spooned some loose-leaf tea into the pot strainer. "I'm afraid that I only have peppermint. Jasmine is better for clairvoyance, but peppermint will do in a pinch. I don't have any sugar or milk I'm afraid."

"That's okay, I like it without." Jackie said.

"Good good, that's so wonderful as I have none to give you. Come in, come in, dear lady. Your cat is welcome too of course, though I don't have anything for him and wouldn't know at all what kitties his size drink. Being a cat, I would assume milk, but I've already said that I don't have any, I'm so sorry."

"It's okay. Do you have any water?"

"That I do have in great abundance, and I will put some in an extra saucer for him, will that do?"

Jackie smiled, charmed. "That would be fine."

"Good, good; now sit and here is your tea. I don't read tea leaves or the crystal ball I'm afraid. The tea leaves are too inaccurate, and the crystal ball is far too moody. Having to stroke something to get it to work? Could you imagine? No, no, I'm a card slinger." He gave her a roguish wink. "As are you my dear."

Jackie was taken aback. "How could you possibly know that?" She wasn't afraid, though now she was wary of this man, whoever he was.

"Why a fortune teller never reveals his secrets." He put two mugs of tea on the table. "Come sit, sit. Here's a saucer of water for your friend the mighty lion." He reached down and patted the lion on his head. "Such a noble beast and a good companion. You were smart to bring him with you this time."

Jackie sipped her tea and it tasted wonderful. "I don't mean to be rude," she said quietly.

"But so often, so many of us are." He declared.

"Yeah, anyway. Who the fuck are you?"

He was genuinely shocked. "Oh my goodness, I have not introduced myself! Well, you would know my name from the placard outside my tent of course."

"There is no placard. The whole village here looks deserted and there's blood all over the place." Jackie said. "There's so much blood all over the ground, all over." She paused. "Do you know what happened?" She asked.

"We try not to speak of it. We focus on other matters instead, such as your tarot reading."

"Yes, but who are you?" She asked. "What's your name?"

"I am the great Ronaldo, Seer of the Stars and Beyond!"

Jackie raised an eyebrow. "Is that your official title? Or just your job description?" She asked with a smile.

"Well, dear lady, we all have names, different names. Names we use for different situations. This is the name I have chosen for myself, and Seers of the Stars and Beyond is just advertising."

"Okay then. I'm Jackie."

"Yes, dear lady, I know who you are. You've sat at this table many times now and each time I send you off into the beyond, I wonder where you will go and what you will do. As I said, this is the first time you've had a lion with you. I think that's progress, don't you?" He gave her a small smile and took a sip of his tea.

"You're not the first person to say that I've been on this route before."

"Nor will I be the last. Now, dear, you know what to do. Shuffle the deck until you are done and put them back on the table."

"Don't I need to think of a question?"

"My dear, aren't you living in a question right now? Just open your mind and let it go clear and open. Let the cards tell you what they need to tell you."

"I've never done a reading like that before. I've always asked a question to give the cards guidance."

"Well, I am not you. Please shuffle the cards and then put them back on the table. And remember, there is no right way to shuffle. Though please don't do what one client did and throw them on the floor. The cards are sensitive as you know. You have to treat them kindly, but I don't need to tell you this."

Jackie shook her head. "No, I treat my cards like a connection to spirit."

"My dear lady, that is exactly what they are! I must say you are using better language this time around. So much swearing last time."

"Well thank you very fucking much.."

A pained expression passed over Ronaldo's face. "I spoke too soon, I see. Oh well, no help for it now." He gestured regally to the cards. "Shuffle please!" He took a sip of tea before putting his hands primly on the table in front of him.

Jackie tried to let her mind go blank, but she had difficulty doing this. She had always thought of a question, something to guide the cards, even though she knew that sometimes, the cards answered what they wanted to and didn't bother to answer her question. She knew that the cards would tell her what she needed to know, whatever question she asked.

She approached the tarot from a place of personal growth, but she knew that on this entire journey, she had been doing nothing but growing. Her life was not the same as it had been and nor should it be. As she shuffled, she focused on nothing but the sound of the shuffling of the cards. This was difficult for her, but Jackie shuffled to a rhythm that ran throughout her mind and the sound of the whispering cards. All she heard in the end were the possibilities.

Finally, when the cards felt right, she put them down on the table. Ronaldo smiled at her. "You know the drill, dear lady. Break the deck into three piles and arrange the piles in the order of best to worst. Use your intuition to guide you."

Jackie did so, letting her left hand hover over the cards for a moment before stacking the deck back into one pile.

"Good, good dear lady." He said.. "Let's see what the cards have to say for you, shall we? Now I know that you are skilled at cartomancy and have even started spirit journaling, but please try not to interpret what you see. That is *my* job as the reader here, not yours. Though you may form your own opinions over time after this reading, that is entirely up to you." He smiled kindly at her. "Are you ready, dear lady?"

Jackie sat back and watched him flip the cards over. She was expecting cards like the Sun, the Tower, the Two of Swords and the Ace of Wands. The cards she was looking at didn't make any sense to her and she looked down at them with confusion.

Ronaldo had flipped over three cards.

The first one was The Broken Man. He looked as if his body had crumbled beneath him, and he wore a look anguish on his face. He was laying on an outcropping of rocks, a cliff high above him. The next was a card called The Screaming Banshee. A woman kneeled on the ground and all around her there were signs of darkness and violence. People in the background behind the woman had come to blows and there was blood on the ground and on the woman's clothes. The third card was The Spinning Wind and showed a Ferris wheel, not unlike the one that had drawn her to this place. In the background, Jackie could see carriages and they contained children who wore looks of fear on their faces.

"Oh, now this won't do, will it my dear lady? No no, not at all. Here now, we'll draw three more cards." Ronaldo said. While the first three were placed horizontally in front of her, the other three came down vertically, one above and two below. The layout of cards looked like a cross. She wondered if that was intentional on his part. Jackie often used a spread called the Celtic Cross when she read cards for other people, but she had never seen a spread like this. "Is there a name for this spread?" She asked Ronaldo.

"No, nor should there be. You need to stop trying to interpret my reading, dear lady. Just let me tell you all about what is going on here. Look at the cards I just laid out for you."

She did so. The first vertical card was called The Lady of Shadows. She wore the shadows that moved around her on the card like a cloak or a cape. Rather than look frightened though, she looked more serene. A lock of blond hair peeked out of the cloak's hood. The second vertical card was called The Laughing Cat. It featured a black cat that had entwined its tale with a white cat. That would be simple enough, but both cats were surrounded by sprigs of fire and flame, safe on the only spot of land in a sea of lava. Neither cat looked as if it were laughing. The final card was the only positive one. This one was called The Cascade of Leaves. On the card, a woman stood underneath a large rowan tree. Jackie looked at the tattoo on her right hand and then back at the card. The woman stood with both arms stretched out, and she stood in a shower of leaves that swirled around her, a look of happiness and even joy upon her face.

"What the fuck do those cards mean? They aren't like any cards I have seen before." Jackie said.

"And yet, you just decided to go on a jolly holiday, didn't you?" Roland replied with a smile. "Sometimes, the things we don't understand give the most clarity when we finally understand them."

"But I can't read them."

"I know you can't, and I told you not to try. Trying to read the tools of another mystic and wielder of cards will drive you crazy. Added to that, you must let the cards read you first, which you have."

Pointing to the first card, Ronaldo gave her a sad glance. "The Broken Man. Not a nice card to receive at all. This tells me that you arrived here broken in some way, hurting and in pain, but unable to run from yourself anymore. The rocks that this man lies upon indicate to me that whatever you ran from gave you a very difficult landing.

He pointed at The Screaming Banshee. "Whatever situation you found yourself in after your landing left you in turmoil. The lady on this card finds herself in pain. Unable to find a physical release for it, she lets her primal reactions take over. There is no comfort to be found as there is carnage and violence all around her."

Jackie thought that so far, this reading was bang on. She actually shivered. Ronaldo pointed to The Spinning Wind.

"There is a question here, my dear lady. This card is asking you whether you are repeating the same cycles that you have done before. Are you making the same mistakes in your relationships or your life? Remember, you get back whatever you put out in the world, so this card is karma, yes, but it is a reminder that sometimes you need to get off the ride."

Ronaldo pointed at the next card. "Lady of Shadows, oh she is a mighty warrior. She sees the shadows around us and within herself, and rather than fight against them, she welcomes them to her and befriends them. She knows them well and wields their power."

Jackie pointed to the next card. "Why is this card called The Laughing Cat?" She asked. "This doesn't look like the cats are laughing."

"Well, my dear lady, you know as well as I do that appearances can be deceiving. This card is asking you what those you know may be hiding from you. More importantly, what you could be hiding from yourself? These cats are laughing because after everything they tried to do, they still ended up in a soup of hellfire." He gestured to the cats. "I like to think that they are laughing on the inside. It's a very ironic card, don't you think?"

Jackie let out a snort. "Fuck yes."

"Yes, fuck indeed." Ronaldo said, giving her a wink. "Thankfully dear lady, we end on a happy note after all this fire and brimstone. The lady on this card is being blessed. The leaves are of the tree which is of the earth. It looks fresh and green and bright, and the lady in this card stands underneath the branches, waiting for its bounty; hoping for release and light and comfort of the soul and the spirit." Ronaldo looked at her with a wide smile and a twinkle in his eyes. "There now, that's the perfect card to end on, don't you think dear lady? So much better than all that doom and gloom!"

"Well, what does all this mean?" At the question, she heard the pen scratches in the leather-bound book that was in her bag. The pen was scratching loudly, and Jackie knew that she would have a lot of reading to do later.

"What do you think it means? I've just told you what I see and my interpretations." Ronaldo said. "Do you want to know what I think?" Jackie nodded. "When I look at these cards, I see someone who is lost within herself who is entering a period of metamorphosis. She is becoming, and despite the hardships she has experienced, she continues to grow." He raised his left eyebrow sardonically. "Sound like anyone we know?" Ronaldo gave her a soft chuckle. "You mustn't fret, my dear. You've been on this journey before, but you may beat it this time. You may yet find your way."

He took one more sip from his teacup. "Would you care to go for a walk with me, my dear? These old legs need to be moving every once in a while, you know."

Ronaldo held out his arm, and she took it. The lion followed closely behind as they walked through the opening of his tent. Outside, the landscape still hadn't changed; everything looked as decrepit and derelict as it had before.

"What happened here, Ronaldo?" Jackie asked softly.

"A great many things, dear lady. A great many things."

He led her with purpose towards the Ferris wheel. It was already lit up and a soft tune was coming from it, one that she remembered from the fairgrounds of her youth. Jackie wondered who had turned it on, for she saw no one else here.

Ronaldo gestured to a seat. "Hop in, dear lady. We'll fit in one of the seats. Your lion friend might have to wait below here on the ground. I do think he's too big for the seats."

The lion let out a snort and sat down in front of the Ferris wheel, looking somewhat dejected. Jackie approached the lion and ran her hands through its mane. "It's okay. You will be able to watch me the entire time, okay? I won't be going far."

"Oh, but you will. You'll be going up!" He gave her a smile. "Well, you'll be able to *see* far anyways, which is more or less the same thing."

They settled into their seat and Ronaldo brought the bar down. They went slowly upwards, the music tinkling merrily as they rode. "Why do you want to take me on the Ferris wheel?" Jackie asked.

"Aren't you tired of not knowing what is coming? Of encountering new landscapes and having no idea what comes after? This will give you a birds-eye view, dear lady. That will be to your advantage."

As they rose above the dried-out trees that dotted the landscape around them, Jackie began to see. She saw rivers and forests and roadways. She'd had no idea that the land went on this far, though she supposed that this was still her world, even if it wore a different face.

"Do you see now, my lady?" Ronaldo asked her. "Your next stop will be there." He pointed at a castle that sat a little way off. "You will find her there."

"Who will I find? Will she help me?"

"Not in the way you want, but in the way that she can. She is a stickler, but if you follow her rules, you should be fine. Mind her, though."

She made note of the path that she and the lion would have to take. "I will. We'll set off now."

"You'll do no such thing. It is almost night. You will spend the night in my tent, it's quite roomy and there is space enough for the three of us. I'd like you both to be my guests."

Jackie was silent as they rode back down. Finally, she asked, "Why are you helping us?"

Ronaldo took her hands in his. "My dear lady, I'm trying to make sure that you don't repeat the same mistakes and end up here again. Why would you look kindness askance? Come, I will make you another cup of tea and you can rest your feet while I make dinner. The night is young, but there are dreams ahead for you and I, yes, many dreams are to be had."

Jackie was surprised to find that she was smiling as they made their way back to the tent, the lion walking beside them.

*

Ronaldo had given them a place to sleep for the night. Part way through the evening, they woke to sounds that no human or animal would ever make. Jackie had cuddled closer to the lion, trying to draw strength from it, to find the courage she needed.

Lying there in the darkness, with the sounds of Ronaldo snoring and the inhuman noises from outside, she was comforted by the lion's presence. Jackie supposed that the lion was allowed to remain with her, as it was on this journey with her, every step as new for the lion as it was for her. She fell asleep again, being lulled by the beating of the lions heart and the sounds of its breathing.

When she woke, Ronaldo was already up. He made them both some more tea. "I hope you like mugwart tea." He said. "I found some this morning when I went to make my peppermint tea. Do you know that mugwart tea is good tea for clairvoyance? It's supposed to open the pathways to the beyond that we cannot see and give us access to the worlds we thought we knew but only knew so well."

He placed a plate in front of her. It contained bread covered in butter, several strips of bacon, and eggs. "This is wonderful." Jackie said. She meant it too, as she hadn't had anything quite so lovely in a long time to eat.

"It's the last of my eggs, I'm afraid, but you're worth it. You have to be prepared for the journey ahead, dear lady, you will need your energy about you and your wits, also an open spirit and mind." He motioned at her cup. "Hence the tea." He set down another plate for the lion and it was covered in thin strips of meat and some rough looking vegetables. There were a few strips of what looked like beef in on the plate as well. "I was able to take the life of a bird this morning and cook it for the lion. I know that he is probably very hungry." Looking down at the large cat, Ronaldo nodded to it. "I'm afraid it's a meagre feast for a king such as you, but I do hope it will suffice." The lion nodded, blinked once and then set to eating.

"How can I ever repay you?" She asked. "You've been so kind to me. I hope that I remember the reading."

"Oh, I'm sure every word of it is inside your little book that I heard scratching away before, plus a bit more besides. Do you find that books are able to see more than we do? That just by having them around, they can bring us knowledge and sight and clarity?" He gave her a warm smile.

They ate in silence except for the clink and clank of cutlery and the sounds of the lion devouring its own meal. Jackie took a sip of the tea and, while she didn't love the taste of it, she thought it might have brought her a moment of clarity. Jackie didn't know what Ronaldo meant by clairvoyance; she certainly wasn't psychic. In fact, she didn't know what she *was* anymore.

When the meal was finished, the seer cleared away the plates and the mugs. Jackie put her swords back on, and went to grab her bag, but Ronaldo handed it to her. "I've placed a few things in here for you. There is some food for later, and a half-litre of wine for the evening. I've also mended your clothes and placed a few charms inside for you to help you on your journey."

Jackie was taken aback. She didn't know if she would ever get used to other people's kindness, especially in the world as it was now. Taking her bag, she looked within it to see a trio of crystals and a small bag filled with wine and food. She was touched. "Thank you, very much. I don't know how to repay you."

Ronaldo blushed. "Your happiness is thanks enough, dear lady. You have quite an adventure ahead of you, the cards are never wrong, my dear. Never wrong at all, as you well know!" He squeezed both of her hands in his own and kissed the back of her left hand. "I know that great things are on the way for you, you just have to make sure that you head towards them, okay? No matter what comes?"

She almost asked him to elaborate but didn't. This was her journey after all. Jackie knew that even if he told her what was coming, she would have to face it anyway. Looking at him, she saw something in his eyes that let her know he understood the internal dilemma that was going on within her. He patted her hand, and didn't say a word, and she was okay.

He bent down to pet the lion and run his hand in his fur. "Will you take care of her as you move forward into the unknown?" The lion nodded its head. "Then I am giving you over to your charge, fair sir. I'm glad to know that she will have you and you her." Ronaldo looked into the lion's eyes. "Make sure that her every step is true, won't you? I would hate for her to lose her way."

The lion nodded again, and Ronaldo smiled a bright smile at them both. "I have a feeling that you will succeed, you really will. Off with you now before I ask you to stay another night and share the stars with me. You go on now before I can't bare to see you go." He shooed them lightly towards the curtain and bowed them out. "I know you will do great things, Jackie Queen of Swords."

A shiver ran down Jackie's spine. "How did you know that I was called that?"

"Why you must have told me."

Jackie looked at the lion and it shrugged its shoulders at her. "I don't think so. I didn't even show you my cards."

"Well, you must have." He looked away and then back at her again and smiled at her. "Either way, you have to get going, the day is still young and the castle is just over that hill. It will take you a while to get there so you will have to walk quickly if you want to reach the castle before darkness falls."

"Thank you again. Really."

"You're welcome, really." He smiled. "Now go. There are more people waiting for you on your journey and you will have to meet each one of them if you are to finish where you began. I have great faith in you Jackie." He gave her one final smile and bow and stepped back behind the curtains.

Jackie looked down at the lion. He looked at her as if to say 'What the fuck was all that about?'

Jackie shrugged. "Fucked if I know."

With a loud sigh, Jackie took one final look at the Ferris wheel as it spun lazily around above them. It was as if it were gazing down on them, watching them on their journey like a giant eye in the glaring light of the sun.

XI

Jackie and the lion started to walk.

The landscape around them changed once again. The green grass decorated with blood droplets and empty houses gave way to grass but surrounded by the wild trees that she had seen when she was in the Ferris wheel. The land had looked as if it went on forever.

The castle hadn't seemed like it was far away, but Jackie knew that appearances could be deceiving here. She though of the mountain and what she had done to reach it, wondering if a similar step had to be taken.

She decided to stop for a moment and catch her breath and sat down on the grass. The lion sat down on the grass beside her, letting out a grateful sigh. After just having a reading, she didn't feel like taking out her cards, and though she knew that her book was probably filled to the brim with words for her to read, her head was so full of information at the moment that she didn't think she could stand to take in anymore.

Instead, she sat there with the lion and ran her fingers through its fur. She marvelled at where her path had taken her so far and she felt like she was living out someone's idea of a quest.

With a sigh, she stood and kept going, the lion standing and walking beside her. The land around them began to change. The trees looked more gnarled and gangly, with large shoots of leaves that tried hard to block out the sky.

She knew that her journey forward would be a difficult one. The cards that Ronaldo had pulled for her told her so. However, she also knew that the journey, though difficult, would bring her a lot of growth and hopefully end happily. Jackie knew that this might not be the case. Tarot was funny that way. The cards had shown her how things would progress in that moment. If she strayed off her path, or did something to change the flow of events, the cards would change, too. Jackie loved tarot for that - it wasn't an exact science. More, it was a window into one person's soul in that given moment. She used the cards for personal growth. If this journey wasn't personal growth, she didn't know what was. Jackie knew that the next steps in her path would challenge her, whether she was ready for it or not.

The trees looked less threatening than they had when she had seen them from the Ferris wheel. They marked a border around the castle, and as she got closer to the trees, she could see its stone walls through the foliage and in between the trunks.

Her nervousness grew as she neared. As she came to the trees and stood there with the lion, Jackie was finally able to take in the complete size of it. The castle seemed too big, impossibly so. It was made of dark stone, pockmarked with white limestone. There were large windows that shone out like a sea of eyes watching her. She didn't see a garden, only a moat that surrounded the castle, and a drawbridge. It didn't look or feel welcoming. When she imagined castles, she thought of palaces of gold and jewels so bright they shone. The castle in front of her didn't look as if it had ever shone a day in its life.

She heard scratching from inside her bag. "Fucking book," she said out loud. Looking down at the lion, she asked "So what do we do?"

The lion let out a gruff snort and shrugged its shoulders as best it could as if to say, 'It's your journey, I'm just along for the ride'. Jackie sighed and moved forward beyond the border of the trees. At that moment, she was very nearly blinded. The castle went from derelict and downtrodden to a brilliant shine. Where there had been grey and falling bricks before there were now bricks of opalescent white and the windows gleamed as if they were made of crystal.

Jackie looked back down at the lion. "What the actual fuck?"

The lion snorted out a breath as if to say, 'I have no fucking idea.'

Smiling, Jackie made her way down a small hill, the lion following beside her. The castle in front of her continued to shine and, as she got closer, she noticed that the white brick had stones inlaid in its surface, accounting for some of its lustre. She noticed white and clear quartz, selenite, and she even recognized some crackle quartz. What the hell had happened to the dark castle that she had seen when they were approaching? The windows looked as if they would have fallen out a moment ago, and now they were shining so brightly that it hurt to look at them.

As she got even closer, she could hear the sound of water somewhere in the distance. Looking around her, she also saw no drops of blood. Jackie thought this odd.. She had seen carnage and blood everywhere she had been on this journey; the town and the fairground being the worst of it aside from the altar in the mountains, and Aldrich looking as if he had bathed in it. Why was there no carnage here? Where had the blood gone?

It didn't just disappear. Why was there no signs of violence? Jackie did take a moment to appreciate the fact that she found the lack of blood splatter odd but pushed that thought away. The lack of blood didn't make any sense in this world where it had been everywhere before this. Why did the absence of carnage frighten her so much? She wondered what that said about her and the person that she had become.

Looking down at the lion, Jackie said "This place is fucking creepy." It nodded in agreement.

They had no choice at this point but to move forward, so that's what they did. They came upon the sound of the water. It was a small reflecting pool with water that was aqua green. It was fed by a small fountain shaped like a pair of brass scales. The water would pour into the scales, then trickle down into the water. Looking up, she saw that the brass scales were held by a woman made from stone. Her stone face was turned, but there seemed to be a smile on her lips. She held the scales almost lazily, as if she could care less about them. The woman's stone eyes seemed filled with a delighted amusement.

Jackie wanted to sit somewhere and pull a card, but she didn't think that this was the right place. The shining castle and the woman with the scales seemed to be watching her, following her every move. She wanted to find the entrance, find what she was supposed to be here for, and get out. She didn't know why the place was giving her a bad feeling, but it was. Jackie already wanted to be far away from here and whatever was housed in this castle. Another thought struck her: what did it say about her that she was less creeped out by arcs of blood over grass than a completely clean and shining castle? She knew why almost instantly: nothing in this world had been clean, nothing in this world had been kept in one piece, yet somehow this castle stood in front of her with a fucking fountain. It just wasn't possible. She knew there was magic here; she could feel it.

Taking the long swords out of her scabbard made her feel better, more prepared for what was to come, whatever that may be. She walked slowly towards the bridge that covered the moat. The water that had been dark and brackish was now a light aqua, rippling below her as if it were waving to her. The bridge over the moat had changed too. When she had seen it from the other side of the trees, there had been rough planks of giving her a path over the water. Now, it was a stone bridge that arced itself over the stream. There was even iron railing on either side, a filigree of flowers worked into the metal. When she set foot on the bridge, the metal flowers began to bloom until the railings were filled with more flowers than she could count, all made out of different hues of metal. They continued to grow and reach and stretch themselves until they framed a door on the other side of the bridge. She supposed that this was where she was supposed to go, but she didn't think that she would be able to get past the iron flowers.

The lion shivered a little as they walked across the bridge and she wondered whether the lion was afraid of the iron, or the water. She ruffled her fingers through its fur and then reached out to push open the door. The door slid open almost as if someone were waiting for her, which of course there was.

Jackie stepped inside slowly, the lion following close behind her. There was the sound of flute music from somewhere in the distance as the door closed. Jackie tried not to be afraid of her own shadow. She was terrified of what she would find. If only there was some blood, she had grown so used to seeing the gore.

A voice spoke from somewhere in the darkness. "It's a shame you find the cleanliness frightening since it's a reflection of who you are."

The voice had a slow drawl to it, as if the person speaking was amused at her presence. "Who are you?" Jackie said. She hated how much the fear wanted to take hold of her. It made her words come out as if she were being choked.

The lion put its paw on her leg, and she looked down at it. He bowed his head and Jackie ran her fingers through his fur. His loud purrs reverberated through her and when she bowed down to pet it some more, it licked her hand. Looking into the lion's eyes, she saw strength there. Jackie knew that this strength was also within her.

Standing up again, she held out her right hand with the lamp tattooed on her palm. It lit the darkness with a soft light because that was all Jackie wished for. She knew instinctively that she could make the light grow brighter or softer at a moment's thought.

It illuminated the darkness in front of her, which helped her to see as her eyes became adjusted to the shadows within this chamber. She walked onward, the lion following close behind. There was the scent of tiger lilies and chrysanthemums. In the light from the lantern on her hand, she took in the sight of them; the flowers covered the walls of the chamber and they looked like jewels. Their smell was overpowering but wonderful all the same. Jackie wondered if the pattern of flowers on the curved bridge was made to mimic the flowers that surrounded her.

"Oh, that's a good one. No one else has registered that." The voice said. "You're very observant."

"Who's speaking?" Jackie asked forcefully. She made her way further into the room. With her lamp, she could see that the room was floored in a dark red wood. The walls that she could see through the flowers looked to be done in a soft lilac colour. "Why is it so fucking dark in here?" She yelled out. "How do I turn on the lights?"

"You merely have to wish it so. Most would like to stay in the darkness, but only the truly enlightened want to see things in the light. That's good on you." The voice drawled.

'*Turn on the fucking light*,' Jackie thought. In a moment, where there had been darkness there was now light. The room was indeed panelled in lilac-coloured paper and the floors were a dark cherry wood. There was a fireplace to the left of her. She held her lamp hand to it as if she were firing a gun, and when she pressed her thumb down a small fire popped to life, as if it had been burning for some time.

"See what your actions bring? They bring light and warmth. Others would bring only deprivation and starvation, but that's them. This is about *you*."

The voice was coming from a room beyond the foyer in which she stood. Looking at the lion, she motioned with her free hand that she was going to move into the room beyond. Now that the place was lit up brightly, she didn't need to fear the dark so much.

With her sword in her left hand and the lamp in her right, she moved forward into the room where the voice had originated. If the foyer had been opulent, it was nothing compared to this room. The walls were lined in bookshelves that were filled to the brim with books. This library would have put Em's to shame. Thinking of her made Jackie realize how far she had come. She would continue onward, no matter what.

The room housed a baby grand piano, and its black body shone like obsidian in the light. She wondered idlily whether it had ever been played. There was a settee and a wingback chair arranged around a coffee table made out of what looked like lapis lazuli. The bookshelves were made of the same cherry wood as the floors she walked upon.

Sitting in the wingback chair was a man who looked impossibly young. She wasn't sure whether he was older or younger, or somewhere in between. His face made him look like a teenager, but it was his eyes that made him look like an old man. His hands were clasped gently in front of him, and he regarded her with eyes that had seen too much for one so young.

"I'm much older than I look, Jackie. Sometime within the last thirty years or so, I stopped aging physically so that I could focus entirely on growing mentally and spiritually."

"That must make it fucking hard to date." Jackie said before she could stop herself. *Fuck*, she thought. *Reel it in!*

The man didn't take offense, though. He actually gave her a little grin, though it could have just been a soft curving of his lips rather than an actual smile. His face didn't give much away.

He walked toward her, and he held out his right hand. "I'm pleased to make your acquaintance." He said, his drawl heavy.

"You already know my name. And you also know what I'm thinking apparently?" She gave him a quizzical look. "How the fuck do you do that?"

He let out a sigh and gestured to the settee. "Have a seat, please. I'll pour you a drink."

She wondered about whether or not to take anything from him. "I'll have what you're having. My friend will have water."

"I would assume so. It's not wise for lions to drink wine. And I assure you that the beverages here are quite safe." He went to a sideboard that she hadn't noticed before and poured out two glasses of rich, dark liquid. "I do hope you like an aged wine. It's a cabernet sauvignon that I've grown quite fond of." He brought the glasses over. "This bottle is from 1960. I have older vintages in the cellar, but I prefer this year. 1960 was a happy year." He raised his glass, and she took hers in hand. They clinked and there was the sound of birdsong from somewhere in the house.

Jackie sat there and wondered if she had somehow fallen into a rabbit hole somewhere. The castle had changed, she was sitting here having wine with a mysterious stranger and there was not a drop of blood in sight. *Why did this frighten her so much?*

"You *should* be asking yourself why there is so much blood everywhere else rather than why there is no blood *here*." He said.

"Get out of my fucking head."

He bowed his head slightly at her. "Not my fault when you're thinking so loudly, but I will pretend I don't hear anything from now on, will that be sufficient?"

"Yes, thank you."

They drank their wine in silence until her little book began to whisper, the sound of pencil scratches on paper filling the room. Jackie itched to pull the book out and read what was inside, but she wondered if that would be rude to do in front of company?

"Yes, it would be." He took a sip of wine. "You wanted to know my name?"

"Yes, I do." She tried to see if she could think of something in a deeper area of her mind, but she had never had reason to try to go deeper. She didn't like the fact that he could hear everything. Why did he hear everything?

"Because I'm judge and jury. It's what I do and what I've always done." He sounded tired and seemed bored with it all. Jackie decided not to take him to task for pretending not to listen.

"Do you know how many others have come here over the years? How many others that I've had to judge worthy or unworthy?"

"Who says you need to do any of that?"

"Because it's what I *do*." He sighed, then sat down, and took a large swig of wine. "My name's Colburn. You can call me Cole."

"Okay, Cole. It's nice to meet you." Jackie said, thinking that she wasn't sure if she meant it. She knew that Cole could hear that thought because he gave her another small grin.

"You're wise to be cautious. I could be anyone."

146

"Well, yes. There have been a lot of colourful people on this journey so far." Jackie said. "I just wanted to find out where you lay."

"Well, I'm the judge. I'm impartial. I have to be. I am neither good nor bad. I have been cursed with seeing all and hearing all, but I can say nothing."

"Funny, you're doing a lot of talking so far." Jackie said. "You seem to be doing fine. So, why don't you do me a favour? Start at the fucking beginning and stop trying to be all mysterious. It's giving me a fucking headache." She took a sip of her wine.

"I guess I didn't start things off on the right track, did I? You were a surprise. You've never made it this far before."

"Yeah, well you see all and hear all, right? So, you should have known I was coming." Jackie punctuated with another sip of wine.

"I didn't think you would make it, didn't believe it. You've tried so many times before."

"Everyone keeps saying that but trust me this is the first time I've taken this journey. Either way, you're getting off topic. The castle? This place? What about you, Cole? What's your story, what drives you? What's your motivation?"

"I don't appreciate your sarcasm," he said, not unkindly.

"Then how about you tell me what's going on here? This place is giving me the creeps."

"Please don't let it creep you out. This is meant as your reward."

"I'm listening." Jackie said and held out her glass. "And I could use more wine."

Cole rose, brought over the bottle and filled her glass. He left the bottle beside her. Jackie thought this was an altogether wise move.

"When did the castle change its appearance?" Cole asked.

"When I stepped past the line of trees."

Cole nodded. "That's when it normally changes. It all depends on what you've put out there into the world."

"Like how? Artistically?"

Cole shrugged. "No, more like the deeds you've done. Did you see the woman holding the scales outside?" Jackie nodded. "Those are the scales of justice. Those trees are the border of this part of the world. They are a representation of what I do."

"I don't understand you." Jackie said. "Thanks for making everything so clear, I wish you had told me all that before." She rolled her eyes at him and couldn't help giving Cole a sarcastic grin.

"I'm not finished." Cole said. "When you step beyond the line of trees, you will see before you what you've accomplished, what you've put out into the world, shown back to you. Most people don't see a castle, they see a lovely little house or a cottage. If they've been nothing but an asshole in life, they will see a rundown hut. There was one time that one guy saw a fucking trailer home and another who saw a wooden shack that did not have electricity of plumbing. Those were not fun, but in the end, they were just physical representations of the help they would receive, or the shelters they had built."

"So, they get back whatever they put out..." Jackie said, thinking out loud. "Kind of like karma?"

"Exactly like karma." Cole said. "We used to measure the weight of one's heart against the weight of a feather, but that got so messy, and the cleanup was a bitch. You can imagine the kind of riffraff that the blood attracted. No, instead we decided to let the karma be the deciding factor. We wanted to measure a person's worth, and by we, I mean all other judges who have come before me, for we go very far back. It's not easy, watching those that take this journey and wondering whether they will be judged."

"Others have been here before me?" Jackie asked. "Others that have completed this same journey?"

"You know that it doesn't work like that. Yours is based around the tarot cards in your bag and the mysticism you carry within. Everyone's journey is different. This is yours."

Jackie thought about it for a moment. "So, I could have shown up here and the castle could have been a cottage?"

"Yes, it could have, but *this* journey is important. You've learned so much about yourself, but there is also much left to learn."

"But then *why* a castle?" Jackie asked. "Am I supposed to be impressed by that?"

"Yes, you are actually. In all my years of doing this, the castle has never remained as a castle. As I've told you, it's been a great many different things, but it has never retained its form and grown even more beautiful. There are rooms here with treasures waiting for you to find as a reward for all of your hard work."

"There must be some mistake." Jackie said. "I haven't done anything amazing. I've just lived my life until I ended up here, wherever here is. I don't know what I'm fucking doing."

"Maybe it's the fact that you started on a journey from which you had no idea what to expect."

"I thought you saw and heard everything. You just told me that you were the judge of whether people were worthy. So you must know what I've done and know that not all of it's good, right?"

"I do and see all but I don't tell all. I will tell you this, however. It has a lot to do with the journey that you've been on currently." Cole's voice was tired, and Jackie wondered if he always had the weight of the world on him, or this was his natural tone of voice.

"There must be some mistake." Jackie said again, not willing to believe him.

Cole turned and looked at her with something approaching kindness in his eyes. "Why do you think yourself undeserving of good fortune? You've come so far, Jackie."

Jackie let out a harsh bark of laughter. "Far? Yeah, right. I've come so far. I ran away from everything I knew because some guy screwed me over. I ended up in this bizarre fucked-up version of my world and I have no idea how to get out of it. I have no idea what I'm fucking doing! I have no idea what to do!" She was shouting now, unable to stop her voice from growing in volume. Her words resonated around her, and she could have sworn that she heard an echo. She wondered how big this castle was.

When Cole spoke, his tone was soft but kind, and his voice carried over to her. When he spoke, she could feel the kindness in his words. They wrapped around her like a mantle. "You must stop judging yourself as unworthy of something good." Cole said. "This castle is your home as long as you want to remain here. It's your reward for the work you've done on yourself. Only *you* judge yourself as unworthy."

When Jackie replied her voice was calmer, and she looked at Cole's eyes when she spoke. They were gold and brown and green. "I don't know what to do. I know that the tough stuff is coming, my cards showed me that. I don't know what to do and I'm afraid." Despite her stoicism, a tear slid down Jackie's cheek. The lion licked her hand and gave her hand a nudge with its head and Jackie began to run her fingers through the lion's fur. The lion calmed her, and she took comfort in the animal's purring that reverberated around them.

"Only you judge yourself as unworthy, Jackie. Sometimes, life doesn't go the way we planned. However, all of our actions have consequences. Surely, you've realized that by now?"

"And this is my consequence?" She said, gesturing around at the world around her.

Cole stood and held out a hand to Jackie. "Come and have a walk with me. Feel free to bring your wine."

Jackie stood and held on to her wine glass. Cole refilled it slightly and put the bottle back on the bar. He left the room, and she followed him through a hallway. What she saw as they moved through the hall and into a new part of the castle left her breathless. The room was opulent and grand. There were wide open windows that let in the sunlight, and she almost had to shield her eyes because of the amount of gold and silver she saw. The lion was following behind her, its footsteps making soft thumping noises on the marble floor that shone as brightly as the gold.

"What the actual fuck."

"Is that an exclamation of pleasure?" Cole asked, turning to her with a wry grin on his face.

"You could say that again. But there's no way I did enough good to earn all of this. It's too much, this is too much. I don't deserve all of this."

"You do." Cole said simply. "You judge yourself unworthy because of what others have told you. However, if you were a child, would you have questioned your good fortune?"

"No," Jackie said without hesitation. "No, I wouldn't of. This would be a dream come true to a child. It would have been more than I could wish for as a kid. What child doesn't dream of being a princess in a castle?"

"But yet you question your worth against this now, as an adult, and all that you have done?"

Cole let the question hang in the air without an answer and walked out to the courtyard. She expected a opulent courtyard to match the grandeur of the castle. Instead, the courtyard held only a fountain in the centre of stonework. The fountain gurgled with black water that was like sludge made from oil and mud. It slopped into the water at the fountain base, where bubbles appeared and emitted a noxious smell.

The garden was filled with flowers, but not roses or chrysanthemums or violets. Instead, this garden was filled with flowers that wore black petals and had thorns that covered their stems. Then there was the blood.

The blood was splattered across the stones of the courtyard, the blood that had been missing this entire time. *What does it say about me that I'm happy to see the blood, that it makes me more comfortable?* Jackie thought. She didn't like the fact that she was happy to see it again.

"What is this place?" She asked.

"Well, for every positive judgement, there is a negative one. You said before that you didn't find yourself deserving. Well, here you will find every bad decision about yourself, every time you put yourself down, every time you told yourself you weren't worth anything at all. This place holds every moment you judged yourself unworthy.." Cole replied.

Jackie was silent. She looked all around the courtyard. At the trees with black trunks and dark purple leaves. At the roses that were black and already drooping on the stems; at the black lily pads that floated in the water. There was no sound of birdsong, and there was a gorgeous slash of blood on the stones. "Has the garden been here all the time?"

Cole nodded. "Just like what the others see instead of the castle, the garden differs in size and shape and foliage." He looked Jackie in the eyes. "Your journey is a worthy one, Jackie. You are a worthy person to take it on, and I truly believe you will see the end of it this time."

Jackie merely nodded, not sure she wanted to hear more about how she had died previously. "Thank you."

"You're welcome." He paused. "You know, you can stay here for as long as you want to. You don't have to go on just yet."

Thinking about it for a millisecond, Jackie shook her head. "I'd love to stay, this is really good wine, and you are good company, but I have to go on, you know? Please tell me that you understand."

Cole nodded. "That is very sound judgement. I have something for you, will you wait here?"

Jackie nodded and handed him her wine glass. The lion and Jackie waited. The fresh breeze that came by ruffled Jackie's hair and the lion's fur, and they wondered what would come next and what awaited them on their journey.

Cole returned carrying a small bag. He handed it to her. "I packed a few things for you and your friend so that you don't go hungry. There is also something else in there for you. I hope it will help you on your journey."

Jackie reached into the bag and pulled out a gold pocket watch. She opened it and realized that instead of mere clock hands counting time, the sun shone from the centre and two of the rays were the hour and minute hands. The planets represented the numbers, with an extra two she had never seen before. Jackie knew that anything was possible here, even unknown planets. "This is beautiful."

"Thank you. I want you to have it so that you can look upon it when you are making an important decision. Though it may not seem like it now, time is on your side."

Jackie went to Cole and hugged him. She put the bag of food and the watch inside her duffel bag, which was getting a little full. The watch clinked against the talisman that Xander had given her. "How can I ever repay you?" She asked Cole.

He thought for a second. "By making sound decisions and being a better judge of yourself. I'd hate to see your garden grow."

"Deal."

As she and the lion made their departure, Jackie felt like Dorothy in the Wizard of Oz, walking on the yellow brick road, except for the fact that the yellow brick road wasn't covered in blood and Dorothy had worn better shoes. Her own feet were clad in comfortable sneakers without an iota of sparkle.

"Fuck." Jackie said, and she and the lion walked onward.

XII

The leather-bound book in her bag was constantly scratching now. She would pull it out from time to time to read what it said and try to absorb its wisdom. It was a retelling of the journey she'd been on, but with added insights. She took these insights as a comfort, knowing that she would have made them eventually. For instance, within the chapter that dealt with her visit to the carnival, the book had said **"As Jackie travelled up again, she could see part of the castle ahead. Each time the Ferris wheel made a rotation, she could see more of what was coming ahead of her. Sometimes, you had to repeat a cycle many times in order to know where you were going."**

Jackie knew that the book contained her own thoughts, and also other thoughts which belonged to her spirit. It still amazed her that her spirit could think for itself. She was kind of jealous of it for a bit, having deeper thoughts than she did, when she gave her head a shake. They were *her* thoughts too, even if she wasn't aware of them. She had to make time to read the book further and listen to what her spirit was thinking. Jackie gave a silent note of thanks to Em for her gift. It seems it really *was* the book of knowledge. Jackie wondered how it could be big enough to hold everything that she was seeing and doing but came to understand that magic didn't need an explanation. It simply was.

She had no idea what came next but knew that whatever came she would face it. Jackie understood that she had no choice, it was what she had to do. Her cards and the reading that she had received from Roland had shown her this. She only wished that she had faith that everything would work out. That was what the cards were to her though, a little piece of faith printed on cardstock. She always felt that she was talking to her spirit when she laid out a tarot reading and so she had to believe that spirit had an idea of what was coming for her. She just had to let go of her expectations and realize that this world, whatever or wherever it was, defied them.

The lion let out a soft growl and looked around in confusion. Jackie shared the sentiment. The cobblestone of the courtyard looked as if it continued onward for a long time, making Jackie think of the Wizard of Oz again. She stopped for a moment and tried to figure out where the stone pathway ended but she couldn't see over the hills and the valleys. Who knew how far this path wound?

"Well, I guess we're going to find out, aren't we?" She said aloud.

She didn't mind the walk, even if the stone pathway was covered in slashes of dried blood. *What the fuck bled all over this place?* She thought. *And is it still alive?*

A shiver ran down Jackie's back and she gave her head another shake. "I have to stop thinking like that. I'm going to be frightened of my own shadow if I keep this up."

The lion let out a snort; Jackie chose to ignore it.

Jackie let out her own snort. "Two can play at that game, you know." The lion rolled its eyes at her and kept walking. Despite herself, Jackie was smiling widely.

They kept on, the only sound being the air around them. Jackie heard words within the wind. Trying to make them out, she found that it was a lost cause. *The wind was playing tricks on her again, like most of this fucking place*, she thought. It was hard to know which way was up and which way was down.

She would find her footing one moment, only to lose it the next. The grass was green here, even if it was covered in droplets of blood. Jackie saw flowers blooming some distance away in the grass, and for reasons unknown to her, she stepped off the path and made her way toward them. They weren't too far from the path, and their deep purple colour calmed her. She knew their scent, and remembered her grandmother always wore lavender oil. Her house smelled like a valley of flowers. Looking at the lavender in front of her, she thought of her grandmother. She could see her so strongly at that moment, Jackie would swear that her grandmother was right here with her. "Don't fight the path," She often told her. "It has something to teach you. Sometimes, it's best to just let it be and see what it has to say." She had been full of phrases like that. Thinking on that now, mixed with the scent of lavender, Jackie felt more rooted and grounded. She bent down and pulled a few stems of lavender blossoms. She brought them back to the path, wove a couple of them into the lion's hair, and made a bracelet for herself.

She knew that eventually, the blossoms would fall from her wrist, but she liked to think of the lavender marking the way she had been, as if she were Hansel and Gretel with the breadcrumbs. What was with all these literary references? Jackie pondered.

A soft wind blew across her skin and ruffled the lion's fur. Jackie felt the sun on her skin and the wind on her face and for the first time since she had come to this place, she felt alive. She didn't know what was coming, but she looked forward to what would.

As they moved forward, their feet making a kind of music as they continued on the cobblestone, they began to see signs of civilization. The occasional hut and cottage, a small field that looked as if it had once held livestock. At one house, she saw laundry still hanging on the line. Veering towards the house, she went into the backyard and looked for signs of human habitation. She didn't see any, so she helped herself to a couple of pieces of clothing, a shirt and a pair of jeans. The nights had been getting cold and, though she never planned be to be out in the middle of the night, she would need warmer clothes.

"Why hello there."

She turned towards the voice, knowing already who it was. Xander hung from a branch in a tree that was in the backyard , only he hung from one foot that looked as if it had been tied to the branch with a piece of twine.. He looked almost happy to be in his predicament and, with the way the sun was shining, it was as if his head were surrounded by a halo.

"Xander!" She went to him. "What are you doing here?"

"Me? Well, I could just be hanging around waiting for you." He said, a smile on his face that looked like a frown from Jackie's right-side up viewpoint.

"You've been waiting all this time?" Jackie asked, touched.

"Well, what is time really?" He gave her another frowny smile. "Sometimes, you just need to get a different perspective on things, you know?"

"No, I don't fucking know, and did you want me to let you down?"

Xander looked as if he shrugged. "I'm good. But I think there is something waiting for you inside that house."

"I can't go in there. What if the people who live there are inside?"

"I can assure you that they are not. I've been hanging here for quite some time, and no one has come out. But I can see the flicker of the television. I see it most clearly at night when there is nothing else around here. You should go in and have a watch." He said coyly.

"What aren't you telling me?"

He folded his arms across his chest which was odd to watch him do upside-down. "You should go in and have a watch." Xander insisted. "The lion can stay with me and rest."

Jackie nodded, not sure what else to say, and she wondered what the television would be playing here in this world that was so much like her own, yet so different. She looked at Xander. "I'm afraid. Why am I afraid?"

Xander upside-down shrugged again. "Sometimes, part of being strong is knowing your fears and facing them."

She huffed out a breath. "I just knew that you'd have something fucking mystical to say."

"That's me, mister mystical. Go on." He urged.

Jackie tried again. "Don't you want me to get you down?"

"In a moment. I'll be perfectly okay here with your lion nearby. Go on now, quit stalling."

Jackie nodded and walked up the small flight of stairs. When she got to the sliding door for the deck, she saw that there was a flickering light in the living room which was otherwise in darkness. Carefully, she slid the door open, and heard voices. It took Jackie a moment to realize that the light and the voice was coming from the television.

"...In these times it is important to remember that we are only as strong individually as we are together..."

She followed the sound of the voice into the living room. There, she saw that the room was almost stopped in time. There was a half-finished drink on a side table, a cigarette in an ash tray that had burnt down to the nub, leaving a finger of ash. The television was on and a man was speaking. She recognized him. He was the President. He looked so frightened. In the corner of the television screen were the words *previously recorded*.

"...I know that you are afraid. We all are. This virus is a test to our people unlike anything that we have seen before. As you know, the social distancing that we put in place to prevent the spread of the virus was not followed.

Though it was mandated by law, some people felt they were above the law. Ignoring the rules has caused the spread of the virus to continue."

Jackie thought back a bit. She remembered that some people were whispering about a new medical problem that had been affecting many people in Italy and Spain, a virus that started like a cold and then quickly developed into something more. *Is that what he's talking about?* She thought.

"Of course, you will know that we were unable to flatten the curve of this disease. Those of you who have lost family members will know the signs, and we thank you for doing your self-quarantine so diligently. You have my respect, and you are heroes. I also know that quarantining yourself with someone who has contracted the disease is most likely a death sentence. You are the new heroes of this generation. Our country thanks you."

Death sentence? Jackie thought.

"By now, you will all know the symptoms. It starts like a common cold and then morphs into a fever. As the skin grows hotter and hotter, those infected will turn on those around them. They attack and they do not leave survivors. After they attack, the body seems to shut itself down and they die, but they have already spread the virus. The amount of death that this country has seen in a mere handful of days cannot be counted."

"Shit." Jackie said. "Shit fucking shit."

"We know that these are dangerous times, that there is anxiety and fear. However, we want you to know that we are doing everything we can to find a vaccine. In the meantime, there are some things you can do. If you do sneeze, do so into your elbow. Go out of the house only if it's absolutely necessary. When and if you do go out, please wear masks and gloves. There are tutorials on how to make your own non-medical masks on our web site."

"What the fuck happened here?" Jackie whispered to the television, knowing that the President wouldn't answer her, but asking anyway.

"I know that you are all in peril. People have lost their jobs because they have had to self-isolate or self-quarantine. However, you have *not* lost your life. We thank everyone who could listen to our advice and acted quickly. You may have helped flatten the curve."

"What the fuck?" Jackie whispered.

"We know that supplies are running low, and groceries have grown scarce. Those that are still working on the front lines, nurses and doctors and food service workers, we salute you. You are the unsung heroes. You will be remembered. It should be noted too that all borders have been shut down and locked. The world is in lockdown. If you try to cross a border into another country, state or province, you will be shot on site, as you are considered to be a threat. I have spoken on this many times, but it still needs to be said. You will be shot on site, so do not cross borders, do not leave your homes, do not leave.

"There are tens of thousands of people who have died. Though this may feel like the end of times, it is not. We have proven as a country that we are strong, that we will survive. That we will overcome. I commend you all for the work you have done so far. We are looking for a cure for the disease, and we *will* find one. Stay strong, stay home, and hopefully we will succeed at flattening the curve."

The television was filled with snow and static for a moment, and then the news clip started over again. It was on replay forever now. Jackie thought that there was a good chance that they didn't find a cure, that no answer was ever found. She stood there in that empty living room, watching a news clip from who knew how long ago and felt incredibly, totally alone.

Feeling as if her feet wouldn't support her, she made her way to the porch door and stepped back out into the sunshine. Xander and the lion were still there, the lion lying on the grass by Xander's head. Jackie walked towards them.

She just stood there, unsure of what to say or what to ask or how to feel. Finally, with no other alternative left to her, she sunk to the grass and let the lion lean into her until Jackie wove her fingers through its fur.

"You okay?" Xander said.

"Define okay." Jackie said. "Actually, no, fuck no. I'm not okay." She ran her fingers through the lion's fur and enjoyed the purr it gave her in response. It was loud enough that Jackie could feel it throughout her body. "Is that what you meant by a different perspective?"

"Yeah." He said. "Sometimes, it helps to see things in a different way so that we know what to do, or how to move forward."

"Do they know what caused the virus?" She asked.

"No, they don't. They do know that it moved from person to person by touch. It started as a respiratory disease and then took on a life of its own. It grew and changed and doctors the world over were never able to figure out a way around it, a way to destroy it."

"How long did all of this take?"

Xander spoke while he reached up to untie himself. Jackie stood and began to help him. She didn't want him to fall and hurt himself. "It took a ,a matter of days." He said softly.

"That's it?"

Xander nodded. "A little over two weeks to affect the whole world. It stated in Russia and then moved onward from there, never staying still, never staying in the same form. It was a day or two before doctors realized that all these people experiencing illnesses were suffering from the same thing. Then they tried to cure them with the usual cold medications and pills and anti-biotics. Then they realized that the only way to kill the virus was if it couldn't feed on people. So, they kept people apart from one another."

"Only that didn't work." Jackie said. "Obviously."

"Well, it did for a while. For a few days, they thought that they were making a difference, and that good things were happening. Then those that were infected started becoming something more..."

"You mean the people who changed. What the fuck did they change into?"

Jackie had been working at the rope that tied Xander to the tree. She released his foot and he fell, only a short way, to the ground. Xander stood and his face looked grim. "I don't know. They just changed into something *more* than themselves. They attacked the people around them, attacked as many as they could. The blood they spilled spread the disease further. Those they attacked wouldn't change into one of them for some time, giving them more opportunity to spread the disease until they did transform, usually about forty-eight hours later. The authorities believed that having people self-quarantine would help prevent the spread, but they were wrong. The virus kept spreading, people kept turning."

They were both sitting on the grass again, both petting the lion. The lion was purring up a storm now and the ground around them rumbled. "The news said that they would just change, that they would attack. I haven't seen anyone here except for you and the others. Was there really that much violence here?"

He raised an eyebrow. "You walk in a world touched by blood and gore and signs of destruction, and you have to ask that?"

"Okay, I'm sorry, but all of this is a little hard to take in."

"Yet, you've survived for a number of days in a world that is so much like your own but can't possibly be, am I right?" Xander said. "Think on the violence and where you've seen it. What areas have been marked by blood? How do you think the blood could have gotten there?"

Jackie thought back through this world that she had been walking through. She thought about where she had seen the blood. There had been blood on almost every step of her path. The worst was with Aldrich at his altar of blood. The runner-up for that was the fairgrounds with Ronaldo, the blood stretching across the ground in long arcs.

A thought bloomed inside her head: The arcs of blood that flowed across the grass from the Ferris wheel. She thought she knew how that had happened. The people riding the Ferris wheel had been sick already, they had all been sick, they had attacked and ravaged the bodies of the people with whom they shared seats, and they in turn had attacked the attacker, spraying more blood across the velvety green grass.

"Dear God," Jackie whispered. "This whole place is like a funeral barge or a burial ground."

"That's why there are still fires burning around here." Xander said. "They tried burning piles of people to get rid of the bodies, but that didn't help much. That just spread whatever was in the bodies into the air. It made the virus travel faster."

Jackie sat there, utterly stunned. She knew now that every splash of blood she had seen had been a spot where someone had lost their life or where someone had fought to save their own. Images ran through her mind: She saw the stone walkway covered in slashes of blood, the blood and gore that soaked the grass of the airport, on the streets outside of Em's house. She looked at Xander and he nodded. He knew that she finally understood.

Looking at him, at the depth of his eyes, at the sea that they contained, Jackie swooned a bit and longed to touch his skin, but she gave her head a shake. Even though they now shared the knowledge of the horrors that had taken place, it didn't make her want him any less; the fact that there was someone who understood the horrors that were going through her mind right now made her want him even more. *What the fuck does that say about me?* She thought.

"We did this to ourselves?" She asked.

"No, the virus did. The virus took what remained of those people and made them into something else, something capable of the unspeakable."

"Why are you telling me this?"

"It was time for you to know."

"Just like that? You decided to tell me now, just fucking because?" Her palms erupted with sparks from the right and light from the left, the rowan leaf and lantern tattoo coming to brilliant life and coming to her defence in her agitation.

"I didn't just decide. Don't you see, you've never made it this far before, you've come so much farther than you ever have. You have to know this before you go forward."

"Are you going to tell me what the fuck you mean by that bullshit? Everyone keeps saying that, that I've never come this far before. What the fuck does that mean?"

"I can't tell you that."

"Jesus fuck!" She flung out her right hand lazily without much effort. The light coming from her caught Xander and threw him against the tree from which he'd been hanging. He slid down and lay in the grass. Though he looked at her and did not move, flashes of blue light ran down his body. "I should have left you hanging from this fucking tree. You're such a fucking bullshit artist."

She stalked forward and kneeled down at him. "Why are you always leaving and coming back? Why have I only seen Gabriel one more time, but I've seen you three times now. Why are you helping me when you're not supposed to be helping me according to Marie-Claude? What's the fucking talisman for if I keep seeing you on what is supposed to be my fucking journey?" She clutched at the star shaped talisman.

The questions came from her in rapid fire, and she could hear her journal scratching away in the bag that lay in the grass close by. *I guess I'll have some fucking reading to do later*, she thought. She was furious. Looking down at him, she knew that he couldn't be the target of her fury, she knew it was just the situation that she found herself in.

Xander spoke quietly and quickly as if he feared that Jackie would cast out her hand in the same way again. "I keep coming to see you because I care for you. Marie-Claude doesn't know, or if she does, she's allowing it. I would be dead otherwise, or at least made to suffer. I am telling you now because you are running out of time, and you need to do one final thing. You have to find out what caused the virus and how to make it right."

"I have to cure the fucking world?" She nearly yelled at him.

"Yes." Xander said quietly. "Yes, you do."

Jackie just looked at him, mouth agape. Then she closed it again and turned to look at the wind as it ruffled the grass around her, and the blood that dotted the grass in darker and darker patches as she looked further away. She turned back to Xander.

"Well fuck me."

XIII

The fact that Xander had not answered all of her questions was not lost on Jackie.

With the sun quickly going down, they chose to spend the night in the abandoned house. The television only played the one channel, on a continuous loop. Turning it off, Jackie felt like the big grey box was like an eye that was watching her. She went to turn on the radio, but all that played was static. "I guess I shouldn't be surprised." She said to the lion. It blinked at her in response.

Not knowing what to do with herself and still humming with anger, she went to explore the house. It was filled with the kind of things that her mother would have called knickknacks: Royal Dalton figurines, decorative plates, vases filled with dried flowers. She scoured the surfaces for framed photos and was rewarded when she found a handful on the living room walls. The couple depicted looked middle-aged, but the house felt as if it belonged to people decades older. Perhaps they were the children? Either way, she couldn't get over the idea that she was intruding upon their house, even if they were no longer here.

She avoided Xander for most of the evening. The lion came upstairs with her, and they sat on one of the beds in the largest bedroom. Jackie examined the trinkets and knickknacks scattered around this room. This appeared to be the daughter's room. There was a music box that played a soft melody with a little doll that looked like a ballerina. She would twirl as long as the box was open. Jackie found herself opening and closing the box several times.

There were some photos on the walls above the desk, too. The girl looked to have been popular and had a multitude of friends. Jackie wondered what had happened to the girl, what had befallen her. Whether she had become one of the people lost within themselves to the disease, or if she had somehow escaped it to perish later?

Shivering, Jackie said "I have to stop thinking that way. It doesn't change the situation thinking on the past, all I can do is think of the future, no matter how fucked up it may be." The lion gave her a wink as if it agreed with her; maybe it did.

There was a light knock on the door, and Xander came in with a tray. It was laden with cups of tea and left-over biscuits. "I'm sure the cookies are dry as shit, but the tea is wonderful."

"Thanks." Jackie said only slightly waspishly.

Xander poured the tea from a pot decorated with snapdragons into two cups that were decorated with lilacs. "Look, I know you're pissed off. I'd be angry, too."

"Gee, would you? You're sure smart! Look at how smart you are! Your mother must be so proud to have raised such a smart son."

Xander sighed and took a sip of tea. "I'm sorry. I'm so sorry, Jackie. I know that it's hard to walk this path without knowing what you are doing or where you are going. I know that it's frightening to battle your way along, fighting when you need to and being slightly lost the rest of the time. I know it's a lot, and it's a lot to ask of someone. Especially someone who didn't sign up for it."

Jackie let out a snort. "I guess I as good as signed up for this when I slid down the emergency slide."

"The beginning changes but yes, you're right. Once you take the leap, you're committed to seeing it through, no matter how it ends."

"I figured as much." She took a sip of tea and then another. Xander handed a saucer of milk to the lion. "I've never liked not knowing. I always have to find out everything I can about something, so the fact that you know shit that you won't tell me drives me crazy."

"I can't tell you everything. I could share what I did, because you'd seen what was on the television, you'd heard the President speak. I could fill you in on what happened because there was no other way for you to find out. I can help you somewhat, so can Em and Gabriel, fuck even Aldrich if he's having a clear day. We can help you, but we can't lead. We can aid, but we can't take over. It's why Marie got so pissed at us before. We were keeping you cooped up and trying to make sure you knew what to do before we sent you on your way. It doesn't work like that. You've learned to fight on your own, you've learned to trust your instincts on your own."

"It still doesn't mean that this doesn't suck serious shit." Jackie said.

Xander cracked a smile. "You're so right."

They drank their tea and Jackie tried not to look at his face, at the dark eyebrows and eyelashes that fanned his face like a caress. Finally, she spoke. "Was it different for you?"

"Was what different?"

"Your journey. You sound like you've been on one of your own?" She said, her voice rising up in a question.

Instead of answering her, he put down his cup of tea and rose. Xander walked to the bedroom window and looked out. Jackie wished that she could see inside of him to know what he was thinking, but she had a notion that even if she could see into him, he would still be able to hide what he knew.

"I can't tell you." He said with his back to her. "Everyone must go on their own journey. Mine was so different from yours. I had a role to play, and I play it still."

"You make it sound like we're chess pieces on a board." Jackie said. "Like someone is moving us around."

He turned to face her and there was a blue fire in his words. "No one is moving us around. We are not someone's playthings. You have to understand that you are responsible for your own actions. I need you to understand that!"

His eyes burned so fiercely that she actually shrunk back and the lion rose, its hackles expanding. "I do, okay? I fucking do!"

"You are an...unexpected complication. I care for you too much."

"So, is calling me a complication supposed to woo me into bed with you?"

"You know what I mean."

"Obviously not or I wouldn't be asking you. What are you talking about?"

He shook his head and the fire in his eyes faded slowly. "It's only that there are challenges coming up, trials that you have to be ready for. A lot of people don't survive and they have to start their trial all over again."

"Well, if they get to start over again, it can't be that bad, now, can it?"

Xander's face grew solemn. "This is only the first of three trials. There is so much left to do and so much left to see. I want to make sure that you can get to the end of this in one piece." He came closer. "There is something about this place that changes you. You have to focus on the task at hand which is getting through this intact."

"Well thanks for having faith in me." Jackie said quietly.

"I do have faith in you, I really do but-"

"No buts." Jackie stood, not noticing the gold light that flamed at her right hand. It seemed to be an automatic response to her anger. "You stand there, lecturing me on what I need to do, but where the fuck have you been? I've been on my own for this journey and I've been doing a pretty good fucking job of it, too!"

"Jackie, I-"

"No. You stand there telling me what I need to, and you don't even stop to think for one fucking moment about everything I've been through."

"Look, I know-"

The gold flame flared ever larger. She stood there holding up her hand as if she realized that the flame was coming from her for the first time. "No, you *don't* know. Everyone has their own journey, right? Well, this is mine."

"You don't know what's coming!" Xander said desperately.

"And you wouldn't tell me even if you could." Jackie said.

"No, I wouldn't." He sighed and his head hung slightly. "I'm not able to. I wish I could tell you but that would ruin everything. All I can do is see that you're prepared enough for what is coming. You have to be strong."

Letting out a mirthless laugh, Jackie pointed at the lion. "Strong like him? Yeah, I think I'm strong, I'm a fucking *champion*." Her golden fire came to life again, but she used control, managed to reign it in and pull it back into her. "Why are you telling me all this? What are you not telling me? Do you know what is coming?"

Xander looked away. When he looked back, she saw something different in his eyes. The storm that normally moved and flowed there had grown still. His eyes were just a bright and piercing blue. She was not reminded of the sea when she looked at them, but an abyss.

"Things are about to change. I just wanted you to be prepared."

She nodded. "I am prepared, or as much as I can be." She reached a hand out to him, and then let it fall weakly to her side. Something was different between them. Something had changed and she didn't know how to fix it. "I have you to thank for that," she said quietly

Jackie left the room and the lion followed. She didn't know where she was going, only that she had to get out of this house and breathe in some fresh air. She could almost hear the sun, wanted to feel it on her face. Everything felt different now and she no longer knew where she fit, especially in this world that was so different from anything she had ever known.

The lion made a soft mewing sound beside her. Jackie saw the lion looking up at her with large, worried eyes. "I'm okay," Jackie said. "I'm okay. I will be okay." That was a lie, and she knew it. That was a fucking lie.

As soon as she got outside, she wanted to go back inside. The sun felt too strong, too bright, too brilliant, too fierce. She shielded her eyes and sat down on the edge of the back deck, looking at the tree from which she had found Xander hanging. She remembered the gold crown of light and wondered if everything that she had seen in this world was real. Nothing felt real to her, but at the same time everything felt too real.

"What am I supposed to do now?" She asked the lion, running her fingers through its fur. "What the fuck am I supposed to do now?" The lion nudged her hand, Jackie let out a watery laugh and rubbed the lion's fur some more.

Turning away from the fence post, Jackie looked at the world that surrounded her, really looked at it instead of taking it for granted. She noticed something white in the grass. She blinked a few times and the whiteness didn't disappear. Jackie was immediately drawn to go and see what it was. What would be white in a sea of green grass, and would it be safe to walk in the field?

She was feeling reckless, so she stepped into the grass, and heard it whisper around her. The wind blew hard, making the trees sound like they were whispering and telling secrets to the grass underneath her feet. Looking up at the sky, she saw the sun bright and incredibly beautiful.

She wanted to feel free, even if only for a moment. She wanted freedom, to change the path that had been thrust upon her. Jackie wanted to find another future for herself, one that was different than the one that she was heading towards. Even though the leatherbound book was in the room with her swords and her bag, she could swear that she could hear it whispering from here, much like the grass under her feet. She wanted to remove her shoes but thought it unwise. She saw splotches of gore and bright red blades of grass not too far from the white thing in the grass, so she kept them on.

The grass still whispered with every step she took, and the wind was picking up around her, though there were no storm clouds. It was as if the universe, such as it was, knew that something was happening within her, something was changing.

Picking up speed, Jackie ran towards what she thought was a rock. She didn't know why she felt so compelled to see what it was, only that it gave her an escape from Xander and all of his truths untold. She hated the fact that he knew so much but that he kept it to himself. He wanted her to be prepared for her journey forward, but wouldn't help her? Or had he helped her a much as he could?

She ran, the grass whispering as her feet dashed along, wind whipping through her hair. She was closer now and could finally see it clearly. Coming to a halt, Jackie looked down and saw the white object for what it was: the skeleton of a bird.

Looking at the wingspan, she guessed it to be a crow or raven. She thought of the birds that had attacked her outside of Em's house by the forest. That seemed like it had happened years ago. How much had changed and yet how many things had stayed exactly the same? Jackie snorted. "Fucking nothing. Nothing is the same."

Jackie leaned down to get a look closer at the skeleton. The lion nudged her leg and Jackie looked down. "It's okay. It's only a skeleton. The bird can't hurt us anymore."

She crouched and reached and touched one of its wings. It crumbled beneath her finger, as if it had waited all this time for her touch. She let out a soft noise and watched as the rest of the skeleton began to crumble, the breakage flowing from the point where she had touched the bone.

Looking at the dust and bone, Jackie had an idea. "It's time to make this bird fly again."

She gathered up some of the dust in her hands and lifted them up into the sky. Opening her hands, she let the wind take the powder that had been an animal's bones. It felt good, she thought, freeing. Jackie began to gather more of the dust and let it go in the wind, handful after handful. It felt freeing to let it go. In this way, the bird would fly again. She hoped that it would have a good flight.

Soon, where the bird bones had been, there was nothing. It was as if the bird skeleton had never been here. Looking back to the house, she was surprised to see the back deck was father away than she had first thought. She tried to run back to the house and the wind helped her along. It was at her back now, and she was being rewarded for her long trek through the grass. She almost leaped across the grass and let the wind push her back from where she had come. She felt like she was flying.

When she reached the back deck, the wind let her go and carried on its way. She stood with the lion and looked up and around her. The air was filled with facets of light that shone, only for a moment, and the sky was filled with the soft sound of music that sounded like the tinkling of bells. The dust faded, and the music disappeared with it. The lion let out a soft mew and looked at the sky with her.

Hearing the patio door open, she heard footsteps approaching and she turned to find Xander watching her. His eyes swirled a brilliant blue once more, but she was no longer entranced by them. Something inside her had changed, had made room for a light of her own that didn't need to be filled by another person.

Looking up at him, she saw someone that she could have loved, but everything was all tied up in what was going on within her. She was surprised by the idea that she could have loved him, and the fact that she probably did love him anyways, however that couldn't be helped. This was her journey, right? This was what she had to do.

"Hey."

"Hey yourself."

"I came to see if you were all right."

She thought about it. "I'm not but I will be. I don't have any choice, do I?"

"You always have a choice." Xander said. "That's the point of this journey, it's all about choices."

"You're right. I do." Looking at the lion, she nodded and the lion blinked in return. Though there was no real language shared between the two of them, she was sure that the lion understood.

Moving up the stairs, she made her way past Xander and back to where her bedroom had been. She didn't say anything to him, didn't know what to say. She took a pause in the bathroom; when she came out, Xander was waiting in her bedroom.

"What are you doing up here?" She asked him.

"I came to see if you were all right," he said again. "You seemed a little off downstairs."

"Me? No, I'm fine. I'm better than I ever have been, actually. It just took me a moment to realize it, that's all."

He looked at her and the blue in his eyes shone. The tattoos that were inked along his skin glowed so brightly they showed through the fabric of his clothes. She could see the sword that he held on his right leg, what looked like a wand on his right arm. There was also a cup that was tattooed below his heart, and Jackie could see the edge of what looked like a shield tattooed on his back. He was a sparkling blue wonder, and what she was about to do would hurt him, but it was the way that this had to be. It was her path after all.

"Something about you is different." He said. "I'm looking at you and you seem harder somehow, more focused."

She thought about it and nodded. "I suppose I am." She said "I know what I need to do now." Going about the room, she gathered up her duffel bag and put that on first. It was a little heavier now with the extra trinkets that she had been given and the extra clothes that she had pilfered, but that was all right. Next, she made sure that the long sword and the short sword were secured in the holder and hefted those on. She secured the harness and then made sure her most prized procession was in her duffel bag. She reached in and felt the leather-bound journal and made sure that her cards were there too. Taking them out of the bag, Jackie held them close for a moment, as if they would be able to give her guidance merely from touch. They brought her such comfort and such peace. It was a blessing to know that she held a part of her spirit and that she could decide the path that it was on.

It was odd, but she wasn't afraid anymore. Jackie had been wandering on this path for so long, frightened of what she would find every step of the way. Now she knew that she would take on whatever came her way.

QUEEN OF SWORDS

The entire time that she readied herself, Xander watched her. His eyes had stopped swirling as madly as they had before, and he regarded her as if she were a mystery he was trying desperately to figure out. Jackie tried not to look too deeply into his eyes or look too long on his face. The look he wore while he examined her would make her want to stop and forgive him, as if everything was okay. The sad truth of it was that everything *was* okay, at least within her. She had let go of the desire she felt for him the moment she had raised up the powdered bone from the crow and let it fly into the wind. Something within her also flew away, and by the time she had made it back to the house, she had decided what she must do.

"I can help you." Xander whispered softly. "I can come with you. You shouldn't be alone."

His voice seemed loud in the room, but it was because her heart was beating so hard that the words seemed so powerful. She did take a moment to look at him then and saw that every line on his face was etched with misery. A part of her broke away then, that part that loved him, and she felt it fall between them as if a piece of a chalice that she carried inside of her had fallen away.

She gave him a soft smile. "This is my journey. You told me that yourself. I have to do this alone." The lion softly batted her legs with its nose. "I mean, I won't be totally alone, I'll have the lion."

Making her way slowly past him, Jackie took a moment to inhale his scent, that heady mix of sandalwood and bergamot. Her heart beat a little more quickly and her breath sped up, but she kept going, kept moving away from Xander, no matter how much her heart wanted her to go back to him. Maybe she had fallen in love with him because of his kindness in this world, or the fact that every time she saw him, he represented a moment of hope that she would be able to make it and go forward.

Now, she knew that she would have to go forward alone with the lion and leave part of herself here in this house. Jackie hoped that Xander would be able to find it when she left. Jackie stared when Xander gently grabbed hold of her wrist.

"Let me come with you."

"You know you can't." Jackie said. "Marie-Claude will be angry, you said so yourself. You keep talking about how this is my journey, so you have to let me go and let me complete it. I can't go forward by going backwards." She went down the stairs quickly and heard the soft pad of the lion's feet behind her.

She kept going, through the back door and out again into the sun. Unlike before, feeling the sun on her face didn't bring her any joy. Now she felt empty, but this meant that there was more room inside of her for whatever else her adventure brought.

Much as she wanted to, she didn't turn back to see if Xander had followed, if he had come out to watch her from the porch steps as he had done before. Instead, Jackie and the lion went back to the path and left the small house and a piece of her chalice behind; the duffle bag and swords making a comfortable *thap! tinkle!* as she walked on.

XIV

"Fuck," Jackie said.

Though she didn't say it with as much vigour as usual. It came out sounding like a rather quiet damnit instead. The lion rubbed her leg gently with its head, and she reached down to rub its fur. The lion whined and nudged her harder.

"It's okay, really." The lion turned its head and gave her a look. "Well, it will be even if it doesn't seem like it now."

They had been walking for what seemed like forever. She wanted to put as much distance between her and Xander as possible. Even though she knew that he hadn't hurt her intentionally, she also knew that they couldn't be together, at least until she was finished her journey, whenever the fuck that may be. She sighed and spotted a bench not too far away, on the side of the cobblestone path that seemed to go on forever.

Making her way there, she sat gratefully and took out a bottle of water and some food she had scrounged from the cupboards of the house. She gave the lion a drink of water, and while it drank, she pulled out her cards.

They always helped her in moments when she needed guidance, and now she needed guidance more than ever before. She needed to see a light in the path in front of her, or at least get some direction, some sort of guidance. Just because she was no longer afraid of what was to come didn't mean that she wanted to go into the future completely blind.

She shuffled and cut the deck and chose the pile that spoke to her. Then she stacked the deck together again and pulled her card. "Mother fucker!" She swore out loud. "Fuck you Queen of Swords, fuck you very much. I know already, *okay?*" She almost threw it down but placed it gently on the bench instead. She drew two more cards, the Tower and the Sun. That meant a crumbling of foundations, and joy at its basest meaning. "So, something is going to suck and I'm going to happy about it? That's fucking great." Jackie knew she was being flippant, but she knew the cards probably had the right of it. If she was the Queen of Swords, and by this point she had to assume as much, then it only made sense that part of her foundations had crumbled. She briefly looked back from where she had come, and thought of Xander.

Shaking her head, she looked at the Sun card and thought of the joy that this card implied. Did that mean that she was successful in finding out how to cure the virus, now that she knew the cause?

She pulled one more card, the Ace of Wands. She knew that card was all about the spark that lit up the spirit, and it represented the start of a new cycle that would bring joy to her spirit and the core of who she was. She didn't have time for anything creative, she had to finish the task before her before she took anything else on. She shook her head and put the cards away, tucking them safely back inside her bag. Though she wasn't clear on the message, she knew from years of using tarot cards that sometimes it took a while for their meaning to become clear. "Hurry up and make it clear then, fucking cards." Jackie said. "I don't have all day." The lion let out a snort.

With a sigh, Jackie stood and walked, the lion following closely by her side. They walked on a bit, and both lifted their faces to the sun. The cobblestone path they had been following for quite a while now began to change. The stones underneath their feet and paws gave way to dirt and gravel, mixed with something that looked like diamonds. Looking more closely, Jackie saw that it was actually small pieces of quartz and other stones. She recognized lapis lazuli and aquamarine. She leaned down to run her fingers along the ground, picked up a small handful and let them fall from her hand. To Jackie, it looked like she was letting rain fall from her grasp.

She stood and looked at the lion. "Look, we need to find you a name." The lion sniffed. "Well, I can't keep calling you lion, or hey you, can I?" Jackie said. "Besides, we're on a journey together. You deserve a name."

The lion rolled its eyes. Jackie smiled and regarded it. She tried to think of lion like names. "How about Beast?" The lion stuck out its tongue. "Lion-O?" The lion made a gagging sound. "King?" The lion pulled a face. "Mustafa?" The lion shook its head.

"I'm drawing a blank here. I need a little help. What should I call you? I mean, you are strong, obviously, and you're brave. You've protected me a few times and you've journeyed next to me through some pretty weird shit." She tilted her head to the right and looked at the lion with the sunlight shining behind it. The lion was lit up like mountain, full of brawn, bravery and loyalty. From the moment that Jackie had shown the lion how strong she was, he had never left Jackie's side. She thought about it for a moment, but then something within her clicked.

"That's it!" She spoke. "That's fucking it! How about Brawn?" Jackie asked.

The lion looked at her quizzically. "Think about it. It's better than just calling you Brave outright. It's *more* than bravery. It's like bravery with muscle!" Jackie said.

The lion looked at her and blinked once. Then, just to make itself clear, it nodded its head. "Brawn? I can call you that?" The lion let out a short growl in response.

"Excellent!" Jackie said. She held out her right hand out in front her as if she were expecting a high five. Jackie waited a few moments but then the lion, Brawn, put its paw in Jackie's palm. It was done, Brawn was born.

It was easier walking next to a beast that had a name, rather than walking with an unnamed one. She now looked at the lion differently. *It was funny how having a name did that*, Jackie thought. The walking became easier now that Brawn had his name. It was easier to walk with a friend than with someone who was nameless.

Jackie watched as Brawn leapt off the path to stalk and kill some birds that had unwisely chosen to land nearby. While he ate, she sat down on the cobbled path and took out her leather-bound book. Taking a pen out, she saw that there was a new entry. She read: ***Sometimes, I wonder why I'm even going through this. What does this journey want me to learn? What does it want me to change about myself? What do I need to let go of and what can I absorb and integrate into my life?***

Jackie sighed. She supposed that the book, like the cards, was a tool for delving deeper. Sometimes there are no answers, only questions that begged to be answered. Life was like that too, she imagined. It didn't mean that she didn't wish for an easy way sometimes. She had always taken the hard road, but the one she was on right now was certainly the most difficult yet. She had to find a way to balance herself, to bring the many pieces of herself together: the person she had been, the person she was, and the person she was becoming. There was no way to remain unchanged after this experience.

The lion came back, its eyes wide from the hunt, a speckle of blood on its muzzle. She rubbed its mane affectionately. "Ready to go, Brawn?" The lion nodded. Jackie stood, and they were off. They walked a little further, the houses having disappeared long ago. Now their only company was the wind and...was that the sound of water?

"You thirsty after your meal?" She asked Brawn. "Sounds like you can get a drink too. Can you find out where that sound is coming from?" Brawn nodded and leapt away from her, running down the path to parts a distance away from her. She watched Brawn slide to a stop not too far away. She didn't have far to go, but the sun was hot on her skin, and she was tired. She hadn't been this tired for a very long time. She thought back to the last time she had felt fatigued on this journey, and a thought struck her: *change is coming*. That had certainly been the case before, and she supposed it would be the case now. Jackie just wished she knew what the change was and what it would bring.

Following Brawn, the sound of water became louder. There was also the sound of music, as if someone was playing an instrument; it wasn't an instrument that she recognized offhand. She kept walking and smiled when she heard a splash. Brawn had found the water. Jackie walked faster, eager to join him. That water would feel amazing. She would jump in with all of her clothes on, at this point it didn't matter. She just wanted to feel clean again.

She rounded the bend and almost stopped entirely. There was a small meadow beside the stream in which Brawn was swimming. It wasn't this that had made her think about stopping, it was the leather-clad man standing next to a black monster of a motorbike, resting in the grass a short distance away from the cobblestone path. That, and the fact that the man had wings made from black feathers.

The closer she got to him, she saw that there were other colours within the black: blues, dark purples, darker blacks, some the colour of stone and others the colour of night. When she was almost in front of him, the wind ruffled the feathers, and she swore that she saw some of the tips sparkle. The wings were black but not black, dark yet full of light.

When she was directly in front of him, he spoke. "See something you like?"

"Yeah, I was admiring your wings. They're beautiful."

"I like to think so. You gotta take care of them you know? I have to add feathers one at a time."

"Really? Aren't angels born with wings?"

"I'm no angel and no, we earn our wings one feather at a time." He shook his head. "Born with wings. Could you imagine pushing that out?"

Jackie led out a loud snort of laugh and then couldn't stop. She was laughing so hard that she had trouble catching her breath, and a stitch was beginning to burn on her left side. She looked at the angel through tears in her eyes, and he reached into his leather coat and pulled out a handkerchief. He reached into a compartment on the motorbike and handed her a bottle of water. "Take a drink of that. It'll help."

She wiped her eyes and then, still trying to catch her breath, took a swig of the water in the bottle and almost spit it out. At the last second, she swallowed thickly. "That-that's vodka!"

"Well, it sure as fuck isn't water." He gave her a smile. "That lion yours?"

"Yeah, his name's Brawn."

At the sound of his name, the lion got out of the stream and shook his fur out his fur and came over to them. "Of course it is." The man said. He reached out to pet Brawn and the lion leaned into his touch. "That's a cool name." Brawn let out a soft purr.

Jackie handed back the bottle and the handkerchief. "Thank you."

"Welcome. Name's Cosmo Virtue. I know who you are."

"Yeah, that seems to be happening a lot, people knowing who I am before I even know who I am."

"It happens a lot around here." Cosmo said. "People who shine are known about; you dig?"

"People who shine?"

"People like you, like your magician friend. People who shine brightly."

"I don't shine." Jackie said, blushing under his gaze. She wished he would take off his sunglasses; not being able to see his eyes was slightly unnerving.

As if he heard her thoughts, Cosmo took of his glasses. She had thought the would be blue like Xander's and that they would somehow contain the ocean, but they were a black so deep, they defied colour. She could have sworn there was even some purple in them, much like his wings.

"Not that I'm not happy to see you, thanks for the drink by the way, but what the fuck are you doing here?"

"Em and Gabriel sent me. Hence the motorbike. I had to get here quickly, before you went too far."

"Went too far for what?"

"For what comes next. You're almost ready, but you're not there yet."

"Not ready for what?"

"That's for me to know and you to find out." Cosmo said.

"Gee, that clears things up. I'm glad that we had this talk, things make so much more sense now!" Jackie said with a touch of sarcasm. "Thanks a lot."

"I assume you know that shit here is on a need-to-know basis? Like if you need to know, we will tell you?"

"I'm beginning to have an understanding about that."

Cosmo smiled, and his grin made him even more handsome. His dark hair was wavy and curly. Jackie had never thought of angels as heartthrobs before, but there was a first time for everything.

To distract herself, Jackie reverted to bitch mode. It always worked to keep her mind on things and gave her a focus that she needed right now. "What kind of angel rides a motorcycle?"

"Who says I'm an angel?"

"Duh, the fucking wings."

"Wings don't necessarily mean I'm an angel."

"What are you then?" Jackie asked. "Some kind of Peter Pan wannabe?" She saw the sting hit his face but pushed on. "We all know that he needed magic dust to fly. Why don't we go find you a fairy and tap her on the ass and see what happens?"

Cosmo gave her a very long look with his intense black eyes. She was surprised to see a smile begin to slide across his face. "Are you always such a bitch?" He asked.

She felt her cheeks blush. "Not always."

"Good, you're not very good at it. As if I would tap a fairy on the ass, I mean really. Have you ever met one?"

"No."

"Well, I can tell you that if you did tap one on the ass, you'd live to regret it." Cosmo said. "I mean, they are all pretty and what have you, but piss one off and that will be the last thing you do. No, I'm here to help you."

"You've been such a big help already."

"I know I have. I'm here to help you with your powers and learning to manage them."

"I don't have any powers." Jackie said.

"I'm sorry, you do have powers if I say you have powers." He reached out and took hold of both of her hands and pulled them to him, palms up. The left one was tattooed with the sign of the lantern and the right had the rowan leaf tattoo. "I'm here to teach you how to use these together."

"I don't think they're supposed to be used together." Jackie said, not at all feeling sure in what she was saying.

"Really? You don't think it would help you to know how to direct your main power and balance it with the one you've been given?"

At the mention of her powers, her right hand began to sparkle. "Well, maybe that would be nice."

"And have you even turned on the light yet?" Cosmo asked, pointing to her left hand.

"No, I haven't had to, yet."

"Then turn it on now." Cosmo said. He leaned back on the seat of his bike and crossed his arms carelessly in front of him. "I can wait."

She let out a nervous laugh, but the lion pawed head butted her leg gently. Jackie looked at Brawn and was surprised when the lion nodded and looked deep into Jackie's eyes. Jackie knew that Brawn was telling her that he believed in her, even if she did have a sarcastic pain in the ass angel in front of her, goading her on.

"Do you have to work at being such an asshole?" Jackie said with a grin.

"No, it comes naturally. Go ahead." Cosmo said. "Turn on the light."

Jackie nodded. She looked at Brawn one last time and the lion winked at her. If anything, she wanted to shine brightly for him. Taking several deep breaths, she put her hand out and...nothing happened.

Cosmo gave her a little grin, but he didn't laugh at her, she had to give him credit for that much at least. "What am I doing wrong?" She asked.

"You have to...turn yourself on if you get my drift."

"Excuse me?" Jackie was trying hard not to be turned on right now.

"Well, you must imagine that inside of you is a switch of some sort. You've used the rowan leaf before. How do you turn that on?" Cosmo asked.

Jackie shrugged. "I don't know. It's always at the ready, waiting to be called into action."

"Well, you'll have to try to put the lantern on the same setting. It would have been unfortunate if you had reached a part on your path where a little bit of extra light would have helped you and you weren't able to use the lantern."

"You don't have to tell me." Jackie said. "How do I turn it on?"

Cosmo gave her another small smile. Instead of infuriating her, it soothed her for some reason;either that or she wanted to smack him in the face. She wasn't sure which impulse she wanted to give in to, so she did nothing.

"Close your eyes."

"That's all I have to do? Close my fucking eyes?"

Cosmo sighed. "Look, this can be easy, or we can do it the hard way." His feathered wings ruffled yet there was no breeze.

"Why is everything you say a double entendre?"

He shrugged. "You're just hearing what you want to hear. Just close your eyes for me." He paused and then added "Please."

Jackie closed her eyes. It was the please that had done it. Inside of her head, there was darkness. She became aware that Cosmo had moved closer to her and was standing nearby. Jackie could smell his cologne, a deep woodsy scent. She thought briefly of Xander, then pushed the thoughts of him away. She could hear the lion purring beside her, so she knew that she wasn't in danger. She focused on the sound of Cosmo's voice when he spoke.

"Now, I know that it's dark within you now, but can you see two spots of light in the darkness? Two seeds of brightness that light up the dark?"

Jackie focused and could see two small dots of light. They looked like seeds, and even from a distance, they thrummed. One of them was brighter than the other. "I see them." Jackie said.

"Okay, good. I want you to go toward them. Can you do that? Think of it like swimming. Just swim towards them."

"Okay." She resisted the urge to do the breaststroke, and simply kicked her feet in her mind. She moved through the darkness and the shadow, and the lights came closer to her. The closer she got, the more they began to move apart from each other, the brighter one on the right and the softer one on the left. "They keep moving farther apart."

"That's okay, just let it happen. The light goes where it needs to go. Just swim towards it, okay?"

Jackie nodded, and only felt like a fucking idiot for a moment, so concentrated was she on getting to the light before it drifted away from her entirely. She had the sneaking suspicion that it wouldn't, that this light was within her; why else would Cosmo say to close her eyes and look within?

She swam further, and she felt the dark run along her skin like water. Jackie could see the liquid dark moving through her fingers like water and could almost hear it; a wet sound that was welcoming and nurturing at the same time, like a heartbeat within the water. She got even closer to the two small seeds of light and, without being told, stretched out her arms to grasp both of the lights, one in each hand. The light warmed her body, the right one warmer than the left.

Looking down at the light in her hands, she saw a rowan leaf on the small globe of light and she understood. "The lights are my powers, aren't they?"

"Not all of them, but yes, those are the ones that we're concerned about for now. See how small the one on the left is?"

"Yes, it's like a seed." Jackie said with worry.

"It's okay, you have to help it grow. See how big the light is under the rowan leaf?"

"Yes, I do." Jackie could see the outline of the rowan leaf as if it were super imposed on the orb. The light shimmered within, and it was hard for Jackie to believe that this light was within her, that she held something so beautiful in a body. It was like the light had been dipped in shadows for so long. *Has this light been growing the entire time that I've been on this journey?* She thought.

"Good," Cosmo said, and his voice had taken on an ethereal quality. It was as if he was speaking within her and also outside of her, like his voice was the wind itself. "See how much bigger that light is?" He asked her.

"Yes."

"I want you to share the light. Can you pull of a bit from the rowan leaf and give it to the lantern? The rowan leaf symbolizes bravery, and there's no reason that your light can't be as brave as you are."

Jackie tried to pull some light away from the rowan leaf, but it was made of stone. "I can't."

"You're picturing a stone. Light has no actual form, Jackie. It is beyond form. Can you see it in a different way?" He asked. "Look at it as liquid."

Jackie did what he asked, and the moment that she chose to look at the light in a different way, to see it as liquid light instead of a stone orb, the light morphed and changed underneath her fingers. "It's working!" she said. "I can see it changing."

"Good, now try pull some of the light away and give it to the seed of the lantern. See what the light has to show us, Jackie." There was urgency in his voice now, but it was not angry. His voice was filled with wonder and amusement. It sounded like he was close to laughter but it wasn't directed at her. It was the sound of laughter waiting to break free, that indescribable sound of joy and wonder, and Jackie had the same feelings running through her.

She pulled some of the light from the rowan leaf and moved it over to the seed that was the lanten. Jackie was surprised by how blue the lantern light was. Where the light from the rowan leaf was warm, the light from the lantern was a cool blue, and the light from the rowan leaf helped the lantern to grow. Jackie watched as the seed grew to the size of the rowan light. The rowan leaf looked like the sun and the lantern looked like a blue moon. It shone just as brightly, even though it seemed to be made of a different material. Jackie looked at the two orbs of two different lights, cupped one in each hand, and Jackie felt a moment of wonder that this light had been inside of her all along.

"Okay Jackie, we're almost there. Can you put the lights back and then come back to me?" Cosmo said softly.

"Yes," Jackie said.

She placed the orbs in front of her and tucked the darkness around them to keep them in place. As she slipped away from them, letting the liquid dark slide along her skin, her procession was lit by the light she carried within her, filled with blues and golds, shades of periwinkle and a gold so bright that it defied colour. She landed back in her body, and when she opened her eyes, the whole world felt different. Jackie felt more complete than she had before, more whole, as if a part of herself had been missing this entire time.

"So, feel turned on?" Cosmo said giving her a grin.

Jackie grinned back. "Yes, I do."

Holding up her left hand closed in a fist, she opened it and a light appeared, glowing softly in her palm. It was a pure white light except for the blue tinge on the edges. She marvelled at the fact that she could do this.

"That's excellent Jackie!"

"I know, right? I can make it grow stronger or lessen it if I need to. Why did I never feel this light before? I can feel both of my lights running through me now. Why am I just feeling them now? Have they always been there?"

Cosmo shrugged. "How do I fucking know?" He gave her an actual smile. "Now, can you do one more thing for me?"

"Sure, what?"

"I want to see if you can use your lights together. See what happens if you use the lantern with the rowan leaf. I want you to aim them together and we'll see what happens."

"Sure, what do I am at?" Jackie turned and spotted a weeping willow not ten feet from her. "Will that do?"

"Sure, have at it and let's see what happens."

Jackie nodded and held both of her hands out. She felt a small click in each of her palms as both lights came to the surface. She let the lights go, let them combine and integrate themselves around each other, the gold light twisting around the blue.

They both watched as the tree began to grow, the vines becoming longer and the trunk growing thicker. The growth continued, and even though Jackie took her hands away, the light going dark when she put her hands in her pockets. The tree continued to grow until there was an ear-splitting crack and it exploded. Pieces of leaves and vine ended up at their feet.

Jackie was quiet for a moment, and then she asked "What hell was that?"

Cosmo grinned at her. "That is what happens when you use both together. Alone, one is a light into the dark and the other a weapon and a true expression of you. Together, your powers are an explosion."

Jackie looked at where the tree had been standing. "Well, fuck." She said.

*

"You gotta be fucking kidding me."

Cosmo was showing her how to use her powers now that she had turned on the light within her. He showed her how to aim and how to use enough of the rowan leaf and the lantern so that she didn't exhaust herself. Now he was telling her that while she could destroy and defend, she could also make things grow.

"It's true. Take a look at the tree that you destroyed."

"It's not hard to look at it. The tree is in fucking pieces all over the place."

"Yes, I know. But you can bring them back together."

"Like I said, you gotta be fucking kidding me."

"What? You don't believe me? This from the woman who walks with a lion through a ruined landscape full of beasts that shouldn't be and, oh yes, she can shoot light out of her palms?"

He gave her a cheeky grin and she knew that he was laughing at her on the inside. *Smug bastard*, she thought. "Okay, point taken. What do I have to do?"

"Well, it's all about what is inside you. You pictured the light breaking the tree apart, so now you have to bring things back together. Just think of yourself like a magician of sorts."

Jackie felt a stab at the mention of the word 'magician'. She pushed the vision she had of Xander out of her head and concentrated. Working with her magic was a lot like conducting music, she thought. There was a flow to all of it. The flow had to come from inside her if she wanted the magic to work well. Thinking of the word magic gave her pause. It astounded her that she was capable of anything that could be considered magic. She wondered if what her mother had once said was true: *"We are all made of stardust, Jackie. Remember that."* She found it comforting that her mother still came to her in the world as it was now. It somehow brought her past and her present together clearly in her mind, giving her a moment to pause. She needed to breathe deeply and focus on what she needed to do.

Keeping her eyes open, Jackie went within herself and pictured all the pieces of the tree scattered around the liquid black sea that she held inside. She could picture them floating separately and they shone slightly, thrumming with the light that was still within them.

Still using her imagination, Jackie reached for the pieces of the tree, the leaves and the branches, the seeds and the twigs. She placed them all around the trunk of the tree. Jackie watched all the pieces moving through the air towards the tree, mirroring her actions within herself.

"Good Jackie, good. You're doing wonderfully."

"I fucking know that." She said, but she was smiling.

When all the pieces of the tree were assembled in front of what remained of the trunk of the tree, she began to let her light shine, a little at first but as the light grew, she heard the music that she had grown to love that came from within. She knew that the music was her magic singing. It sounded like the tinkling of glass given to the wind, and she thought this was rather fitting. The music was so beautiful to her, as was her magic.

Inside of the liquid sea, Jackie began to put the pieces of the tree back together. She didn't know how she was doing this, how it all felt so natural to her, but she didn't care. She was a force of creation as well as destruction. Cosmo and Jackie watched as the tree came to life, somehow larger than it had been before. Cosmo told her that her light had the power to make things grow, and it looked like this was true.

After what felt like forever but was really only minutes, the tree stood in front of them, shining brightly with the white light of the rowan leaf, and the blue hue of the lantern. The tree was the most beautiful thing that Jackie had ever seen. She put her arms down and the tinkling music faded away, though the tree still hummed and glowed softly. Jackie looked at the tree, at what had once been a symbol of the destructive power of her magic and now looked at it again. She could see the cracks in the trunk and along the limbs of the branches, but now those cracks glowed with light. She was reminded of the Japanese art of Kintsugi; the art of mending broken things with gold to make them whole and beautiful again. She was using her own kind of gold, but it came from within her. The tree shone so brightly now, and Jackie was proud to have left her mark on this world in some way. She was glad that it was something beautiful. She didn't know where she was in the world or if she would be able to come back to this spot in the future, but she was glad that a little piece of her was here.

Jackie turned to look at Cosmo. "What happens now?"

"Now? Well, you go onward and so will I."

"You can't tell me anything about what is coming?"

His black eyes grew even darker somehow. "There is a reason why I've taught you how to use your powers and turn on your light. Did you not think of that?"

Jackie rolled her eyes. "The thought did occur to me. Everyone I've met on this path keeps warning me that something awful is coming. I suppose it's about time that I find out what that is."

"Yes, it is. Not everything is light." He motioned to the tree. "There is darkness in this world too."

"Gee, you fucking think so?" Jackie scoffed. "I would have thought I was on holiday if it weren't for all the fucking blood around here."

Cosmo smirked. "I think you'll do fine, Jackie Queen of Swords." He leaned in and kissed her cheek softly. "May we meet again."

"Do you think we will?" Jackie said.

He shrugged. "I think many things and many of them have come true. Maybe this will, too."

"Thank you, for all you've taught me. You're my favourite angel."

That grin became a full-fledged smile. "I've already told you. I'm no angel." His feathered wings ruffled, and reaching backward, he plucked a feather from his left wing. Holding it in his left palm, Jackie watched as it began to shrink and change until it was a small silver feather. When he pulled it out of his palm, there was a silver chain attached to it. He took the chain and fastened it around her neck. "For when you need to fly and can find no other way."

"Thank you." Jackie was touched by the gift. "I have nothing to give you."

"You've already given me everything I need. You've given me hope and that is a gift beyond anything else."

He climbed onto the motorcycle and revved the engine. "Blessed be, Jackie. May we meet again."

As he rode away, Jackie and Brawn watched him. The dust that rose up from his motorcycle obscured him from view for a moment, and when the dust cleared, they saw a large crow flying into the sky, away from them. Jackie saw flashes of purple and blue within the feathers.

"May we meet again, you smug bastard." Jackie said with a grin.

XV

Jackie and Brawn walked onward.

The lion found animals to eat along the way, and Jackie founds some edible plants and berries that sprang forth in abundance. It was somehow amazing to her that something so beautiful could grow in the desolate landscape. She also had the last bit of food from her bag.

As they walked onward, the landscape around her began to change once more. Instead of cobblestone, grass, or pieces of quartz under her feet, the ground grew darker so that it looked as if she were walking on black sand. Indeed, there were a few parts of the pathway where it felt like she was walking on quicksand, and she would have to ride on Brawn's back.

The land around her also began to change. Gone were the trees, grass, and other vegetation. There was more blood than anything else here, more destruction. Jackie saw fires and smoke in the distance, and the very air here smelled burned. She saw the carcases of animals and was sure she saw one or two that looked human in shape.

"What the fuck is wrong with this place?" Jackie said quietly. Brawn looked up at her and shook his head as if to say, "I don't fucking know." She wasn't sure whether lions understood the concept of swearing, but she figured he wouldn't mind her putting words in his mouth this one time.

The amount of blood also began to increase. Though they still walked along a ground that looked as if it had been burned, Jackie had to walk on patches of blood that had dried darker than the black sand that surrounded her. In some spots, the spatters of blood were still wet, and Jackie and Brawn had to step around them. With each spot of blood that Jackie stepped around, on or through, she wondered who the blood had belonged to, and whether or not the victim had been human. It seemed odd that she was contemplating such a thought, and she wondered if anyone here was really human anymore, herself included.

With each step that she took, the air grew warmer, but not in a good way. The air felt thick instead of filled with the warmth of the sun. The smoke she had seen in the distance was increasing too, and she wondered what could be the cause.

"Are you afraid?" She asked Brawn.

The lion nodded his head.

"Good, it's not just me then."

Jackie reached into her pocket and touched the talisman that Xander had given her. For some reason, the amulet didn't bring her sadness, even though it had come from him. She supposed that was because it was a symbol of power for her; but then she thought of him and pushed the vision of his face away, further into the black liquid sea that existed within her. She attached no light or signpost to his face, and hoped that he would remain lost, but she didn't think that would be the case.

The air grew rancid, and she clutched the amulet tighter with every step forward. It never occurred to her or to Brawn to turn back and venture in another direction, especially because there didn't seem to be any other paths. There was only one way to go on the path that she found herself, and that was forward, even if she didn't want to take another step.

A hot wind swirled around her, and she watched as the black sand began to rise up and dance with the hot wind, and then settle back down when the wind had quieted. Jackie finally knew what the black powder she walked on was: ash, not sand. It was black ash, and she wondered what had caused it, but she also didn't want to find out. Considering the amount of ash, the fire must have been enormous. *What the fuck had burned all of this?* She thought. And what was it *before* it was ash? She looked forward on the path and saw even more blood than before. *Was it the virus that had caused the blood?* She hoped so but knew in her heart that it wasn't the virus. It was something more.

Looking down at Brawn, she saw that he too was feeling the effects of whatever this place was. He seemed to be walking slower, testing each step before taking another. The whole landscape was barren, filled with ash and blood.. She knelt down and looked into Brawn's eyes. "Help me be brave, Brawn. Help me to be strong."

There was fear in the lions eyes, but instead of backing away from her touch and leaving her, the lion ran its face along hers, almost as if he were petting her. She heard the deep rumble of his purrs, and she knew from reading about cats that they purred when they were happy, afraid, or when they were trying to heal. She knew that Brawn was trying to heal her, so they would be strong together, in order to move forward.

She stood and put her right hand in Brawn's fur. She tried to balance him as much as he was balancing her. "We can do this...right?" The lion nodded and gave her a wink and that was good enough for her.

They walked onward even though she wanted to turn back with each step. She wondered if this is what Xander meant by telling her that there were dark times coming, and that she didn't understand everything on her path that was to come. Jackie also wondered if this was why Cosmo had worked so hard with her to get her to use her powers and learn how to use her magic. He knew that there was darkness coming, and he wanted her to be ready for it. She didn't know how long this part of the path went on, but she kept the lantern and the leaf on standby, just in case she ran into something fouler than what she was walking through. She really didn't want to know what was causing the ash but had a bad feeling that she would find out sooner or later.

As they moved forward, their steps began to crunch as they walked. Looking down, Jackie saw that there were bones among the ash. She looked up and tried to focus on the burnt blackness around her; the tall grass that whipped back and forth in the wind that sent the smoke closer and closer to them, instead of what was under her feet. Whether animal or human, she didn't want to find out to whom the bones belonged. Again, Jackie had a feeling that she would be shown anyway, regardless of how she felt.

The sound of crackling that reached her didn't inspire her to walk any farther, but she did. She wasn't ashamed to admit to herself that she was afraid, and she walked on. They were approaching a rockface, and Jackie knew that the crackling sound was coming from beyond the outcropping of rocks. They framed the path of ash as if they were a gate, and Jackie didn't want to step through, but they did. Brawn had become hyper-alert, and inside of herself, Jackie made sure that both of her switches were turned to on.. She wanted to be ready. She needed to be ready. Xander had taught her that much.

Jackie walked on and held her head high, knowing that she would face whatever waited beyond the rocks on either side of the path. She looked down at Brawn, and he nodded at her as if to encourage her along. She nodded back, took a deep breath, and stepped between the rocks.

The living room that she entered looked so comfortable. It was done in soft pinks and pastels, with the occasional bright splash of red. The couches were a deep rose colour, and the curtains were white with swirls of scarlet. The windows were open to the sunlight and the sound of birds singing. There was a squat woman with white hair wearing a red cardigan, and she was busily laying out a tea service. "I'm so happy you got here on time. Please take a seat, Jackie. The tea is ready to pour! I also have those delightful cakes that you so enjoy."

"Cakes?" Jackie looked around her. She had been moving past something, stepping through something. She didn't remember what she had been doing. "I'm sorry...?" Jackie said because she didn't know what else to say.

"Quite all right, dear, quite all right. We don't want to make the same mistake as last time, do we?"

"No, no we don't." Jackie wasn't sure what mistake she had made.

"You can take a seat anywhere dear, and I'll pour the tea."

A cat meowed at her feet. Looking down, Jackie saw that she was now wearing sensible shoes, and not the sneakers which had been there before...at least she seemed to remember sneakers. Where had these shoes come from? The cat meowed again, and Jackie bent down to pick it up. As she did, she saw something peripherally in the corner of the room. For a moment, Jackie thought she saw chains leading from someone, but when she blinked, the vision was gone.

"I'm sorry, but..." Jackie paused. "I seem to have forgotten your name. I don't know who you are..."

"Darling, you remember me, don't you? I'm Rigby. We've been friends for a long time now. Oh, you've found your little cat friend!" She smiled, but Jackie didn't think the smile looked very happy. "How lovely!" The cat hissed at her, and Rigby's smile turned into a small frown. "Yes, well there is no accounting for taste, now is there pus?" Rigby carried the tea tray over to Jackie. "I don't know what you take in your tea dear, do you like one lump or two?"

"Um, two?" Jackie said, taking hold of the tea cup

The cat meowed at her again more urgently, and she began to pet it automatically. The cat's purrs began to fill the small sitting room, and Jackie found herself getting sleepy. Then two things happened at once: the cat dug its claws into her left leg, and Jackie flung out her arms. Jackie's left hand tossed the hot cup of tea towards Rigby's face, and the woman let out a scream as she was drenched in the scalding liquid. Hot tea also splashed onto Jackie, and this added to the pain from the cat's claws made Jackie close her eyes. When she reopened them, everything was different.

The chains that she had seen only briefly were now entirely evident. They were flowing from a chair and a lamp that were towards the back of the room. "I'm sorry," Jackie said. "My cat dug its claws into my leg." Her cat? She thought. Yes, that sounded right. It looked up at her from the comfort of her lap and slowly blinked at her. When that didn't produce any reaction, the cat blinked at her several times.

"It's quite all right, dear, these things happen!" Though her voice sounded cheerful, there was steel underneath. Her skin was blotchy and red from the tea where it had burned her skin. "You have such a charming, lovely pet. You should know, however, that I do not allow pets in my living room. I'm afraid that your pet will have to leave."

Putting down the tea tray, Rigby went to grab the little ginger cat, but the cat backed further into Jackie's lap and started to hiss at Rigby.

"I'm sorry." Jackie said. "I don't know what's gotten into him."

"Well, animals are just wild beasts, really!" There was a manic look in the woman's dark eyes that wasn't helped by the redness of her skin, and the closer Jackie looked at Rigby, the more it looked like part of the woman's skin was beginning to fall off from where the tea had splashed her. She approached the cat, and it began to hiss more loudly, and let out unearthly screeches. To Jackie, it sounded like the howls of a banshee and she remembered something that she had read years ago: banshees were harbingers of death. They would make their song when someone was about to enter a situation or a place that could result in the persons death.

Jackie was moved to put her arms around the cat. Was the cat even hers? She looked down, and it blinked at her and nodded its head. Jackie nodded back to the cat, and Jackie could feel a thrum of energy between them. The cat seemed to relax momentarily but let out another screech as Rigby made to grab it again.

"Would you mind handing me your cat my dear?" Rigby asked.

The cat in question let out what could only be described as a roar. The sound shook the walls, and Jackie watched as paint began to flake off and fall to the floor. Rigby paid that no mind and made a lunge for the cat.

The cat leapt off of Jackie's lap and roared as it landed on the floor, its shadow thousands of times larger than its physical size. Jackie looked for the light source that would make the cats shadow seem so large, but there wasn't one. Jackie peered at it more closely and saw that it was a lion. A word came up to the surface of her mind and she spoke it aloud.

"Brawn?"

The cat turned to her and blinked, and Jackie could see the shadow of a mane on the wall fluttering in a breeze that wasn't there. "Brawn." Jackie said again and she sounded surer this time, more positive that this was the animal's name. "Why don't you look like your shadow?"

Rigby turned to look at the cat's shadow and let out a sound that was dangerously close to a scream. "Will you *please* give me that cat, dear?" Rigby demanded, all niceties in her tone gone. "Give. Me. That. Cat."

Jackie stood and plucked the cat off the floor. "No, I don't think I will. The cat is mine. And I am his. That's how it's always been." Jackie heard the purring coming from the animal and it started to grow larger in her arms. "I know we've been through a lot together."

"Are you *sure* of that, my dear?" Rigby said in her cool voice. "I mean, you could be delusional you know, it could all be in your head. You could have imagined everything up to this point. Now, give me that *cat*."

"No. I won't" Jackie said. "I won't give him to you."

The cat had grown too big for Jackie to hold, and she let it tumble to the floor. It turned its head to her and let out a roar that was so loud, it not only shook the walls, but it also shook Jackie. She felt something within her break open as if she had been encased in a cocoon and she let out her own roar, its sound joining Brawn's, the volume rising until the walls around them cracked and fell into black dust.

When the roar was spent, Jackie almost fell to the floor, but Brawn caught her before she could fall. When she was able to stand again, she looked around, and saw where she really was for the first time.

The walls around her were made of pitch-black rock that shone, like the two pillars that she had passed through. Looking behind her, she saw that those pillars stood where the entrance to the "living room" had been. The rocks looked more menacing from this side because of the way they shone. They looked like mirrors, and Jackie could see how frightened she looked.

The lion stood beside her, and Jackie gratefully put her hands in his mane. He purred under her touch, and Jackie took strength from that purr. She let a little of her light flow into him and his fur glowed beneath her touch. His purr grew louder, and Jackie found that she was standing straighter.

Turning, Jackie saw two people chained to a spear of rock that went from floor to ceiling. They had their arms around each other, and they were naked underneath all the soot. Though they looked at her, Jackie doubted whether the man and the woman chained together could actually see her. She sighed inwardly and felt a moment of sadness for the lives that these people lost and then turned to look at Rigby.

Jackie was surprised to see that she was the same. The same squat woman, the same greying hair cut in a neat bob. The same grey-silver eyes were looking at her, and the same smile that didn't meet her eyes, were observing Jackie with a look that promised only problems.

"I've always hated fucking cats." She went over to the table that was now made of black stone instead of glass and picked up her cup of tea. "They know too much for their own good."

Where the tea had struck her face, there was a red mark, but that was all. She had expected the mask that Rigby was wearing to fall away, revealing another face underneath, and yet here she was looking at the same person. Jackie couldn't say she was surprised. Some people didn't wear masks.

"What the fuck were you trying to do to me?" Jackie asked.

"I wasn't trying to do anything to you. You were doing that all yourself."

"That's bullshit and you know it." Jackie said. She kept the rowan leaf and the lantern at the ready, but she didn't unleash them. She needed her wits about her, and she couldn't lose herself to this world, whatever it was Rigby wanted from her.

"But don't you *like* a little distraction?" Rigby swept her right arm around and the couple who were chained to the black stone were gone, only to be replaced by her old apartment. The window was open, and she could hear the noises of the street and they sounded like music as they always had: the chatter and yells from people on the streets and sidewalks, the traffic and the cars as they sped and honked their horns. She could hear rain, which added to the cheerful noise that was filling the air. The burned smell was also gone, the ash on the floor replaced with the carpeting she had picked out when she'd moved into her apartment. She walked forward slowly as if she were in a dream; she wondered if *this* were a dream, if the whole path that she had been following had been some sort of epic dream quest and she had really woken up from a long and deserved sleep.

Moving forward, Jackie ran her fingers along the book she had left on the bedside table: Wild, by Cheryl Strayed. The book was well-travelled as Jackie had read it four times and had been in the middle of reading it for a fifth time. She had chosen to leave it behind when she departed on her impromptu trip. She hadn't felt brave then, and the book had mocked her. Jackie sure as fuck felt brave now.

The lion made a noise behind her, a loud purr capped off by a small roar. Jackie looked at the lion and blinked to show that she understood, that she knew what it was trying to say. She wasn't only brave anymore. She was fucking courageous.

"This is all junk." Jackie said. "All of it."

"This? Your bedspread that you spent so much on, the clothes that you spent a fortune on?" The closet doors opened and Jackie could see the aforementioned clothes. They spilled out onto the floor, as if beckoning her to put them on and feel them against her skin. "How about the trinkets that you spent so long collecting?" The trinkets that were lined up on her baker's rack and on every surface glittered and shone even brighter than they had before. "Everything you have is in this place, in your *home*. You would turn your back on it, on everything you've done?" Rigby asked, her voice taking on a soft and sweet quality. She turned to face Jackie and wore a look of caring and concern on her face, but Jackie could see that there was something underneath all of that, the darkness that rode beneath her skin.

"Yes, it's all junk." Jackie said. "None of this *means* anything. It's all just junk and trinkets. I wasn't really living before. I'm living more now, on this journey, than I have in the past forty-five years. I've lived more in the past few days to make up for the fact that I haven't lived. Do you think that you can distract me from the path I'm on?"

Rigby let out a laugh that started out soft but began to grow in volume. Soon, Rigby was having to hold herself upright by leaning on the entertainment unit in her living room. "Oh, you are so fucking funny!" Her voice was high-pitched with mirth, but Jackie heard a deepness to it that reverberated around the room. "Standing there so tall and proper, so filled with righteous anger! I commend you, Jackie, but you aren't strong enough. Why don't you lie down and fall into slumber? When you wake, all of this will disappear, and it will be erased from your mind. It may be like waking from a dream. Cast down your swords and your shield and sleep, child. Just sleep."

God help her, a good night's sleep on her comfortable bed did sound appealing, but there was more that she had to do, more steps on her path, she was almost done. Jackie could feel it within her. She didn't know how she knew, but she did. It made sense to her that there would be someone standing in the way of her path at this point, when she was so close to seeing this through to the end. She could do this; she knew that she could.

"What the fuck is in it for you?" Jackie asked.

"What isn't in it for me?" Rigby smiled and approached Jackie. "I get what I want, and you get what you want. You get your home and your life back, and I get to keep this world as it is now. It's so gloriously beautiful, don't you think?" There was something in her voice that went inside of her, inside Jackie's mind. As Rigby spoke, she could hear the woman speaking in front of her, but Jackie could also hear her within; her voice echoing off of the walls of her skin, ricocheting along her bones and muscles. She could feel the woman inside her and while she was disgusted, while she wanted to do nothing more than take her short sword across her skin to bleed out Rigby's voice, she found herself being lulled by the melody of it, by what the voice wanted. The woman, if she really was a woman, was smiling now as if she knew the effect that she was having and was relishing it.

Rigby came even nearer, and the room around Jackie took on a brighter hue, the pastel colours of her bedspread looking even more alluring and comfortable. "Don't you *want* to give in? You've been walking for so long, you must be so tired, *Jackie* dear. To think that you ran away from one man who mistreated you, only to fall into the metaphorical arms of another who told you nothing but lies." Though she didn't touch her, Jackie felt a hand caress her cheek as if to offer comfort.

"You are so *tired*, Jackie. Don't you want to stop walking and take a rest? Don't you want to give in and let sleep take you? If you want, I could let you have the memory of the magician. He lied to you. He is proof that all men are worth nothing and you are worth everything. You must treat yourself as such, and rest." She almost hissed this last word, and Jackie swore that Rigby's eyes changed shape and colour for a second, making the woman look almost reptilian.

It was the mention of Xander, the magician who had lied to her, that broke her out of the reverie that Rigby had woven around her. It was only a dream and none of this was real. The path was real, her journey was real, and she couldn't deny that journey or that she was almost there. She had come so far, and she wouldn't let some fucking bitch stop her.

"No." Jackie said.

"I'm sorry dear?" Rigby said, her voice like honey and strychnine.

"I fucking said no." Jackie repeated, struggling against the bonds that Rigby had been tying around her. She could feel the chains even if she couldn't see them. Even though Rigby didn't move, Jackie knew that the woman, this bitch, was forging the chains one link at a time, and soon she would be like that couple who had given in and had lost themselves in their need for what was comfortable.

"I don't understand dear." Rigby came even closer now, her breath smelling of brimstone and ash. Seeing her up close, Jackie saw that the smoke was in the cracks of her skin, could see the wrinkles that surrounded her eyes. She watched as the skin of her face rippled, and Jackie wondered what lay underneath; what shadows did the woman hide that ate at her until she was only shadow and no stars?

"Are you fucking deaf?" She moved to get her short sword, each movement of her arm painful and torturous. It hurt more than anything she had ever done before, but she pulled the sword from her scabbard and held it out in front of her. "I said fucking *no*. I know you're not told that very often, but you can't give me what I want."

"And what is it you want?" Rigby said in her sweetly saccharine voice, but with a note of desperation. "Tell me and it will be yours."

"I want to find out what is at the end of this path." Jackie said. She meant every word, whatever came, whatever the path put in her way; she would surmount it. "It's my path and I'm meant to walk it. That's what I want."

Rigby let out a little laugh, and the chains that had wrapped around Jackie pulled a little tighter. "Well of course you asked for the one thing I can't give you. Your place is here by my side."

"No, you're not fucking listening." Jackie said, her voice calm. "I don't belong here." She felt the lion stand beside her, could feel Brawn's power beside her and his presence was a comfort.. She took strength from him and kept looking at Rigby. The woman had seemed almost wholesome when Jackie had first seen her, but she knew that this wasn't true. Her wholesome face hid darkness. "Everything you say is a lie. You're pathetic. Why hold on to me anyway? What can I give you that you want so badly?" She turned the woman's own question on her, but she wasn't really expecting an answer.

To Jackie's surprise, Rigby was honest for the first time since they had met. "You shine so fucking bright." She hissed. "Brighter than any light that I've ever seen, Jackie Queen of Swords. I will have you and your light for my own."

"You fucking think so?"

"Yes, as a matter of fact, I do. Do you think you can just cut through the chains which even now I'm weaving around you?" Rigby let out another little laugh, and it made Jackie's skin crawl. "It will take something stronger than a fucking sword to cut through them."

"Well, it's a good thing I came prepared then, isn't it?" Jackie said.

She pulled out the long sword and kept that pointed at Rigby. She turned on the switch within her that powered the rowan leaf, and Rigby shrunk back from her light. As much as she wanted to feast upon it, the light was too bright for her. Using her short sword in her left hand, Jackie turned on the light of the lantern so that she could see. Where she could see nothing before, with the light of the lantern Jackie saw the coils of chains that surrounded her. Slashing with all of her might, Jackie heard the tinkle of the chains falling away. With every swipe, she felt freer, father way from the devil's grasp. She took one final stab, one final cut with the short sword, and the last of the chains fell away to the ground with a dull, wet thud.

Rigby made a lunge to grab at Jackie, letting out hiss as she did so, and Jackie did the only thing that she could think of: she pierced the woman with the long sword. Jackie thrust it into the woman's stomach as far as it would go.

With a sigh, Rigby opened her mouth, and a swarm of black moths began to fly out from between her lips. Just one at first but soon hundreds of moths began to fly into the air, until with a final sigh, Rigby fell away until she was nothing but black ash. Jackie's sword fell to the ground, and she looked at Brawn.

"Fuck." She whispered.

Brawn blinked his eyes to show he understood.

XVI

Jackie wasn't sure what to expect from this world.

She knew that, in some ways, it was her world, the one that she knew and had grown up in, as it grew up around her. In other ways, it was as if she were walking around in an alternate reality. This world went beyond the one that she had known, no matter what similarities it may have.

The ground began to get even more difficult to traverse. The black ash that had consumed the part of this world that Rigby had inhabited covered the ground for a little bit here too, but it was far rockier, and the land was jagged, as if some great beat had torn it apart. . Walking away from that place, Jackie knew that Rigby wasn't dead, that the moths that had flown from her mouth would find a way to regroup and come together again. Jackie knew that evil, whatever it's form, never truly died. Her ex-boyfriends were proof of that. Goodness knows that she may have wished them dead many times over, but they still continued to live.

Stopping for a moment, she put her hands in Brawn's fur, and took comfort from him as she surveyed her surroundings. The black ash still continued here, but she saw that it lessened and gave way to gravel again, with the occasional rock. Nothing was uniform here, the rocks jutted from the earth like uneven teeth. There was glass shattered over the ground, and she could see the wreckage of a plane in the distance still smoking away. She wondered if the plane held people and if anyone had survived or had they long since been claimed by the world around her? She thought the second option was far more likely. The air smelled like burnt hair and plastic.

Brawn let out a whimper and she saw the sadness in his eyes. Letting a little of her light flow into him, Jackie looked Brawn in the eyes and let him know that she carried the same sadness within her. "It's okay, my friend. You and I will get through this together. We've been on quite the journey, haven't we?"

The lion blinked and Jackie blinked back. Brawn nuzzled her hand with its nose, and she let a little bit more light flow into him. "I love you too." Jackie said. "I never thought I would find a man that I could love with my whole heart." She said, and a momentary vision of Xander filled her mind.

She pushed him away and looked down into the lion's eyes. "Thank you for your love, Brawn." The lion purred and Jackie stood upright again.

She didn't feel like walking toward the plane, but it there was no way around it. There was a house before the plane, a small cottage. Like the plane, the cottage looked weatherworn, and she was pretty sure there was blood on the door, but they were still too far away to make it out clearly.

Both the cottage and plane were still some distance away, so as they walked, she would see if she could spot a way around it, even if it didn't seem likely right now. She thought of when she tried to approach the mountain where she had met Aldrich, or the castle where she had met Cole. Both had changed their appearance and her path when she had found a way to approach them differently. She wondered if that would work here?

Looking at the path, Jackie saw that it curved past the cottage and twisted until passed the smoking plane. She glanced at the grass alongside of the path. The long grass was swaying gently in a breeze that made the scent of burnt plastic grow even stronger. She moved to step off the path and into the grass, but Brawn let out a growl and stood in front of her. It shook its head and Jackie paused. She watched as Brawn went into the grass a few feet from her and as he walked, the grass began to rustle a bit more. Without any warning, dark shapes leapt from the grass and Jackie tried to see what they were. They looked like birds, but smaller than the ones that had attacked her at the forest near Em's house. There was a cloud of them, three or four of them that cawed and tried to bite at the lion. Brawn took one of them out at a time, clamping its jaws down on their wings or their bodies. The blood that flowed from them was a red so dark that it was black, and when the blood hit the grass, it sizzled and burned. When the birds were dead, Brawn went to a stream that flowed at the edge of the field of grass and drank some water. When he made his way back to Jackie, the grass shivered and shook but nothing else came at him from within the tall blades of grass.

As soon as Brawn came back onto the path, Jackie bent lower to hug him, to rest her face in his mane and to hold him closely. "Thank you for that, my friend. You probably saved my life. I may be good against a fucking bitch, but those birds creep me right the fuck out." Brawn gave her a half smile and rolled his eyes.

They walked onward, the only sounds being the *whap! tinkle!* of her swords, the whispering of the leather-bound book in her satchel, and the sound of their footsteps on the path. Jackie had grown used to not speaking much. She saved her words for when they mattered or when she was uttering a well-chosen expletive. They stopped and found food; Brawn found some birds that were suitable for eating and Jackie found some nuts and berries and a small pond for water. With every step, the plane came closer.

"I don't know why that plane bothers me." Jackie said to Brawn. "I mean, shit around here has been smoking before, but it's always been far away, right?" Brawn looked at her and blinked. "Maybe I'm just growing tired."

The lion nodded and let out a small roar, aiming its muzzle at the small cottage. It was just a few more steps in front of them and, though it had probably belonged to people that had lived here, or maybe another traveller like herself who had made it to this point on the path, she felt odd about using a place that had belonged to someone else. Still, it was either that or risk sleeping outside, or keep going in the dark. She didn't relish that idea either. Jackie nodded to let Brawn know that she understood. "Okay, mister. Let's go."

The front door had been splattered with blood. Jackie could almost picture how the blood had gotten there, an image forming of someone trying to escape, being caught and pinned against the door as the virus ravaged what had once been a human being. She shivered was careful to take hold of the doorknob where there was no blood. Jackie was surprised to find the door open. She had been prepared to break a window in order to gain entry, never mind that it would have left them vulnerable to whatever waited for them in the dark.

The door slid open quietly, and Jackie had a small moment of trepidation before she stepped inside, with Brawn following after her. They looked around the cottage. There was a small sitting room with a fireplace and a small television. There was a large picture window on the side of the room that looked out onto the field of tall grass. They made their way further into the cottage, closing the door behind them with a soft click.

The whole room was quiet and still. There was no noise inside the cottage, and they seemed to be alone. They moved into the next section of the building , and found a small kitchen and a bathroom. The fridge had some items of food in it that were still fresh, and the freezer held lots of frozen meats. The cupboards were occupied by other items like cereal, and crackers, and boxes of cookies. Jackie wondered if the people that had lived here had left or been taken by the virus. It must not have been too long ago if there was fresh food in the fridge and cupboards. Jackie wondered if it was wise to stay here of if the people would return. She sighed. They had nowhere else to go and night was fast approaching. Jackie knew that they didn't want to be outside when night fell. They were left with no choice really, as they were out of options.

Before they made themselves comfortable, they went to explore the rest of the cottage. There was a small bedroom, and a pantry that held cleaning supplies and gardening equipment that had long since rusted over. Judging by the look of the grass, Jackie figured it had been a long time since any gardening had been done. It was a good thing the gardening shears were rusted shut, Jackie thought. They could do serious damage to someone.

There were also two more bedrooms, a large one was done in earth tone colours, and the other in shades of pink. While there was no blood in the room with the earth tones, the pink room looked as if someone had tried to redecorate and had used a thick red paint. . The walls had large splashes of blood across them, in giant arcs that covered the ceiling and the floors. Jackie saw a collection of dolls on the bookcase, and they seemed to be grinning at her hungrily through an arc of blood which had covered all of their faces. Stepping out of the room, Jackie closed the door behind her and looked down at Brawn. "Let's sleep in the other room, okay? Those dolls are fucking creepy." The lion nodded.

Jackie set about defrosting and then cooking some of the meat from the freezer for both of them. She thought that the chicken should be okay, and it would be easy enough just to fry it up. While Jackie cooked, she thought of what might be still to come. She had found out what had caused the world to become this way, but now she had to find a way to cure the pandemic and return the world to what it had once been. Shaking her head, Jackie thought that was wrong. She didn't think the world would ever be what it once was. She just had to get it to a point where the earth could begin to renew itself, instead of the cycle that it had been on. She just had no idea how to do that. Although she was thankful that Xander had pretty much told her what had happened, it still left her no closer to figuring out an ending to the situation she found herself in. While she cooked, she looked inside the leather-bound book, but it was just as confused as she was, being a link to the thoughts that she had and the deeper ones that came from her spirit. One page had one line that summed up things perfectly: **"Though I have no idea where I'm going, I have to continue on. I have to step through my spirit to find a way forward, only when I step through, all I see is the blackness of the void of the unknown."**

Jackie let out a snort. "Ain't that the fucking truth."

When the chicken was done, she put a plate in front of Brawn along with a bowl of water. She served herself some and ate gratefully. She hadn't tasted anything so good in a long time. While she ate in the small kitchen, she listened for the sounds of birds or other animals. There didn't appear to be anything truly alive around her and she wondered if it had to do with the black birds that were in the tall grass. She thought that was probably the case.

After she was done eating, she did the only thing she could think of doing. She moved her swords out of the way and reached into her duffel bag to get her tarot cards. Bringing them back to the table, she shuffled, cut the deck, and then pulled a card. It was the Queen of Swords. "Of course, it's you, you fucking bitch. You won't leave me alone, will you?" Drawing another two cards, the saw The Sun and the Ace of Wands. "Yeah, like anything about this mess will bring me joy." Jackie sighed. The Ace of Wands was about using her magic, letting the creative spark feed her spirit so that the creativity could flow. "Well, that doesn't do me any fucking good." Jackie said. "What the fuck am I supposed to do creatively in all of this shit? I can't do anything creative and I'm already on a fucking journey, I don't need another one. Why can't you tell me how to end this?" She almost threw her tarot cards against the wall. "Why won't you tell *anything*?" Brawn looked at her and blinked as if he understood her frustration.

"I just don't understand what I'm supposed to do." She told Brawn. "I mean, I know what caused all of the destruction, but what caused the virus? How am I supposed to end something that I can't even *see*?" She looked around the kitchen. "Shit, I wish there was a bottle of wine here, or something." Brawn blinked at her and let out a small growling sound. "No,

I supposed getting shitfaced wouldn't help matters, would it?" Brawn shook his head. "I didn't think so."

Before she threw her tarot cards out the window, she put them back in their box and wrapped them in their cloth and tucked them back into her duffel bag. She knew from experience that the cards told her what she needed to know, regardless of the question she might have asked. They didn't have to answer her question, it's not like spirit was obligated to remain on speed dial for her alone.

She went to the living room, and Brawn followed. She made space for him on the couch, and they sat there for a while, the woman and the lion, listening to the sound of the wind outside the cottage. She tried the television, but unlike the one in the last house she was in, this one didn't work. Jackie thought again of Xander and again, she pushed the thought of him away. She noticed a stereo and reached out a hand to turn it on. The air of the cottage filled with static. Jackie wasn't expecting anything. She figured that if the television no longer worked, there certainly wasn't going to be anything on the radio.

However, she was wrong. After turning the dial for a few seconds, Jackie heard voices. "....don't want to alarm anyone, but with the situation that we find ourselves in, there is little to do but worry. There is no rhyme or reason to the way the disease effects people. Some get the virus through the air, others through a bite, and still others remain immune. The disease continues to spread and there is nothing that seems to be able to stop it. Those that have been tested and proven to be cured have recontacted the disease. It is sending the body through a cycle that has no ending. There are those that succumb and then fall apart, those that bite others to spread the disease and still those that somehow become better only to get the disease again..."

Jackie was chilled by this. If even those who were cured got the disease again, what was the point of trying to find a fucking cure? How was she supposed to cure a disease that had no fucking cure?

"...I don't know if anyone can hear me or if anyone is listening. I am broadcasting from my basement, and I haven't left in weeks. I'm afraid to go out, afraid to see what's left of the world out there. The government haven't been able to put a stop to what is happening. No one knows what to do. Has anyone tried anything? Shit..." The voice paused and he suddenly sounded young, as if he had somehow become younger, aging in reverse. He sounded hopeless."It doesn't fucking matter, does it? No one can fucking hear me. I don't know what's going on outside anymore, not really. I only look out from my basement window once a day to find out if the world is still alive..."

Jackie felt the same way. It had been a feeling growing within her, ever since she had stood in that living room and listened to the President talking about the disease behind the pandemic and the people dying. She just felt so lost within herself, even with Brawn there beside her. She had no idea what to do anymore.

"...I'm going to sign off. It doesn't matter if anyone is listening, does it? No one has a way of getting in touch with me. I'm just talking out into the nothing because I can't stand being alone and talking to myself..." There was a click and then there was nothing but static again.

Jackie sat there after hearing another person's voice and felt the world within her shake a little. It was good in a way that someone else was experiencing the same emotions she was. It meant thatshe wasn't alone in this and that there were other people trying to find a cure, however many of them were left. She just felt so alone. Why had this weight been put upon her? Jackie felt like she would crumble, as if it were too much for her to be the only one holding up the fate of the world.

Leaning into Brawn's fur, she let herself cry as she hadn't cried in a long time. In those tears, there were the feelings she had over her ex boyfriend and what he had done to her, the torment that she felt over the journey that she had been on, and what she had seen and experienced. She let visions of Gabriel, Marie, Em Aldrich, Cole, Ethan and everyone she had met on her journey pass through her mind. She was angry at all of them, and especially at Xander. They had all known more than they ever told her. Jackie was just expected to pick up the fucking mantle and strive forward, while they watched with hope in their eyes. She was fucking done. She was fucking totally done. She felt hollow within herself, all of the tears letting the frustration out of her, and she still didn't seem any closer to finding and ending to all of this.

"All I've got in this world is you, Brawn." She stood and looked at him. "Thank you, my friend. Although it probably helps that you can't speak, right? That's why we get along so well?" Brawn rolled his eyes and Jackie was surprised to find herself laughing. "Come on, let's go to bed. It's dark and maybe things will look better in the morning."

They went to the small bedroom and Jackie lay on the bed. Brawn lay down beside her and his warmth and purring sound were incredibly comforting to Jackie. "I love you, Brawn." The lion licked her arm in response. Jackie fell asleep to the sound of his purring.

*

Jackie was awoken by what sounded like a cry of pain.

Looking beside her, she saw that Brawn was no longer there. She sat up and looked around for him but didn't have to look far. Brawn was lying on the floor a short distance away and he was looking up at her with wide, terrified eyes. Brawn let out another sound of pain and reached a paw out to her. Horrified, Jackie moved closer to him and that was when she saw the girl.

Her face was buried in Brawn's stomach. It had been ripped open and she was devouring him from the inside. Jackie saw that his intestines had already been thrown aside and they lay like worms on the carpet. Brawn let out another sound, and this time the noise he was making was weaker, softer. Jackie made her own sound then, one that defied the use of words. It was the pain at seeing her only friend in this world suffering and knowing that she held that pain within her too. It was as if her own heart lay on the floor, bloody and discarded.

When Jackie made the primal cry, the girl looked up into Jackie's face. She recognized the girl underneath the mask of red meat that was now her face. She had seen a picture of her in the living room, it was the daughter who had lived here with her parents. Jackie wondered where she had been hiding; how long she had waited for darkness so that she could come outof the shdows. Jackie cursed herself. She thought of the small kitchen and a door she hadn't checked. Had it led to a cellar? Had the girl lay in wait there, listening to the sounds of Brawn and Jackie moving above her? It didn't matter, all that mattered now was revenge.

The girl hissed at Jackie and made a movement as if she were ready to pounce. The girl, watched Jackie's movements. She tilted her head to the right in an almost quizzical motion, as if trying to figure out what Jackie was.

Jackie didn't think the girl knew what it was to be human anymore. That didn't make what she would have to do now any easier. Even though her face was a red mask of horror, one that reminded her of Aldrich, there was nothing human in the girl's eyes where Aldrich's had been lively and full of life. The girl's eyes held nothing but hatred and hunger.

Jackie reached for her short sword. Before sleep, she had laid them out beside her. With the lion at her feet and her swords beside her, she felt safe. Now, Jackie felt only terror and rage. Her hunger was different than the girl's. It was a hunger for flesh, but not at all in the same way. She had no desire to eat the girl, Jackie just wanted to end her. She also knew that she would not use her magic in any way. She wanted the girl to die by her sword, and her sword alone.

With a cry of rage that once again defied the use of words but described all the anger and sadness that she felt, Jackie sliced through the air with short sword. Her aim was clean and true, and the girl's head flew from her neck and through the air, an arc of black blood trailing behind. The head hit the wall with a loud *splat!* and slid to the floor. The girl's eyes were still bright with what passed for life, and Jackie leapt from the bed and plunged the short sword into her head with all the strength that remained. She felt the sword slide through the bone of the skull and land solidly in the grey matter underneath. Jackie worked the sword so that it went further in, and she watched as what passed for life in the girl's eyes began to fade and eventually go dark, and the head was still.

Pulling her sword from the girl's head, she threw it onto the bed and ran to Brawn who was watching her with its wide, terrified eyes, yellow and green in the dark and so big, too big. They were like moons in the dark, and she used them to guide her through the dark. Kneeling beside him, she was careful of his ruined body, and she looked into his eyes. "I'm going to fix this." She said. "Don't leave me, Brawn, I'm going to fix this, do you hear me?" She let her light flow out of her then, and the light from the lantern and the rowan leaf flowed through her. Jackie let everything she had, every ounce of her light flow from her and into Brawn, but no matter how much light she gave him, she watched as the light in his eyes continued to slowly fade.

"Don't leave me, please don't leave me, I don't know what I'll do, I don't know what to do without you!" She was sobbing now, her face covered in streaks of tears, but she could not stop, she could not stop. She let more light flow from her body into Brawn's. "Please, please don't go. We're almost at the end, Brawn. We're almost there, I can feel it. I can feel it, Brawn. Don't you want to see the end? Whatever it may bring?" She sobbed again, and for a few moments, the words coming from her mouth once again defied the use of words or syllables. What came from her mouth was a sound of sorrow deep and so complete that it shook her light until it went out.

"Please." She said when she was finally able to form words again. "Please, Brawn. Please, I love you. Please stay. Stay with me. Please Brawn. Please."

Looking down at his face, she saw that Brawn was shedding tears her his own. Jackie reached with shaking fingers to wipe them away Brawn blinked his eyes slowly. "Please," she said again. "I don't know what to do. I can't go through this without you. I love you. Please stay…"

Brawn let out a low, soft meow, almost like that of a kitten and he reached out one of his paws to touch her face. She watched as a final tear slid from one of his eyes. He licked her hand with his tongue and winked at her one final time.

Then Brawn closed his eyes, and he was gone.

XVII

Jackie didn't know how long she had lain there.

Even though she knew that Brawn was gone, even though she knew that he had left her, Jackie still laid with him. His blood flowed out of him slowly and soon she was covered in it. She didn't move though, she stayed until he was cold, and for a long time after that until the blood flow had stopped completely. She stayed not because she didn't know what to do, she stayed because she couldn't picture herself doing it without Brawn by her side.

Occasionally, she would look at her sword and the body of the girl. Sometimes, she would look out the window and watch the sun rising into the sky and she would pretend for a moment that when she turned her head around and looked, that Brawn would be there, there he would be alive, and that he would lick her hand or rub his nose against her face.

She lay there on the floor, pressing her face to his nose and she could pretend that she still felt some warmth in him, that she could still feel some life in him. For a moment, Jackie thought about sending more magic into his body, but she knew that it wouldn't do any good and that thought brought on a fresh wave of tears.

Jackie was lost inside of herself. She didn't know how long she had been lying here, how many days she had mourned Brawn. She got up to relieve herself and then would curl up beside him on the floor again so that she could look into his eyes that were only half closed. She could pretend that he was mid-way through a blink, that he would nod his head, that he would let out one of his small roars. She could pretend that he was alive.

For quite some time now, the whispering from her bag had been growing louder. It rested beside the bed where she had left it, but she didn't care about the fucking whispering, the stupid nagging journal that knew better than she did about herself. What was the fucking point of having a book that was supposed to hold all of her knowledge if she had grown to hate it? What good was a book that made her feel stupid every time she read it for not understanding her own fucking thoughts?

Jackie was angry and there was a whirlwind growing inside of her mind. She was thinking of all the gifts she had been given along the way; the book, the swords, The fucking talisman from Xander. She both missed and hated him the most. The whispering reminded her of the time they had stayed at Em's house, when this whole adventure had seemed like some kind of a game...until the birds came.

So fine, she thought. *Fucking fine.* She would go out into the grass with the swords and see what she met, stand up against what was waiting for her there; even now she could hear their whispering. *Fucking demon crows,* she thought.

Standing, she grew angry when the whispering reached a fever pitch, almost screaming out a hiss of sound and white noise. Jackie was so goddamned tired of being told what to do. She would destroy every talisman, starting with the first one, the fucking star from Xander. She would break that fucking thing to pieces, throw it to the ground and spit on it. She would set it on fire, and dance as it burned. Fuck everyone and everything, all of these people that knew more than she did but told her fuckin *nothing*. Fuck that.

Grabbing the bag from the floor, she rooted through it and found the golden star right beside her tarot cards. It glittered at her from the bottom of the bag, and she squeezed her hand around it so hard that the points of the star dug into the palms of her hand. She wanted the pain; it made her see more clearly.

She wanted to feel something else other than hollow.

As she had lain there in mourning, Jackie had begun to realize that Brawn was more than a companion. He had been her rock, her source of bravery and strength personified. He had been her friend and her confidant. He had looked at her without judgement and wanted nothing from her, only her love and friendship. Brawn had protected her and loved her without restraint, which was a lot more than could be said for anyone else in this fucking place. She clutched the star in anger and fury. She knew that stars were to be wished upon, but she didn't feel like wishing upon a fucking star. She wanted to die. At that moment, she wanted to die and for it all to end.

Jackie thought again of her short sword and how she could draw the blade across her wrist. She squeezed the star shaped stone harder and closed her eyes. She took a deep breath and then took another. And another. Tears were sliding down her cheeks now and she was sobbing. She let the star fall to the floor, its yellow colour tinged with the red of her blood. Jackie heard it clatter to the floor but didn't watch to see where it went. She didn't fucking care.

Closing her eyes again, she saw the light within her. It reminded her of starlight in the darkest part of night. She opened her eyes again. Jackie didn't want to look at light. She wanted to die, but she knew that she couldn't. She couldn't let the world as it was take everything from her. Jackie knew that she had given too much of herself to it to let it take everything. She left the gold star on the floor where it had fallen. She would go out into the world tonight when it was dark and look at the real stars. If something attacked her, so be it. She would be ready.

In the meantime, she would rip every page out of the leather-bound book. It was still whispering at her, practically screaming at her and the hissing had grown to a volume that was shaking the glass in the few windows in the cottage. She was so fucking sick of that book, of this journey, of everything. All she could do was stand inside the cottage and look at the body of the lion, listening to the sound of the hissing whisper of that fucking book. She would start with that.

Pulling it out of her bag, she grabbed the front and back cover and tried to pull the book apart. It didn't bend or tear. She grabbed at the paper and tried to pull them out of the book, she would rip the book apart page by page if she had to. The paper wouldn't tear. She screamed out her rage, let it fill the cottage so that it was louder than the *whisper hiss* of the paper in the leather-bound book. She screamed again when she realized that she couldn't shut it up, that the whisper was in her head because the book was a part of her. Looking around for something to set it alight, she let go of that thought knowing that in her current state she was more likely to set the cottage on fire than the book.

Letting the book fall onto the bed, it fell open at a page and the whispering stopped. Where before, her mind had been filled with the hissing of the book, there was now blessed silence. She lifted the book off the bed to look at what the book wanted her to read. "Don't fuck with me," she said. "Please. I'm not in the mood."

The page the book had fallen open to read: **"Though I was loathe to admit it, I was glad for their company. Though I could not leave this moment without harm, they offered me hope for the journey to come."**

"Oh *fuck* no. I don't want to see anyone right now. And I would never use a word like loathe."

"No but your spirit would." A voice said.

Jackie turned and saw Gabriel and Xander standing there. Gabriel gave her a bright and welcoming smile. Xander just looked rather sheepish and slightly uncomfortable. *Good*, Jackie thought. *You should be, you fucking bastard*. She knew that she was angry with him because he had hurt her heart, and yet they had never had the conversation, never really discussed their feelings, it was only ever the journey that she was on. She pushed those thoughts away before they materialized in front of her.

"What the fuck are you two doing here?"

Gabriel, larger than life, came at her and wrapped her in a hug. He held her for a few moments, not saying anything, just holding her with love. It was this love that kept her together, though more tears fell from her eyes. She couldn't be bothered to stop them now, wouldn't have even tried. All she could do was let Gabriel hold her, and eventually she gave into the embrace, the warmth of his hug that enveloped her. For a moment, she pretended it was Brawn, but she had to push that away too. It was still so raw.

When Gabriel stepped away, he looked at her, tilted her face softly and looked into her eyes. "Honey, you are wrecked." He said.

"Fuck you too." She said softly.

Gabriel laughed. "Honey, it's okay. I've just never seen a hurt this deep. Was it the lion did this to you, or having to kill that child?" He asked. "I don't know if I would have had the strength for it, myself. I'm all about loving everyone and everything, even this guy behind me."

Laughter nearly broke the surface, but Jackie held it in. "Well, he's a hard man to love," she said.

There was silence for only a second, but it was filled with everything that she couldn't say, that they hadn't said to each other. Fuck, she didn't even know if he liked her back; maybe this was a one-sided crush? Either way, she couldn't treat him like crap because he was doing what he was supposed to do, making sure that she got as far along the path as she could, at least she assumed that's what his job was. She couldn't continue to be angry with him. It was taking up too much room inside of her, and she only had room for Brawn right now and the loss of her friend.

"Nice to see you, Xander." She said.

He looked surprised to be addressed. A look of happiness spread across his face and the blue of his eyes intensified. "It's so good to see you."

"Okay, niceties over. So, can either of you tell me what the fuck you're doing here?" Jackie said. "I'd offer you something to drink but I couldn't give a shit right now."

"We're here to see you through this time." Xander said.

"What the fuck does that mean?" She walked away from them. Going into the kitchen, she pulled out a bottle of vodka that she had seen before while looking through the cupboards with Brawn. It had been nestled into the freezer. She pulled out the bottle and drank it straight. She always was a simple woman when it came to her drinks, no fancy cocktails for her. Just straight vodka, scotch, whiskey and gin. If she wanted to get really fancy, she would add a slice of lime and maybe some tonic water, but that was about it, so she was fine with straight vodka. Fuck, at this point, she'd settle for turpentine if it tasted good. She put the cap back on before she had too much.

"It just means that you're going through grieving." Gabriel said. "It's understandable."

"What is?" Jackie said. "The fact that my best friend in this godforsaken place was taken from me, or that I killed a kid? Or maybe the fact that my life as I've known it is over and I don't know where I fit in this new world or what my place in it is?" She unscrewed the cap, took another swig, and let the warmth spread through her. *Fuck it,* she thought. "Or maybe I'm freaking out because I have been given the task of solving this shit show and I don't know how to do that. I have no fucking clue. I feel as if without Brawn, half of me is missing and I can't see the road ahead!" She was crying again, the tears sliding down her cheeks, and she made no move to wipe them away.

"That's part of the journey." Xander said gently. "Sometimes, part of finding the way forward is not being able to see what is coming but stepping forward anyway."

Jackie looked at him with narrowed eyes. "I could do without your sayings. I can do without a lot of things." She took a breath. She tried to find that moment of calm within her. She knew it had to be there somewhere.

"C'mon honey," Gabriel said. "Let's you and me take a walk under the stars."

"Stars?" Jackie said. "It's daylight out."

"Honey, you've lost track of time. Grief will do that to a person." Gabriel motioned to the windows. "See, it's night out."

"It was daytime a moment ago!" Jackie said, reaching out to touch the windows as if she didn't believe what she was seeing.

"Well, time passes, as does grief." Gabriel said. "C'mon Jackie, let's go. The cosmos beckon."

Jackie nodded and picked up the harness and her swords. She would not be without them now. They were like a protective vest against the world as it was, and the darkness that was out there waiting for her.

Gabriel watched her slide the harness on and then held out his hand. "Here, take my hand, honey."

Jackie took his hand and immediately felt the warmth. . She remembered it well, that lovely feeling of heat that emanated from him. She held on tighter, willing to take that warmth right now. She was cold from the inside out and didn't know if she would ever be really warm again. She took all the warmth that she could get.

As they left the stone cottage, Jackie turned back to look at Xander. He was looking at her with pain in his eyes. The seas within him were riling again. The door closed behind them, and Jackie looked up at Gabriel. "Will he be okay?" She asked softly.

"Honey, he'll be fine. Right now, I'm more worried about you."

"I'm okay." Jackie said. She had to be tough, had to fight against this. She could not break down again.

Gabriel stopped walking. "No, you're not." He took a flask out of his coat pocket. "Here."

"I'm okay," she said. "I don't need your handouts."

Gabriel let out a heavy sigh. "Honey, just because you're the Queen of Swords doesn't mean you have to be a bitch all the time."

Jackie bristled. "What did you say?"

"Only that I'm trying to be kind to you and you're throwing it back in my face. You don't have to keep this pain all to yourself, you know. You can talk to me. That's why we're out here. C'mon, letsgo sit down. We can get cheerfully wasted and look at the stars." He motioned to a picnic table that had been set up near a tree. There was also a tire swing hanging from a tree branch. The girl that had been in the house had probably swung there. For a moment, Jackie pictured the girl in her mind's eye as she had been, a child laughing with joy, caught in a moment of delight. This eased the pain that Jackie felt at taking her life, whatever kind of non-life she may have had in the end.

"Sure," she said. "That would be nice."

They walked toward the table, and although the grass around them rustled, nothing attacked them. "Why aren't the birds coming for us?" She asked.

Gabriel shrugged. "Cause we give off too much light. It frightens them."

"I certainly don't feel like I'm giving off any light."

"Well, you can't see it, but you are. You shine, honey. Even when you can't see it, the light's there."

Gabriel passed her the flask and Jackie took a sip. It was a heady mix of flavour, sweet, but not overly so. "This tastes like wine and chocolate fucked and had a baby." Jackie said. "What is this?"

"Frangelico." Gabriel said. "My preferred drink of choice. It will get you sauced off of a few sips and it doesn't taste like shit." He took the flask back and took a sip, then another. "It also leaves your breath smelling great, not that that matters much now, though."

They sat there and drank in silence. There didn't seem to be a need to fill up the emptiness with words. Jackie had questions and things that she wanted to say, but for the moment, they could wait. For now, Jackie sat with someone she liked and admired, and looked up at the stars.

Gabriel let her lean back on him and he put his arm around her. She should be cold sitting out in the night, but there was so much warmth coming from Gabriel. She felt comfortable, and though she still felt the pain and the ache of loss, there was a seed within her that she hadn't notice before that let her know she would be okay.

"Did you want to talk about it?" Gabriel asked.

Jackie didn't know what she wanted to ask first, but just let the words out as they wanted to come. "Do you think it will ever stop hurting?"

Even though she couldn't see him, Jackie could feel him shaking his head. "No, the pain never really goes away. Anyone who tells you that is lying or trying to bullshit you. The pain lasts, but it lessons over time. A little of it falls away each day, but it never truly leaves you."

Jackie let out a sigh. "I don't know if I can live like that."

"Well, you're going to have to. Besides, hurting the way that you do proves that you're human and that you have a heart. Hurting is part of life, honey."

"If it never goes away, does it get easier?" Her voice was so quiet that her words were almost a whisper.

Jackie could feel him nodding. "Yes and no. We don't forget the pain, but the urgency of it goes away. It gets easier to live with. We just adapt to a world where we hurt, and eventually it hurts a little less. That's part of grieving honey. It's a cycle and it's part of life. A horrible one, but ultimately good."

A pain flared in her chest. "How can *this* be good?" She whispered.

"Because you will keep the memory of Brawn alive. He's not gone from you, sweetheart. He lives on inside of you. If you need proof, you just have to look up at the stars."

Jackie did so and for a moment, she was entranced by their beauty. They said so much without saying anything. She felt like she could lose herself in their depth and majesty.

"Why was the talisman a star?" Jackie asked. Gabriel was pleased to note the question was thoughtful, and that there was a lot less pain within it.

"Well, you're looking up at the stars now." He said. "What do they make you think of?"

She shrugged. "God, I guess. Except I'm not that religious, so maybe something else, a creator of some kind, a higher power." She shrugged again. "I often look up to the night sky when I'm talking to someone I've lost or someone who has passed on."

"Good honey, that's good." He passed her the flask again. "I like to think that the sky is really full of spirits, but we can only see them at night." He took the flask back and took a sip. "I'd like to think that everyone we've ever lost is always with us and always looking down, watching us. It gives me a lot of comfort when I'm alone some nights to know that I'm not alone, you see?" He handed back the flask.

Jackie knew that more tears had started to slide down her cheeks, but she didn't bother to wipe them. "I don't know what I'll do without him, Gabriel. He was my *friend*." Her voice broke on the last word. "Brawn didn't want anything from me but my companionship. I miss him so much already."

"Now haven't I just told you that the stars are really the spirits of all those that we've lost looking down upon us? Here, look there. Brawn is already in the sky looking down upon you. See that grouping of stars? It's the lion." The stars seemed to shine brighter as he pointed them out and Jackie wondered what kind of magic he had within him.

"It looks like an iron or a seasick cow." Jackie said.

"Nope, it's the lion. He has always been up there looking down upon you. You were just lucky enough to have him with you in the physical form for as long as you did." He could feel her sobbing now, her body shaking against his.

"You really think so?" Jackie knew that the voice was thick with sorrow, but she didn't care.

"I do. He's looking down upon us right now. Even more than that, he's within you, in your heart. No one can ever take that away from you, Jackie."

They were silent again for another few moments and Jackie enjoyed the sound of the wind and Gabriel's breathing, the thud of his heart that seemed to reverberate through her. Finally, Jackie spoke. "I know that the cluster of stars that make up the lion have been there since before time began."

"That's what your mind knows. But your heart and spirit know that the lion was always watching you and always within you. It's where you get your strong spirit from."

Jackie let out a small sob and sat up, turning around to look at Gabriel. "Thank you."

"Don't mention it." He said.

"Why does it have to hurt so much?" Jackie asked.

"So that we can remember what it feels like to love someone so deeply." He told her. "Healing takes time You can't do it in a day."

They stood and began to walk back to the stone cottage. They took their time and listened to the sound of the black birds as they talked to themselves in amongst the tall grass. Rather than make her feel afraid, the fact that they were able to walk past them made her feel brave. She wasn't sure why this was, but she embraced that feeling. Jackie liked to think that the lion would have been proud.

They went back into the stone cottage and Jackie felt her mouth fall open. It was like they had walked into a different cottage. There was a fire burning in the fireplace and everything was clean and bright. It looked as if the entire place had gotten a new paint job or was cleaned at the very least. Wood glowed and metals shone. The hardwood floors they walked on had been swept so that everything was clean.

Walking slowly further into the cottage, she saw that every surface had been cleaned and that the place seemed warmer somehow; it was more than just the fire in the grate. As she looked around her, she wondered if this is what the cottage felt like before the virus had wiped out the world.

She turned to where the lion had been, to where Brawn had lain, cut open by the girl who was no longer a girl. The blood was gone, the girl was gone, and Brawn was nowhere to be seen. Turing again, Jackie looked once more to where she knew his body had lain, to where she had lain with him for what felt like all the time in the world and no time at all. She turned to look at Xander, with her heart empty and yet full of so many feelings she didn't think she could ever name all of them.

"What did you do?" She asked softly. The words came out almost in a whisper. "Xander, what have you done with Brawn?"

He held out his hand to her. "Come with me."

She nodded and didn't think of telling him no. She let him take her hand and she willingly went with him. "Why was the talisman a star?" She asked him and Jackie wondered if he would sidestep the question like Gabriel had. Instead, he surprised her and answered, his voice quiet as they went back out into the night in the front of the cottage.

"Because stars are symbols. They represent lots of things: magic, wishes, hopes and dreams. It was my hope that when you would used the star talisman, you would be thinking of me. You know that stars mean that someone is thinking of you. I wanted you to wish for me, but more than that, I wanted to let you know that should you need me, you would not be alone." He had the grace to look sheepish. "Silly, I know."

"No." Jackie said. "It's not silly." She was surprised by the warmth that ran through her at that moment, at the heat that bloomed where it had once been a cold wasteland. She was surprised by this because she had been trying so hard to forget him, but that made her think of him all the more. They stopped by a tree that grew in the front yard. She had never really looked at it, more concerned with finding a place to rest her head as night fell around her. Looking, she saw that there were orbs that shone in the tree that she hadn't noticed in the light of day. They hung in the branches, and Jackie couldn't help but be reminded of the Tree of Life that was one of the underlying themes of the tarot. Nine orbs of different colours hung in the branches, each of them made of a different coloured light. She reached up to touch one of them, a purple one, and was surprised when her hand went into the light. The orb shone brighter when she touched it, and when she took her hand away, the brightness of the glow remained.

"I thought this was a good place for him to lay at rest." Xander said. "We all carry some sort of tree within ourselves, whether it be one of story or the veins that run through our bodies. This way, he'll always be with you."

He looked down and Jackie saw that he had dug a small grave for Brawn. He had lain the lion inside the grave, and to Jackie, Brawn looked as if he were sleeping. She wished that she could see Brawn's eyes one more time, but she wondered if she looked up at the stars what she would see there, if he would be looking back down at her.

Looking at Xander, she felt tears again, but these weren't ones of sadness. These were ones of joy. "Thank you." She said. "Thank you so much. He would have loved this tree."

Xander nodded. "Did you want to say anything?" He asked quietly.

Jackie started to shake her head, but then stopped herself. She didn't think of these as her last words to him, for she knew that she would always be speaking to him in some way. Instead, she thought of Charlotte's Web, a book she had read as a child. "Salutations." Jackie said. "I know that we will meet again. So this is not goodbye, but so long for now." She let her tears fall into the dirt of the grave and the coloured orbs within the tree branches began to glow brighter. "Thank you for being my friend, for coming with me on this journey." Jackie almost stopped speaking then, the words catching in her throat, but she pressed on, let them fall from her lips as her last gift to him. "Though I continue on this journey without you, I will not be alone. I will carry your strength with me wherever I go. Thank you, my friend."

There was a humming in the air, and she closed her eyes to listen to it. She wondered if it was the song of the orbs or if it was Brawn's spirit that was singing to her. Jackie heard a soft *thump* and opened her eyes. Xander had lain the soil softly on top of his grave. She let one final tear fall to the soil and she watched as her tear spread out to form the tree of life, winding its way through the soil on top of his grave, mirroring the nine orbs that hung above the grave in the tree. She thought that was the perfect tombstone. She reached down to touch the earth and when she did so, Jackie felt a warmth flare along her right inner forearm. When she pulled back her sleeve, she was unsurprised to find that a tree had been tattooed there, its branches growing up her arm like the veins that she had underneath the skin. *Every step of this journey had left her changed or marked in some way*, she thought. *Why should this be any different?*

Looking at Xander again, Jackie saw that his blue eyes were calm and hopeful. They shone brightly in the night, as did the tattoos that graced his skin. She knew then that he was hers and even though she had to travel the last part of this journey alone, he would always be hers in some way.

Without saying anything, for no words seemed needed at this moment, she went to him and embraced him. It felt good to feel his arms encircle her, it felt safe. She leaned in and tried to say everything that she wanted to say with a simple kiss. Jackie knew that he understood, and Xander kissed her back, the lights in the tree growing brighter even as the darkness of night grew more complete around them.

"I hate to pull you two lovebirds apart," Gabriel said softly. "But we gotta go."

Jackie didn't know how long She and Xander had stood there, communicating with touch instead of words, but they pulled away from each other softly, as if afraid that they would lose whatever had happened between them the moment they moved apart from each other. Thankfully, the light was still there, and it bloomed even brighter when she looked into his eyes again and he looked into hers.

"Fuck." Jackie said softly.

Xander grinned, and the sight of that made the light in Jackie grow brighter. "My sentiments exactly." Xander said. "But Gabriel's right. We do have to go. You must go the rest of the way alone. If anyone can find a cure to the disease that has taken over the world, it's you."

Jackie felt a thrum of fear run through her. "How can you be so sure?" She asked, her voice softened by fear and the emotion that still ran through her from Xander's kiss. "How do you know I'll be able to do this?"

"I feel it in here." He took her right hand and put it to his chest, and she could feel his heart moving and beating underneath his skin. "You've never come this far, never found a way past barriers that stood in your way before. Now I know that you will see this through to the end, and I can feel it in here. Just like you carry Brawn in your heart, I carry you in mine."

Jackie took in a breath. It was the closest that he had come to saying that he loved her. She wanted to hear the words, but not yet; not yet. Now was not the time. It was enough to know that her anger with him had faded away, and that losing Brawn had shown her what really mattered. Besides, her heart hurt too much to hold on to too much hate and anger. If she was going to go forward in this, it was to do so with love.

"When do I go?" She asked Gabriel.

"You have to go now. We wanted to help you grieve and start you on your healing process, but you really have to continue Jackie."

She looked around her and at the stars above her. "Do I really have to start walking now? Can't it wait until the morning?"

Xander shook his head. "No, it can't, Jackie. We're sorry. This is the path you are on, and this is the way it has to be."

She knew this. She knew this but wasn't happy about it. "I guess it's a good thing I have my lantern." She held up her left hand and let a little of the light flow out of her.

"Yes, but you also have the light of the stars and moon. It won't ever be completely dark with them shining down upon you." Gabriel told her.

"Sometimes, you have to do things when we are afraid." Xander said. "It brings the truth from within to light."

"There you go, being all fucking mystical again." Jackie said. She didn't hate him for it this time. She hadn't hated Xander for it last time either, but she had been so angry. There was no anger now, there was only a stillness

221

where before there had been an angry sea of emotions. She much preferred the calmness within her than the anger. She could see further than she had before. This would help her on the long walk ahead.

Jackie went into the cottage and took one final look around. She had changed here, she had grown. Gathering her swords, she fastened the harness around her. Her duffle bag felt heavier than it had before. Looking inside, she saw that it had been filled with food and water for the journey, as well as her talismans. The star talisman had been found and cleaned and put back inside her bag. Looking at it, Jackie knew that she wouldn't use it again. Though she knew that it still had power, Jackie also knew that she carried more power within her. Still, it felt comforting to have it in her bag and to know that part of Xander was with her as well.

She went back outside and found Gabriel and Xander waiting for her under the light of the tree. The orbs continued to shine brightly, and Gabriel and Xander were cast in multiple hues of colour. "I suppose neither of you can tell me what happens next or where I'm supposed to go?"

Xander shook his head. "I'm afraid not. That's not the way this journey works, you know that."

"I know, but I had to ask anyway." She said.

"I know you did."

Again, the words they wanted to say were not said. They would have to wait for another time. Jackie kneeled down at Brawn's grave. "I'm going to go on now, Brawn." She said. "I just wanted to thank you for being with me. Though I leave your body behind, your spirit comes with me."

She stood and placed a hand on Gabriel's cheek. He covered that hand and then placed his flask in her free hand.

"I've refilled this. Use it when you need to."

"Thank you." She tucked it into her duffel. She looked at Xander, and again something passed between them. Jackie knew that if she went to him, if she embraced him, she wouldn't want to leave.

She turned her back on them and walked in the only direction that she could. The path only led one way, so she followed it with only the moon and the stars to guide her.

XVIII

"Fuck." Jackie said.

Whatever she had told Xander and Gabriel, she was afraid, at least a little bit. Even so, she hadn't known what was coming any step of the way on this journey and she had gone forward anyways with]grit and verve. She would do the same here, she had no choice really. Jackie knew that she had her talismans in her bag, but she knew that the real power came from within her.

Jackie also knew that she would be wandering this land in complete darkness, except for the glow of the moon that shone above her. She had always been able to stay safely inside somewhere during the night. That wasn't the case this time and she knew it. She wasn't safe, she was afraid, and she was alone. Thus far, the dark hadn't been too kind to her, and it was filled with a fear so real that it would take away one's breath away. Jackie knew that it was her fear that the fear lived within her, but that didn't make it any easier to deal with. She tried to swallow it down and realized how much having Brawn with her calmed her. She looked up into the sky and tried to see the lion constellation. When she found it, when she found Brawn in the sky, Jackie felt calmer.

"It's so dark out here." Jackie said. It felt odd to hear her voice, it sounded loud in the darkness, and she wondered if there were animals waiting to pounce on her. *I will not be afraid,* she thought. *I will not be afraid. I will embrace the lion in me, and I will shine brightly.* That gave Jackie an idea and she almost smacked herself. Here she was in the dark and she didn't have to be. She held up her left hand and turned the switch on, just a little so she could see the land around herself.

The path that she was on was made of gravel and the occasional cobblestone. Jackie would have to be careful not to trip and fall, but then if she did, she would just pick herself back up again and keep going. "We got this Brawn." She whispered. "We *got* this."

She was shaking inside; she was so afraid. However, she kept walking and kept the lantern tattoo lit, her left hand shining on the ground so that she could see her way in front of her. She was terrified of what could be waiting in the dark for her, but she kept walking. She thought of Brawn and the comfort that he would have been able to bring her at this moment, and the terror within her went to new heights, as if it was a bird trapped inside of her chest that kept flapping its wings. Jackie wanted to scream so that the bird inside of her would be able to fly out of her and find its place in the night sky. Only, Jackie knew that if she did that, if she screamed, she didn't think she would be able to stop. She screamed anyways but only on the inside. It was as if the bird within her had a song without words but only emotions.

Jackie was so used to hearing noises on the path that she had been on; the *thwap!* of her duffel bag and the *tinkle!* of her swords, the crunch of her footsteps on the gravel. Strangely, there was no noise and even with her lantern, she could only see a few feet in front of her. She made the light from the lantern brighter, turning around in a circle to see it that would make a difference, but it didn't. A few feet around her was all she was able to see.

She stopped walking, and she could hear the soft whisper of the leather-bound book. That sound, however muffled, brought her comfort. She would look forward to what the book had recorded of her thoughts, but for right now, she had to choose what she was going to do.

Would she continue forward even though she could not see where her path would lead? Or did she go back the way she came and try again when it was light out? Thinking about it, Jackie knew that this part of her path would always be in darkness and shadows. Jackie didn't even know if she would be able to find her way back. She pictured herself lost in the dark, stumbling over rocks, black dust covering her skin. She could feel the bird in her chest singing even louder and wondered if it had always been there.

"Darling, haven't you realized that you are the creator of everything?"

Jackie looked around her, shining her light to where she had heard the voice, but she couldn't see anything. The bird inside of her chest was growing more and more frantic which made her feel more agitated. She had to get out, she had to walk onward, she had to breathe, *she had forgotten how to breathe!*

"Breathe now, darling. It's okay. Look, I'll brighten things up, shall I? Will that make things easier? I don't know why it has to be so damn dark here."

In front of Jackie, a soft light began to glow. Then Jackie saw another pop into life, and another, each of them like seeds in the dark. Jackie wondered what would grow from these strange luminous seeds. Jackie watched as other pinpricks of light made themselves visible and she longed to reach out and cup her hands around the wishes in front of her and bathe in their light, make a wish to take her far away from all of this. She didn't though. Something told her to wait, to watch, and see what would happen.

It was like watching a flower bloom in slow motion, Jackie thought. Eventually after some time, Jackie could make out the shape of someone in front of her made entirely by the stars in the night sky. The person shook their head and Jackie saw a mane of gorgeous hair made of stars flow out into the sky then settle itself around the face that wasn't a face, merely a handful of stars to make up the person's features, but Jackie could see them. Jackie could see *her*. She stood there with her hands on her hips, a little bit of stardust slipping into the night sky.

"Who are you?" Jackie whispered.

"There's time enough for that yet. Let's get walking," she said.

"I don't know what to *do*." Jackie said.

"That's the easy part." She replied. Her voice was soft and warm. "You just put one foot in front of the other."

"I've been doing that for so long already." Jackie said, trying to keep the impatience from her voice. "I'm exhausted. I really am. I could also use a huge glass of wine."

The woman made of stars regarded her. "The truth about journeys is that they don't end when we want them to. They go on for as long as they need to for us to learn a few things about ourselves." She talked with her hands and Jackie could see stars leaping off of her and floating towards the sky. "Come on now, walk with me."

Jackie did, even though she didn't want to walk anymore, partially from exhaustion and partly from fear. *Nope*, Jackie thought, *mostly from fear*. She didn't know where she was going, who this star lady was or what she wanted. "Why are you here?" She asked her.

Jackie saw the star woman tilt her head. "I'm here because you are here. You've got some things to face up to and I will help you as much as I'm able. I mean to see you through to the next part of your journey."

"Why are you helping me?"

"Darling, is this where I pretend like I'm a jinnee and you get three questions? Wouldn't you rather ask for a million dollars?"

"That wouldn't do me much good, as nice as it would be." Jackie said.

"I suppose not. Come on, get walking. One foot in front of the other, Jackie."

Jackie took one step, and then another. It was easy once she began, though she knew that if she stopped, she didn't think she would be able to continue. She would have to walk the dark lands with a star woman that may or may not exist for all time. That was not an encouraging prospect. Jackie kept walking, kept putting one foot in front of the other. The star woman walked beside her, and if Jackie's footsteps were quiet, the other woman's footsteps were made of starlight and dreams and quiet as the night.

"Who are you?" Jackie whispered.

"You'll know soon enough. We're almost there."

"Almost *where*?" Jackie asked. "Please tell me. I'm so afraid." It hurt her to speak the words aloud. "I'm so afraid and I have no idea where we are or where you're taking me."

"Darling, I'm not taking you anywhere. I'm following *you*. This is *your* journey, I'm just along for the ride."

Jackie took each step, her lantern held aloft, and her rowan leaves held down towards the ground, but she still felt fear. It was as if the bird within her chest was trying to come through her ribs now, not just trying to come up out of her throat. It was as if it would rip through her ribs. Jackie hugged herself to try and hold it in.

"You have to trust in yourself, Jackie. You've come so far, and you've done so much that you didn't think possible but look, we're almost there!"

Jackie saw her hand point towards a light that was growing in front of them. They were walking towards what looked like two towers that were taking shape from within the darkness. They shone in the darkness as if they were made of the same glass-like stone that had surrounded Rigby. As they neared the towers, the woman made of stars spoke again.

"What do you want to do most, right at this moment?" She asked.

Jackie didn't have to think of her answer. "I want to find the end of this pathway. I want to reach the end and finish this journey."

"Those are some lofty dreams, Darling. What are you so afraid of?"

They still walked forward, the towers becoming taller and more fully formed. "I'm afraid of what I will find at the end. I'm afraid of what will happen afterwards and what the next step will be."

"It's okay to be afraid of the unknown, as long as it doesn't stop us from moving forward."

"But why me? Why is this my journey?"

"Do you want to succeed?" She asked, her voice light but full of meaning.

"More than anything. I want to find the end more than anything I've ever done before."

"Then that's why. You can't let your fear distract you from finding your dream and chasing after it. You lose parts of yourself that way."

Jackie thought of the men that she'd been with and the things she'd given up to be with them, just because it was easier than being alone. She thought of every job that she had taken just to pay the bills rather than to do what she loved. Now that Jackie thought about it, she had been living most of her life afraid of something. Maybe afraid of herself, and what she really wanted.

As they came nearer to the towers, Jackie saw that there was a small river that ran across the grass. She could hear water and when they came upon it, Jackie saw that the water itself shone inky black. She stood there with the woman made of stars because, as far as she could see, they could go no further. What was she supposed to do?

"Wait." The star woman said as if Jackie had voiced her question out loud. "Just be patient and wait. Sometimes, that is the key to battling fear. Other times, it brings clarity. Just stand here and watch with me, okay?"

Jackie nodded and watched. She felt the woman take her hand, and though the hand was somewhat solid, it also felt as if it were made of smoke and was cold to the touch.

Jackie almost asked her what they were waiting for, what was supposed to happen, when it happened. She watched as a silver crescent began to show itself from above the horizon. They stood watching it grow bigger and bigger, a yellow orb of such beauty that it took Jackie's breath away and calmed the fluttering bird inside of her chest.

The sphere began to rise higher, making decent progress as it travelled along the sky. The higher it went, the more the light from the orb began to brighten the world around them. When the moon was at its peak in the sky, Jackie looked at the world that had changed from darkness and shadow into bright and beautiful colour. The water in front of her was a dark and rolling blue, and the grass was as green as jade. She saw that the path that she was on was briefly interrupted by the water, but it continued on the other side. Jackie let the light of the lantern and the rowan leaf fade. Though it was still dark out she could see so clearly in the moonlight, and the two towers looked as if they could stretch to the stars themselves. Jackie turned to the star woman and her mouth dropped open.

The woman was made of shadows. The moonlight had revealed her to be made from the night sky. When she looked at the star woman, Jackie could see someone familiar within her. It was as if another layer rested on top of the darkness of her. Jackie could make out a face and hair that fell to her shoulders, kind eyes that were filled with more stars but were a startling light blue, just like her own.

"You could be my sister." Jackie said.

The woman shrugged. "In a way, I guess I am."

Jackie reached out to touch the woman's hand and a thrum passed between them. The air around them swirled briefly and then went still. The thrum grew into a beat that Jackie could not only hear, but feel as well. "What was that?" Jackie whispered.

"It happens only when two halves meet. It is a coming together of spirit and soul."

"What do you mean?" The flutter was starting again, and Jackie was growing agitated. "Who the fuck are you?"

The woman, or whatever she was, smiled at her. "Don't be afraid. I'm your shadow half. You know the part you that yearns and dreams and hopes? The part of you that wants to fuck Xander's brains out event though you would never admit it to yourself much less to him? The part of you who's a badass when you need to be, even if it isn't in your nature? When you look in the mirror and you swear that you can see someone within your eyes? That's me."

"I don't understand." Jackie said. She waited for the flutter of wings to start in her chest again, but they didn't come.

"Darling, I'm your wants and your needs, your darkest desires. I'm also your intuition and your spirit. You should consider yourself lucky, most people don't ever get to communicate with their shadow selves. They're too blinded by what they think is going on to pay attention to what is being said."

"Then why can I talk to you?"

Though her facial features weren't well defined, a swirl of stars caused a flurry in the shadows that passed for her skin, and she let out a light laugh that sounded like the stars themselves had learned to make sound. "Because you're you and you're *here*."

"What do I call you?"

The shadow woman tilted her head in thought. "That's a good question. I've always thought of myself as Jackie, but that would make things confusing, plus it's the name that you're using in this lifetime. Call me Shadow, it will do as a name as well as any other name because it's what I am."

"What do we do now? The river is blocking our way to the path." Jackie looked at the two towers made out of the glass-like obsidian rock that leered at her from the other side of the river. She was exasperated all of a sudden. "What the fuck are we supposed to do?"

"Well, that depends on you." Shadow said. "It won't bother me none to cross a river. So, I return the question to you: what the fuck are *you* going to do?"

"We have to continue on the path." Jackie said.

"Do we? Is that what you really want to do?"

"I thought you were supposed to help me here."

"I'm your shadow self, not your aid. I exist because we are all made of stardust in some way. You have an easier time than most because you use your tarot cards. They help you to connect to your spirit more clearly than others can. That's all I am, stardust filled with desires, wants and things left unsaid. Therefore, I ask you again, what are you going to do?"

Jackie looked at the world around her, at the water, grass and path that were cloaked in shadows, and the brilliant moon that shone so brightly. She couldn't see everything in front of her, but she *could* see enough so that she could move forward. She could go back the way she came, or get lost in the shadows behind her, but Jackie knew that she wanted to find her way forward. She needed to go on, to discover what was waiting for her between those two pillars of black glass rock. Though the thought of not knowing what was waiting for her was frightening, it was also somewhat liberating. Jackie held the lantern and the leaf and felt she had the heart of a fucking lion. She would do this, and find a way to beat back her fear, one step at a time.

"We go forward." Jackie said, her voice strong with conviction.

The Shadow gave her a wisp of a smile and the stars within her burned brighter for a moment. "That's my girl! You got this." There was pride in her voice. "I knew that you would choose the right path."

"Like I had a choice." Jackie said sarcastically.

"Darling, you've always had a choice. You could have headed back to the plane the moment you left it. Goodness knows it would have been comfortable and had a lot of food. However, it wouldn't have been this much fun."

"I wonder if I've had this much fun on the other times I've done this. They keep saying that I've never gotten this far before."

"Yes, I did wonder at that, too. Well, like everything we've done, if at first you don't succeed, you try again." Shadow said. "Shall we continue?" She held out her hand filled with stars.

"Fuck yeah." Jackie said.

They went to the edge of the pond and Jackie looked into the water. She could see a crayfish underneath the water. As they watched it, the crayfish made its way over some rocks and then scuttled out, breaking the surface and heading to the waters edge. When it got to land, it veered off of the path and disappeared in the grass.

They looked at the river. Though the current looked strong, it didn't look that deep. She looked around her for something to use as a bridge to get to the other side, but there was nothing around. Being that it was nighttime, Jackie didn't want to walk in this strange unknown land looking for planks of wood. There was no other way around it. She would have to forge her way across.

"I'm going to just cross it. Are you okay if you get wet?"

"It's sweet of you to worry, but I don't really have any physical form. This one," she said, motioning at the body she wore. "Is for you, so you don't feel uncomfortable talking to yourself, though I must say that talking to yourself is often thought of as a sign of genius."

"So, short answer is you won't get wet?" Jackie asked.

"Correct."

Looking at the water, Jackie had another moment of fear flutter within her, and she felt the bird come to life again. "No," she said. "No, I'm braver than this. I can do more than be afraid."

Without thinking about it any further, she took her first step into the water. She had been right, the current was strong, but it felt as if it was welcoming her rather than fighting her presence in the water. Shadow floated beside her.

"Do you feel any better? Water is supposed to be cleansing." She said.

Admittedly, Jackie did feel better. The water wasn't that deep, merely covering her leges up to her ankles. There was a loosening of the fear and after a few deep breaths, it was gone. While she stood there, a deep feeling of calm came over her and, while the two towers of black glass should frighten her, she now regarded them with open curiosity. She wondered what was beyond the two towers and what answers they might hold.

Jackie didn't know if it was the water or everything she had been through, but she actually felt connected to this place, right here and right now. She knew that this might change the moment she took another step, but for right now, she just listened to the water and everything that it had to tell her. When she had listened to the water's secrets, she took another three steps and crossed to the other side. When she stepped out of the water and back onto dry land, she couldn't hear the whisper of the water nearby, but she could hear it within her.

As Jackie was about to take another step, a wolf moved quietly through the grass. Jackie could see its shadow moving and her eye was drawn to the wolf. It seemed to realize that someone had spotted it because it turned and looked directly at her. It had yellow eyes, so dark they were almost golden. Jackie couldn't help but think of Brawn and the way that he had looked at her, and the way they used to communicate with each other without using words. The wolf stopped and blinked twice at her; then the wolf nodded, and it turned and leapt into the tall grass and was gone.

Jackie felt as if she had seen her old friend, or if it had been him but in another form. She had no idea how this world worked, even though it was her own. Was it a trick of her imagination or did she hallucinate the whole thing?

"You okay, darling?"

"Yeah, just saw an old friend, that's all."

"Sometimes we meet friends in the most unlikely of places. Isn't it funny how things work?"

"No," Jackie said. "Not really. I don't find any of this fucking funny."

Now that they were on the other side of the water, the tower of black glass looked even more menacing. The moonlight made it seem as if the two pillars of rock were alive with a light that shone from within them. She remembered the black rock from her dealings with Rigby and how the black rock had made her feel trapped, but these rocks before her filled her with a sense of fear and one of anticipation.

"Are you afraid?" The Shadow woman asked.

"Yes, I am." Jackie said.

"There is a lot to be learned from fear. It can show us what we really need to know about ourselves. It can show us the way when it may have been hidden before. Sometimes fear can reveal desires that have been hidden within us for a long time. You need to embrace your fear and let the light of the moon show you what it really means." Shadow said.

"Yeah, well if I could do that, do you think I would be here?"

Shadow smiled at Jackie. "Yes. You would have ended up here eventually. It's not the first time that we've been on this journey and it's not our first time through this cycle. Have you ever considered that maybe the path hasn't always been the same?"

Jackie looked at the black glass again and shook her head. "No, I suppose not."

She stepped forward, the path beneath her feet whispering to her as she walked through the sand as much as the water had done. Jackie wondered if the water and the sand on the path were trying to tell her what to expect, what to know; she cursed her overactive imagination. The whispering got louder the closer she got to the stones, and that bird inside of her, the one that she thought she had let go of, began to flutter once more. She tried to clam herself, told herself that there was nothing to be afraid of, but she was afraid. She had to admit that to herself.

Turning to Shadow, Jackie asked "Have the two towers been here forever?"

Shadow shook her head. "No, it's different for each person. It all depends on what they fear the most and whether they are brave enough to walk through to the other side. What do you fear the most?"

Jackie tried to close her eyes internally to what she saw, to the mental images that came to life inside of her mind's eye. She tried to turn her eyes away from the fresh earth and what it held hidden underneath, the life that the earth held within. She had never been good at endings; it had always been this way. That was why she had had so much trouble leaving relationships that didn't honour her. She was terrible with endings. Looking at her shadow, Jackie saw her nod.

"It's okay, Jackie. It'll be okay."

"How can you be sure?" She tried to keep the fear from her voice but wasn't at all successful.

"I can't be. But I will be right there with you when you walk through. Here, take my hand, okay?" Shadow offered.

Jackie nodded and took Shadow's hand in hers. She took a deep breath in and squared her shoulders. Then with her shadow beside her, she walked forward. She was right in front of the stones now, and when the light of the moon shone down, she saw that between the two towers of black glass there was a shimmering veil. She touched it and watched it move, the gossamer-like fabric rippling. Jackie took a breath.

"Are you ready?" Shadow whispered.

Jackie nodded and then shook her head. Then she nodded again. "Yes and no."

"You don't have to do this, Jackie. You can just go back the way you came. Everything will be the same." Shadow whispered.

Jackie shook her head. "Nothing will ever be the same again. It's better that way."

Jackie felt a tear slide down her cheek and the bird within her chest began to flail around, but Jackie walked forward with calm steps, her Shadow part of her now, no longer a separate entity. The fabric of the veil touched her skin and began to embrace her and wrap all around her. Her body started to come apart, bits of her floating into the ether. She could see her skin floating away like rain, and she watched her blood swirl around her as if it were dancing. She was reminded of the arcs of blood that had covered most of this land, particularly the blood that had covered the fairground where she had met Ronaldo and they had ridden the Ferris wheel. Jackie watched her blood with fascination.

When her skin and blood had been given to the darkness, there was only her mind left, but even then, she could feel the darkness eating away at it, could feel it floating away into the void. She gave in to the inevitable and let herself float away. Before the darkness took her, Jackie had one last thought: *So, this is what dying feels like...well fuck me.*

Then the world around her went black.

XIX

The first thing she became aware of was light.

It started as a pinprick, far in the distance. She tried to reach towards it, but it wouldn't come closer. She didn't have hands to reach for the pinprick, so she just watched it as it approached her. As it moved closer, floating in the dark sea around her, the light began to grow. No, it wasn't just a light, it was a seed, a seed that was growing. It looked as if the light was blooming in front of her.

She floated in the darkness and tried to will herself closer to that light, to that shining seed of joy. As it moved ever closer to her, Jackie experienced a joy like she had never known. It warmed her skin, and the warmth ran through the idea of her body. She tried to look down at herself and could see only darkness and shadow, though she was not afraid as she had been before. The worry and fear had been left behind her; now there was only the light in front of her.

As she watched the light move even closer, Jackie thought of Brawn, his kind eyes that shone like a bright light and had brought her so much comfort in the darkness. She thought of Xander and the love that she felt for him but had never voiced out loud. At the thought of two beings who she loved with all of her heart, the light in front of her grew even bigger and brighter. She wondered what else brought her joy, what else brought her contentment. Jackie thought of Gabriel and Em, she thought of Ronaldo and of Aldrich. She thought of what she had overcome on this journey and how it had shaped her as a person and as a spiritual being.

The light continued to grow brighter and larger, the seed of light blooming into what looked like a flower made of light. She reached for it and was surprised to find that she had a hand, that she could move it and watch her fingers dance. Jackie marvelled at the sight of her hand and looked back to the light which had grown bigger still.

Jackie thought of Xander again, of the light within her that he had taught her to use, and the swords which he had guided her with in practice. She thought of his blue eyes that swirled with want when he looked at her, and she wondered if her own eyes had done the same. Jackie wondered if she would ever feel his touch again and wished that she had told him how she felt about him, how their connection was not just a physical one. Jackie felt a yearning move through her and watched as the flower of light grew even more substantial.

Thoughts of Xander made her think of her tarot cards and the joy that they brought her. The connection to spirit that they represented, and the counsel that she received on a daily basis as she tried to work out the meaning of the cards and understand a little bit more of herself, one facet at a time. With every card she drew, she knew herself a bit more. It had always been this way for her.

The flower in front of her grew even larger and more vibrant. She could see veins of colour moving throughout the bloom now, oranges and golds, the occasional petal of red with a centre of warm white and gold. It was the most beautiful thing that Jackie had ever seen. Rather than blind her with its light, it invited her to look upon it and to study each petal, each tongue of flame.

She thought of her mother and father, long since gone from this world, but still a part of her, their strength and love still running through Jackie to this day. Her mother had been wise beyond her years and had filled Jackie with an endless need to know more, to always question what was in front of her, and to learn the lessons that she needed to learn. Her father had been an explorer, never content to sit and be idle. He had always loved travelling to unknown places and seeing all that could be seen until they were no longer unknown. She knew that both of her parents were with her on the journey even now and knowing that brought her comfort.

That feeling of warmth grew stronger within her, and she was happily surprised to see that her legs had taken shape within the dark sea. Jackie saw that the sea was not as dark as she had previously thought. Looking around her, she saw the flower in front of her had filled the dark shadows with little seeds of light, and as they swirled around her, they reminded her of the stars in the night sky. Jackie thought of Gabriel and how she had leaned against him, the warmth of his body and the booze running through her body, a moment of simple and uncomplicated joy. This led her to thinking of the kiss that she had shared with Xander, the heat that had run through her at the touch of his lips against hers, and the depth of feelings between them that had yet to be spoken out loud.

The blossom of light grew even brighter. As Jackie watched, it looked as if petals were opening up, and there was a hum in the air that made her spirit sing out with it. There were no words, but Jackie knew that there didn't need to be. Some things went beyond words and syllables and sentences. Some things just were.

Growing, the blossom filled her vision, and she could see every flickering flame of fire on its surface. She reached out to touch the flame, and it reached out to touch her. It welcomed her touch and Jackie let the warmth of the flame run through her body. The flower grew larger until it was all she could see, and Jackie finally realized why the bloom was so familiar to her: it was not a bloom, or a flower, but the sun. She was gazing at the sun and could see every flicker of flame on its surface. Jackie placed both hands upon it and could feel the joy radiating from the sun and closed her eyes as the warmth travelled through her.

Though her eyes were closed, she could still see the warmth and the fire of the sun. Gradually though, it began to fade, though the warmth of the sun stayed with her, the brightness began to dim. She found that she couldn't open her eyes and so she simply floated there in the not quite darkness, watching as the light from the sun in front of her faded bit by bit, though she now felt music that moved through her. When her eyes were filled with nothing but darkness, and her ears were filled with the sound of spirit song, Jackie was able to open her eyes.

She lay on a grassy knoll. There was a white flower that grew near her, and it stretched towards the sun that shone down upon her. Jackie was no longer in darkness and was warmed by the sun. She knew that it was the same sun that she had looked upon in the dark sea. As she lay there, she felt immense joy coming to life inside her, blooming much as the flower filled with flame had bloomed inside her mind's eye.

Sitting up, Jackie looked around. The sun was bright and warm on her skin, but what took her breath away was the view from where she sat. The grassy knoll was on the top of a small mountain. Jackie could see the rockface leading down to the ground below. While the ground looked to be marked in streaks of blood, like the rest of the ground had been on her journey here, the knoll on which she was siting and the mountain below her were unmarked.

Seeing her swords and her duffel bag close by, she reached out and grabbed hold of them, pulling them close. Jackie had never been so comforted to see a physical object. The swords were her mind and the bag held pieces of her spirit; she knew that now. She sat there, one hand hugging the bag to her chest and the other hand laying on the swords, still in their harness. They brought her comfort and both the swords and bag grounded her. When the tears came, she let them fall and didn't wipe them away. The tears were multifaceted, full of sadness and also full of joy, for this moment and for the next that would follow and for every moment after that.

Jackie knew that she had died. She had conquered her fear, thinking that death was the worst thing that could happen to someone, when really it was to live a life unlived, even with so many things to experience and cherish. That was the worst thing that could happen, Jackie thought. To go through life and to have not lived at all. She wondered if she had been on that path, and that was why she had ended up on this one. It didn't matter now.

She stood and looked at everything around her. In the far distance, she could make out the shape of the airport. There was still smoke rising from the grass, and she could see curls of it floating into the air. She could see the mountain in the distance where she had met Aldrich at his bloody alter. If she turned her head a little to the left, she could see the carnival where she had met Ronaldo and the castle where she had met Cole. She could even see the treetops of the forest where she had met Marie and had been marked with the rowan leaf. She saw the river that led to Ethan's hut where she had outrun the black mass. She saw the outcropping of black glass rock where she had met Rigby and her temptations.

Jackie could see every part of her journey. Looking at the path that had led her here, she wished that Brawn was with her. She missed him so much it was a physical ache in her body. He should be beside her, looking at all of this. Though she had only met him part way on her journey, it had felt as much his journey as it was hers, however she knew that she would have to finish it alone. She could feel in her bones that she was close to the end.

That led her to think on something else, the final puzzle that she had been given. While Xander had shown her what had caused the devastation of the world as she had known it, Jackie was still not even close to figuring out how to end the virus that had wiped most of the earth clean. That she had been given this responsibility was something beyond thought. How could she cure the world when she could barely cure herself?

Sitting back on the ground, she pulled her bag to her. She took out her cards and some of the food that had survived wherever the blackness had taken her. That she still had her duffel bag filled with her food and talismans and her cards was so incredible to her. She hugged the bag, grateful that it had come with her on this journey.

She picked up her leather-bound book and let it fall open in her hands. She was hoping that she would find some wisdom contained within the pages that she hadn't thought of. She read *'I wondered what to do. It's not fair being responsible for the fate of the human species, but these are the cards that I've been dealt, so I can't turn my back on this part of my journey, perhaps even the sole purpose of it. I merely need to find a way to share my light with as many people as I can.'*

Looking at the words, Jackie thought about them and wondered why these thoughts hadn't occurred to her waking mind. Still thinking on this, she picked up her cards and shuffled them, cut the deck and pulled a card. It was the Queen of Swords. "Ugh, I fucking know already, piss off and tell me something that I can use." She pulled another card. It was the Six of Pentacles. Jackie knew that the Six of Pentacles was all about giving and receiving, being open to give to those who need it, and also being willing to accept generosity. She would have to think on that until the meaning was clear to her.

Putting her cards and the book back in her bag, she stood and looked down at the path that she had taken to get to where she was. She was so thankful for every step, even the difficult ones. They were the ones that taught her the most about herself. Fuck, this entire journey had taught her what she could handle. She had learned so much and had come so far. Hell, she had disembarked the plane, something that at the time she had never thought that she could do, and now look at her and everything that she had accomplished. She had done things she had never dreamed of, let alone thought she could survive. She had come so far and had only a little farther to go.

To think that she had left to outrun another failed relationship and had landed on the path that led her to this moment in this time. That brought her joy, along with the people she had met along the way, and she had learned what she was really capable of. She thought of what this journey had taught her, and what it had cost her. Rather than let thoughts of Brawn and Xander make her sad, she considered herself fortunate for the chance to develop those relationships, and that she had loved so deeply and been loved in return. This made a special kind of happiness fill her body.

Giving in to the joy, she stood and lifted her arms up towards the sun and the sky and the air around her. Jackie felt alive and wished that there was someone here with whom to share this moment. She wanted to dance, to laugh with joy at everything that had happened to her and who she had become, but she only had herself.

A thought came to her then, one that made her put her arms down and gaze at the sun in wonder. She would have to think of a way to end the disease, but it would have to be creatively done. If there was anything that she had learned about this world, it was you couldn't approach many things head on. You had to look at it in a different way and try to find your way around the problem before the solution would make itself known to you. That had been the case for her previously, and she knew that it was the same here and now. She wondered what she would have to do.

She looked at the way the sun was hitting the land, how the earth seemed to breathe it in, and Jackie stopped to do the same thing; to take a deep breath of the air around her and to take in some of the sun's warmth.

Staring down at the land below, Jackie knew what she wanted to do. She had told herself that she wouldn't do it, that she would make the rest of the journey alone, but she reached into her duffel bag and withdrew the star talisman that Xander had packed in the bag. She held the star in her hand and wondered how to manipulate it. The blood had been cleaned off, and it shone again like a bright golden fire in her palm.

Jackie knew that she didn't want Xander here, that if she saw him now, he would ruin her concentration, but it was the one thing that she had that connected them in some way, something physical that she could hold on to and touch. Rubbing the star, she tried to determine how to use it, how to talk to him without having him physically present.

Grasping the star talisman, Jackie closed her eyes and thought of love, and she tried to send that feeling out into the world and the cosmos. She knew that she really needed to find a way to cleanse the world, but she needed guidance. Even though this was her journey, she needed help to figure out what to do, and she wasn't ashamed to admit it.

Jackie didn't know how long she stood there, holding the star and basking in the sun. She could feel the wind and the light and realized that something had happened when the sun became warmer on her face and the wind whipped around her briefly. When the wind died down, Jackie opened her eyes, and her hand went to her mouth.

"Mom?" The word came out in a whisper.

"My darling girl." Her mother said. "I'm so proud of you."

Her mother looked the same, even if she was made from blue and silver vapour. She had the same short hair, and the same eyes that sparkled with joy behind a pair of horn-rimmed glasses. The same smile that she had grown up knowing lit up her mother's face, and Jackie let the feelings of joy and love wash over her.

"What are you doing here?"

"You called for help. I suppose you were expecting that handsome boy to show up?"

"That was the plan, yes."

"Well, I wouldn't kick him out of bed. He asked me to come and see you instead. He thought you could use a mother's love."

A tear slid down Jackie's cheek. "He was right."

Her mother approached and reached up to hold Jackie's face. Her hands were cold and warm at the same time. Jackie welcomed the touch. "My darling girl, why are you so afraid?"

Jackie looked into her mother's face and tried to imprint the sight of it on her spirit. "I don't know what to do, Mom."

"I think you do. If you look way down within yourself, you already know the answer."

"I don't know how I'm supposed to cure the whole world, Mom. That's too much for one person, how do I cure all the people that remain? How can one person do that? It's too much."

Her mother took her hands from her face and Jackie missed the touch instantly. "You know, you just said two different things." Her mother looked thoughtful. "How are you supposed to cure the world and how do you cure all the people that remain? Did you stop to think that the those that are still on this earth are here because they are fine? That they aren't susceptible to the disease?" She turned to look out at the peaks and valleys below, and Jackie went to stand beside her.

"If I look out at the world below us, I see a lot of darkness. There is blood, there is fire, and people have suffered. But if you cure the world, or at least show it some love, that will be a step towards helping the others that still live on this planet with you. You have the power within you, my darling girl."

Jackie shook her head. "I don't think I do. I'm only one person. What can I possibly do to change the world?"

"Sweet girl, didn't I always teach you that one person can move mountains if they put their mind to it? I repeat: You have the power within you." Her mother turned and took both of Jackie's hands and turned them palms up, so that both the lantern on her left palm and the rowan leaf on her right palm were visible. "There is so much light within you. What have I always told you about the dark?"

"That it holds no power when you shine light within the shadows." Jackie said, remembering when she was a child and she had woken up from a nightmare. Her mother had held her and told her the same thing, and she had always turned on a light afterwards. It was something that she had forgotten over time.

"That's right." She looked away for a moment, and then back to Jackie. "I can't stay much longer. Know that I am always with you, darling girl. Know that I'm within you always, okay?"

"Okay Mom."

"I am so proud of you; your father and I both are. We are watching you from above, with the rest of the stars. We will see you again when the time is right."

Her mother hugged her, and the sensation was like being hugged by cold water. It sent thrills of joy and sadness through her at the same time. "I love you, Jackie. You're so close to the end, so close. You know what you have to do."

Jackie held onto her mother, even though she could feel the coolness of her mother's touch fading away. "I love you, Mom. I'm so afraid."

"Good," Her mother said, her voice fading. "It's when we're afraid that we can achieve great things, darling girl."

She stood back from Jackie and she watched as her mother's spirit faded away, until all that was left was a sparkling speck of sand taken by the wind. Jackie watched it for as long as she could, until it too disappeared.

"Well, fuck." Jackie said.

XX

Jackie could hear the scratching of a pen coming from her duffel bag, but she paid it no mind. She didn't want to read what the leather-bound book would have to say about the visit from her mother. She already knew what it would say.

Looking down at the world and the path that she had taken, she felt like her path was about to change if only she could figure out what to do. She looked down at her palms, at the tattoos of the lantern and the rowan leaf and remembered something that Cosmo had said when she had been trying to teach her how to use the lantern and the leaf together: *"Alone, one is a light into the dark, and one a weapon and a true expression of you. Together, your powers are an explosion."*

Looking at the lantern and rowan leaf, she thought that she knew what her mother had been trying to tell her; that she had to use the light of the lantern and the light of the rowan leaf together and thought about how her mother had turned her hands palms up. It was so that she would see them both, and hopefully know what to do.

"What do I have to do, Brawn?" Jackie asked out loud. "The last time I used these together, they only destroyed. There's no way that they could heal." Brawn of course remained silent.

The scratching inside her bag became louder and more insistent, and she dug the book out and let it fall open to where it needed to. Looking at the page, she saw handwriting that was not her own. It was a curling and beautiful script that reminded her of flowers from a garden for some reason. Touching the words, an image of Em floated into her mind. Looking down at the words again, she could hear them in Em's voice:

'Idiot woman, you have been given all the tools you need! You know what to do! You can do this, and I believe in you. I can't tell you what to do, but I can tell you to **use the tools that you've been given** *to direct your energy!* <u>I believe in you!</u>*'*

The last four words had been underlined twice. Jackie wondered if Em had written in Jackie's book of knowledge so that she would be able to read the message. If so, she was taking a big risk in communicating with her this way. It was a shame as it still didn't make things clearer.

She took a look in of her bag for the tools that she had: her tarot cards, the leather-bound book.. There was the star talisman that Xander had given her. None of these things would help her now, not in any real way. She looked down at her hands and saw the rowan leaf and the lantern. A thought struck her. What was she supposed to do? It was something that her mother had said: *"There is blood and there is fire and people have suffered. But if you cure the world, or at least show it some love, that will be a step towards helping the others that still live on this planet with you. You have the power within you, my darling girl."*

Jackie knew now that she had been put on this journey so that she could learn about her true path and the ability to be honest with herself, but did she really have the power to change the world, to cure a disease that had wiped out most of the population? Looking at her hands, she began to wonder and then think some more. The wind sang to her while she waited and thought, and though it had nothing wise to say, it seemed to be urging her on.

"Enough fucking thinking." Jackie said. "I have the fucking light. What if I gave that to the world? What if I showed it some love?"

She stood at the edge of the rockface looking down at the world below her. She was high up, and from this angle, the blood dotting the land looked as if it had formed some kind of bullseye. Jackie widened her stance and held her hands out in front of her, aiming for the centre of the target. Then she let the lights from the rowan leaf and the lantern flow out of her at full blast.

It had a less than desired effect. The lantern light was taken away by the wind and flew into the clouds. The light from the rowan leaf splintered all around her, and the air crackled with electricity that had no place to go and no focus. She supposed that she could go back down to where she had been and just direct her energy into the ground, but that would mean having to go backwards and who knew how long that would take. No, this journey was all about going forward. She just didn't know how.

"Thanks for being so fucking descriptive!" Jackie yelled. *"Use the tools you've been given!"* She said in a mocking tone. "Fuck you Em! What the fuck tool am I supposed to use? I can't get my fucking magic down to the earth from here! What the fuck am I supposed to do?"

Beside her duffel bag, her swords glinted in the shifting sun, sending an almost blinding light into her eyes. "Fucking swords!" She yelled. Jackie took hold of the long sword and was about to throw it off of the mountain when the golden magic from the rowan leaf sent a tongue of enchantment up the blade. Instead of being pulled away by the wind or crackling around her as the magic had before, she watched with wonder as the streak of magic continued down the blade of the sword until it faded.

She stood holding the sword, looking down at the blade. Jackie stayed that way for a few moments, thinking, and finally said "Do you think it could work, Brawn? Do you really think it will work?"

Standing with her feet planted securely on the rock, she held the sword with both hands, her arms and the blade pointed down to the earth. Jackie tried to aim for the bullseye made by the blood that marred the earth, but at this point, she didn't think it mattered. Presently, it was all about intent. Though she had tried using both of her hands together, she had never used a sword to focus that energy. She held the sword in her hands, and it felt different to her, like it had emptied itself and was waiting for her contribution.

"It's going to work." Jackie said out loud. "It's going to fucking work, right Brawn? Because I'm the fucking Queen of Swords. You bet your fucking ass it will work!"

Jackie had one moment of hesitation, one moment of self-doubt. It felt like every moment, every step, every battle along the way had led up to this moment, right here and right now. She wondered what Xander would say and thinking of him brought her so much joy. At this moment Jackie felt like a caterpillar leaving the cocoon, transforming into the shape of a beautiful butterfly. All she had to do was spread her wings and fly. She had to trust herself herself and know that what she was doing was the right thing to do. She couldn't lose confidence now. Jackie had to shine, and she had been trying to do that her entire life.

She turned the rowan leaf and the lantern on at the simultaneously. She watched the bluish white light of the lantern and the golden light of the rowan leaf twist and turn their way up the blade of the sword. As the magics intertwined, the light grew brighter and took on a deep green hue. Jackie was reminded of the colour of emeralds being lit from within by the sun.

Jackie had one brief moment where she could see herself as if she was watching from above. She was standing on the mountain with a sword lit with a green flame, her clothes, body and face marked by the path that she had taken, her blond hair whipping in the wind around her, and all she could think was: *I'm a mother fucking warrior!*

With a force that surprised even her, the light flowed in the direction she wanted, focused to a point, and with wonder, Jackie watched as her magic - her *power* - arced across the sky and down into the earth. When the green light connected, she felt a shifting inside of herself, as if this were the final step in her transformation and change. She felt the earth in that change, could feel it within her as if she were made of the very soil her magic was flowing into. At that moment, she was not made of skin and bone; she was made of stardust that had taken shape and been given form.

Jackie watched as her magic flowed from her into the earth, she watched as a ripple began to form on the earth's surface. The ripple increased so that it looked as though the earth were made of water, instead of soil and rock. She wondered how long she could keep this up, but her power felt endless, the cycle of it coming from a deep well of magic within her. Jackie just kept giving the earth more. It didn't pull it from her, but held its arms open wide for the gift that she was giving it.

Soon, the blood that marked every bit of the earth she could see began to dissipate. To Jackie, it looked as though the earth were healing its wounds. *No,* she thought. I'm *healing the earth's wounds. I'm healing the earth.* As the wind blew around her, as if to cheer her on, she heard the sound of bells, and thought momentarily of her mother and father looking down upon her. The sound increased until as if all the stars above her, hidden in the blue sky by the light of day, were singing to her. That sound amplified the power that flowed out of her and down the sword, and strengthened the power that flowed into the earth.

When all the blood that marked the earth was gone, there was a loud crack that sounded like thunder above her, and the skies opened up. Rain began to shower the earth, and Jackie, let herself breathe and stopped the flow of energy from her body to the earth. She moved back a few steps, let her long sword fall to the dirt beside her duffel bag, and just stood there; looking at the world below her, being washed by the rain. She held her arms above her head, and let the rain wash off all the dirt and grime and blood, until she felt clean again.

The rain fell for a minute, an hour, a day, Jackie didn't know. She didn't have any concept of time anymore. She just knew that the rain was washing everything away so that the earth could start again. So that *she* could start again. When it stopped, she felt rejuvenated. Jackie felt more alive than she had ever felt in her life.

A smile broke out on her face. "Fuck that felt good!"

XXI

Jackie wondered what she was going to do now.

It felt as though she had always been walking, always been on this path. She didn't know what she was going to do, only that she was ready for what came next. She put her duffle bag on and strapped her swords to her back.

As she looked down at the earth that she had helped heal, she heard the music of bird song. She felt complete and whole. Jackie knew that she had completed the cycle of the path that she had been travelling on and knew that she was ready for her next adventure. Jackie had learned so much about herself and what she was capable of, but now she wanted more. She wanted to see what else she could accomplish, and how much more she could change herself and the world around her.

She took her deck out of her duffle bag and shuffled the cards carefully. Then she pulled one card for herself after asking "What happens now?" She drew The World card and she smiled. No fucking Queen of Swords, because *she* was the Queen of Swords. The World was a card of endings and beginnings. She wondered what her next adventure would be.

There was a noise behind her. The sound sent shivers down her spine. She knew that sound, has missed that sound, had yearned for it for what seemed like forever and yet it also seemed like only a moment in time.

Turning around, Jackie saw Brawn standing there, looking proud and so wonderfully beautiful. This was her heart and soul in front of her, and she ran to him, kneeled down and buried her face in his fur, tears of joy flowing down her face. He was warm and vibrant and real. Brawn was *real*. Inside of herself, Jackie felt the last piece of her heart click back into place.

"My friend, oh my friend. I fucking missed you!" She leaned back and looked into his golden eyes. Though she wondered how he could possibly be alive, she realized that it didn't matter, she was so glad to have him back. He blinked at her, and she blinked back, and when Brawn put his paw on the side of her face, she held it there and just gazed at him.

Finally, she stood. "Well, I don't know how we're going to get down from this fucking mountain." Jackie thought of Xander and his blue eyes that looked like the sea. "There is someone who I must find."

Brawn went to the edge of the rockface. He opened his mouth and let out a roar that shook the very earth itself. Jackie stood there watching, and stared open-mouthed as a path started to form, one rock at a time, down the mountain. It curved and bent up the mountain and stopped only when it reached them. When it was done, the path looked as if it had been made from glass instead of rock, as each stone shone like the sun. The path down the mountain was filled with light, and she could see every curve and bend of it. The shining rocks looked like a waterfall down the mountain and she wanted to swim within it.

When the roar stopped, she heard its echoes reverberate around her, and she watched as birds flew into the air. She wished for a moment that she could join them, and then realized that she already had. Jackie had finished her transformation and now she had to use her own wings to fly.

"So, what happens now?" Jackie asked. "How do we get down the mountain?"

Brawn let out a snort and turned his head to look back at his body. Jackie understood right away, and gently climbed on to the Brawn's back. Brawn started to purr, and Jackie could feel the vibrations in her body. She had never felt so wonderful.

As the lion made his way down the path of stone glass that marked their way, Jackie wondered what would come. Whatever came her way, whatever new journey she was about to embark upon, Jackie knew one thing with certainty:

She was ready.

Acknowledgements

This novel has been with me on a long journey.

In 2013, my life changed forever. It was new years eve day, and when I woke, I had no balance, motor control and I couldn't walk. I was afraid and worried about what was causing the issues with my body. Over the next few months, it became worse. I would lay there in the darkness of my bedroom, unsure of how I was going to continue or how I would overcome something that I could not see. I would lose the ability to type, to walk and to speak coherently.

To distract myself from the turmoil within me, I would let myself be taken away by the seed of an idea, a story about someone who would wake in an unknown world and having to find their way along the path, no matter what obstacles stood in front of them. They would find a way to go on and move forward.

I was diagnosed with relapse and remitting multiple sclerosis in 2014. In a sense, that diagnosis was a gift. I now had a name for the unseen enemy, even if it was inside of myself. I worked on learning to walk again with a cane, type again one word at a time and to speak. I felt like I was waging war against my own body. To distract myself, I took a variety of different workshops including reiki, manifestation and tarot.

I had a love affair with the Tarot several years before and finding the cards once again was like a revelation. In learning the cards once more, I was reminded of my idea that I had in 2013 about that person that woke in an unknown world. I thought it would be a neat idea to tell the story of the Fools Journey from the Major Arcana but in a novel. The only problem was that I had no idea how I would go about telling that story. There were twenty-two cards in the Major Arcana. It seemed too big, and I wasn't sure that I could tell it.

Then two things happened. I began having a dream about a woman on a plane. She was drawing Tarot cards. The kept drawing the same card over and over again, no matter how many times she shuffled the cards: The Queen of Swords. I thought that was a really cool dream and tried to reflect on what was trying to tell me, but that was it.

It wasn't until June 2019 that the seeds that had been planted were given the spark they needed. I was watching the news and there was a story about a woman named Tiffani Adams. She had fallen asleep on a plane while travelling from Quebec to Toronto and when she awoke, she was still on the plane and buckled into her seat. Looking around her, she realized that the plane was in the airplane hanger, and everything was dark. She had no idea where she was at first and no idea where anyone else on the plane was.

The idea for this novel fell into my head at that moment and it was like my mind was full of light. I thought of the story I had wanted to tell way back in 2013, the idea I'd had in 2014 and the dream I had about the woman on the plane reading her Tarot cards. I finally knew the story I wanted to tell about the Fools Journey. I knew that it would be set in a dystopian world and that mirrored our own and it would follow a woman along on a perilous journey as she came to know how strong she was and what it really meant to be brave. I asked my friend Jackie if she would mind being the main character and I started writing the novel that night.

As I wrote, I realized that I was going on my own journey with Jackie. It wasn't lost on me that I was writing about my own journey with multiple sclerosis and the terrain that my body had become. I loved the parallels between Jackie's journey and my own and I thought it added something to the novel. I wanted the Fools Journey to be *my* take on the cards and I knew that each chapter would focus on one card in the Major Arcana. It seemed the way that made the most sense. I put so much of myself into every book I write, and it was no different for this book. Then in March of 2020, everything changed again.

That was when the pandemic hit, and the world had to deal with the Covid virus. I almost stopped writing the novel at that point. I didn't feel like writing a novel about a virus that has wiped out the world when a very real one was doing the same thing around me. I put it aside for a week or two and tried to work on something else, but Jackie called out to me. She wanted to find out how her journey would end, and I couldn't help wondering the same thing.

It was my Wonder Mom that got me writing Queen of Swords again. During one of our conversations, she asked about the book, and I told her that I had stopped writing it and why. She took a breath before she spoke.

"I don't know, Wonder Son. I'd say that you've been given a pretty rare opportunity. Not many people get to write about a catastrophe while actually living one. Imagine how much the Covid pandemic will influence your novel."

I took that advice and ran with it. The whole novel feels somewhat claustrophobic and there is an unseen threat in the book. I wanted to convey what it was like for me in lockdown, worried about a virus that could kill me, and it's my hope that this influenced the urgency of Queen of Swords.

The whole novel took me almost five years and multiple drafts to finish. It's been with me for ten years from seed to publication and I know that this novel was my journey as much as it was Jackie's. It feels surreal that my little seed of an idea that appeared shining in my head way back in 2013 is finally seeing the light of day.

I've learned a lot after years of studying and working with tarot cards, however the one lesson I learn again and again is that life, like the tarot, is a cycle. It's what we learn along the way that shapes what will happen on the next cycle. I'm thrilled that this novel represents the end of a cycle for me and also a new beginning.

I can't wait to see what will come next.

A lot of people helped me along the way.

My husband Michael has my love and my gratitude. He has been a constant sounding board throughout the writing of this novel and many others when I find myself stuck or lost in a plot hole. He is always my support, my best friend and my husband and it's a joy and a pleasure to love and be loved by you. Michael, over the past couple of years, we've both had our share of health challenges and even though it's been difficult, I'd like to think that it has also brought us closer together. Thank you for coming with me on this crazy journey. I love you, Michael, more and more with each passing day.

My Wonder Mom and Wonder Dad saw me through a lot during the writing of this novel. They have always been unfailing pillars of support and love for me. They love me an inspire me to try and be a better person.

They've both seen Michael and myself through a lot during the writing of this and they have seen me through so much and been my champions. Thank you, Wonder Mom and Wonder Dad. I love you both beyond words. Your support means the world to me, and I hope that you are proud of the man that I've become.

I would like to thank my Wonder Mom in Law, Bev, my brother-in-law Steve and my sister-in-law Leeanne. Your unfailing faith in me makes me want to shine brighter. I'm honoured to have you and all of the Bellefeuille's as my family. You opened your arms and your hearts to me from the moment I met you and I'm blessed to know you and be loved by all of you. To think I went from having just my Wonder Mom and Wonder Dad as my family and now I'm loved by so many people. I'm so grateful for all of you and I love all of you.

I would be remiss if I didn't thank some members of my spirit family: Christine Gilmour, Meaghan, Karine, Alexandra and Kimberlee, your support and your love for all the years I've known you has been a blessing that defies words. You are the sisters I never had but always wanted, the confidants when I needed to share words with another and my support network when it felt like I was going to fall. I am so thankful, and I don't have enough words to say how much I love all of you.

There were a few people who helped bring Queen of Swords to life.

Jackie, thank you for letting me put you in this novel and take you on a journey when I didn't know how it would end. You truly are the Queen of Swords. Dominic, thank you so much for the beautiful and amazing cover. You truly brought Queen of Swords to life and thank you doesn't really capture everything I want to say to you, but I hope it's enough for now. Christine Moore, thank you for your editing prowess and for falling in love with this story as you worked. Thank you for your friendship and your guidance when I felt lost at sea.

To my Bubble Friends: Cousin Michael, Sharon, Marg, Catherine and Brenda. Thank you for seeing Michael and I through the ups and downs of the pandemic. Having you as our bubble made the frightening world less terrifying and the abnormal seem normal once more. I love you all so much and I'm sending you buckets of sparkles!

And thank you, dear reader. Some of you may have followed me on each journey that I've taken and for others, this may be the first time that you lost yourself in one of my stories. Thank you for reading this book. It's meant so much to me and it's a wonderful thing to have someone read it.

The only thing left to say is that another seed has popped into my head, another book waiting to be told. All I have for now is a title and a little spark of an idea. I just hope that King of Wands doesn't take me so long to write. The tale wants to be told.

I will just have to see what's in the cards.

Jamieson Wolf

About the Author

Photo by Susie Shapiro

Jamieson has been writing since a young age when he realized he could be writing instead of paying attention in school. Since then, he has created many worlds in which to live his fantasies and live out his dreams.

He is a number-one bestselling author—he likes to tell people that a lot—and writes in many different genres. Jamieson is also an accomplished artist. He works in mixed media, charcoal, acrylic and oil pants. He is also something of an amateur photographer and poet. He is also a Tarot reader.

He currently lives in Ottawa Ontario Canada with his husband Michael and their cat, Anakin who they swear has Jedi powers.

Learn more about him at www.jamiesonwolf.com

Other Books by Jamieson Wolf

Lust and Lemonade
Life and Lemonade
Love and Lemonade
Beyond the Stone
Little Yellow Magnet
Captain Maven and the Shadow Man
Covidly Speaking